PRAISE FOR

# THE ANATOMY OF DREAMS

"The way that Benjamin gives equal weight to both the romantic relationship and the novel's more cerebral, philosophical questions is impressive—and a feat we hope to see in many more books to come."

—*Nylon*

"After reading Chloe Krug Benjamin's *The Anatomy of Dreams*, you'll never dream the same way again. Benjamin's debut is a majestic collision of sci-fi thriller and love story that explores, as the title claims, the anatomy of dreams—their power, both chilling and beautiful—through the lens of a young couple. Sylvie and Gabe meet as teens at a California boarding school and, years later, become sleep researchers investigating lucid dreaming under the instruction of their former teacher, an intelligent and mysterious man with potentially sinister intentions. Though anchored in reality, their story takes surreal turns. It's a riveting tale that will instantly transfix readers, like a dream you're not quite ready to wake up from."

—*Bustle*

"A sly, promising, and ambitious debut."

—*Publishers Weekly*

# THE
# ANATOMY
# OF
# DREAMS

...........................

A NOVEL

CHLOE BENJAMIN

**ATRIA** PAPERBACK

NEW YORK   LONDON   TORONTO   SYDNEY   NEW DELHI

**ATRIA**
PAPERBACK

An Imprint of Simon & Schuster, Inc.
1230 Avenue of the Americas
New York, NY 10020

This Atria Paperback edition September 2018

**ATRIA** PAPERBACK and colophon are trademarks of Simon & Schuster, Inc.

For information about special discounts for bulk purchases, please contact Simon & Schuster Special Sales at 1-866-506-1949 or business@simonandschuster.com.

The Simon & Schuster Speakers Bureau can bring authors to your live event. For more information or to book an event, contact the Simon & Schuster Speakers Bureau at 1-866-248-3049 or visit our website at www.simonspeakers.com.

Interior design by Kyoko Watanabe

Manufactured in the United States of America

10  9  8  7  6  5  4  3  2  1

The Library of Congress has cataloged the original paperback as follows:

Benjamin, Chloe.
    The anatomy of dreams : a novel / by Chloe Benjamin.—First Atria paperback edition.
        pages cm
    1. Dreams—Fiction. 2. Sleep—Fiction. 3. Trust—Fiction. I. Title.
    PS3602.E66347A53 2014
    813'.6—dc23
                                                            2014009655

ISBN 978-1-9821-0503-7
ISBN 978-1-4767-6117-6 (ebook)

PART ONE

# DUSK

# 1

EUREKA, CALIFORNIA, 1998

When Gabriel returned to me, I was twenty-one, and I was in the middle of the long summer before my senior year of college. At the time, I was a realist. I was at the top of my class, and I didn't think there was anything anybody could tell me that I couldn't figure out myself. Coincidences, accidents: I believed in those. But it took such effort to unfold other possibilities. That meant opening myself like a paper fan, the ridges flattening to reveal parallel worlds.

My first clear memory of Gabe is from our junior year of high school, though I was aware of him before that—you knew everybody at boarding school, especially one as small as Mills. He was part of a rowdy group of boys who were always getting into trouble. Not pranks or fighting—they were just too investigative for their own good, regularly uncovering some conspiracy: what was actually in the cafeteria meat hash, or what Mr. Keller, the headmaster, was growing in the garden behind his house. I didn't pay Gabe much attention those first few years. I was preoccupied with my courses, especially English; the hard sciences came easily to me, but I couldn't think in metaphors. Maybe that's why I was annoyed by Gabe and his friends, for whom one thing always stood in for another: the corned beef in the hash was dog meat, and among the strawberries and celery and mint I had seen with my own eyes, Mr. Keller was growing oleander to make poison.

In our third year, though, a lunar eclipse brought us together. Mr. Cooke, our physics teacher, had been talking it up all semester, and our class had permission to see it. It would be at 6:51 P.M.—dinnertime—but that night we ate outside. It was cold but not snowing: in Northern California, January brought steamy haze that lent each evening a feeling of dark eventfulness. We carried out blankets and trays and huddled at the top of Observatory Hill, where Mr. Cooke had once shown us how to chart the phases of the moon. I sat with Hannah McGowan, my roommate and best friend, who was telling me a story in a rapid, hushed voice and at one point said, "Sylvie. Sylvie . . ." but I could hardly hear her. Her voice trailed into the air like fog as we waited for the moon to change.

Mr. Cooke had told us that a lunar eclipse could only occur when a full moon was perfectly aligned with the earth and sun. For just a few minutes, he said, our planet would cast two shadows and the moon would travel through them. Light from the sun, passing through earth's atmosphere, would bend toward the moon, and our rock would transform: dyed by the planet's sunrises and sunsets, the beginnings of days and the ends of them, she would turn red.

I knew all of this, but I was still unprepared for the feeling that came over us when it happened. Slowly, earth's shadow moved in front of the moon, covering it almost completely. But the moon fought back. Like a phoenix, she shed her ashes and caught fire. We gaped at her change in costume: she hung, a blood orange in darkness. The trees and the sky and even the hill vanished, and we had only each other.

And then, of course, it was over. The moon faded back to gray, and we all laughed in a jittery, scattered way, as if shaking off the remains of a fear. By 9:00, small groups had formed and left the hill. I stayed, along with a few others. Gabe was one of them. As we started to talk, he asked, "Who wants to see something I found?"

There was something bold and vulnerable about him, standing on top of a rock to the left of the group. We looked at him with mild interest and amusement, the deluded but well-loved member of our small town. He was no taller than five feet six inches and slender then, though he became stockier as he got older. He had the square, densely determined face of a pit bull, hazel eyes, and a thick swath of brown hair that whipped around in the wind like a wild halo. Sometimes the girls on my floor gossiped about him, saying he had a Napoleon complex. Now another boy shouted at him to get off the rock. But Gabe stayed, his eyes swooping from face to face like a low bird before landing on mine.

I shivered. Was it dread? Pity? Or perhaps, somewhere, the thrill of election.

"I'll see it," I said.

There were whoops and catcalls as we left down the hill, but Gabe plunged silently into the redwoods. The trees surrounded Humboldt County and its bowl of bay, filling our campus with a sweet, grandfatherly smell. I thought of turning back—I'd never had a violation before, and if we were found in the woods, we could both be suspended—but I decided against it. Just as I knew Gabe's reputation, I knew my own: a goody-goody, uptight, not a daredevil like him and his friends. I found them irritating, sure, but when I watched them laugh raucously at lunch or play soccer before dinner, falling whole-body into the mud, sometimes I wished I wasn't always a spectator.

We emerged in the clearing beside Mr. Keller's house. Trespassing here was much worse than being caught in the woods. Mr. Keller was forty-five, a firm-bodied man with a bald head and stark, Germanic features. Besides being headmaster, he taught an upper-level psychology course that people practically fought to get into. Dynamic, creative, and impishly appraising, he demanded more of us than any other teacher. He was the harshest, too.

"Jesus Christ, Gabe," I hissed.

"Don't freak out," said Gabe. "I won't do anything untoward."

He said the last word—one of Mr. Keller's favorites—with special emphasis. The headmaster's house was a two-story brick structure with small, turreted rooms rising up like pointed attics. But Gabe led us around to the garden, a square plot inside a silver-gray fence. Two stories above us, the tall windows glowed with light. Gabe barely glanced at them before stepping lightly through the unlatched gate.

I edged inside the gate and followed his footsteps—he wound through the plants with such dancerlike precision I suspected it was not his first time there. The sun was long gone. In the moonlight, the flowers and vegetables Keller tended glowed with the otherworldly iridescence of deep-sea creatures.

"Everyone's probably back in the dorms," I whispered. "So find whatever you want to show me or don't."

"Keep your voice down." Gabe held my eyes. "Come here."

He was in the corner of the garden, pointing to a little patch inside the ninety-degree angle of the fence. Below his finger was a flower, large, a fuchsia color so vibrant I could see it in the dark. When I bent closer, I saw it was not one flower but two—or one and a half. The flower had two faces, rimmed with slender pink petals, which shared the same central disk and the same stem. What was notable about the disk—that saturated, mustard-colored eye—was that it looked like the infinity symbol, as if someone had pinched the middle. I touched it, and when I pulled away, there was fine gold dust on my fingers.

"This is what you wanted to show me?" I asked.

Gabe's eyes shone, two small moons.

"This is what we're breaking curfew for? We're trespassing on Mr. Keller's property—do you realize we could be suspended?"

Gabe clamped his jaw shut. His eyes flitted across my face the way they had through our group on the hill. Then a different, steely sheen came over them; it was as if someone had let down the blinds.

"Forget it," he said, stepping over the fence.

He began to walk rapidly toward the dorms. I hopped the fence and ran to catch up with him. I was almost five feet seven, taller than he was, but I felt like a kid bobbing at his side.

"Was it some kind of joke?" I asked. "Push the Goody Two-shoes, see how far she'll go? See if you can get her in trouble?"

He made a snorting noise and kept walking. I could tell I'd disappointed him, but some resentment deeper than I was capable of moderating was rising to the surface.

"I really thought you'd be into it," he said, keeping a step or two ahead of me.

"How could you know what I'd be into?" I asked. "We've barely even spoken!"

By then, we had reached the dorms. To the left was the boys' dorm, and to the right was the girls'. I half expected him to grin at me, confess it had all been in play. But he continued toward the door, as if I was the one who had wronged him.

"I'll tell people about it!" I said, the words flailing out of me. "I'll tell the girls in my dorm!"

It was the only thing I could say to disempower him. I had figured out by then that it wasn't a joke, what he'd found, that it meant something to him and that, for some reason, he had chosen to share it specifically with me.

He turned; his face seemed to hang with resignation. Then he walked through the door to the boys' dorm, leaving me alone on the path.

I didn't tell anyone, of course. I already felt guilty for the way I'd snapped at him; or maybe it was something else that held me back, the curled edges of belief. While we washed up in the bathroom, the other girls teased me, asking how it felt to kiss Napoleon. I told them it felt good.

• • •

During the rest of that year, I barely spoke to Gabe. The flower incident had ended so badly that we were skittish around each other, prideful and embarrassed. But something uncomfortable and magnetic glowed between us. When we found ourselves inescapably close in proximity—in line at the dining hall, or seated at one of the dreaded two-person desks in Keller's classroom—our silence was as loaded as any acknowledgment. Finally, one of us would break: "'Scuse me," I'd say, reaching past him to grab the 2 percent milk; or Gabe would clear his throat and ask, "Pencil?" his body angled the tiniest bit toward mine, until I reached into my zip-up case and wordlessly handed one to him.

If the eclipse brought us together the first time, our next real meeting was equally serendipitous, orchestrated by forces that felt as fated as the phases of the moon. Summer had passed in a close, muggy blur, and now it was late August, the beginning of senior year. My flight from New Jersey had been delayed, and it was nearly midnight in the Arcata/Eureka Airport. The student shuttles ended at nine P.M., so I was slumped at the Delta desk at baggage claim, calling the dorm phone without success. I hung up and dragged my bags—two massive duffels and an overstuffed, twenty-pound backpack—to the nearest bench. Outside, it was cool and dewy. Drops of moisture clung to the parking meters and the slick yellow uniforms of the crossing guards. In ten years or even five, most of the students at Mills would have a credit card or a cell phone, and being stranded at the airport would be easy to fix. Having neither, I felt like a forgotten piece of luggage myself.

"Patterson?"

I turned. Gabe was outside the sliding doors of Baggage Claim 3, wind ruffling his hair as the doors whooshed shut behind him. He stood wide-legged in a pair of too-small flip-flops and worn cargo shorts; he'd slung a bag over each shoulder, making his T-shirt ride up around his waist. A dark fuzz of hair extended down from his belly button, and his skin was sun-browned. He grabbed the bottom of the shirt and tugged it down.

"Lennox," I said.

"You're late. Late for senior year."

"So are you."

We regarded each other, wary. Then I scooted over on the bench, and he lumbered over, dropping his bags on the sidewalk with an inadvertent, gruntish sigh.

"Well," he said. "I guess we're stranded."

"Shipwrecked."

"Marooned."

We grinned at each other, at our senior-year banter, at the strange August night that was as wet as early spring on the East Coast. I looked at Gabe's shirt. It was holey around the neck and worn thin, with a blown-up image of Darth Vader on the front. Below, it said in block capital letters, WHO'S YOUR DADDY?

"Nice shirt," I said.

"Ditto."

I looked down. I'd forgotten I was wearing an old T-shirt

of my dad's, a comfort on plane rides back to school. GET YOUR REAR IN GEAR, it read: 5K WALK FOR COLON CANCER.

"Touché," I said.

We sat for a few moments in slightly bashful silence, both of us knocked down a peg. Absentmindedly, as if he'd done it a thousand times before, Gabe stuck his thumb through one of the holes at the neck. I'd heard he was on scholarship; there were rumors that his family was broke, that his dad had died penniless, though others held that his dad was just a living asshole who refused to pay child support.

"Where'd you fly in from?" asked Gabe. "Jersey?"

"How'd you know that?"

I was genuinely curious. I had never discussed my family with Gabe. Then again, we'd never discussed his, either, and I still knew that he lived in California with his mother. I knew, too, that she was morbidly obese, a consequence of some medical condition, though no one knew exactly what it was.

Gabe shrugged. "I listen," he said.

"What about you? Where'd you fly in from?"

"Michigan—I was visiting my gran. She lives on Lake Superior."

"Was your flight delayed, too?"

"What?" Gabe looked confused, then shook his head. "Oh—nope. I just forgot the shuttles ended at nine."

"You would," I said, but it didn't sound mocking; it came out downright affectionately, much more than I'd intended, and Gabe laughed in surprise. My cheeks warmed, and I fiddled with the zipper on my suitcase. We fell into another silence, but this time, it was relaxed. Maybe it was the late hour or the unusual circumstances; neither one of us knew whether our new amity would last once the clock struck midnight and we arrived at old, familiar Mills, where the social hierarchy was as firmly set as the granite foundation. Right then, though, it didn't matter very much. We had a delicate understanding, a connection like a spiderweb, and we navigated it with earnest, clumsy excitement. It felt like being outside after curfew: an extra hour tacked onto the day, wondrous and strange.

"So," said Gabe. "What say you? Are we sleeping here?"

"God, I hope not," I said, but the truth is I was buzzing with excitement. I pictured us making a nest of sweatshirts, a pillow of old tees, searching the airport for coffee and bloated muffins the next morning. Back at school, we would have an inside joke—a raised eyebrow, a *Remember the night we spent in baggage claim at Arcata/Eureka?* We would groan for effect, making it sound much worse than it really was. So my heart went limp when we saw the wide, maroon-colored Mills student shuttle careen around the corner. It pulled up in front of us and ground to a halt.

The door popped open, and out blundered Sandy, the hulking, enthusiastic grounds manager. His curly red hair was pulled into a low ponytail, and he huffed as though he'd run to the airport instead of driven.

"All right, all right, you're saved," he said, grabbing our bags, giving each of us an amiable clap on the shoulder. "Load 'em in and let's get a move on."

"How'd you find us?" asked Gabe as we climbed into the carpeted body of the shuttle, which always smelled faintly of Cheetos. Was it possible I detected a strain of disappointment in his voice, the same one I felt?

"Hall monitor noticed two of you buggers were missing," said Sandy, eyeing the rearview mirror and pulling onto the road with a lurch. "We checked the phone in the girls' dorm—knew *you* wouldn't be the one to call, Lennox—and what do you know, five missed calls. Number traced right to the airport."

"Five?" Gabe looked at me, grinning.

"Well . . ." I said in protest.

"Anyway," said Sandy, "no harm done. Just a little excitement on a Sunday night. I should be used to it by now."

With Sandy in the car, Gabe and I went mute again, staring out of our respective windows. But there was a presence between us, a fullness, and the molecules in the van seemed to shift to accommodate it. The drive to campus was only twenty minutes long, but it felt like hours. At one point, Gabe shifted his large boy-foot, and his calf—warm, hairy—rubbed against mine. I shivered, and his calf muscle tensed. But then the shiver passed, and his leg relaxed, and we stayed that way: linked by the barest touch as we wound toward school, stars winking in the windows.

When I woke up in my top bunk the next morning, Hannah snoring vigorously below me, the previous night felt like a dream. But when I saw Gabe across the dining hall at breakfast, sitting at a round table with David Horikawa and Michael Fritz, he stuck his arm in the air and motioned me over with the exaggerated enthusiasm of an air traffic controller.

"Yo!" he called. "Patterson!"

A few of the other seniors craned their heads around in surprise—Hannah and I usually sat with the girls on our hall—but I grabbed Hannah by the wrist and walked over, feigning confidence. Teenagers have a nose for insecurity, which is probably why we so often pardoned Gabe: everything he did had a robust aplomb that sent us sniffing elsewhere.

"Patterson and I had a little adventure last night," said Gabe as Hannah and I took our seats. ("*What the*—" asked Hannah, who had heard none of this, before I jabbed her thigh under the table.) Soon, the five of us were eating breakfast together almost every day. By the end of September, Hannah had entered into a passionate, ill-fated liaison with David Horikawa, but Gabe and I still hadn't kissed. We'd had plenty of opportunities—late-night meet-ups in the multipurpose room; riding cafeteria trays down Observatory Hill, Gabe and I crashing at the bottom in a tangle of legs and plastic—but whenever the laughter stopped, we could only stare at each other, red-faced.

"You guys hang out all the time. I just don't get what you're *doing*," said Hannah. Blotchy, blackberry-colored hickeys had started to appear on her body in surprising places (collarbone, inner elbow, and once, she showed me, smiling wickedly, her inner thigh); she was baffled by our restraint, not that it was intentional.

"We're *talking*," I said helplessly, and it was true: we'd become expert in the kind of simpatico conversation that usually only fell into place after years of friendship. Tucked between the redwood trees in the forest behind school, we traded stories: our secret plans ("To be a physicist," I whispered, hot-cheeked), our childhood fears ("Pill bugs," said Gabe), our families. What I'd heard of Gabe's was partially true: he lived with his mother in Tracy, California, a humid town in the San Joaquin Valley—"best known," said Gabe, "as the place where people stop to pee on the way to Tahoe." His mother worked from home for a telecommunications company and was heavily medicated for a chronic pain condition that made her yell, he said, or sleep. His dad wasn't dead, but he "wasn't in the picture"—a phrase Gabe said with such swift automatism that it sounded like something he'd been trained to say.

I didn't push him. Instead, I told him about my family. We were closer, maybe, but not cuddly. My parents prized their intellects and encouraged the same in my brother, Rodney, and me. Rodney was five years younger, thirteen during my senior year, and he was the softest one of all of us: a boy unusually gentle for thirteen, who kept a pet newt and wrote short stories on my father's hand-me-down laptop. They lived in New Jersey, ten states and six hours away, and most of the time I kept them tucked in one compartment in my mind—a compartment I opened up when I went home but otherwise kept firmly lidded.

A narrow channel had opened between Gabe and me, and we wriggled through. What we had was a likeness, an understanding of the way that solitary people could and had to drift together. Though Gabe was often surrounded by a troop of boys, he was more reclusive than most people knew. He took long, tangled walks alone on weekends, returning to the dorms with dirty fingernails and forearms scratched by brambles. He did his homework in the attic of the library, a tower that one of the headmasters in the 1960s had dubbed a place for silent thought—Gabe claimed he couldn't think if anyone else was around. Having spent most of the past three years at Mills ("It's like this weird alternate universe," he said, "where everyone is sixteen"), we were both independent by design, expert in adopting friends and in letting them go. As solid as Mills felt while we were there, we knew we would have to relinquish it at the end of senior year, just as we had our real families. Against our better judgment, in defiance of our transience and the rush of time, we built a raft and clung to it.

When I was with him, I longed to kiss him, but I was starting to despair. ("We couldn't do it *now*," I said to Hannah, rolling around in my bunk. "We're already friends. It'd be too weird.") On Halloween, Hannah—sick of my whining and already to third base with David Horikawa—came into our room armed with a trough of makeup and a minidress purchased at the thrift store in Eureka.

"Tonight is the night," she said. "Women's intuition."

She was right. In the middle of the annual Halloween party—a teacher-patrolled affair in the multipurpose room, with an epic snack table to offset the booze we seniors snuck into the punch—Gabe pulled me into the boys' bathroom and took my face in his hands. He was a hamburger with pool-noodle fries, I a Roy Lichtenstein comic girl. We kissed pressed against the stalls until one of the resident advisers came in to pee, his eyes bulging; then we ran, hysterical with adrenaline, our hands clasped tight as sailor's knots. We took the fire escape to the first floor and burst outside. It was raining faintly; above us, the windows of the multipurpose room had been pushed open to release the collective heat and Cheez-It breath of two hundred teenage bodies. Their voices floated out to us, free and high-pitched as loose balloons.

"So," said Gabe.

"So."

I could barely get the word out. I felt like I'd swallowed my tongue.

Something—not love but its precursor, a love embryo—loomed between us. I moved toward him again, and this time our kiss was tentative, investigative. We covered more ground, moving from mouth to ear to edge of cheek as if to memorize the topography of each other's faces. That night, we fell asleep outside, and though we got in trouble for it later—Sandy glowering as he lumbered toward us through the trees, his red ponytail slapping his back—I still remember the first few moments of that morning: the sun blushing over the hills as the sparrows trilled the day's first song, their notes soaring through the air like streamers.

I couldn't believe we'd done it—that one of the most beloved boys in our class had kissed my cheeks and chin and eyelashes until the red dots that Hannah had so painstakingly applied (bent over our art history textbook, lip liner in hand) smeared my whole face blurry. If Gabe was a pit bull, I had the pert, close features of a dachshund: quick brown eyes, small pursed mouth. A snub of nose, a dash of freckles. It was a utilitarian face: focused, unobtrusive, fine to look at but nothing that would make most people look twice. I was as lean and agile as Rodney, even at sixteen; I kept my chestnut hair in a taut little ponytail, my widow's peak a dark point. Sometimes I envied girls with voluptuous features—plump lips, lush movie-star hair—but just as often I was grateful for my inconspicuousness. There's nothing more dangerous than a teenager who looks like a librarian, because we can get away with anything. On the day of the Halloween party, a group of us snuck out to the closest corner store that sold alcohol, and I was the one who purchased it. I was never ID'd; I looked so plain, so earnest, that the paunched owner gave me the benefit of the doubt. That Gabe wanted me was just as thrilling as buying a bottle of whiskey at the age of eighteen: both meant, somehow, that I had passed.

Gabe and I began to sit together in class, scribbling notes on old homework assignments whenever the teacher turned to the board. He saved a chair for me at lunch, his beaten-down black JanSport marking my spot. I still remember how it felt to walk into the dining hall and see it there. My stomach rose, as if pulled by strings; I moved not by foot but by hovercraft. Most surprising was how little I resisted. Some of my friends had boyfriends, and I'd always scoffed at how distracted they became, how easily they relinquished their former selves—and here I was, vaulting away, leaving behind the tidy rows of my independence.

It took us weeks to figure out how to sneak into each other's rooms at night without the resident advisers catching on. The trick was to go between hall checks, walking nonchalantly past the monitor's station as though you were just going to pee, then taking the fire escape to ground level. The boys' dorm was separated from the girls' by a thin path, but if you snuck around the back of the buildings, James Bond style, you could avoid the Cyclops gaze of the security camera. Those first few nights were deliciously illicit; we clung to each other even more fiercely for having made the trip successfully. But one morning, I woke to find that Gabe was gone. That time, I chalked it up to the discomfort of fitting two people in one pancake-mattressed twin bunk. But when it happened a second time, and then a third, I was hurt.

"Different people like it different ways," said Hannah, who was not bothered by Gabe's presence at night. She slept so deeply that our friends had started to call her Hannah Van Winkle; the only thing that woke her up was our CD alarm clock, blasting Stevie Wonder's "Signed, Sealed, Delivered" at full volume. "Could be he's trying to send you a subliminal message, say he doesn't really want to have sleepovers after all."

Hannah was the baby in a bright lineup of sisters—sisters who knew how to braid hair, who flattened cardboard boxes and slid down the hills that surrounded their father's farm, and who handed down to Hannah a complicated mythology about boys in addition to old sweaters and winter jackets and bicycles. But Gabe didn't seem the type for subliminal messages. His face was open and readable as a dog's. When we talked, I could tell if I'd offended or pleased him just by the tightness of his mouth.

One Tuesday in November, I saw him leaving Mr. Keller's garden. I had woken up at four thirty and hadn't been able to fall back asleep, so I pulled my pillow over to the window that overlooked the grounds and began to read with a flashlight. Soon I caught some motion in the corner of my eye, and when I looked outside, I saw it was Gabe. My dorm faced the front of Keller's house, but Gabe appeared to be coming from the back, where the garden was.

My first thought was that he was still stuck on Mr. Keller's flowers, and a wad of dread gathered in my chest. Neither one of us had mentioned the doubled flower since the night of the eclipse. I was embarrassed for him—his interest in it, his suspicions about the school as a whole, made him seem paranoid. So when I saw him in the dining hall that morning, I meant to bring it up. But his skin was pale and his eyes were sunken, the lower lids rimmed by sallow half-moons. It frightened me—I wondered if something much worse was going on. I made him a plate of food, and we ate together by the windows that overlooked Observatory Hill, where we had watched the eclipse almost one year before. By the end of the meal he seemed to perk up, the color of his cheeks becoming more beige than white, and for the moment, that satisfied me.

# 2

Six years later, as Gabe and I drove a U-Haul from Fort Bragg, California, to Madison, Wisconsin, I found myself sorting obsessively through my memories of Mills and the years after I left. There was plenty of time on our drive, and more space: first the California redwoods, then the sliced-open rock of the Sierra Nevada and Utah's red hills. In Colorado we saw rivers so glassy and clear they mirrored the land above them, so that the river ceased to be a river at all and instead became a double of the sky.

We looked at all this without talking; we felt as though it belonged not to us but to the natives and travelers who hiked those canyons by day and slept with the sun. We had forfeited our right to day by accepting a different offer. And though I had accepted it, I had always been the harder sell, and there were still moments when insurgencies would spark unexpectedly inside me. It was as though there were thousands of little soldiers in my gut, most of whom were aligned with the cause but some who wrestled free and fired at it. It was one thing to say we would participate in Keller's work; it was another to make it our lives. Or perhaps I clung to that skepticism because it suggested that choice had not been lost—or at least, irreversibly muddied—at the very start.

Our new house in Madison was a rental on East Main Street, in a neighborhood called Atwood. It was a historically blue-collar district that had undergone a sort of half gentrification: the old porn house had been converted into a theater that showed art films, and there was a little chocolatier between Trinity Lutheran Church and St. Bernard Catholic Church. But there were also wide lots penned in by wire and filled with low warehouses, or nothing at all. Madison is known for the two lakes that bracket its isthmus, and Atwood felt like an island, hemmed in by bodies of water.

The house was square, painted a faded, wheaty yellow, with a steeply triangular roof; the previous tenants had left a couch on the front porch. The house's combination of shabbiness and sweetness was typical of Madison. Unless you went to the west side, where the university professors lived, or to Maple Bluff, the governor's neighborhood, most of the apartments looked a little cobwebby. Inside our place, the wooden floors were faded and the kitchen drawers jammed. The refrigerator door routinely got suctioned stuck, opening only when I braced one foot against the freezer and yanked with all of my strength. The brass doorknocker had rusted to the color of tea, and the light fixtures—beautiful fixtures, made of decorative metal and glass—swung precariously on their cords.

In Fort Bragg, we had lived in a garden apartment—half underground, that is—that Keller paid for, subtracting it out of what he owed us for our work. Our place in Madison was huge in comparison. Upstairs was the bedroom, the bathroom, and, above that, an attic. On the bottom level were the living room, the kitchen, and the office. Gabe preferred to work on campus, so the office became mine: a room with large windows and a domed ceiling. I loved the clarity of its shape, the sense of being tucked away in an egg, and when I left it in the evenings, dazed from work, I felt like a hatchling, vulnerable and disoriented.

There was one other house on our block, separated by our two driveways and patchy lawns. Structurally, it was almost identical to ours, but it had been painted violet with pink trim. The porch was strung with multicolored lights and hung with wind chimes I could hear from the office. And for most of August, that noise, along with the two recliners on the porch, was the only evidence that people actually lived there. Most of the bright, floral drapes were drawn, but the curtains on the upstairs window had fluttered open, and I could see the edge of a bedside table, a salmon-colored pillow.

I was eager for the sight of other people because our house was so secluded. It sat in the center of a nearly barren block: to the right was the neighbor's house, and to the left were freight-train tracks, which were clearly the reason for our affordable rent. We were separated from the tracks by a chain-link fence, four feet high and overrun with wild greenery: messy, verdant trees keeled over them from each side. The trains came most often after dark, making low bellowing noises that kept us awake. It was almost a blessing that so much of our work with Keller took place at night.

Usually, we went to the lab around seven, a couple of hours before the participant went to sleep. It was our job to explain the procedure, soothe them—you'd be amazed how many seemed to treat the experiments like therapy—bring them water, if they asked for it, but no food. Often, the anxious ones asked for Gabe instead of me. I was more businesslike, explaining the procedure matter-of-factly, but Gabe didn't talk about the study. Instead, he got the participants to talk about their children, their partners, their ailing parents. Once they fell asleep, I monitored the polysomnogram in an adjoining room while Gabe stayed next to the bed, watching closely for signs of movement or speech and intervening as necessary.

On days when we didn't have a procedure scheduled, we worked at the university sleep clinic with Keller, where our tasks were more routine. Some of the higher-ups at the clinic knew about our project, which had been commissioned by the Center for Neuroscience, but most of them didn't. They didn't seem to find our caginess odd—it wasn't uncommon for researchers to keep their work close to their chests—but I can see now that it prevented us from feeling at home in the university community. The department's interest in Keller's work had been a surprise: his research was so experimental that getting mainstream validation was always an uphill battle, and we felt like we were working on borrowed time.

We worked in the lab about four nights a week, and on those days we slept from the time we got home until early afternoon. We had brought our eclipse curtains with us from Fort Bragg, made of a tightly woven fabric that blocked light completely. It was part of our work to be interested in dreams, and we always listened intently to each other's stories—not that I had many. I was rarely able to remember them; no matter how vivid my dreams felt at the time, they slipped through my hands in the morning. All I had was a faint sense of space and emotional residue that lingered, like a bad taste in the mouth. Gabe dreamed, most often, of transportation: helicopters and planes, commuter trains, and ships that crossed vast bodies of water with impossible speed.

When he told me about them, he looked not at me but at the ceiling, or out the window to the neighbor's house, an arm bent behind his neck. He was my height, five feet seven, and by then he was stocky and muscular, with a head that almost looked to be too large for his body. With me, his face softened: his mouth untensing, the wide-set brown eyes, which narrowed when we worked, becoming gentler and more open.

Other women seemed to find him attractive, though I suspected that had less to do with the way he looked than with his confidence. He was decisive and convincing in speech, but he could also drop into a low tone of intimacy that was, for Keller's participants especially, profoundly comforting.

We worked in the old neuroscience building, a mile away from the quad of undergraduate classrooms and dorms near State Street. It was a flat, drab structure the color of brown eggs. Most neuroscience operations had transferred to a newly constructed, multistory building closer to the heart of campus, but this one still housed experiments, and Keller had a five-room complex in its north wing. Only one of the rooms had windows, so the wing felt like a collection of cells.

A petite, red-haired woman and an older Hungarian man conducted experiments in other parts of the building. I never knew exactly what they did, but I always stopped and made small talk when I saw them. In fact, I was rarely the one to end a conversation with anybody; I became so friendly with two of the checkout men at our local grocery co-op that Gabe accused me of flirting. I denied it at the time, but perhaps I was—flirting not with them, but with the idea of another life. We kept such irregular hours that neither of us had much opportunity to develop outside friendships.

This was the way our lives went for that first month of August—muggy, static days filled with fatigue and the little caffeine pills Gabe bought online—so I would probably have been grateful for any shift in our routine. It just happened that the shift came in the form of Thomas and Janna.

I remember the evening they arrived because there was a terrible thunderstorm, the kind I learned was common during Midwest summers. The rain was warm and steady, but the sounds were violent: great, piercing cracks, the taut sky shot open. Thunder like this used to terrify Bo, my family's dog; I had always talked in my sleep, and my brother told me

I often comforted Bo in that state. I was packing dinner for the lab with Gabe, thinking about Bo cowering in the closet, when we heard the garage door open next door.

Instinctively, we gathered at the kitchen window to watch. We'd been wondering about the neighbors. Gabe thought they were a family band, folk performers gone until the children were required to be back in school. Hypothesizing about them gave us a small, secret pleasure, like reading a cheap magazine, and when we heard the garage door, I thought they might be better left unknown. Whoever got out of the car would certainly be more ordinary than we'd hoped.

It was a small blue Honda with a bent-in bumper. Before it reached the garage, the car halted abruptly, and the passenger door swung open. A pair of shoes hit the pavement, and that was when we first saw Janna. She was a tall woman, practically at eye level with our kitchen window and maybe ten feet away, though she wasn't looking at us. First she stomped several times; then she grabbed the bottom of her white, sack-shaped dress and shook it, as if brushing out crumbs. She wore chunky motorcycle boots, laced and buckled up to her knees. The combination of the black boots and white dress made her look eerily spectral. Up close, I would see her skin was very pale, with undercurrents of veins so visible it seemed she lacked a layer the rest of us had. Her light hair was shot through with red and black; in the rain, the blond parts were almost translucent. She turned and walked inside before I could see her face.

Next, there was Thom, coming out of the garage as the wide door descended behind him. He was even taller than her and slender, his reddish-blond hair matted like grass. Behind him, he pulled two suitcases, his shoulders hunched. He wore a white T-shirt, blue-striped scrubs, and scuffed brown moccasins. Right before he reached the porch, he pulled off his round glasses and held them up to the rain. Then he ducked through the screen door and rubbed them with the underside of his T-shirt, leaving the suitcases outside to be splattered. When he finished, he slipped the glasses on again, hoisted the suitcases onto the porch, and walked into the house. The lights inside came on just as he disappeared from view.

"Bad trip," joked Gabe, turning away from the window.

"Maybe she felt sick," I said.

I was still looking; I thought one of them might open the drapes, and then I felt silly. It was night—who opened the drapes at night?

"Could have at least helped him with the bags," Gabe said.

He wrapped our sandwiches in foil and put them in the cooler. I was filling water bottles up from the tap. The water was cloudy and tasted faintly metallic, but the landlord said this was normal.

"How old do you think they are?" I asked. "About our age?"

"Probably," said Gabe. "Late twenties, I'd say."

We were twenty-four. Most of the neuroscientists we worked with were in their fifties and sixties, and Keller was over fifty himself.

A light came on in the second floor of the neighbor's house. Gabe and I leaned toward the kitchen window.

"What is it people do around here, when someone new moves into the neighborhood?" he asked. "Don't they bring over a casserole?"

"Casserole," I said. "That's pretty antiquated, don't you think?"

But we each harbored the hope that casserole would be delivered to our porch the next morning, that we would all eat together in the dim light afforded by the old dining room bulb. We hoped for the arrival of the Welcome Wagon, something we had heard our parents talk about, as if the Welcome Wagon would drive right out of their generation and into ours. But weeks passed, and we heard nothing from the neighbors, though we spotted them now and then. Evenings, I saw the woman getting out of the Honda, her arms covered in a gray film of dirt. Other times I saw her on the porch, wearing satiny pink shorts and a thin tank top, as if she were lounging in the privacy of her bedroom. She also had an array of little dresses that she wore with the black boots—ruffled miniature things in shades of coral and lime, or stark black-and-white shifts with pointed shoulder pads. But she didn't seem to go anywhere in them: whenever I saw her coming or going, she was in shorts and a T-shirt, her body covered in that sheer coating of dirt.

In each incarnation, I found her beautiful, though I couldn't quite say why. Because she never looked our way, I had ample time to study her without fear of eye contact. She had a narrow face with angular bones that rose prominently beneath the skin: high, sharp cheekbones, wide-set eyes, a long nose that pointed toward the line of her mouth. Her lower lip was pierced with a ring, and she had a barbell through her left eyebrow. I had a visceral reaction when I first saw it—a slight clench, as I imagined she did when the needle went through. It gave that brow an appraising, arched appearance that was at odds with the glaze of her eyes.

She walked with an elfin bounce that came from her knees rather than her feet and gave her a look of youthful awkwardness. But her body was a woman's body. Her height had given her large feet and long, slender legs. She had broad hips and a soft dumpling of a belly. A long tattoo curled up her left forearm, though I was too far away to tell what it was. I knew I could pass for decent looking: I had a narrow build, small features, and brown hair the color of coffee with milk, which had been cut the same way for most of my life. But I was fascinated by the neighbor's turns and bows, her breasts. They were rounder than mine and emerged from her undershirts in firm slopes, like islands coming out of water.

# 3

EUREKA, CALIFORNIA, 1998

Janna reminded me of Nina, a Ukrainian girl who transferred to Mills when we were juniors. She and Gabe dated on and off that year. Nina was a tall brunette with large gray eyes and a pursed button of a mouth. She had Janna's combination of airy nonchalance and unexpected vigilance, something I would see in Janna only later. It was as if she had a number of extrasensory probes, sent out every which way to gather information, while she sat on the porch and feigned disinterest.

Nina's mother was a celebrated mathematician, and Nina was my biggest competition in statistics. Once Mr. Lee called the two of us up to the board and wrote a logic problem between us. It was meant to be a playful competition, but I could feel myself beginning to sweat as I started in on it.

Nina finished before I had even drawn my truth table. As we were walking back to our desks, she said, "You shouldn't focus so much on the little details, Sylvie. You'll miss what's coming."

I bristled, but I knew she was right. I had a habit of zeroing in on the specifics to the exclusion of the whole, and I didn't have very good foresight. That night in November, for instance, when I saw Gabe leaving Mr. Keller's garden—

despite how much it disturbed me, or perhaps because of it, I tried to forget it when Gabe seemed to return to normal. There was a several-week stretch when I found him beside me in bed every morning, and I convinced myself that he must have been sleepwalking, like I'd done as a kid. How could this warm and peaceful body, this person who had become more precious to me than anyone else at school, have done anything so strange on purpose?

That year, we both decided to stay at Mills for Thanksgiving. We were puppyish with infatuation—after a rocky, bitter breakup with David Horikawa, Hannah had started to call us the Moonies—and the idea of eating turkey and canned cranberries with our families was wildly undesirable. I told my parents that the six-hour plane ride was too long for three days at home, with finals just around the corner. Gabe called his mother and received surprisingly immediate clearance to stay, too.

We spent most of that long weekend exploring the woods around campus, the little hill-dips and streams, kissing on Observatory Hill with grass stains on our jeans. We found a pile of dusty board games in one of the common rooms and played deep into the night, betting over who'd win, wrestling for the best pieces. In the dorm kitchens, we cooked ambitiously: stuffing with pecan and thyme, real cranberry jelly that didn't come from the can. We drove to a nearby market in Hannah's clunker Honda and got a whole turkey that we roasted and took out too soon, pink juice streaming down its legs. But even this made us laugh.

One afternoon, we walked to the top of Skinner's Hill, where the Rock Shelter was. It was a massive stone, hollowed out by erosion and open on the inside like a cave. We lay down on the cool, smooth floor. It began to drizzle, then pour. I climbed on top of him. I could feel his erection through his jeans, his belt buckle digging into my stomach.

"Hi," I said.

"Hi," said Gabe.

We peeled off our wet jeans, our sweaters, our socks. My body seemed to vibrate, in hunger and in terror; I had only kissed a boy before. I played with the elastic band of his boxers, then put my hand inside to touch him. His body was tight and dense: muscles cabled through his back, and the tendons in his neck rose like a sculpture in relief. He followed me with his eyes as I stripped off my camisole and pulled down my underwear, then his. We fumbled and grasped at the puzzle of sex, the strange angles, Gabe gasping, open-mouthed, when he came; for me, there was only pulsing discomfort, which faded to a dull throb. The next day, in Gabe's room, I held his chest as he lurched and rocked above me; and then I was the one who was lurching, rocking, tentatively at first and then with a voraciousness I didn't know I had. We moved together brutally, our teenager's need as aggressive as it was ravenous, shoving until we seemed less to be having sex than pushing outside our own skins. It was as though there was something to be found beyond sex and we were running for it, clasped together but somehow in competition. Which is not to say it didn't feel shared; we were together in those moments, the only ones who knew what it was like.

Around this time, I started to have dreams I could barely remember and that left me physically exhausted, as if in them I ran great distances. Once, I woke with a bloody scrape on my left knee. I showed it to Gabe: the scrape glittered red under my desk lamp, as if it were not a wound but a jewel I had been given. I attributed the dreams to sex, both their physical manifestations and their psychological features. I was always exploring a space I never had before—walking across an empty room or through an unfamiliar forest. There were never other people, but sometimes, there were animals. In the forest I saw squirrels whose rustles of movement startled me, but I was most afraid of a cat in the unfamiliar room. It was a small creature, silky and mustard colored and not overtly intimidating, but I felt loathing when I saw it. Often, the cat circled me or pushed against me with its head. Now I think my aversion had more to do with my resentment at being left alone in the room than the cat itself—probably it could sense my fear and was trying to comfort me. But I felt strongly that some wrong had been done in putting me there, and I directed this bitterness at the only creature I could.

On the last night of the Thanksgiving break, Gabe and I fell asleep together: our legs braided, our chests stacked spoons. The next morning, though, I woke up alone. I'm not sure how I knew he hadn't gone back to his own room—call it instinct or intuition, the last cry of the subconscious. Before I could convince myself otherwise, I shoved into my sneakers and yanked on an old sweatshirt, grabbing a flashlight on the way out of the dorm.

It was cold outside, wind sighing in the trees. Fog had turned the sky cottony, so it was difficult to see Keller's house—only its smudged outline, faint as the sun's corona, before a scrim of trees. As I came closer to the house, I could hear the stream that ran behind it, making noises like little licks. I intended to go all the way to the garden, though I had no idea what I'd do when I got there. But I didn't have time to decide, because Gabe walked right out of the front door.

"Sylvie," he said, stopping in front of me.

I was stunned. Even if I feared I'd find him here, I hadn't actually expected it. Still woozy in that early-morning hour, I almost felt I was dreaming. I reached for him.

"No, don't." He stepped back. "You're not supposed to be here."

"Not supposed to be here?" We were both whispering, though my voice was getting louder. "You just walked out of

Keller's house. I saw you—out of Keller's *house*. And *I'm* the one who's not supposed to be here?"

"It's part of the—" Gabe turned his head, and his eyes flickered to the left, as though searching for someone. "Remember what I told you, Sylvie. It's part . . ."

His mouth hung open for a few seconds, then closed. But before I could tell him that he hadn't told me anything, another voice came from the doorway.

"Gabriel."

Mr. Keller stood in the arch that led into the house. Keller didn't often appear among us students when he wasn't teaching, but when he did, his presence was electrically charged. If he was ever in line at the dining hall, the entire row of students fell silent in a current. He had a light, charming way of interacting with us, but his power and influence always ran underneath it. Nobody wanted to disappoint him in case his amiability cracked and something else surfaced.

It was more than that, though. He had an attunement to us, an awareness of our inclinations and desires, that was unusual for an older teacher. Once, he came upon a group of us standing in the foyer of the library, with a boy named Will Washburn off to one side. Prone to colds and dramatic, exclamatory falls in gym, Will was particularly on the outs with us that day: another boy had ribbed Will about his lack of athletic skill, and Will had shouted insults until one of the hall monitors gave our entire class early lights-out for the week. Keller could have continued into the library, but instead he paused.

"William Washburn," he said. "Just the person I was hoping to see."

Keller's body was angled toward Will, but not so much that he shut the rest of us out completely. Will looked up nervously.

"Me?"

"Indeed. I meant to ask about those papers I gave you. You've not had a chance to go through them, I assume?"

This caught our interest. There was a persistent rumor that Keller was working on a project and that he selected certain students to serve as research assistants. Some people said you got money for doing it, like a sort of work-study. Others said it was more the honor, the prestige—that if he chose you, you were pretty much guaranteed an acceptance to the college of your choice. We all wondered if this was what Keller was referring to now.

"No, not yet," said Will. His face had a scrunched-up look, as if he was trying to contain something—shock, or maybe pride.

"Well, I'm glad to hear it," Keller said. "I've made adjustments, so we'll have to scrap them. Bring them to me when you can and I'll go over what's changed."

"Yeah, okay," Will said.

"Right, then," said Keller, before turning, for the first time, to the rest of us. "Afternoon."

We all made our feeble hellos, and he nodded amicably before disappearing into the atrium of the library.

Whether Keller really had given Will something to work on or not, Will's troubles faded shortly thereafter. So on that day at the end of the Thanksgiving break, when Keller followed Gabe outside, I was almost relieved; I hoped he could diagnose whatever was going on with Gabe and bring it to an end.

He walked to Gabe and put a hand on his shoulder. An expression of nervousness and new clarity came over Gabe, as if he now understood he might really get in trouble.

"Mr. Lennox and I were just having a conversation." Mr. Keller spoke softly, but his voice was a blade. "A conversation about boundaries."

"I couldn't sleep so I went for a walk," said Gabe flatly. "I went out of the dorm and across the field. I meant to go into the woods but when I came to Mr. Keller's house I got curious about his garden and stopped. I walked into the garden and looked at all the plants. I was only going to stay for a minute or two but I know it was wrong and I shouldn't have."

The whole speech of apology was so continuous it seemed programmed. Maybe this was something he'd decided he would say if he got caught. But if that was the case, I couldn't understand why he was telling me.

"Also known as trespassing on faculty property," said Keller. "Now, it's a very nice garden, I won't deny that; I've spent years raising my little collection, and you're not the first young botanist to show an interest in it. You're perfectly welcome to stop by during the day and have a look, with permission. But not this way."

He walked to Gabe's other side, his hands clasped behind his back. My heart was throbbing. All I wanted was for Keller to get to the end of the speech so Gabe and I would know what his consequences would be.

"Secrets," said Keller. "Mr. Lennox and I were having a talk about secrets. I invited him inside; I saw no reason to leave him out in the cold. So we sat down in my dining room and had a very frank talk about secrets and what comes of them."

I looked at the house. The shades on the first floor were drawn and rimmed by light. I caught a sliver of the living room, though I didn't see any furniture.

"Consequence number one," Keller said. "Reduced night privileges. I expect Mr. Lennox to be in his room without visitors by eight thirty P.M. The monitors will see to that."

This was to be expected. We waited mutely for what would come next.

"Number two. An essay of at least one thousand words to the tune of what it means to be a respectful citizen in an academic community. Typed, carefully proofread, et cetera, with points deducted for each word misspelled."

Mr. Keller was standing at Gabe's side. Instead of his usual daytime uniform—black suit pants, a navy button-up shirt—he wore scrubs and a green sweater with ragged edges. It was unnerving to see him dressed so casually, though of course it made sense: he had probably been in bed. Gabe's expression was blank. But every so often, he looked at me, and some muscle seemed to flicker.

"Number three," Keller said. "He has agreed to convey these rules to his peers. It's now Gabriel's responsibility to make sure others don't repeat his mistake. I'll rely on him to serve as an example, and if I find someone else out of bounds—in my garden, say—Gabriel will be the person I turn to first."

Mr. Keller fell quiet. The only sound was the wind threading through the trees, and I felt even more alone. But I was not just uneasy for Gabe. The more I stood there, the more I seemed to remember something about the place we were in, like the edges of déjà vu.

Gabe and I walked back to the dorms without speaking. There was a bright ball of fury in my chest, and I knew it would burst if I opened my mouth. But it was something deeper than anger that made me quicken my pace until Gabe, scrambling behind me, gave up and hung back. I felt betrayed. We had chosen each other: we had lain in my top bunk twined in conversation, our secrets loosening through the night like slipknots. He knew me as well as Hannah—maybe better. But he had lied to me about where he went at night, and for no reason better than his own pathological need to stick his nose where it didn't belong. His dogged interest in Mr. Keller's garden was so peculiar that it made me feel humiliated—for believing that he was different from other boys, for believing that he had grown up.

Classes resumed the next day, and I avoided him. When I did see him—sitting across the room in physics or walking to the dining hall, lagging behind his friends and trying uncertainly to catch my eye—my stomach vaulted, and I looked away. I spent most of my free time with Hannah in the workshop, a high-ceilinged warehouse at the edge of campus. During the day, it housed art classes, but in off-hours it was available to students. In our first year at Mills, Hannah and I signed up for Introduction to Painting. We thought it would be a steal: two periods a week to mess around with color, periods when we wouldn't have to use our minds. But it was the hardest class I took. Physics required logic, but the logic of painting was different—one that came from a place below the neck rather than above it and required hours of experimentation.

"I want you to mix a color," Ms. Mildanovich had said, winding her way through our tables. "A color only you know." I chose the dusty gray-blue of my old baby blanket. And though I could picture this color exactly in my mind, everything I mixed looked wrong and too potent on paper. The blanket was airy, diffuse, a tone I could better describe by feel than color. It was twilight, soft and shadowed; it had volume, like sheep's wool. Later that semester, I found an old sponge beside the workshop sink and layered paint until I got it right. That was when I realized that colors had shapes as well as tones. To find them, I had to use touch as much as sight, invention as much as memory.

Now I abandoned the painting of objects—the curved bowls and closed hands, the hard little apples—and studied *Nocturne in Black and Gold*, a crinkled page in the "Abstract" section of our art textbook: its smear of fire and light, its luminous darkness. The appeal of abstraction was psychological, too, for I could paint a piece whose true subject only I knew. I could hide things there: the angles Gabe's body took in bed, or the way I felt when I woke from my dreams of him. Sitting on the pale floors of the workshop, I did more than tell those stories: I encrypted them. Beneath layers of oil, in a box within a box, were shapes only I could read.

Now that I knew what Gabe had been doing with his nights—or at least where he'd been going—the idea of him was tainted for me. There seemed to be something shameful about him, something sordid with which I had unwittingly become involved. He'd plucked me out from inside the person I'd always thought I was and made me question my own judgment. But I cared too much to let go of him. I was insatiably curious, hysterical with late-blooming girlhood. What was he doing? Was there someone else with him? I pictured him clasped in the woods with Diana Gonzalez, the curviest girl in our senior class, or exploring the garden with Nina; once, I dreamed of her pearl-gray eyes, iridescent as nail polish, her bare body pressed to his.

In a strange way, I felt I had a responsibility to protect him. Nobody else knew where he went at night, and after Keller's warning, I wanted to make sure he didn't sacrifice his tenuous parole. I woke each morning around five, when the mountains were barely outlined in light, and sat at the window. For three nights, I didn't see him. But on Thursday, at five thirty, he came around from the back of the house and walked swiftly toward the dorms. There had to be a pattern, I thought, and I was right: he was gone over the weekend, but he was back on Tuesday and Thursday. This schedule continued for two weeks, during which the dreams I'd been having, and their strangely correlating physical injuries, were absent—which made me even more convinced that something about my relationship with Gabe had inspired them.

December brought no snow: in Humboldt County, winter was cool and wet. At forty-five degrees, you could get away with a sweater, though the moisture in the air would cling to it as it did to the soft, bright bark of the redwood trees. Among us students, there was an atmosphere of feverishness. We had gotten a taste of vacation over Thanksgiving, and December was a mad dash to winter break, hurdled with final exams. During our history exam—rain splashing the windows, the furious scratch of thirty pencils on paper—Gabe was absent. I rushed through my essay on Spanish colonization and slapped it on Ms. Callaghan's desk, Hannah staring at me in wonder. Then I stopped by the dorm for my raincoat and set out in search of him.

I found him in the attic of the library. He was leaning against one of its octagonal walls with a physics textbook in his hands.

"So you ditched our history final, and now you're studying for physics," I said. "Waste of time. At the rate you're going, I doubt you'll even make it to the end of the semester."

Gabe looked up. His knees were tucked in toward his chest, and notebooks were spread out around him. Faint light shone through the tower's windows, and his eyes looked bare and squinty, as they did in the morning.

"What do you mean?"

"I've seen you," I said. "Tuesdays and Thursdays, like clockwork. You're lucky if Keller hasn't spotted you again, but he will. The thing I can't understand is why you keep doing it."

Gabe put the physics book down and straightened his legs.

"It wasn't me," he said.

"Please, Gabe."

"It wasn't." He raised his eyebrows. "How can you be sure? It's dark out at that time of morning. Have you ever seen my face?"

"You sound pretty defensive for someone who supposedly wasn't there."

"Hardly." Gabe's features relaxed, as if on command.

"Oh, come on," I said. "Who else could it be?"

"David Horikawa. Michael Fritz. It was Mike who told me about Keller's flowers, you know—those ones with the doubled disks. He's been convinced for months Keller's running experiments in that garden. I'm not the only one curious about it."

"You expect me to believe there's a whole band of kids running around Keller's place at night?"

"All I'm saying is it wasn't me."

"But I know you," I said. It was the only thing I could hold on to, the only thing that convinced me I wasn't delusional. "I know the shape of your body, what it looks like when you walk."

I was almost crying. After the months we'd spent together, this cool confrontation was excruciating. I knelt down in front of him, putting my palm on his knee.

"Gabe," I said.

But he only looked out the window, putting his hand over his eyes like a visor. When he turned toward me again, his face had the same blank look I'd seen that night at Keller's.

"I'm sorry," he said. "I have to work."

He picked up the physics book again. When he opened it and began to read, underlining every so often, it was as if I wasn't even there.

• • •

That evening, I collapsed in my bunk. Hannah was out, and being alone made me cry even harder; I blew my nose so loudly that someone in the room next door banged on the wall and shouted, "*Je*-sus Christ, cut it out with the foghorn!" I fell asleep in my clothes, my eyes swollen shut. When the door opened, I thought it was Hannah, coming back from the common room at lights-out. But when someone climbed up to my bunk, the wooden ladder creaking more than it ever did beneath Hannah's ninety-five pounds, I realized it had to be Gabe.

He was disheveled, greasy-haired, and his eyes were blood-shot. He stopped in front of me and knelt.

"What are you doing here?" I asked, scrambling into a sitting position.

"I can't stay for long, but I needed to see you. I have to tell you something."

He exhaled, looking up at the ceiling. When he faced me again, his jaw was set.

"I'm sorry," he said.

"Okay." My head was pounding. "For what, exactly?"

"For acting like a total weirdo. For freezing you out in the library. For—for not being honest." He put a hand on my knee. "The truth is, Sylvie, I'm not doing so well. My head's in a bad place. But I don't want to lose you."

"Then don't," I said.

"It's not that simple."

"What's wrong? Is it your mom? Or your grades? Did you hear from your dad?"

"No, no." Gabe shook his head.

"What, then?"

He seemed more impenetrable than he ever had before, and I was exhausted. Embarrassed, too, that he had seen me this way. The waistband of my jeans had ridden up, digging tracks into my stomach; one sock had fallen off and somehow wound up on my pillow. I hadn't bothered to take my hair out of its bun, and now it sagged over the side of my head, bobbing above one ear whenever I spoke.

"Do you trust me?" he asked.

"I want to."

"Well, can you try?"

"I *have* been trying."

I could feel my eyes filling again. *Stop it*, I told myself. *You're being a girl, a stupid girl.*

"Hey," Gabe whispered. "Don't cry"—and his thumbs were below my eyes, scooping the moisture off my cheeks and wiping it on his jeans. He was frustrated, thinking hard; when we spoke again, it was labored.

"All I need is a few days. A week, tops, to sort everything out. Then we can go back to normal—to how things were. I'm serious this time."

I stared at him, trying to understand. For a moment, I almost gave in, but I was still angry: at his audacity and his withholding, his request for me to trust him when he wouldn't tell me anything. I pushed him by the shoulders, pulling my knees up to my chest so he couldn't come closer. But he pushed back, and we struggled against each other, Gabe trying to calm me while I wrestled even harder. I shoved my knee into his stomach, and he made a low noise of pain, but he didn't pull away. Thick, sloppy tears rolled down my chin and onto the chest of his T-shirt.

Gabe was making snuffling noises, noises that I thought were from exertion before I realized he was crying, too. His head was limp, hanging forward from his neck like a scarecrow's, but he held me just as strongly.

I had never seen him cry before. Against my better judgment, my resistance softened. What did I know of his secrets, and what right did I have to know them yet? Gabe laid his forehead on my chest, wrapping his legs and arms around me until I stilled. I don't know how long we stayed like that; the next thing I remember, it was the middle of the night, the moon a sliver of fingernail in the window. We were lying down, Gabe breathing steadily with sleep. His knees were tucked behind mine, and one of his arms was around my waist. I must have moved slightly, because he stirred and looked at me, his eyelids flickering.

I turned to face him. There were four inches, maybe less, between us.

"Are you sure you don't want to break up?" I asked, keeping my voice low so I didn't wake Hannah.

"I'm sure."

"Why?"

"Why am I sure I don't want to?"

He grinned at me, lopsided.

"Yeah," I said. "Because it kind of seems like you don't know what you want."

"Sylvie," Gabe whispered. He tucked his forehead into the nook of my shoulder; I could feel his breath against my ear. "You're my person."

The words vibrated inside me, and I grinned despite myself. *You're my person*: he was mine, and I was his. But when I woke up the next morning, I wondered if I'd dreamed it. The light was pale and bluish as water, Hannah was snoring softly below me, and Gabe was gone.

• • •

That day, he wasn't in the dining hall at breakfast. I thought he was avoiding me until he was absent at lunch, and again at dinner. Gabe could scarf down three sloppy joes before belching loudly and declaring himself satisfied; there was no way he'd subsisted for an entire day on granola bars from the dorm vending machines. That night, I stood in front of the dessert window, staring at that night's special—whipped-cream-topped Jell-O in plastic cups—while feeling increasingly nauseous. There was a whiff of perfume, and then Nina, Gabe's ex, appeared at my side. She grabbed my arm.

"Sylvie," she said. Her long dark hair fell forward in a sheet, and her silvery eyes were wide with urgency. "Have you heard?"

"Heard what?" I asked, but my stomach was already curdling.

"He's gone," Nina said.

It spread through the dining hall within minutes. The rumor was that Gabe had been asked to leave after he ditched our history exam, but that didn't make sense—Mills would never expel someone because of such a minor transgression. Everyone asked me what had really happened, and the fact that I was just as clueless made me burn with resentment. How could he have told me nothing? I was convinced his departure had something to do with Keller, but I shared this with no one and couldn't prove it even to myself. After dinner, I ran to Gabe's room, but when I burst inside, it was empty: his bottom bunk stripped of sheets and his dresser bare. Beneath a pushed-up window, one open drawer rattled in the wind.

Hannah was the only one who wasn't shocked by Gabe's disappearance. The rest of our group picked over the rumors in the dining hall, hushing in sympathy when I sat down. But she was silent and evasive. One night, while doing homework in our room—Hannah sitting in the chair by the window and I in her bottom bunk, leaning against her enormous frog-shaped pillow—she swiveled abruptly to face me.

"I'm glad he's gone," she said. "There—I said it. Everyone acts like this whole thing is some Shakespearean tragedy, but he wasn't exactly a great guy to begin with."

"That's not true," I said. "You didn't even know him."

"Neither did you!" burst out Hannah. Her curly, corn-silk hair was wrapped in a towel; below it, her cheeks were the color of strawberries. "No one else will come out and admit it, but he was using you, Sylvie. You think it's a coincidence that he only came over at night? That he left before you woke up the next morning?"

"We were *talking*, those nights," I said, but Hannah only

raised her eyebrows. "What? You think he was using me for sex?"

"He wouldn't be the first guy to do it."

"That's a really shitty thing to say, Hannah."

"I'm not saying it to hurt your feelings," said Hannah. "I just don't want you to look back through rose-colored glasses."

It was one of our inside jokes, a phrase our English teacher favored. ("Now, it's Gatsby's nostalgia that gives him life, but it's also what destroys him—he can't help but look back through rose-colored glasses.") But I didn't laugh.

"I'm not," I said.

I turned back to my math sets and looked down at them, hard. I could feel Hannah's eyes on me.

"It's not like you were in love with him, were you?" she asked.

A wave of heat washed through my body. My cotton pajamas felt like wool, and Hannah's blanket was stifling. Hannah stared at me, but I couldn't answer her; I pushed out of bed and ran to the bathroom in my socks, slowing as I passed the hall monitor's office. At the sink, I splashed cold water on my face until the heat passed. I had never been in love before, and I couldn't explain to Hannah how I knew I was now. But my love for Gabe was as recognizable as anything I had seen with my own eyes. Mr. Keller's garden, for instance: its unlatched gate, its shapely darkness, and that strange doubled flower, so vivid a color it could be seen without light.

For months, I was sure I would hear from him. But he didn't call or write, and my own calls to his mother's house went unanswered—there was only her drawl on the machine, the cool beep, and then my own voice, cryptic, tentative ("Gabe, it's me . . ."). It would have been easier to move on if I thought our relationship had been a fling, but I knew that wasn't true. Our conversation in bed, that final night, was a hook in me; I returned to it again and again, searching for meaning I hadn't found before, trying to tease it out of the skin.

Hannah and I returned to our old group of friends, but the girls on our hall seemed colorless and uninteresting now, their conversations petty. At mealtimes, I dragged my fork in circles until Hannah asked me if I was hypnotized. When I went home for winter break, I couldn't sleep. I was groggy during the day, prone to mistakes that startled my family: I put scissors in the refrigerator, ketchup in the freezer, dishwashing soap in the laundry machine.

"It's a breakup, Sylve," said Rodney, "not the zombie apocalypse."

But I couldn't snap out of it. When I got back to school in January, I left my duffel on the floor and climbed onto my bunk, spreading my arms and legs like a starfish. With Gabe gone, there was too much space. It was raining outside, sloppy and plashing; when Hannah walked in, her hair was slicked to her cheeks. She stood in the doorway—huffing from the stairs, a puddle pooling at her feet—and looked at me with her eyebrows raised. Then she dropped her bags.

"Okay," she said. "No."

"No what?"

"No," she repeated, climbing up the ladder to my bunk. "You are not doing this all semester."

"You're getting everything wet," I said in protest.

"Try to stop me," said Hannah, and then she was tickling me as I yelped for leniency, both of us laughing so hard the bed shook. "Come on, Sylvie. You don't want to spend your last semester of high school as some miserable blob of longing."

Over dinner, we plotted a self-betterment program. We took frigid runs before physics, dragging ourselves out of bed at six thirty, racing so fast downhill we were practically falling.

We spent even more time in the workshop, using charcoal to draw our hands open, shut, twined together. Over spring break, we drove to her family's farm in the Sacramento Valley. We sped down Route 101 with the radio turned all the way up, howling at the redwoods, sugar-high on Blizzards from the Petaluma Dairy Queen. Hannah's sisters had all left home, so we had our pick of bedrooms in the farmhouse. During the day, we helped her mother, Ingrid, in the nut orchard. I preferred the almond trees: their hulls fuzzy and green as unripe peaches, their delicate ecology. They needed five years of pollination to bear fruit. It was our job to find and shuck the seeds, tapping each shell with a hammer until it split in two along the seams. At night, we spread out in the unused barn with our charcoals and worked in easy, simpatico silence.

There, I felt peaceful—not ecstatic or despairing, as I had with Gabe, but fine. Even content. It's the physical sensations I remember most: the sun close as a hand pressed to my neck, the relief of a crack in the almond's stone shell. Each nut was a small adversary, a minute-long accomplishment. By the time we left Sacramento, I had almost convinced myself it was possible to let go of him. I could live on my own, I thought, or on a farm with Hannah; maybe I didn't need the highs and lows that came with love. Maybe this quietude—these small, daily pleasures—could be enough.

• • •

That April, I got into UC-Berkeley, and I began to map the pillars and floorboards of my new life. I missed Gabe most in moments of camaraderie among us seniors—reading by the lake in early June, or crowding around someone's computer, looking at photographs from a college visit. But I tried not to dwell on his absence, and with each month, it became a little bit easier to leave him behind.

By the time graduation came around, I had almost done

it. After the ceremony, everyone congregated on the lawn in front of Keller's house, eating cheese cubes and drinking out of plastic cups—champagne for the adults and sparkling cider for us. I stood with my parents and Rodney at a center table, talking with Mr. Keller, when I felt something soft brush against my leg.

I jiggled my foot, thinking it was the tablecloth. But then I felt it on my other leg, and when I reached down, I found a moving, velvety body, its muscles rippling against my calf.

It was a small cat, tawny in color, with rust-colored flecks on its forehead and paws. But what I noticed most was the pressure of its head on my leg, a firmness, as though it wanted to push me into the table.

I dropped my hand and straightened as if I'd touched something soiled. I must have knocked the table with my elbow on the way up, because Rodney's glass began to quiver. Mr. Keller reached for it, but he wasn't fast enough, and the cup toppled lightly into the grass, where the sparkling cider barely missed the cat's tail.

"Is that your cat?" I asked.

"Indeed she is," said Keller. "Lucy."

He had been talking to my mother, a cup of champagne in one hand. I could tell she wanted to continue the conversation and wished I hadn't interrupted it, but I couldn't pretend I was fine.

"I had a dream about her," I said.

Keller's face hardly moved.

"You wouldn't be the first. Lucy's always lurking around the dining hall and the library. Come finals, everyone's dreaming about cats."

There was a pause while my family looked at me. Then my father started to laugh, and Keller smiled briefly before turning back to my mother. But I still felt as though every nerve in my body had been lit with a match, and I couldn't concentrate on the reception. The whole thing gave the end of my time at Mills an uneasy feeling. Soon, I began to avoid thinking about the school at all. It became easier and easier until the summer before my last year of college, when Gabe returned.

# 4

One Wednesday in late September, when the heat was just beginning to lift, I went to our neighbors' house for the first time. I was standing at our kitchen sink, washing water glasses with the window open, when I heard someone call to me.

"You want lemonade?"

I looked up. It was the woman next door, hanging out of a second-story window that faced our house and the train tracks. She leaned from the waist, so that her upper body tilted out of the frame, her hair streaking the sky.

"Sorry?"

"I said would you like lemonade. I saw you looking at my porch. Sometimes I sit there with a drink but I'm in today, it's too goddamn hot. So I thought I'd invite you."

I had planned to go to the office to enter the data from last night's session. Our participant had wriggled out of his leg straps and walked down the hall to the building's emergency exit. When Keller brought him back to the lab, he had no recollection that he'd been there before; eventually, he became so agitated that Gabe had to sedate him. We woke him several hours later.

We hadn't lost control like this since patient 222, a woman

named Anne March. She was the first person I worked with, and she left our study abruptly, though I tried not to conflate these two facts. I still wondered if we'd helped her at all; sometimes I thought we'd actually made things worse. Every so often, I forgot about her, but then, like a fussy, chronic injury—a pulled muscle or a bad ankle—she made herself known again. But I didn't want to spend the day thinking about Anne, and I was too curious about the woman next door to turn down an opportunity to meet her.

"Okay!" I shouted back. "Thank you!"

I put my last glass upside down on a towel and crossed the driveway that separated our houses, the screen door hissing shut behind me.

The woman had left her front door ajar. She stood by the refrigerator, her large feet turned out. She wore a ruffled white dress, and up close, her legs looked even more like a calf's—shins longer than thighs, with hyperextended knobs for knees. When I stepped into the kitchen, she came to greet me, a glass pitcher in one hand. The liquid inside was bright yellow, topped with little pieces of cucumber and strawberry and torn mint.

"I'm Janna," she said. She pronounced the *J* like a *Y*—*Yanna.*

"Sylvie."

I held out my hand. Her fingers were long and thin, cool from the refrigerator.

"Sylvie. That's fascinating. Do you like it?"

The barbell above her eye raised along with her eyebrow. Her irises were the iridescent gray-blue of abalone shells.

"Like it?" I asked. "I guess so."

"I do," she said. "Very much."

She walked to a large standing cabinet, painted yellow and peeling, and took out two ceramic cups. The kitchen's layout was identical to ours, but the two rooms looked nothing alike.

Here, a mix of pots and pans hung from multicolored pegs, and the kitchen table—wooden and water-ringed, one bad leg wrapped in duct tape—had a *matryoshka*-doll centerpiece. The nesting dolls reminded me of my paintings: the bright figures resting inside each other like secrets, increasing in detail as they decreased in size.

"Janna's not a name you hear often," I said. "Are you from the States?"

"Nope. Finland. But the name itself is Hebrew. Mother started out Lutheran, but Daddy's a Jew and she converted. His family's from Israel, but he met Mother in Helsinki, where he was born. There are a little more than a thousand Jews in Finland, you know, and that's where most of them live."

"I didn't know. Are you practicing?"

"Ah, no." She shook her head, and the strands of red and black rustled together. "I left a lot of things behind. But I appreciate it, the ritual. Ritual and ceremony and songs and bitter herbs. And the sweet things, too. Charoset is sweet. You've had it?"

She set down the cups, one blue and one green, and poured the lemonade hastily. Drops splattered the table.

"I haven't," I said.

"Are you religious?"

She put the mug of lemonade at my place and sat down across from me, waiting for me to drink. But I was trying to keep up with the conversation: like a wild bird, it kept jumping unexpectedly, then resettling on delicate claws.

"No," I said. "Neither were my parents—my mom is a microbiologist, and my dad's an ancient historian. He studies ancient history, I mean—the Sumerians. He himself is very modern."

Janna smiled, distant. "Funny," she said.

"Anyway, I suppose that's where I get it, the atheism. I'm in academia, too."

"What do you study?" asked Janna. But she was examining the fingers on her left hand, her knuckles bent; eyeing something, she brought the fourth finger to her teeth and tore at the jagged skin around the nail bed.

"Oh, it's complicated."

I could tell this upset her. Her face and neck flushed, and I became more conscious of the blue veins beneath her skin. Is it terrible to say I was delighted? It was a small moment of leverage—my foot wedged in a cranny of rock, my body muscled above hers.

"I'm not sure I can say much about it, honestly," I said.

Gabe and I could talk about our work within limits—Keller asked us to be vague, and we were to never share information about individual patients—but we had never done it. Both of us feared we would be seen as quacks—or worse, interrogated, doubted, and criticized. It was safer to keep the truth between us.

"I see," said Janna. She took a gulp of lemonade and looked out the window to the street, as if waiting for someone to join us.

"What do you do?" I asked. "Sometimes I see you coming back in the evening."

As soon as I said it, I reddened. I didn't want Janna to know I'd been observing her as closely as I had. But if she was surprised, she didn't say so.

"I'm paid to garden. *Landscaper* is the term, I suppose, but I prefer *gardener*. I work for one couple at the moment who've got a big plot of land, several acres. It's like a bunch of needy babies crying out for me. That's what Thomas says: I'm raising my children."

"Thomas," I said. "Is that the man who lives here?"

Janna nodded. She put her spidery fingers on either side of the mug and began to rotate it.

"My husband," she said. "He's in academia, like you—the

English department. He's a Romanticist, studying for his PhD."

I wasn't sure whether he was studying the Romantics or if she meant to imply that university work was a romantic gesture in itself, a comment that had to be directed in part at me. Then and even months later, it was difficult for me to gauge Janna's slyness, to sift it out of what was sincere.

"And you?" she asked. "I've seen someone else coming out of your house. Is he your husband? The short man?"

"My boyfriend."

I was irritated by then. I finished off my lemonade, ready to make an excuse about work. But Janna leaned forward in her chair and began to tell me about her courtship with Thomas— how they met in college when he was studying poetry and she was in botany; back then, she said, she thought she might be a field researcher. Something delicate in the bright sheen of her eyes, her quick, pale hands, stopped me from resenting her.

The tattoo on her arm was a plant, black and white, with slanted flowers and sharp leaves. It traveled from her palm to her elbow. Her skin seemed too thin to withstand such inkiness. But most disturbing was the piercing on the back of her neck, which I only saw when she turned: two balls spaced an inch or so apart without a bar. I couldn't tell how they'd been inserted, and that was what unnerved me. Keller had shaken my notions of privacy, and though I was now tied to his work, it made me fiercely protective of my core. There was something about the piercing in Janna's neck that seemed invasive, even if she had chosen it. That was what struck me: her allowance of invasion, her desire for it.

• • •

As it turned out, Gabe spoke to Thomas the next day. He told me that night while we did our exercises. In Fort Bragg, we had begun to feel the physical toll of our lifestyle, in which we were either sleeping or observing the sleep of others. Our lower backs ached; our knees popped. Because our work schedule was so irregular, it didn't make sense to join a gym, so Gabe suggested we use DVDs. We rented stacks of them from the library, our tote bags clattering on the walk home. Today, we were using *8 Minute Abs* with *8 Minute Buns*.

"I went over to the neighbors' house yesterday," I said. "The woman invited me—Janna."

Gabe grunted. When we finished our sit-ups, we sat up and took a sip of water.

"Funny," he said. "I met the guy this morning. At the Laundromat."

We started bicycle crunches.

"You didn't mention that," I said.

"It was a little strange, to be honest. He sat down next to me by the dryers. I thought he recognized me, but he didn't say anything. He took out all these books. And then"—we stood for lunges—"when I was leaving, he asked if I would wait for him, so we could walk back together."

"So you talked then?"

"Not much. He mentioned the weather—asked did I think it was humid. I said I did. He was sort of looking around like this."

Gabe dropped his shoulders so his neck was long and his chin lifted, like a prairie dog. He turned his head from side to side, as if searching for someone in a crowd.

"Well, the woman wasn't any less awkward," I said, though it occurred to me that *awkward* was the wrong word. It was more that she made me feel uneasy—as if she didn't understand how to do small talk or wasn't playing by the rules.

"The weirdest part," said Gabe, squatting, "was that when we got here, he suggested the four of us get together for dinner. He said his wife had thought of it."

"Really? I didn't think she liked me very much."

"Why not?"

The tape ended. Gabe turned off the TV, and we flopped to the floor, our stomachs rising and falling in unison.

"It was just a feeling I had."

But the more I thought about it, I couldn't be sure I was right. The next morning, I slipped a note under their door inviting them to eat with us that night, and despite what Gabe had told me, I was still surprised when they accepted.

• • •

Kraft macaroni, tomato soup, cream of mushroom casserole: these were all things that my mother had made when I was growing up and that seemed painfully unsuitable now. Gabe cooked more often than I did, in part because he enjoyed it but mostly because I had not inherited certain womanly qualities from my mother, who did not have them to give me. I had never known how to bake scones or how to bounce an infant to keep it from crying. When Gabe approached me in college, I was becoming acutely aware of the differences between me and other girls, and the idea of Keller's work—so divorced from typical gendered life, divorced even from typical human life—felt like a blessedly alternate universe.

Now, for the first time in years, I felt real social anxiety. I wanted to prove I could play hostess. So I told Gabe I would cook and found a recipe for skewered chicken, the breasts slippery as silk in my hands. I set the table with my grandmother's red tablecloth and a small vase, which Gabe filled with daisies he picked along the train tracks.

Janna had called to say they'd be by at seven thirty. But it was eight when our doorbell rang, and the chicken had almost gone cold. Gabe and I had dressed up—he wore a button-up shirt with his jeans, and I had on a knee-length navy skirt—but Janna and Thomas looked like exotic birds in our entryway. She wore a short, canary-yellow dress, he a three-piece herringbone suit that looked much too hot for the late summer weather.

"I'm Janna," she said, turning toward Gabe. "And this is Thomas."

After I began to call him Thom, I found it odd she never did. I still remember the way she introduced him that day, as if it was her duty to preserve something old-fashioned and noble in him.

"Pleased to meet you," said Thomas. He shook my hand, his grip boyishly enthusiastic; he nodded his head at the same time, the fuzzy strawberry-blond hair flapping up and down on his forehead. He wore a bow tie at his neck, and that, combined with his freckles and glasses, made him look like a character in a newspaper comic. But behind the glasses, his eyes were a deeply concentrated brown. They anchored his energy, like a mooring dropped in busy water.

"For you," said Janna, holding out a porcelain dish, fuchsia, with plastic wrap on top. "Blueberry soup, for dessert—something my mother used to make. *Mustikkakeitto*, in Finnish."

The words had a staccato beauty. In her high, lilting voice, they sounded sharp and delicate as glass shards.

"Thank you," I said, taking the bowl. The liquid inside was a deep magenta stain. Gabe reached for Janna's hand.

"Gabe," he said. His smile broke open as easily as it did with Keller's patients, and he held Janna's hand in a firm grip, then Thomas's.

"Quite nice of you to have us over," said Thomas, flattening the front of his vest with his palms and looking around at our walls, which were bare. "It occurred to us too late that we should have hosted you. But here we are, and we brought Janna's soup. Though now I wish we had something better—a housewarming plant or something, yeah? Bit bare in here, unless that's how you like it?"

"Don't be rude," said Janna. "Thomas says the first thing that comes to his mind, and usually the first thing isn't the best. They've just moved in, they haven't got time to get the place decorated. It was that way for us, too, in the beginning—everything packed away in boxes and boxes."

Later, I would marvel at the change in Janna. Alone, she hadn't seemed to worry about small talk and propriety, but with Thomas she acted like a moral handler. As time went on, I began to notice that he did the same to her, however subtly. They seemed to exist in this constant state of checks and balances, one catching the other whenever they swung too far.

But I didn't have time to sort through this then; I was too busy feeling embarrassed about the state of our walls, for the truth was we had nothing in boxes. Gabe had wanted to hang some of my paintings, but I didn't want to look at them every day. Each piece felt like a minor exorcism, a dredging up of all the silt and sludge that collected around my consciousness. When I finished one, I felt accomplished, but I never thought they were beautiful.

As we sat down at the table, a train approached. We paused to listen to it whistle, then howl.

"It's a lovely noise," said Janna, her back erect. "I always like it when I hear one go by."

I found it intoxicating, too, like a missive from another world. The trains came through erratically that year; we never knew what they were carrying or when the next one would come. But if it was at night, and we were asleep, I always woke up.

I'd put the chicken back in the oven to keep it hot, and it had dried, but Janna professed to love it. I felt too jittery to eat much, so I asked questions: How long had they lived here? What did Thomas do? He was a graduate student in the English department, he told us, studying Romantic poets of the nineteenth century.

"My third year here," he said. "But we try to get out in the summers. This year we went to South Carolina to see my mother—didn't get back until August."

"Thomas was studying for his preliminary exam," said Janna. "He read two hundred books, and then he wrote eight essays in eight hours. Doesn't it sound awful?"

"I was *supposed* to read two hundred books," said Thomas, with a bite of chicken. "I read one fifty. No—make that one forty. I shouldn't lie to myself, I skimmed at least ten. How can you skim Lord Byron? The point is, you can't."

"Sounds like a huge task," said Gabe, leaning forward. "And what about you, Janna? Are you involved in the university?"

"Nope," said Janna. She swallowed a sip of wine. "I garden."

"She used to study botany," said Thomas. "Before that it was biology. She likes the way all the little parts of a thing fit together."

"No, if I'd liked it I would have stayed," said Janna, with a sharp look at Thom. "I dropped out our senior year of college. I'd rather be touching things, you know, than reading about them. But let's talk about the two of you—where did you meet?"

Though she'd been effusive about the chicken, she hadn't eaten much of it. Now she picked the chunks off the skewer with her fingers and grouped them on one side of her plate. Gabe and I looked at each other.

"It was in high school," I said.

"High school!" said Thomas. "Fantastic!"

"Thomas goes wild for a good love story," said Janna. "Were you sweethearts back then?"

"We dated for a while," said Gabe. "But then we went in separate directions. We got in touch again partway through college, before Sylvie's senior year."

He grinned at me and put a hand on mine on top of the

table. I was soothed by its warmth, but I wished he had taken my left hand—the one beneath the table, closest to him.

"Those are the best kind of relationships," said Janna. "Ones with a long history. Thomas and I are the same way. We met in our first year of college, in the only poetry class I ever took—Keats."

"'In spite of all,'" said Thomas, "'some shape of beauty—'"

His voice changed as he recited the poem, steadying and becoming lower in pitch. There was something commanding about his presence now. But Janna waved a hand, cutting in.

"Oh, stop, they don't want to hear it. I certainly don't. It's been a summer of hearing him go on about Keats, and Blake, and Coleridge—don't look at me that way, sweet, you know it's true—and Wordsworth, and *Goethe*, and who's that annoyingly emotional man who's always going on about social ills?"

"Shelley," said Thomas, and cackled. "'Oh! lift me as a wave, a leaf, a cloud! I fall upon the thorns of life! I bleed!'"

"Besides, we haven't even asked what you do," said Janna. "Do you see what I mean? We get talking about poetry and then real life goes out of the conversation entirely. Gabe—you tell us."

I wondered if she remembered my own evasiveness at her house several days before and thought she might get a more direct reply out of Gabe. Either way, I was happy to let him give our answer. He was better at it than I was—I got tripped up trying to tell the truth.

"It's not very exciting," said Gabe. "We're sleep researchers in the Center for Neuroscience. Mainly, we're studying consciousness and REM cycles. We look at the point when dreaming begins and the extent to which the dreamer is conscious of that shift."

"How can you tell?" asked Janna.

"Well, there are different ways. We use a polysomnogram

to measure the stages of sleep through brain activity, muscle tone, eye movements, and so on—this tells us when the subject is in REM sleep. That's when dreaming occurs. Our next job is to figure out whether or not they're aware of it."

Thomas leaned back in his chair, dropping his fork onto the plate with a clatter.

"You don't ask them, I presume? 'Sorry, don't mean to bother you, but are you dreaming yet? No? Whoops, carry on then, just pretend I'm not here.'"

"No, we use a mask," I said, smiling. "It's equipped with two LEDs—light-emitting diodes—which we flash a certain number of times once the subject's in REM. They're supposed to respond to the flashes by making an eye-movement signal: two pairs of horizontal eye movements, left-right, left-right, if they're asleep and conscious of it. If no signals are made, we can assume they aren't conscious."

"Like we said," Gabe said, shrugging, "it's not very interesting."

"It's hardly uninteresting," said Janna. "I'd like to try it sometime. You don't need a new subject, do you? Hook me up to the machine—I'll tell you if I'm awake."

She was leaning in, her tattooed arm cast across the table. I was transfixed by her combination of toughness and delicacy, her body pale as a mirage.

Thomas laughed, staring at Janna with his eyebrows raised, and Gabe followed him.

"I'll put you on our list," Gabe said. "Lots of people trying to get in for this kind of research, you know."

"Vying for their chance to be shot through with light and made conscious," said Thomas. "Oh, to be new-born!"

Gabe rubbed my hand. I was relieved that we'd squeezed through without too much probing. This was the explanation we gave to our oldest friends, the nurses at the sleep clinic, even our parents. It wasn't untrue, exactly—our studies started by measuring consciousness this way—but it was only a small slice of what we did. Gabe was in favor of saying we studied sleep medication, but lying so blatantly made me uneasy. And more than that, I wanted to be known, wanted desperately, even then, to be found out.

We cleared the table with Thomas and Janna's help. When Thomas excused himself to use the bathroom, Gabe began to do dishes, and Janna offered to dry them. By the time they had almost finished, Thomas still hadn't returned.

I went upstairs to look for him. The bathroom was empty, its door creaking open. But the light in our bedroom was on, and when I ducked my head inside the door frame, I found him sitting on our bed.

He was perched on the edge, holding up to the light a locket my mother gave me. Usually I left it on my bedside table, but Thomas had hooked the chain around his index finger. The locket had been opened to reveal two photos: one of my mother, and one of me. He tapped the edge with his other index finger, so that it turned around and around, tangling on the chain.

When he saw me, he smiled, bright and sheepish.

"So sorry," he said. "Didn't mean to go out of bounds. I used the bathroom, and then I wandered in here. I sat down to have a look at the trains. Well, the place where trains would be. The empty trainless place."

The locket was still on his finger. I held out my palm, and he gave it back to me.

"I tend to fidget," he said. "I just picked it up to have something to do with my hands."

"That's all right," I said, though I was spooked. I wanted to get him back downstairs, but he spoke before I could suggest it.

"You're welcome to call me Thom."

"All right."

"If you like."

"I'll try."

"All right," he said—my words—and smiled.

The window by the bed was open; outside, a group of flies—the last survivors of the summer hatch—whined softly. Thom turned, swinging his legs around to face me instead of the train tracks.

"What do you really study?" he asked. "What within sleep?"

"Consciousness and REM cycles, like Gabe said. We make physiological recordings—"

"I remember what Gabe said." He picked at the threading on my comforter for a moment, then dropped it down. "It just seemed a bit simplistic. First of all, there's a word for what you're studying. It's lucidity, or lucid dreaming—when a person's aware that they're dreaming. Am I right?"

"That's right."

"Which is why I find it hard to believe that's all you're measuring," said Thomas. "It's been done. I learned about dreaming and lucidity in a couple of intro psych classes—long before you became involved in this kind of research, I presume. Some of the Romantics even knew about it: Thomas De Quincey, Coleridge, Keats."

"You're right—we're not the first to study lucid dreaming. But we're doing something different."

I paused, and Thomas looked at me with expectation. I'm not sure when I made the decision to tell him more than I had ever told anyone else, but I know it was before that moment. Maybe it was when I followed him upstairs, leaving Gabe and Janna in the kitchen, or maybe it was even earlier—the first time I saw them, returning home in the storm.

"Accounts of lucid dreaming have been around since the fifth century," I said. "Saint Augustine wrote about it first, and Tibetan Buddhists recorded their experiences in a funerary text. Back then, it was used to access a higher spiritual plane, even to relieve stress and problem-solve. It was treated like an escape. But we think of it as a return."

"To?"

"To the self," I said. "We dream in metaphors. If you're having car troubles, you're feeling powerless. Failing a test? You're insecure, unprepared. Trapped? Well, that one's obvious. The brain is like an excellent fiction writer: every part of a dream is laden with meaning that can be unlocked, analyzed, and understood. We hide our greatest hopes there, our deepest fears. And when we learn to read our dreams, so to speak—not retrospectively, when we wake up, but right there in the moment—we're reading the story of who we really are."

"Isn't that just Freud?" asked Thom.

"Partly." I sat down beside him, my palms beneath my thighs. "Freud's ideas make up the bedrock of dream interpretation, so it'd be impossible for us to avoid his influence—not that we're trying to. Freud was the first to suggest that dreams give us access to the unconscious mind; he called them the royal road, the king's highway. Dreams are almost entirely visual, but he gave us a language with which to talk about them, and it still holds up. Analysis is essentially an act of translation."

"You're old-school, then," said Thom. "These days, don't most people believe that dreams are meaningless? The brain sloughing off nervous tension?"

"It's true. Our ideas aren't popular. But dreams involve a whole host of brain mechanisms—they're as rich in neurological activity as many conscious processes. There's just too much going on for us to explain them away as random nerve firings."

Thom grinned. "Do you believe in Freud's other ideas, too, then? The sexual complexes? The idea that all dreams are wish fulfillment?"

I shook my head. "That's where we're more aligned with Jung. He thought dreamers could tap into resources of creativity and ingenuity, imagination and adventure. Healing, too. Besides, Freud never studied lucid dreaming. He relied on dream recollection, which means his patients reported their dreams after they woke up. But memory is fallible—it's what makes eyewitness accounts notoriously unreliable—and that means the conscious mind isn't trustworthy. Lucid dreaming allows patients to experience their dreams in real time. It gives them a panoramic view."

"A sense of narrative," said Thom.

"Exactly. Lucid dreaming also vastly improves dream recall, which means patients can work through their issues in the moment—and come away with a more thorough memory of what happened. It isn't enough to go cherry-picking for symbols. Freud looked for the metaphors, but he didn't string them together. He didn't look for the full story."

It was difficult to breathe. But if Thomas was starting to judge me, he didn't show it; when he spoke, his tone was light.

"And why would anyone want to do all that *work* while they're dreaming? Isn't sleep supposed to be restorative?"

I laughed.

"Our patients don't have a choice," I said. "The people who come to us have sleep disorders—disorders that make them talk in their sleep and get out of bed."

Thomas crossed his legs. I could see a childlike interest in him that made me think of what he must have been like as a boy—the floppy reddish hair, the round glasses, the long limbs in miniature.

"Still," he said. "Why do you have to interfere in their dreams? You can't send 'em to therapy while they're awake?"

"These aren't your garden-variety sleep issues—sleep apnea, insomnia. The patients we see have parasomnia overlap disorder and REM behavior disorder, dysfunctions that make

them act out their dreams. Most of us are physically para-
lyzed during REM sleep, but these patients aren't, and there's
nothing more dangerous than a dreamer out of bed. They can
attack their bedmates, trying to fight off intruders who aren't
there. Some have even jumped out of windows. These people
are disturbed at a subconscious level—and in order to help
them, we have to meet them there. Lucidity enables them to
realize they're dreaming. It enables them to intervene."

"So you're hacking in."

His face was pleasant enough, but his voice had a new
edge.

"What do you mean?"

He leaned back on the bed, his elbows propped up behind
him, and cocked his head.

"You're intruders. Robbing the bank of the subconscious."

"We're breaking in, yes. But we're helping them break in,
too. We give patients the opportunity to see who they really
are and how they came to be that way. It's empowering."

"To look at something is to change it," said Thom. "Your
patients have disorders—fair enough. But you're still opening
up a part of the brain that the brain itself has tried desperately to hide. There's got to be an evolutionary reason we
don't remember most of our dreams. Some things are better
tucked away, if you catch my drift. Some books shouldn't be
read."

"But why?"

"Because," said Thom. His brow was furrowed, as if he
were thinking through a particularly difficult math problem,
and his voice was neutral. "Couldn't what begins as an exercise in self-knowledge actually reveal our darkest impulses?
Once we *experience* our dreams—not via recollection, but
right there in the moment—how long is it before we start
to believe that this is who we really are, what we really want,
how we really feel? You're giving people access to their dreams

as they're happening, which must make the dreams feel infinitely more real—more believable. Couldn't they lose track of what's real and what's not? Doesn't the line begin to blur?" He sat up again and looked at me. "When does one's dream consciousness become their consciousness, I mean? Maybe the dreams themselves aren't dangerous. Maybe what's dangerous is putting people in contact with them."

He raised his eyebrows. My body was taut. This was exactly what I hadn't wanted—someone doubting us, rummaging around and jumbling the thesis we had so painstakingly pieced together. I felt a part of myself begin to close off, like a person running to guard a half-open door. But it also felt even more important that I persuade him.

"Okay," I said. "Two years ago, we saw a patient with RBD. She was thirty-five, a single mother of two. Ten years earlier, her house was burglarized while she was asleep, and that's when her symptoms started. Back then, she was living alone. When she met her husband, her symptoms decreased—but five years later, they divorced, and her RBD came back. One night, she thought she saw a man crouched in the corner of her bedroom. She jumped on him, and that's when she woke up, alone and bloody. She'd leapt onto her bedside table—knocked out four teeth and shattered a rib."

"Jesus," said Thom.

"With our training, she was able to become lucid. Once she realized she was dreaming, she could recognize the intruders for what they were—figments of her imagination, echoes of the past. She hasn't had an incident since."

That woman was one of our greatest, cleanest successes; without her, I doubted that Keller's work would have been commissioned by the university.

"So that's the goal, then? Healing the troubled souls of disordered dreamers? There's no other motive?"

"What do you mean?"

Thom shrugged. He looked upward, and his glasses caught the light of the lamp.

"You're looking at human capacity," he said, "and trying to see how far it can be stretched. But who benefits more: the individuals you're studying, or *science?*"

"Well, we hope to benefit both of them."

"Fair enough."

"Why are you looking at me like that?"

"It's just that experimental research isn't usually so charitable."

"Hey," I said. "I'm all for asking questions, friendly debate, whatever you want to call it—but you really don't know very much about us. We've been refining this procedure for years, trying to make sure it runs as smoothly and ethically as possible."

"But smoothly and ethically are two very different things," Thom said. "And sometimes, I imagine, they're completely at odds."

I must have bristled, because he seemed to realize he was crossing a line. He smiled, more warmly this time, his eyes wide with apology.

"Listen, I didn't mean any harm. I tend to ask a hell of a lot of questions. That's one thing you'll learn about me, if we get to know each other better. It's a nervous mechanism, partly." He rubbed his palms together. "Besides, I'm an academic. I like these sorts of exercises. To me, it's a theoretical debate—it isn't personal."

"It's fine," I said. "You certainly have the right to ask questions."

"Thank you," said Thom.

I knew he was trying to pull me out of whatever cramped box I had gotten myself into. But what I needed was some way to trust him. This arch, impish Thom I didn't trust; but I remembered the way he had recited the Keats poem at dinner—or started to, anyway—his voice a heavy, kicked-along stone.

"What was the rest of the poem?" I asked. "The Keats poem, the one you mentioned at dinner?"

In his face there was both pleasure and surprise; he looked like a boy who did not often know the answers in class but who, called upon this time, had only to open his mouth.

"'In spite of all,'" he said, "'some shape of beauty moves the pall from our dark spirits.'"

"I thought it would be more positive," I said.

"But it is," said Thom.

From downstairs there came sounds of laughter: Gabe's raucous and guttural, Janna's climbing higher octaves. When we walked down, Gabe's head was hanging back, his shoulders shaking.

"Janna was just telling me—she was telling me—" It was a kind of laughter I rarely saw in him: keeled over, full body. "It was a terrible joke . . ."

They were sitting at the table, bowls of half-eaten blueberry soup in front of them. Janna crossed her hands in front of her, trying to quiet him. Then she turned to Thom and me.

"Three children walk into the woods," she said. "But only one child returns, carrying a bag of bones. The child's mother says, 'Whose bones are those, my darling?' And the child looks at her and beams and says, 'The ones who walked too slow.'"

She grinned. The points of her canine teeth reminded me of a cat. Thom shook his head.

"It's awful," said Gabe. But it took minutes for him to quiet down, and even when he did, little puffs of laughter escaped into the night.

# 5

BERKELEY, CALIFORNIA, 1999

In August of 1999, I arrived on the UC-Berkeley campus along with five thousand other freshmen. I carried with me my dad's beat-up blue duffel bags and a leather backpack with a magnetic closure, which my mother bought to replace the corduroy JanSport I'd carried around at Mills. I can still picture the softened blue fabric, which had lost all sense of structure from years of carrying my color-coordinated binders and drawn-on, heavy books—none of which I'd brought to Berkeley, believing their lessons behind me.

There was a tangible feeling of precipice that fall. By 1999, theories of climate change had made their way to Rutgers Newark, where my parents taught. Earlier that year, some of their colleagues had attended the Intergovernmental Panel on Climate Change, and over the summer, the heat wave that swept the northeastern U.S. killed forty people in Philadelphia alone. Now they complained about the weather in Berkeley, saying it was too cold for summer in California, that fifty-nine degrees wasn't *natural*, and even though I reminded them that the coldest winter Mark Twain ever saw was the summer he spent in San Francisco—and he had lived in the 1800s—they merely squinted at the campus, uncomforted.

It was more than just the weather, of course. As we drew closer to the year 2000, even the most skeptical among us wondered what the millennium would bring. In my psychology course, we spent a unit on millennium predictions—the Tribulation, the second coming of Christ, the war of Armageddon. Some of the other students complained of nightmares. But I found myself magnetized by the predictions, the Rapture especially—all of the living and born-again dead rising into the sky like paper lanterns, their bodies lit from the inside and translucent as white sheets.

Still, there were moments when all this was forgotten, when we gathered close to the radiator in somebody's room and told stories from what felt like our past lives. My years at boarding school lent me a new exoticism. Even mundane details—the hall monitors, the curfews, the night privileges that came with senior year—took on a new, storied life when told to an audience who had only ever lived with their parents. My roommates—Donna, a pole-vaulter from Texas, and a Southern California transplant named Mallory—wanted to know how I'd ended up at boarding school in the first place. But when I told them that I went to Mills not because I showed exceptional promise, like the recruits, but because my father had gone there and received a hefty discount on my tuition, they seemed deflated.

"Oh," said Mallory from the bunk bed above Donna's, turning again to her *San Francisco* magazine. She'd ordered it to be sent to her university mailbox despite the fact that we lived in Berkeley, an hour away by train. "So you were a legacy."

I'd heard the term before, but I'd never really thought it applied to me. I found little in myself of my father's legacy. Thin and heavily bearded, he studied cuneiform script and made a hobby of erecting tiny wooden ships in glass bottles. When I was little, I thought it was a miracle, and he wouldn't show me otherwise—he presented them to me when he was finished, gleaming with pride, and I gaped at the size of the ship inside and how it was so much larger than the neck of the bottle.

Years later, on one of the shared computers at Mills, I used the Internet to look up how they were made. At home, we used a noisy dial-up modem that required use of the telephone line, so my brother and I were restricted to a half hour each night. Plus, it worked so slowly and theatrically that it was more of a family joke than anything else; Rodney and I had memorized the jerky song of its connection process and parroted it back and forth while setting the table or getting ready for bed. So when I got to Mills, where we could use the high-speed Internet in the library, I couldn't believe what I'd been missing out on. It was so easy to find information, so easy to solve any problem, that I was almost afraid to trust it. The hierarchical structure of boarding school had taught me that information had to be vetted—by a textbook, by an instructor, by an administrative higher-up—before it was accepted as truth. But I was excited by the Internet, too, its free and unchecked passages. It meant that learning could also be passed from the ground up. It meant, in a small way, insurrection.

When I returned home for Thanksgiving that year, I told my father I'd figured it out—that because the fully formed ship could never fit through the opening, the trick was to build it *outside* the bottle, with its sails and masts collapsed. Once you'd eased it inside, you pulled on a string that lifted the masts, and the whole ship unfolded and rose.

I thought he would be impressed. But he looked surprised and mildly hurt, as if I'd broken an agreement we had settled on years ago. He couldn't blame me, I thought—the inflation technique now seemed so obvious that I couldn't believe I hadn't put it together before. But I was irritated about more than that. It felt unfair that our relationship rested on something as fragile and miniature as a handmade ship. And if it did, I didn't think it was my fault.

I'd grown up with the expectation that when high school came, I'd go where my father had gone. I knew my parents thought my education was the most important gift they could give me, but it had consequences, too. My bedroom had begun to feel more and more like a childhood relic, with its museum-like inventory of past interests and art projects. My parents tried to plan special activities when I was home, but this made me feel even more like a guest. Other people knew what their fathers ate for breakfast and how to fight with their little brothers. Rodney and I saw each other so infrequently that we hardly knew which buttons to press, which ones had been updated and no longer worked the same way. We lived together like bears raised in domesticity, their wildness latent and confused, bears afraid to swipe for fear that they would only scrape at air.

• • •

On New Year's Eve, we gathered in the dorm common room with a bottle of Jack Daniels to watch the Times Square special. The dorm had been decorated with shiny, metallic streamers, as if matte colors had become outmoded along with grunge and floppy disks. We'd heard rumors of a problem known as Y2K, or the millennium bug—a technology crash that could paralyze everything from air traffic control to elevators, since computer systems had only been wired to support a two-digit year. On TV, the Times Square ball hung seventy-seven feet aboveground, and we wondered if this would fail, too, and stay suspended atop the flagpole when midnight turned.

We passed around a crumpled article that someone had found online and pinned to the common room bulletin board. It was a piece from the December 1900 issue of *Ladies'*

*Home Journal,* written by John Elfreth Watkins Jr. and called "What May Happen in the Next Hundred Years."

"These prophecies will seem strange," wrote Mr. Watkins, "almost impossible. Yet they have come from the most learned and conservative minds in America." And given the century's lapse in time, we were all pretty impressed by what Mr. Watkins's learned minds got right. Sure, strawberries weren't as large as apples, as some had predicted they would be, and flies did, in fact, still exist. But it was true that automobiles had been substituted for horses, that weapons could destroy whole cities, that photographs could be taken at any distance and replicate all of nature's colors. It was true, too, that there were airships to transport people and goods, but also to act as war vessels and to make observations at great heights above earth. Man had also seen around the world, via what would become the television: "The instrument bringing these distant scenes to the very doors of people will be connected with a giant telephone apparatus," he wrote, "transmitting each incidental sound in its appropriate place. Thus the guns of a distant battle will be heard to boom when seen to blaze, and thus the lips of a remote actor or singer will be heard to utter words or music when seen to move."

*Heard to boom when seen to blaze*—these words looped through my head that night, their old rhythm and their poetry. There was something haunting about Watkins and the human capacity to predict the future, as much as it seemed to elude us. And the predictions that hadn't yet been realized—were they still to come? That winter could be turned into summer and night into day? What of prediction number twenty-eight, his forecast for the animals?

*There will be no wild animals except in menageries. Rats and mice will have been exterminated. The horse will have become practically extinct. Cattle and sheep will have no horns. Food animals will be bred to expend practically all their life energy in producing meat, milk, wool and other by-products. Horns, bones, muscles and lungs will have been neglected.*

It disturbed me more than the others—the animals gutted, made impotent, stripped of their dignity and their defenses. When the countdown began, my breath caught in my throat. As much as I'd scoffed at rumors of the Tribulation, even of the technology crash, what would happen if I was wrong? If human beings vanished, and so did our consciousness of the world—our inventories of plants and insects and endangered birds, our ability to predict weather patterns and measure whole populations—would the planet still know itself? Or would it be better off without our predictions and the ways we made them come true?

But at midnight, the ball slid easily to the ground at One Times Square. The dorm elevators rose and fell just as they had before. That night, before bed, I pressed my face to the sliver of window beside my bunk and watched as a plane flew by, blinking faintly in the darkness.

• • •

By sophomore year, my old interest in physics had flagged, and I'd decided to become a psychology major. Maybe Keller's classes at Mills had ruined me, or perhaps I simply lost interest in the consistency of numbers. Either way, the laws of motion could no longer compete with the thrill of studying other people. The laws of human beings were counterintuitive and absurd, broken as often as they were followed.

In the spring, my adviser suggested a class in the film department. Painting 201 conflicted with my abnormal psych requirement, and she'd heard good things about Intro to Videography.

"At the very least, it'll give you some good material," she said, leaning forward. "It's sanctioned people-watching. Legal voyeurism! A few of my kids got a lot out of it."

Her hair was brown except for an inch-wide silver chunk, as if she'd streaked it that way on purpose. She wore a shawl with various hanging bobbles that shook when she spoke emphatically. The walls in her office were hung with woven Peruvian tapestries and framed diplomas and grisly portraits of human beings in various states of psychic pain. Though she looked too old to have young children, she had recently adopted twin four-year-old boys from Indonesia. When I saw her around campus, she stared at me with her head cocked, as though wondering whether I was somebody else.

She amazed me as much as she terrified me. The next day, I signed up for videography. I gave up painting with only a small pang—it had never stopped reminding me of Gabe. Film was a relief, for I didn't have to create the material; I just had to capture it. That spring, I got a job as an audiovisual technician at the university, taping speech courses and oral presentations. Sometimes the professors greeted me, but often they continued talking as I set up at the back of the room, as if I required no more acknowledgment than the camera. I felt like a professional ghost. In my free time, I rented a camera from the media center and carted it as far as I could. I filmed the punk girls on Telegraph, the yolky desserts at the Russian bakery, the couples twined together in front of Sather Tower.

In the August before my junior year, I moved into a one-bedroom with David, a graduate student I'd been dating since the previous semester. My parents weren't entirely pleased, but I was dying to get out of the dorms, having spent four years in them during high school, and my AV job enabled me to pay my share of the rent. It was a stout, twelve-unit building with peeling beige paint and a purple burst of a garden; our galley kitchen was so narrow that I could only

open the refrigerator door partway before it hit an opposing
cabinet. Often we ordered in from the dim sum restaurant
down the block, filling David's Ikea plates with shrimp dump-
lings and steamed buns, *lo mai gai* wrapped in lotus leaves. I
did homework for my psychology courses or edited videos,
and I began to read fiction—something I had never enjoyed
before but that now gave me a heady feeling of adventure.

David worked on the font he'd created, the cornerstone of
his dissertation in graphic design. I liked his even demeanor
and his realism. Our similarities were comforting—or perhaps it comforted me to think we were similar. David didn't
ask about Mills. He seemed to assume that high school was as
ancient a memory for me as it was for him. At night, we slept
in his double bed, and he was always there in the morning,
his hands crossed over his chest like a corpse.

Every so often, I received an e-mail from Hannah, who
was majoring in environmental science at Colorado College
(*Happy N-Y! How was your x-mas? I sat on a mountaintop—
drank champagne, made drunken angels in the snow. Heaven*).
We talked on the phone sporadically, but by senior year, we'd
lost touch almost completely. She was happy to hear about
David; once she said, "God, remember *Gabe*?" her tone
conspiratorial and incredulous, as if he were a once-beloved
leader or celebrity who had come to a disreputable end.

I couldn't tell her that I'd started dreaming of Gabe—his
taut, springy legs, the way his eyebrows leapt when he laughed.
Sometimes, the dreams followed a familiar story line, something that had happened at Mills—Gabe and I filching trays
from the cafeteria, then sneaking out to Observatory Hill and
sliding down on our backs—but there was something slightly
off. Gabe's head was shaved, while in real life he'd had thick
brown hair that stopped at his chin, or the sky was a dull
black, a chalkboard black, and I couldn't see stars.

It was the feeling of the dreams that I always remembered

most. I was entirely at peace in a way I never was in waking life. But it was different from the sense of self-possession I had when operating a camera and different from the muted, colorless way that David slept. It was a deep-rooted kind of comfort, a feeling of utter appropriateness. This was where I belonged: on this hill, beneath this sky, devoid of stars as it was, and beside this boy—a boy who was, by then, a man, and who for all I knew could be anywhere.

One warm night in May, I dreamed of him again, but this time, my eyes were open. I could see all the details of David's room—his swan-necked adjustable lamp, his tidy bureau, his poster of a cartoon woman begging at her boss's feet, her speech bubble reading, "*Please*, sir—don't make me use Comic Sans!" And I could see, outside the window, a man who looked exactly like Gabe.

I peeled my eyelids open farther, but the scene didn't change. The man was standing at the foot of a lamppost at the end of the block, looking at a piece of paper. He glanced down the block in the other direction, and then he looked toward our apartment.

I stumbled out of bed and into my shoes. I was wearing an old tee of David's and a pair of raggedy shorts from high school that, narrow hipped as I was, still fit. The legs that led me out of the apartment didn't feel like mine—they were only my dream legs, I thought, and nothing I did with them would be of any consequence when I woke up. So I was brave: I didn't stop to grab my keys, and I let the door lock behind me. In the pink glow of early morning, the streets looked softened and empty. It wasn't until I walked uphill, closer to the lamppost, that I saw a body standing behind it.

At first, the man didn't look very much like Gabe. His hair was short, and he was stockier than Gabe had been in high school. But then I noticed his sharp jaw, his chipped bottom tooth and wide shoulders—the same shoulders I had held on to at night and followed, that November morning, to Keller's house. Still, it was difficult to be sure. Like a hologram, he kept moving in and out of focus, flattening curiously into the background before springing alive again.

"Can you see me?" he asked.

I nodded. He was staring at me with such force.

"I think I'm dreaming," I said.

"Is it a dream," asked the boy, "if you know you're dreaming?"

"But I don't know if I am."

Behind me, there was the quick slap of footsteps on pavement, and I turned. "Sylvie!"

It was David. He was barefoot in boxers; he hadn't even put on a T-shirt. It was the most spontaneous thing he had ever done for me. I walked toward him, and he collected me in his arms like a wild rabbit, stroking my face, my arms. Now my eyes were closed, and I could see stars, or something like them—glittery, silver bursts beneath my lids, as if I were going to faint.

But then the silver cleared, and there was David, panting as he held me out at arm's length. I tipped my head back. The sky above us was the warm indigo of new blue jeans, speckled with white lights.

"Look," I said. "There's Venus."

"Venus?" David shook his head. "Sylvie, what was that?"

I remembered and turned around, but the man by the lamppost was gone, and the entire block was empty.

"I saw someone I knew."

"What do you mean? What the hell d'you—"

"I swear, David, there was a man right here. Thinner than he used to be, with shorter hair."

David's voice lowered. "You've seen him before? Some man in the neighborhood? A thin man, with short hair?"

"No," I said. "I only saw him this once."

I was dizzy. I leaned against the lamppost, rubbing my eyes with the heels of my hands.

"What are you talking about? You said you knew him from—"

"Before. I knew him from before. Let's take a look around the neighborhood, okay? See if he's still here?"

"I don't have any shoes on," said David. "I don't even have a shirt. I came out here because I was worried you'd *lost* it, Sylvie—I felt you get out of bed and then I saw you walking down the street in your goddamn shorts, and I didn't know whether you'd been—*compelled* by somebody—"

"I was sleepwalking," I said, more quietly, for suddenly it was clear to me. "I dreamed I saw someone, and I got out of bed. I used to do it as a kid."

David shook his head, blinking. We eyed each other for a moment. Finally, he stepped toward me, and I sank into his chest.

"You scared me, Sylvie. I was really frightened." He paused, lifting his chin from the top of my head, and scanned the block. "You must have dreamed it. If someone had been here, we'd be able to see him now."

It was true. Gabe wouldn't have been able to get very far. The lamppost was uphill from our apartment, higher than most of the neighborhood, and we could see the streets that spread below. Except for a garbage truck making the early-morning rounds, they were empty.

That afternoon, we arranged a picnic to take to Stinson Beach, packing David's cooler with water bottles and the grapefruit he liked to eat without sugar. He had graduated less than a month before, and though we'd talked lightly about whether or not we would stay together, we hadn't come to a decision: we were both reluctant instigators, experts in avoidance. I hoped the beach trip would be romantic, but the strangeness of last night was still with us. As we drove down

Highway 1, we were both on edge. A green Corolla swerved out from behind us and accelerated into the next lane.

"Damn Corolla," said David, slowing to let it pass. "Been trailing us since we left Berkeley."

I leaned forward and looked into the Corolla. A broad-shouldered, red-haired woman sat in the driver's seat, steering ahead of us. I sat back again.

"Everyone's trying to get to the beach," I said. And when we arrived, it did feel that way. Small camps of people stretched down the sand: families setting up beach umbrellas and folding chairs, college students with beers stuck deep in the sand. We spread our towels near the shore. David took out a tube of sunblock and began to slather his legs.

"Something a little disgusting about beaches, don't you think?" he asked as I set up my tripod and camera. "Everyone swimming in this communal . . . *bath*."

He was grinning. Sometimes he said things he knew I'd object to, just to get a rise out of me.

"Stay dry, then. I'm going to bathe. But first," I said, lifting the tripod and camera up with both arms, "I'm going to film it."

"Don't you think you should ask for consent?" called David. "These people are going to be in an Oscar-winning documentary one day—don't you think you should make sure they don't mind? I smell something smelly, Sylvie, and it just might be a lawsuit."

But I was already walking down to the water, laughing, the sun hot on my back. I wore a yellow bikini that I'd bought on Telegraph Avenue that week, feeling daring and unlike myself. I nestled the three legs of the tripod into the sand and took off the camera's lens cap. It was such a bright day that the iris had to be considerably adjusted. I was focusing the camera, squinting at the horizon line, when I saw a body slicing easily through the waves.

I wouldn't have noticed it if it weren't so much farther out than everyone else. The first ten feet of water were filled with children and parents. After that, there were teenagers playing catch, a few loners doing laps. But no one was as far as the person my camera had focused on, a man with the elegant, compact musculature of a dolphin.

His body was familiar to me, even from so far away. I had only seen him swim once, when we signed out from Mills to go to the pool at Michael Fritz's house. Gabe and I had been dating for a month by then, and I was thrilled by the way he tunneled through the water and somersaulted off of the diving board. It was as if he'd grown up not in Tracy, but in San Diego. Diana Gonzalez's parents lived there, and she claimed she could walk to the beach from her house.

"Where'd you learn to swim?" I asked when he came to sit beside me under the shade of the porch. I leaned over and kissed him stickily, my mouth wet with watermelon and the punch Mike's mom had made.

"My dad lives in Florida," Gabe had said, shaking his head with the vigor of a wet dog. Little droplets sprayed my cheek. He nuzzled me, kissed me again, and when he came up, there was a small black teardrop on his tongue. "Seed."

I tried to follow the man's progress in the water, but I kept losing him. For stretches of time that felt impossibly long, I couldn't see anything. Then he burst out of the water in a different part of the ocean, twenty feet away from the view of my camera.

In my first psychology class at UC-Berkeley, I learned that an acute stress response triggers over fourteen hundred changes in the body. Blood flow is increased by 300 percent and directed toward the muscles. Stores of fat and sugar are released. Our pupils dilate, our hearing becomes sharper, and normal processes of the body, like digestion, turn off, no longer important. I stood staked to the ground behind the camera for what felt like minutes, though it could only have been a few seconds. Part of me wanted to jump into the water and leave the camera behind, but I knew I couldn't do that—it belonged to the school and was worth thousands of dollars. So I lifted the tripod and lugged it across the beach as quickly as I could manage.

"Nothing interesting?" asked David. He was lying flat on his back, limbs spread like a starfish. He held one arm over his eyes like a visor.

"David." I was already sweating. "I need you to watch the camera for me. I saw someone in the water."

"Someone in the water?" He sat up. "Did they need help?"

"No, no," I said. David had been a lifeguard in high school. "It was someone familiar. I have to go. I just need you to watch—"

"Was it the person from last night?" He was staring at me intently, his voice a conspiratorial whisper. "The man in the neighborhood—it's him, isn't it?"

I was so flustered that it must have been an easy guess.

"Let me go," David said. "You're a terrible swimmer, Sylvie. You'll never catch him. Point him out to me."

He was right—I couldn't swim more than a few yards, and even with the benefits of adrenaline, I doubted I could make it much farther. I wanted to be the one to find Gabe, but David had a better chance of bringing him to shore.

"We're going to run out of time," said David, scrambling to his feet. His chest was pale and narrow, the sternum concave. Between his nipples was a dark burst of chest hair the size of a small sunflower. "Just point him out to me, will you?"

I pointed to the man. He was still farther than all of the others, swimming surely to the left. David followed my hand, breathing quickly. Then he set off for the shore at a run. I watched him splash into the shallow water and awkwardly navigate the narrow channels between children. Once he passed them, he broke into a quick, smooth freestyle. Gabe, or the man who looked like him, turned his head every so often as he traveled west, though I couldn't tell whether he was looking at David or trying to breathe.

David was only ten or twenty feet away when he paused and punched the water's surface. I didn't know why until I saw a fleet of sailboats making their way toward him— college students, probably, who could rent boats after taking a quick licensing course. The boats were set to cut right between David and the other man, who was swimming closer to the horizon with increasing speed. David tried to speed up, too—I had zoomed in with my camera and could see the water flurrying behind him—but it was no use; he had to tread water to let the line of boats pass, and when they had, the other man was gone.

Not *gone*, of course. No longer visible. He couldn't have disappeared, because this time, I wasn't the only one who'd seen him. David had, too, and this was so validating that by the time he returned, his chest heaving, I almost felt calm.

# 6

MADISON, WISCONSIN, 2004

By October, the air had cooled in Madison, and the trees made quilts of red and brown and gold. On a Thursday afternoon, returning home from a trip to the market, I saw Gabe and Janna kneeling in a patch of dirt in our backyard. They were scooping earth into a large clay pot and packing it down, Gabe gathering large fistfuls, Janna pressing down with precise and expert speed.

I stepped onto the back porch and set my bags down. The milk, sweating, leaned against my leg.

"'Lo," said Janna. "I'm teaching your husband how to grow a dogwood tree."

She smiled in her brief, catlike way before returning to the mound—a flash of a smile, fool's gold in a pan.

"Boyfriend," said Gabe. He looked up at me and grinned.

"That's right." Janna slapped at a mosquito that had landed quietly on her arm. "I forget."

"I thought it would be nice for us to have a little flora around here," said Gabe, still squatting. "A little fauna. What say you"—he raised himself, propping his elbows on his knees—"about that?"

"*Fauna* means 'animals,'" I said.

"Right," said Gabe. "But with flora comes fauna. Spiders and dragonflies and ladybugs."

"You don't like spiders," I said. "And have you ever seen a swarm of ladybugs?"

"It's grotesque," said Janna cheerfully.

"Anyway," I said, "isn't it a bit late to be planting trees? Doesn't that happen in summer?"

"That's what I thought. But it turns out," said Gabe, "that autumn is the perfect time for planting."

"It isn't the only time, but it's really ideal," Janna said. "After a few frosts, you've still got soils that are warm enough through the winter to allow for root growth. Then, when spring comes, the roots are dying for water, and they're much easier to transplant."

Janna stood and wiped her hands on her jean shorts, which sagged around her waist. She'd rolled the legs up to the top of her thighs.

"So they can keep growing," she said.

I thought of the bags at my feet—the twelve eggs, the avocados Gabe liked to eat plain with a spoon. He scarfed them with such boyish enthusiasm that finding the best ones was a secret pleasure of mine. I could spend ten minutes in the produce section, gently prodding their leathery skins.

"I have to put these away," I said.

"But it's so glorious out." Janna stretched her arms, slender but packed with stringy little muscles. "You don't want to join us?"

"Maybe afterward."

"Suit yourself," said Gabe.

I was irritated by the Labrador look of his face, his smile hanging open.

"You'll be ready to leave in a half hour?" I asked.

"Course," he said. "I'm never late."

It was true: Gabe was a stickler when it came to timing.

That night, he was in the car fifteen minutes early, his bag packed with lab work and the dinner he carried in separate Tupperware containers—one for cooked pasta, one for cold sauce, one for salad leaves, one for dressing. His packing process was by now so rote, so obsessively standardized, that it almost seemed like an act of resistance rather than submission.

The sky became dusky as we drove to the lab. We were quiet on these rides: while Gabe stared at the road, I read through the notes Keller had sent about tonight's participant.

"Who do we have tonight?" asked Gabe, parking.

We stepped out of the car and walked down the sidewalk beneath a line of trees. Their leaves were dark cutouts in the royal-blue sky.

"The kid," I said.

Gabe's jaw set the way it always did when he was thinking more than he wanted to say. We both felt conflicted about Keller's use of children. Still, Gabe was near-paranoid about criticizing Keller; he certainly wouldn't do it when we were within spitting distance. Gabe and I had worked with patients as young as fifteen, but we knew that children had been part of Keller's early tests in Fort Bragg. Tonight's participant was seven.

At the heavy metal doors, we fell into a single-file line and took out our ID cards. Gabe held his to the square reader next to the doors, which emitted a short, high-pitched beep. The doors opened automatically to allow him inside before closing again. When they shut behind me, clapping together with a rubbery noise of suction, we started down the left corridor.

"Evening," said Gabe to the Hungarian researcher, who was pushing a young man in a wheelchair across the hallway.

"And to you," said the researcher. He paused and nodded at us; the man in the wheelchair stirred, his head rolling from one shoulder to the other.

We took the staircase to the basement level of the building

and passed three of Keller's rooms, the doors locked, before we came to his office. It was a windowless bunker at the end of the hall. Inside, there were meticulously organized metal cabinets, a closed door that led to a small closet, and a bulletin board with pinned notes and schedules. Keller sat at a large metal desk, facing away from us.

"Just a moment," he said.

He was hunched over, taking longhand notes on a yellow pad of paper—he preferred this to the laptops Gabe and I used, claiming it helped him to write more intuitively. He held the cap of his pen in his teeth.

We waited. After a moment, he capped the pen and turned to face us. His eyes went immediately to Gabe's shirt.

"You're dirty."

Gabe set down the cooler with his dinner and leaned against the door frame.

"I was planting a tree."

"Planting a tree," said Keller, glancing at me.

I shook my head. "This was his venture."

"Our neighbor's a gardener," said Gabe.

"Well, you can tell him," said Keller, mildly, "that if Rosemarie Sillman complains that my assistants look like they've just buried someone, I'll be holding him accountable."

"Her," said Gabe. "The neighbor's a woman. You do know it's the twenty-first century, don't you? Next thing you know, you'll be assuming all scientists are men, and Sylvie will have to put you in line."

Gabe was able to rib this way with Keller; in their relationship, there was always a line being narrowly walked. Over the years, it had become almost familial—something that made me vaguely jealous, even though I knew Gabe had always needed a father more than I did.

"Noted," said Keller shortly, though he was smiling. "Go on and set up. Room seventy-six."

It was seven o'clock now; we had half an hour until Jamie arrived. We walked to Room 76—the only one with a window, though it was a small square close to the ceiling and barred. Gabe rolled the bed to the center of the room. It was similar to a hospital bed, with white sheets and a remote that allowed us to raise or lower it. Gabe left the room for the closet in Keller's office, then returned with straps that he affixed to hooks down the length of each side of the bed. I walked into Room 74, raised the blinds on the large window that allowed me to see through to Room 76, and powered on the polysomnograph machine and telemetry equipment. I made sure that the amplifiers and the CPAP machines were working properly. I set up the montage, the configuration of all the channels we'd be using, and I did the amplifier calibrations.

Finally, I rolled the cart out of the closet, making sure the wheels were working smoothly—it was a finicky old cart; we needed a new one—and began to arrange the tray. From a small cabinet I took out the EEG paste and sleep mask, the tape and black marker. I arranged the electrodes, sensors, and lead wires at the back of the tray, and beside them the cotton swabs, alcohol pads, prepping gels and pastes, and my gloves. The hair clips I placed in a pocket at the front of the tray; sometimes ten or twelve were necessary if the patient had long hair, but I didn't think we'd need more than four for a little boy. In Room 76, Gabe rolled in the camera and turned on the audio system.

We kept an eye on each other through the window, making sure the other person was getting along okay and didn't need help. Every so often, one of us offered a smile, and the other one returned it before getting back to work.

By seven thirty, we knew Keller had retrieved Jamie from the waiting room and brought him to Room 72, his public office, which had a leather couch and a basket full of toys for children. Keller had been working independently with Jamie for eight weeks now, teaching him the same things he had taught Gabe and me in Snake Hollow. "Lucid dreaming can be learned," Keller had told us, standing in the library. The first step was to improve dream recall—patients who developed this skill were almost always able to remember their lucid dreams after waking. Keller also showed us how to recognize dream signs: ill-defined light sources, repetitive symbols, bizarre text or numbers, and flashing lights, which in our study took the form of LEDs. Some researchers used mild electric shocks to indicate a dream state to their subjects, but Keller eschewed this method. He preferred that our patients be able to recognize their dream states cognitively, not physically.

At eight o'clock, I walked down the hall to the water fountain and filled my bottle. The door to Room 72 was cracked, and I could hear Keller talking in the playful voice he used with younger patients.

"Haven't been drinking any alcohol, I presume?"

There was a woman's laugh, though I couldn't hear the child.

"No," said the woman, an older voice, gravelly. "Hasn't been any of that."

He was getting close to the end of the questionnaire. Gabe popped his head out of Room 76, where the bed was stationed, and I nodded, holding up five fingers.

After several minutes, Keller came out of the office, holding a clipboard with the finished questionnaire. Behind him was a woman who looked to be in her seventies: she had a bushel of wiry, shoulder-length gray hair and quick, sweeping eyes.

Gabe and I stood in the doorways to Rooms 74 and 76 like butlers guarding the entrances of a fancy party. The woman held the hand of a small boy, who was partially obscured behind the wide swath of her hips. He wore loose pants printed with brightly colored sea creatures and red socks; Keller must have collected his shoes.

"You must be Jamie," said Gabe. He stepped forward and squatted down in front of the older woman, peering through her legs at the boy.

"That's Jamie-boy," the woman said. "Don't be shy, sweet."

But I could tell she was hesitant. Keller's research was experimental, still in its early stages. Most of our patients had exhausted the range of traditional treatment options, but it still wasn't unusual for them to be skeptical of our methodology.

"My research assistants," said Keller. "Gabriel and Sylvia. This is Jamie's grandmother, Rosemarie."

"Sylvia," said Rosemarie. "A pretty name."

"Thank you," I said, though it didn't feel like mine. Keller only used it when introducing me to patients.

"Spectacular pants you've got there," said Gabe as Jamie moved slightly into the open. "What's that scary thing with the big old fangs? A piranha? No—a blowfish?"

"A blowfish," said the boy solemnly. He was leaning against the side of his grandmother's leg.

"Ah," said Gabe. "A blowfish. Just as I suspected. Also known as a puffer. Or a toadfish."

He filled his cheeks with air and flared his nostrils. The boy tipped his head and released a short, breathy noise, more a wheeze than a laugh. I didn't know how Gabe knew about blowfish, but I wasn't surprised. He was always picking up bits of odd knowledge, coming back from the library with books about metallurgy or obscure British prime ministers or the First Transcontinental Railroad, as if building a base of knowledge that would help him if his work with Keller ever ended.

"They're kind of freaky looking, aren't they?" Gabe asked, still squatting.

"No," said the boy, but he was smiling.

"A fair point," said Gabe. "Freaky looking—that's not the right way to put it. This fellow here"—he pointed to the blowfish on the ankle of Jamie's pant leg—"this fellow is downright handsome. A nice monster—that's what he is."

"A nice monster," said the boy.

One year ago, we'd learned, he was riding with his family in a miniature steam train at the Lincoln Park Zoo in Chicago when the train made a sharp turn toward the bachelor monkeys. A sudden leak in the firebox forced a blast of flame out of the door, and though the train was evacuated as soon as it came to a halt, those who sat closest to the engine—a father from southern Illinois, along with Jamie's parents and half sister, a college student at the University of Chicago—were already dead. It was a freak accident: later, investigators found that a new zoo employee had accidentally packed the firebox with three times the normal amount of liquid fuel.

Bystanders ran to the train to help. One woman, an off-duty firefighter, retrieved Jamie. He had been sitting behind his sister, sheltered from the worst of the blaze, and only his left hand had burned. Doctors at Northwestern Memorial Hospital were able to preserve the use of his fingers, but his skin was waxy and scarred.

Now Jamie lived with Rosemarie in her apartment in Sun Prairie, Wisconsin. For ten months, he had been suffering from night terrors that made him scream in his sleep and bolt out of bed. In the morning, he remembered nothing. For the past two months, Keller had tried to improve Jamie's dream recall—when he woke up each morning, Rosemarie was to gently ask what he remembered, then record his reply on a notepad—but the boy was inconsistent and difficult to read. Still, he seemed to understand the concept of dream signals and knew how to respond to our LEDs, so Keller believed it was worth attempting an overnight study. If we could get him to start dreaming lucidly, his recall ability would likely improve.

The boy yawned, his shoulders quivering.

"It's past your bedtime, isn't it?" said Rosemarie, putting a hand on his head. "Usually he's in bed by eight. But tonight is a special night."

"How late do you get to stay up tonight, Jamie?" asked Gabe.

"Till nine," the boy said.

"That's right," said Gabe. "Till nine. And it's already eight fifteen. I think it's about time we showed you your bed. Bigger than your bed at home, I'd expect."

"How much bigger?" asked Jamie. He hadn't moved from beneath his grandmother's hand, but his eyes were focused on Gabe.

"Well, that depends on the one you've got back home," said Gabe. "I think you'll have to tell *me* how much bigger it is. How does that sound?"

He held out his large, worn hand.

"Okay," said Jamie, though he kept both hands behind his back.

"Just a minute now," said Rosemarie. She looked from Keller to Gabe, and back to Keller. "Now, this is where I—say good night?"

"It all does seem to happen a bit fast," said Gabe.

Rosemarie's wrists were knobby and her ankles soft and tubular, encased in nude pantyhose that stuck out from beneath her pants. But her hand on the boy's head was firm.

"I'm afraid so," said Keller.

"He's in good hands," I said.

"Sylvia will see you down the hall," said Keller.

Rosemarie squatted down to take the boy in her arms. Her knees landed on the linoleum floor with the tired grace of aging animals, the brittle memory of old bone.

"Be a good boy," she said, and he leaned into the soft pillow of her chest. "You remember what we practiced."

Gabe guided Jamie to Room 76 and gently closed the door. I walked with Rosemarie to the stairs. As we climbed, her shoulders began to quiver.

"It's been terribly frightening," she said. She paused on the landing, her back against the wall. "I've been so afraid."

When I returned to the basement, I was annoyed. It had taken almost ten minutes to usher Rosemarie out of the building, and I'd had to console her all the way to the door. When I walked into Room 74 and grabbed hold of the rolling tray, I forgot to unlock its wheels. My sudden push made the hair clips and some of the electrodes fall to the floor.

By the time I had cleaned them, I was late to Room 76 and flustered. I knew Gabe had noticed—it was already eight thirty, and we were supposed to have Jamie fully prepared by nine—but he didn't show it. When I walked into the room, they were chatting about *Calvin and Hobbes*, Jamie narrating his favorite strip while Gabe leaned toward the bed. When the story finished, he turned around as if I'd surprised him.

"Ah," said Gabe. "Here's Sylvie. She's come to show you all the machines you get to play with, and then I'll be back before you go to sleep."

I could tell that Jamie didn't want to see Gabe go. But he was sleepy, and he lay obediently while I uncapped a jar of rubbing alcohol. He wrinkled his nose at its acid perfume as I dabbed the places where the electrodes would be placed.

"Tired?" I asked, smiling.

"No," said Jamie. But his eyes glazed over as I taped each of eight channels to his skin. Every so often, I pinned his hair back with a clip, and this got a laugh out of him, the same short wheeze.

"I'm not a girl," he said. I noticed a small, dented scar on his forehead—two connected semicircles, like a child's drawing of a seagull.

"Boys can wear their hair back," I said, taping an electrode to the left of the scar, at his temple.

"I never saw one," said Jamie.

"Well, I see you," I said.

He was still smiling—his two front teeth overlarge and spaced slightly apart; permanent teeth, I thought, while the rest were baby teeth—as he looked at the camera.

"What's that?" he asked.

"A camera," I said. "It records videos. Movies."

"I'll be in a movie?"

"That's right." I rolled the camera toward him. "Your own movie. Look."

I turned the camera toward the wall, its lens pointed at the small window, and showed him the screen. The camera was already running—Gabe had activated the recording in Room 74—so this would be filmed, too. I rolled the camera back to its place and turned it around again.

"Do you remember your mantra?" I asked.

His eyes were still on the camera.

"What's that?"

"Something to repeat over and over again, to remind you that you're asleep. You practiced it with your grandma, remember?"

Jamie nodded, but I could tell that he was struggling to bring it up.

"'When I see my hand . . .'" I said, prompting him.

"When I see my hand in my dream," Jamie said, "I know I'm dreaming."

It was a simple stimulus-response technique first developed by Carlos Castaneda, a writer and anthropologist. Castaneda reasoned that the dreamer's body was one of the few elements that did not change between sleep and waking life—and that it could therefore be used to anchor the sleeper in an otherwise changeable dream world, reminding them both of their identity and their state of consciousness.

Jamie kept his burned hand hidden: his elbow bent, the little fingers wedged beneath his torso. He held his other hand up, showing me.

"That's right. Perfect."

I stepped back to examine my work. The electrodes were precisely placed and taped; it was why Keller always left this part to me.

"Where did . . ." said Jamie. He paused and looked toward the door. "Where did he go?"

"Gabe? He'll be back in a moment. We just have to run a few tests to make sure everything is working the way it should be, and then I'll go get him."

"What kind of tests?"

"Fun tests," I said. "Like this. Close your eyes. I'm going to time you, and after thirty seconds you can open them—but no more or less."

He did so.

"Now open them for thirty seconds. You can blink, but try not to move. Try to be still as a plank of wood."

Jamie clenched his jaw, his eyes on the ceiling.

We began each session with this series of bio-calibrations to make sure the signals were accurate. I had him look left and right, to mimic the activity of the eyes in REM sleep; cough, which set a standard for snore levels; hold his breath; move his feet; look up and down. When we finished, I looked into the glass window and nodded. I couldn't see in, but I knew Gabe was there, watching me.

"You passed," I said. "You were great. Now let's get you under the covers."

With the setup complete, Gabe returned from the other room, which meant Keller had taken his place. Jamie lay on top of the bed's white sheets and blanket, his limbs spread, as we tried to ease the covers over them.

"I don't want to," he said.

"Don't want to?" asked Gabe. "Who ever heard of that? Not sleeping under the covers."

"I don't want to do it," Jamie said, more forcefully. His eyes shifted from Gabe to me.

"You'll get cold," I said.

"I won't."

"It's a cold building," said Gabe. "Very cold down here in this building."

"I'm not cold."

Gabe glanced at me, then at the window separating Room 76 from Room 74.

"All right," he said. "Your choice. We'll just have to put your belt on this way."

We started at the end of the bed. I eased the first strap from my side of the bed to Gabe's, and he buckled it in.

"What are those?" asked Jamie, moving his ankles beneath the lowest strap.

"Seat belts," said Gabe. "For the rocket ship."

"The rocket ship?"

"Didn't anybody tell you this bed is a rocket ship? That's why it's so big. And when you fall asleep, it blasts off."

Gabe was pushing it here, I thought. Even Jamie seemed dubious. But he was silent as we buckled each row of straps.

"And here's the last thing you need," I said. "It's a mask, with special lights inside so you can see the stars. Do you remember what to do, when you fall asleep and see stars?"

"I move my eyes," said Jamie.

"Exactly," I said. "Can you show me how?"

He moved his eyes four times, horizontally: left-right, left-right.

"Aren't you good," said Gabe.

"When I see my hand in my dream," mumbled Jamie, "I know I am dreaming."

He was sleepy now, his left hand unguarded. Up close, the skin was thick and marbled, pink-and-white fingers curling toward his palm. The hand looked so tender, so damaged, that I had the sudden urge to hold it in my own.

"That's right," said Gabe. "But they feel real to you, don't they?"

The boy stared at Gabe, unmoving. I looked sharply across the bed at Gabe, then at the window between the rooms.

"They're dreams, though," Gabe added. "Just dreams."

When I left the room and walked into 74, Keller was sitting stiffly before the window.

"What was that?" he asked.

"I don't know," I said, closing the door behind me.

"Likes to push the envelope, that one," said Keller grimly, picking up a Styrofoam cup. "Coffee?"

"I'm fine," I said, taking a seat beside him. "Well—what kind?"

"Half-caf. Here."

He took a thermos from the floor and poured its contents into another Styrofoam cup.

"Thanks," I said.

Keller nodded. He was in his fifties now, nine years older than he had been when I first arrived at Mills, but he didn't look much different—he had the same pale skin, the same substantial nose and dark, full eyebrows. I had never seen him with any other facial hair, but he didn't look gaunt. His features were robust and muscular, his skin lined with idle expressions: two permanent grooves between his brows, crow's-feet raying out from each eye. His pupils were a striking, aquatic blue, almost cerulean, the irises lined in black. Our patients probably felt he looked severe, but I thought his dynamism also made him handsome.

It wasn't long before Jamie was asleep, Gabe sitting in the chair beside his bed. He flipped through the *Isthmus*, our local paper.

"Must have been tuckered out," said Keller, inching his chair closer to the window.

We allowed Jamie to sleep through the first REM cycle. Eight minutes after the next cycle began, Gabe put the newspaper on the floor and gave us a thumbs-up. I triggered the light stimulus—eight flashes in two seconds, transmitted through the LEDs in Jamie's sleep mask.

We waited, Keller and I in Room 74 and Gabe in Room 76, still as he could make himself.

There was no response. Keller tapped his Styrofoam cup on the table.

"I'll try again in two minutes," I said.

Gabe relaxed, though he leaned forward again when two minutes had passed. I triggered the light flashes. Jamie stirred slightly, shaking his head, but he didn't move his eyes.

"He's not lucid," muttered Keller, leaning back in his chair.

There was a brief murmur in the EEG. Jamie had moved his eyes to the left, then to the right.

"Wait," I said. "He might be."

Keller craned over the machine.

"Only happened once," he said. "It could be random. We can't count it as an LR2 unless we get both movements."

"We'll try at the next cycle," I said. Gabe looked at the window and raised his eyebrows; then he left the room and came into 74.

"How long do I have?" he asked.

"About an hour, if his last cycle was any indication," I said.

"Right. I'll be back in fifty minutes."

He left to retrieve his dinner from Keller's office. Keller and I sat alone at the desk. In the other room, Jamie was serene, his chest filling and deflating. Keller and I sank into a comfortable silence, watching him as if in meditation. After a long stretch, Keller shifted in his chair and stretched backward, his back cracking.

"Liking the new place?" he asked.

"It's not bad," I said. "Sort of an empty neighborhood, but at least it's quiet."

"Don't you have a dog park around there?"

"Brittingham. It's pretty. Would be better if I had a dog."

"But you do," said Keller. "That's where you take Gabriel. Let him run around."

He laughed, and so did I.

"What about you?" I asked. "Cottage Grove, right?"

It was its own small village, close to the Dane County airport and Blackhawk Airfield. Keller had had us over for dinner when we joined him in Madison, back in August, but we hadn't been back since; we saw him so frequently that sometimes it felt like we all lived together, here in the basement of the neuroscience building.

"Oh, I can't complain," he said. "I have more space than I did in Fort Bragg. Almost as much space as there was in Snake Hollow."

"Gabe told me you sold it," I said, though I hoped it wasn't true.

Keller nodded. "Lot of money to keep up a place like that."

"It must have been an ordeal to pack it all away."

"Mostly papers. I was lucky. Much easier to bring everything with you when your most precious possessions are two-dimensional."

"I suppose so."

My stomach gurgled. Unlike Gabe, I usually ate before we left for the lab, which had its disadvantages.

"I never thought you'd sell that place," I said.

"I know." Keller exhaled, cocking his head. "But we

couldn't have stayed there forever. And who would have lived in the house while we were here?"

"Renters," I said. "Renters could have lived there."

"*Renters*," said Keller. "Nosing around in my library."

I shook my head, grinning. "Should I get Gabe?"

"He's back," said Keller, nodding toward the window, as Gabe entered Room 76 and took his seat by Jamie's bed.

I watched the polysomnograph closely as Jamie entered his next REM cycle. After eight minutes, I triggered the LEDs.

Keller leaned forward with his elbows on the desk. Another LR signal appeared on the EEG—just one movement again, left-right; we still needed a second one to count it as a sign of lucidity.

"I'm telling you, he's not lucid," said Keller.

"Hold on," I said. "He's trying."

There, in the next room, Jamie's head was slowly rotating from left to right, as if charting the progress of a plane. He turned fully to one side, setting his ear down on the pillow, before going the other way again.

"Well, it's some kind of left-right signal," I said.

"Just not the one we're looking for," said Keller.

"Wait a little longer. I think we may have something."

Jamie's movements were speeding up. He turned his head from left to right more quickly now, and I stood over the EEG, convinced he was working up to an eye signal. But then he began to move faster, so fast his head was slapping at the pillow before bucking the other way, and his legs began to shake.

"Adrian," I said, "I think he's seizing."

Such a lot of movement for a little body—Jamie's legs strained at the straps, then his hips and arms, his breath rising in shallow bursts. Gabe was out of his chair now, standing next to the bed. Jamie had wriggled his burned arm out of the straps, and he scratched at Gabe's face. The last two fingers barely grazed him, but Jamie's pointer finger scraped Gabe's eyelid.

"He isn't seizing," said Keller, pushing back from the desk. "He's trying to get out of the bed. Stay here."

Keller strode out of the room and reemerged in Room 76, where he ran to the bed and took hold of Jamie's head. I put on the headphones that hooked up to 76's audio system just as a voice came through.

"He said he sees her," said Gabe to Keller. I could see his mouth moving, but the sound came through with a second's delay.

"I'm sure he does." Keller was facing away from me, but I knew his voice. "Get ahold of his limbs."

"Some help would be nice," Gabe said as Jamie snuck his left leg out from under the strap and sent a flexed-foot kick at Gabe's neck.

"I have to keep his head steady," said Keller.

I began to take the headphones off, ready to join them, but Keller looked at the window as if he could see through it.

"Sylvie," he said, "I need you there."

"Why?" I asked, though I knew it was pointless—he couldn't hear me in the other room. I felt useless and sick, watching through the window as Jamie writhed and hollered—he was strong in the committed way that children are strong, using every muscle he could. But I stayed where I was, afraid to go against orders.

"Ma!" yelled Jamie.

The mask was still on his face; he reached for it with his left hand, but Gabe was too quick. He grabbed the arm and held it back down to the bed.

"Sylvie, send the light stimulus," said Keller, one hand at the top of Jamie's head, the other at his chin. "Respond to him, Gabe. Try to calm him."

I triggered the LEDs, and Jamie's body paused in notice.

"Where?" asked Gabe. "Where's your ma?"

"There are so many stars," said Jamie, his body tensing.

"That's right," said Gabe. "Do you remember what to do when you see stars?"

"At the window," said Jamie. "I see her."

Gabe looked at the window in Room 76, closed and barred as usual.

"What's she doing?" asked Gabe.

"Climbing out," said Jamie. "I lost her at the—supermarket."

The mask had fallen halfway off his face, dangling over one eye. The exposed eye was still closed.

"At the supermarket?" Gabe asked, looking at Keller.

"No," said Jamie. "We were—riding—on the train—"

The shaking began again, more violently than before, and Jamie screamed. His heart rate had skyrocketed, and the underarms of his pajamas were soaked in sweat. Keller strained to keep the boy's head steady. He looked at the window between our rooms.

"Sylvie," he said, "we need a current. Send it through F3 and F4."

These were the electrodes attached to Jamie's frontal lobe. I shook my head, though I knew he couldn't see me. A current to the frontal lobe—this was an electrical shock, which would result in a real seizure, brief but shocking enough to wake Jamie up. I had been taught how to do it, but I'd never tried it on a patient.

"Sylvie," Keller barked, his teeth gritted. I stood over the machines. The paper from the analog polysomnograph moved to the left as the pen made delicate markings, writing the story of Jamie's brain.

"We need you to do it, Sylve," said Gabe. He was holding Jamie's ankles and looking at me in the way he so often did— with appeal so earnest it looked almost like love.

When I sent the shock, Jamie stiffened in Gabe and Keller's hands as if suspended. Then, almost imperceptibly, he tucked into himself: his shoulders rose as his stomach dropped, his back rounding beneath it. Keller took off the mask, and the boy's body went limp. He was facing away from me, but on the video camera, I could see his eyes begin to open.

It was barely ten thirty. We called Rosemarie to take him home; the study had ended, so we couldn't keep Jamie in the lab. While I put away the equipment in Room 74, Keller met them in the hall. It was impossible to tell how much Jamie remembered: he was woozy and confused, but he seemed to stare at the three of us with new distrust. He flinched, moving behind his grandmother, when Gabe tried to give him a pat on the head. Keller told Rosemarie we had been slightly premature: Jamie wasn't ready; his lucidity skills would have to be worked on at home, and we could try again if he made progress. It wasn't far from the truth—in fact, perhaps it was the truth exactly—but I still felt a long-dormant anger build inside me.

"You're welcome to come back in six months," Keller said, his voice muffled by the door. Through the sliver at the bottom, I could see Rosemarie's orthopedic shoes and Jamie's Velcro sneakers, the red bars on his heels that lit up as he walked away.

When I couldn't hear their voices anymore, I rolled the cart into Room 76 to collect the electrodes. As I peeled off the white tape that had attached one of them to Jamie's head, the electrode fell, hitting the floor with a metallic click.

When I tried again, the same thing happened. I looked down at my hands. They shuddered in a way I had never seen before, my fingers stiff and bony as twigs. I closed and opened them, but the quavering didn't stop—not until I leaned against the wall with my eyes closed, arms limp at my sides, and breathed as slowly as I could.

By the time I walked into Keller's office, half an hour had passed. I expected them to ask what had taken me so long, but Keller sat at his desk, finishing the summary report as usual. Gabe was on the floor, eating the last of his sandwich.

"Come back in six months?" I asked.

My voice was quiet, but I'd gotten their attention. Keller turned around in his chair, the wheels squealing on the floor.

"Is that a problem?" he asked.

"We just saw how damaged he is," I said. "We watched him try to claw his way out of bed, we shocked him—and now we're just going to send him home?"

I felt short of breath; I had never spoken to Keller this way before. I suppose I was worried he'd fire me. But a part of me knew that would be impossible for him, and that's where I found my nerve.

"Sylvie," said Keller, "the procedure tonight was no different than it is on any other night."

"But on the other nights we were using adults. Teenagers, even."

"We don't use them," said Keller. "We accept them as participants."

I inhaled sharply, sucking in my mistake.

"We were accepting adults," I said. "Not children. Jamie's so vulnerable—his dreams are horrific. And we're going to leave him like that?"

Keller looked at me closely, his hands crossed in his lap.

"Lucidity is the most basic demand of this study," he said. "We make it very clear that every patient must meet the same requirement: if they aren't dreaming lucidly within eight weeks, they can't continue. No exceptions. Jamie didn't qualify."

"But that means we just lance the wound and leave it open. We help our patients remember what they're dreaming, we intensify their experience of those dreams, and then we leave them behind if they don't make the cut?"

"I don't understand why you find this so disturbing." Keller spoke clinically, his hands crossed in his lap. "You've watched me release a number of patients early. You weren't bothered by them."

"Maybe it's because Jamie's a kid." I felt checked and defensive. "He's so impressionable, and he's experienced more trauma than most adults. Besides, he's in danger—if we hadn't been here, he would have gotten out of bed and followed his parents right out of the window. He could have hurt himself."

"No, he couldn't have," said Gabe. "The window is barred."

I stared at him, wounded; I'd expected him to be on my side.

"Here it is," I said. "Not at home."

Keller eyed us briefly. Then he picked up the notepad on his desk and began to read aloud, Gabe transcribing the notes on his laptop.

"Patient three oh four, age seven, fifty inches tall, forty-eight pounds, came to the lab for his lucidity assessment following a diagnosis of night terrors and/or somnambulism. In one single-night study, patient three oh four exhibited a characteristic lack of paralysis, but he did not meet standards for lucidity. While claiming the presence of a female intruder, patient three oh four exhibited violent behavior—"

"Exactly," I said.

"—exhibited violent behavior," Keller said, continuing, "which included talking, yelling, punching, kicking, turning the head rapidly from side to side, attempting to escape his constraints—"

"Do you really think we have no obligation to help him?" My body was shot through with heat. "Who knows what'll happen in the next six months?"

Keller sighed. He set the pad on his lap and looked at me with a parent's tired patience.

"The focus of our research," he said, "is lucidity. Our stud-

ies are short-term; our goal is the resolution of abnormal behavior during sleep. Yes, we want to encourage self-awareness.
Yes, we hope that lucid dreaming will ultimately lead to deeper
understanding and reduced anxiety, but we can't guarantee it.
It's never been within our purview to meet those particular
endpoints—we don't have the funding to keep a psychoanalyst
on hand, which is exactly why I always suggest that patients
follow up with a mental health professional in their area. We
make recommendations; that's the best we can do."

He took off his glasses and squeezed the bridge of his nose
with his thumb and forefinger, his eyes shut. When he opened
them again, they were kinder.

"You feel pity for him," he said. "Not surprising, given
what he's undergone—and it is horrifying, Sylvie; nobody
is denying that. But you must remember that you're a researcher. Our loyalty is to the research, not to any particular
participant. If we doubted our work simply because it was
occasionally *unpleasant*—if we braked whenever we felt *badly*
for someone—"

"We'd be shit scientists," said Gabe.

He laughed, and Keller smiled indulgently before looking
up at me again.

"You're right," he said. "Our patients aren't happy people.
They've all experienced some sort of trauma, and that's exactly
why they've come to us. It isn't always a pretty process. But
we can't play God."

It sounded right, and I could poke no holes in it. What
was rightness, I thought, if not impenetrability?

"Sylvie," said Keller as I turned toward the door. "I
shouldn't have had you send the shocks. I was wrong, and I
apologize. It was too much responsibility for you. I should
have done it myself."

I was quiet on the car ride home, eating the sandwich
crusts that Gabe had saved for me as blood came back to my

hands. When I finished, I put my palm on the back of Gabe's neck out of habit, but it felt like there was a long corridor between us. I didn't tell him about the sensation in my hands or the strange wash of heat, which hadn't happened since high school. We got ready for bed without speaking and fell raggedly asleep. In the very early morning—it couldn't have been later than four o'clock, the sky still dark—I began to shudder.

"Sylvie," Gabe whispered, wrapping his body around mine. "Oh, Sylvie. It was a hard night for you, wasn't it?"

I was embarrassed to find myself crying.

"I thought you would have agreed with me," I said.

"I did agree with you. I do."

"Then why didn't you say so to Keller?"

"Because I agree with him, too. I agree with both of you." He smoothed my hair back, tucking it behind my ears.

"Jamie reminded me of Anne," I said.

Gabe stiffened, his hand pausing on my neck. "How?"

"I don't know." I felt like I had said something bad, something I wasn't supposed to admit. "Because they both turned out wrong."

Gabe hesitated.

"You're sweating," he said.

"Maybe I should shower." My entire body was sticky.

"Don't be ridiculous," said Gabe. His voice had turned soothing again, a low hum, and I sank into it. "Go back to sleep. I don't mind it."

He pressed his cheek to mine, his ear against my ear.

"We didn't hurt the boy," he said. "We only woke him up."

By the time I opened my eyes, it was almost nine, and the heat had left my body: my clothes were dry, and so was my skin. Gabe was still asleep. It was only a small scratch on his eyelid—pale as a white tattoo, a child's scratch, the skin barely broken—that made me sure the previous night had happened at all.

# 7

By the time Gabe turned up in the coffee shop by my apartment, a week after the incident at Stinson Beach with David, I was almost expecting him. He sat at a small, narrow table, eating a biscotti and glancing around the coffee shop as though he were any other college student. There was a small yellow notebook on the table in front of him, but he wasn't writing in it. At one point, he leaned down to fit a sugar packet underneath the rickety table stand. When he sat up again, I got up from my table and walked over to his.

"You're a real asshole, you know that?"

He had lifted his biscotti and now put it down in surprise. The saucer rattled lightly on the table.

"Sylvie," he said.

I hadn't realized how furious I was until I started speaking.

"Coming to Berkeley, following me around, meeting me at the lamppost? Specifically coming to the beach, my beach, only to swim away from me—and now you're here, at the only coffee shop I ever go to, pretending to eat a *biscotti*—"

"What's wrong with eating a biscotti?"

"Nobody," I said, "goes to a coffee shop just to eat a biscotti."

The people at neighboring tables had turned to look. One of them was a professorial-looking man in a corduroy coat. On his table was a biscotti in a small dish. Gabe looked at him pointedly before turning back to me.

"Besides," he said, in his pleasant way, "it isn't *your* beach, Sylvie. And I wasn't swimming away from you. I was swimming away from some hysterical guy who looked like he wanted to drown me."

"That was my boyfriend."

"Was?"

It was Gabe, all right. The same dogged insistence, the same lopsided grin.

"Is," I said. "But you knew that."

"What gives you that impression?"

"I just have a feeling."

Gabe stared at me quizzically. "What was that you said about a lamppost?"

"Two nights ago. I saw you through the window, and we met at the end of the block. You asked me if I knew I was—"

But I left off there. Gabe's face was filled with a wondering kind of confusion.

"I had a dream about you," I said shortly.

"You did?"

I could tell he was flattered, and I immediately regretted it.

"Forget it."

"You've always been intuitive."

"It's nothing."

I was leaning forward, my hand on his table, and now I straightened up. I needed time to think, to sort out what had happened that summer and how much of it had been real. So Gabe had been at the beach, but I really had been sleepwalking on the night I walked out of the apartment to meet him. Why would he lie to me about one incident and admit the other?

"Sylvie."

I turned around again. Gabe's voice was quieter, stripped of its charm.

"Don't you want to know why I'm here?"

I wasn't sure if I did. Despite how much I missed him, I knew there was a cost to being with Gabe, that other things came with him. Other parts of myself rose to the surface, like fish on a line; other edges of life had their coverings pulled back. But I was too angry to leave him just yet. I had caught him, and I wanted my questions answered before I let him go.

We left the café and took the street that led toward campus. I think I was in shock. Physically, he looked like any other undergrad, but there was something about the way he observed the students that marked him as an outsider. He asked me what it was like to go to college—where I lived, how the dorms were different from the ones at Mills, what my major was.

"Psychology?" he asked. "That's perfect."

"Perfect?"

"Perfect for you. You've always wanted to figure people out—and you're good at it, Sylve."

I flinched when he used my nickname. "I'm not sure that's true."

"You figured me out."

"No, I didn't. You left before I could. And you've never told me why."

We walked into campus through East Gate and made our way along University Drive. It was emptier than usual in the summer, but there were still clumps of students reading on towels or throwing Frisbees, their shadows winging through the grass.

"It's a long story," said Gabe. "And a messy one. Are you sure you want to hear it?"

It was clear he had come here to tell me this story, but also that he felt he needed permission. Whether it was out of courtesy or guilt, I wasn't sure. But he waited until I nodded to continue.

"I came to Mills for ninth grade, just like you." He glanced at me as we passed Hearst Mining Circle, the elegant three doors of the Memorial Mining Building. "I was on scholarship—maybe you figured this out. At the time, my dad was living in Florida. He didn't pay child support, and my mom's health was so bad that I think the school took pity on me. I always wondered, at least. I didn't have terrific grades."

He kept his eyes on the road, but I stared at him as he talked. The feeling of his body so close to mine was so uncanny I couldn't help it.

"Anyway, I was always looking for ways to make a little extra money. I loved Mills; I considered it my home. My tuition was covered, but I imagined I'd repay the school eventually—I'd make a big donation, cover the tuition of another student, maybe fund a new computer lab. You know how it was with the computers in the library—there was always a line out the door.

"So I started taking these odd jobs. I'd do whatever anybody wanted. For a while I gave haircuts in the Moberly Common Room. They didn't mind so long as I cleaned up afterward. I started a group that played poker on Sunday afternoons, but I got too worried we'd be found out. And I worked night shifts in the dining hall."

"I know."

"Please be patient with me," he said. "I know nothing makes sense yet."

There was genuine appeal in his face. I kept us going straight, rather than turning off one of the side paths that would take us farther into the web of buildings.

"In our junior year, Mr. Keller approached me. I'd been

a smart-ass that day in psych, and he asked me to stay after class. I thought I was going to get in trouble. But he sat me down on the other side of his desk, and he told me my problem was that I had too much energy."

"I remember that." I stopped. "We'd been studying—early childhood development, was it? We all figured you were going to get in trouble. I stopped on the hill as we were walking back to the dorms. I tried to look in the window."

"I saw you," said Gabe. "And I thought, *That's Sylvie, she would do such a thing.* You were always loyal, even before we were together."

He started walking again, and I followed him.

"You told us you were fired, that you'd lost your job at the dining hall."

"I was. But that wasn't the full story. Keller gave me this whole spiel—said I reminded him of himself at my age, that I needed something to pour myself into. I tuned out a bit until he mentioned the pay. Twenty dollars an hour for such menial work: data entry, mailings, things I could do in my sleep. I thought he was joking until he had me sign a confidentiality agreement."

"So it was true," I said. "Keller's research assistants."

Gabe nodded. "He said he chose one or two students each semester, students who showed promise and seemed trustworthy, but he didn't want the word getting around. That was fine with me—I already tried to keep my scholarship as quiet as possible, and I would've been an obvious target if anyone had known about this."

"Was Will Washburn his assistant?" I asked. I remembered the time that Keller had come upon us standing on the library stairs, when Will had been excluded from the larger group.

"The year before me." Gabe tore a twig from the dangling branch of a nearby tree and chucked it in front of us. "So I went to talk to him before I gave Keller an answer. Asked him what it was like, how much money he made, whether he was skeeved out by the confidentiality agreement. Honestly, I was kind of offended to think that Keller had put me in the same camp as Will Washburn—you know how Will was, always throwing some fit—but what I noticed that day was that he'd really calmed down. *A thoroughly useful experience*—that was how Will described it. He said he'd made tons of money and Keller had already written a personal recommendation on his behalf to someone on Princeton's admissions committee."

"Will did wind up going to Princeton."

"Exactly. I figured Keller would do the same for me. There wasn't any good reason not to take the job—so I started in January. The January of our junior year."

"That was the month of the eclipse."

"That's right."

Gabe looked at me appreciatively, as though he'd presented me with a riddle and I had solved it. We were in the grass below Sather Tower, where I often set up my camera. I sat down, and he joined me. The entire situation felt surreal—the haziness of the sky, the relative absence of other students, and Gabe, sturdy and tangible before me.

"What did you mean by showing me that flower? The flower with two disks?"

"The infinity flower." Gabe smiled. "I didn't know what it was at the time, though I found out later I was right—it was an experiment, some sort of play with garden genetics. But by then I had seen Stu Cappleman at Keller's house, and I had a whole new set of suspicions."

"Stu Cappleman? The guy who worked in the dining hall?"

He was a gangly boy from one of the surrounding towns who went to public high school and worked nights in our dining hall. His dad did the plumbing in the dorms, which was how Stu must have been hired. He was something of a character at Mills, with his cystic acne and loose, inventive slang. Sometimes he played basketball on campus with a few of our students, Gabe included. Technically, he wasn't supposed to be there when he wasn't working, but none of the teachers ever asked him to leave.

"That's the one," said Gabe. "This was one night in April—our junior year. I was supposed to have printed out a bunch of reports and put them underneath the door to Keller's office in Sellery Hall. But I'd been scrambling to get a history paper done, and I didn't finish until after midnight. Sellery was closed, so I figured I would go to his house and slip it under the door. I thought I could tell him I'd forgotten he wanted me to put it in Sellery, and he'd never know the difference. I didn't want him to dock my pay."

He plucked a blade of grass and played with it: rolled it into a spiral, slivered it at the center.

"When I got to the door, I realized there was light coming out from underneath it. That's when I heard these—noises. High-pitched whines, like a little girl's voice, and then a lot of muttering I couldn't understand. But finally I realized someone was talking about his hands. 'I see my hands,' the person would say—'Here they are, my hands,' all in the same weird voice. Keller would offer some encouragement—'That's right,' or 'Very good, Stuart,' or 'You certainly do'—but Stu didn't seem to notice him at all. He never responded when Keller spoke, and sometimes he talked right over him."

"Are you sure it was Stu Cappleman?"

Gabe nodded. "Positive. The blinds were down, but there was a sliver of space on each side. At one point, Stu came close to the window and I saw him."

A part of me was skeptical; the story was too fantastic. But another part of me believed Gabe as I believed in dreams, while they were happening: with absurd and unconscious trust.

"And that didn't bother you?" I asked. "It didn't seem to be ethically questionable, Keller keeping a school employee locked up in his house past midnight?"

"Of course it bothered me. It took me a few days, but I finally worked up the courage to ask him about it. Keller listened very quietly, not at all ruffled. You would've thought I was asking him about the weather. Then he looked at me in this calm sort of way and said that Stu had volunteered to be a part of his research, the same research I was helping with—as if I'd known about it all along."

"Had you?"

"Not a thing," said Gabe. "Believe me, Sylvie. All I was doing was entering data I didn't understand, long strings of letters and numbers. He'd kept me in the dark, and for good reason. Now that I knew, it was like I had this special power. And I was afraid. I didn't know what I'd gotten myself into. So I went to Keller and asked him to tell me what his research was about."

On the other side of the trees, a group of middle schoolers, here for a summer camp, ran by, laughing. I shivered. The heat wave had long since passed, and I was only wearing a T-shirt.

"You're cold," said Gabe.

He put a hand on my lower arm and rubbed it until the hairs stood up. Then he smoothed them down again. Everything he touched was a nerve. I pulled my arm back, putting it between my crossed legs.

"So what did Keller say?"

"He said it had to do with sleep," said Gabe, "and dreaming. Consciousness, unconsciousness. REM cycles. But it was Stu I wanted to know about. Keller said he had a sleep disorder, which made it so that he didn't stay in bed when he was asleep—he got up, moved around, acted out whatever was happening in his dreams. Keller was trying to find a way to get him to figure out he was dreaming. Otherwise, Stu could hurt himself—he already had. Once, before he came to Keller, he tripped while sleepwalking and came down so hard his chin split open. Needed about twenty stitches."

"So that's what you were doing," I said. "All those nights, when you left my room, and I saw you going to his house. You were helping him? On Tuesdays and Thursdays?"

Gabe nodded again.

"Why?" I asked. "What was in it for you?"

"He upped my pay—practically doubled it."

It was the first time that day I had seen him look sheepish.

"He must have been trying to keep you quiet."

"Yeah, that occurred to me. But it was good, honest research, Sylvie. It was clean. Some of the other teachers knew about it. I didn't think I was doing anything wrong. And I was excited, for the first time, about science—I thought I might want to be a psychologist or a neuroscientist. I started to work harder in biology.

"But it got more complicated," he added. "The farther in I got, the more confused I was. It was so much responsibility, working with Keller. I wasn't sleeping. I couldn't talk to anyone about what I was doing. I felt like a freak. And one night, toward the end of our senior fall, Keller and I got into this awful fight. I told him I didn't want to help him anymore, that I wanted to be a regular student. He said he'd reduce my hours, but he couldn't let me off completely. I'd signed on to assist him until the end of that year, and we were neck-deep in projects—it was too late to train anyone new."

"Is that why you left?" I asked. "In December—were you expelled?"

"It was my decision. I figured I'd already burned my bridge with Keller, and my grades were dropping fast—I wouldn't have been able to get into a decent school without his help. So I went back to Tracy, hopped from job to job. My mom passed the next year, right around the time you were graduating, so I went to live with my gran."

"I didn't know that," I said. Gabe's head was tilted downward, but I could see the tips of his ears turn pink. "I'm sorry."

Gabe shook his head.

"I spent a few years that way. But I couldn't get Keller out of my head. I kept thinking about him, wondering if I'd been wrong. I called Mills, but they said he'd left. I couldn't find anything out about him on the Internet. It was Mr. Cooke who finally put me back in touch. He had an old home phone number of Keller's, a place in Fort Bragg where he thought Keller might be living."

"But why did you want to go back to him?"

Gabe leaned back on his arms. Two honeybees had found their way to us and were circling him. But he was entirely calm; he didn't even wave them away.

"Keller gave me the opportunity to make something of myself. Otherwise, I knew what would happen—I'd stay in Tracy, get a job driving a truck or working at one of the gas stations. I wouldn't go to college, and I wouldn't get out. He'd seen some potential in me. He'd *chosen* me. And it was like electricity, that feeling of being chosen, when he took me back. There were conditions, of course. I had to do a hell of a lot more training. He had me take a bunch of courses by extension—neuroscience, calculus, chemistry. And I had to move to Fort Bragg. You'd like it there, Sylve. Big craggy rocks, beaches with driftwood and glass. Cliffs and cold weather. It's not far off from here."

I stood up, a door inside me slamming shut. I was really cold now, and I'd told David I would be home by six.

"Can I walk you somewhere?" asked Gabe, standing, too. "Where are you going?"

"To my apartment. I live with David."

"I know you must be angry with me, Sylvie. I know you must resent me."

"You left," I said, starting down the path again, "without even saying good-bye. We'd been *together*, Gabe, and I never heard from you again. All those nights I worried about you, stayed up to watch for you and asked you where you'd gone— you made me look like an idiot. And now what? You want to tell me what you were doing back then? Or did you want to apologize? It was years ago. I don't care about it anymore. I don't think about it. So is that all?"

"No, that isn't all."

He was moving briskly, trying to keep up with me. But I pushed ahead, walking so fast I was practically running.

"You said I was your *person*," I said, turning around. "The night before you left—you lay in my bed and you told me that."

I felt humiliated that I'd remembered it, humiliated that I'd said it aloud. Gabe caught up with me now, stepped in front of me so that I couldn't move any farther.

"You were," he said. "You are."

"No. That doesn't make sense. You can't be somebody's person unless you're actually with them."

"Which is what I'm trying to do now." Gabe inhaled. "I'm here to ask you to join me."

"You must be joking." I couldn't help it; I started laughing, as involuntary a response as tears.

"I'm not joking." There was a quiet force to his voice. "Keller needs a new assistant. Someone to help with intake, data entry. The same kind of work I do, but now there's too much of it for just me. You'd be perfect for it."

"Look around!" I shouted. A clump of pigeons rose and scattered from the path, where they'd been pecking at an old sandwich. "I live in Berkeley. I'm about to start my senior year of college. This is my life now."

"I know that. But you could have a different one. You're smart, Sylvie—smarter than anyone else in our class. You've got drive, and you don't shy away from things that aren't normal. And you want more"—he gestured to the dorms, the tall and columned buildings—"than this. I know you do."

I stepped around him and started to walk again. He followed me, moving quickly, but I was faster.

"You don't know what you're talking about," I said. "I'm happy here. You haven't even been to college—do you have any idea what my life is like? I can't just *leave*."

"You're right," he said. "I don't. But I still think you want to be involved in something bigger. I know it because I'm the same way. And because of what you said to me, back in high school. You begged me to take you with me."

"What do you mean? I couldn't have begged you—I didn't know about any of this."

"But you did know. You knew all along. You just weren't conscious."

There was a terrible whirring feeling in my gut. Gabe wouldn't look at me.

"One night," he said, "I was getting up in the middle of the night to meet Keller. I was in your room, getting my shoes on, when you asked me where I was going. I told you about the research, and before I knew it I was telling you everything. At first I thought you were awake. But something seemed off. You could barely open your eyes, and you only seemed to be half listening. I realized you were asleep."

"So I was sleep-talking." We passed the Mining Circle again; East Gate was in sight. "Really nice of you to fill me in, Gabe, but it isn't the same. You could clear your conscience, and I didn't remember any of it. It was a perfectly safe move."

"You could look at it that way," he said. "But I saw it as dangerous. I was speaking to a subconscious part of you—an uninhibited part of you—whose powers were a total mystery to me. I didn't know what you'd do with the information, subconsciously or not, and I couldn't be sure you wouldn't remember it."

"So you were just listening to me babble on all night? What else did I say?"

I tried to play it off as though I barely cared, but the truth is I was terrified.

"You said you loved me."

I snorted.

"I didn't mean it. I was sleeping."

"More than once."

"And what version of me do you think is more trustworthy? The waking me, or the sleep me, totally unaware of what I was saying?"

"The sleep you," said Gabe. "Without question."

"I probably thought you were someone else."

"That's exactly my point. You said things in your sleep, *felt* things, that you could never acknowledge in waking life. We all do. We're too goddamn scared when the lights are on—we're pansies. But the part of you that came out when you talked in your sleep? She shows you for who you are."

"You took advantage of me," I said. "You pried."

I could feel my body heating up and my mouth began to quiver. But I didn't want to cry in front of him.

"Why don't you trust yourself?" he asked.

"Because I trusted you."

It came out with more venom than I'd intended. We left campus and walked down the street again. He stepped closer to me, the curves of his face shadowed by a streetlamp.

"You chose me," he said. "You didn't have to, but you chose me. You told me those things for a reason, just like I chose to tell you what I was doing with Keller."

We came to a crosswalk. The light was red, but no cars were coming, and I bolted across, the wind in my face. Just then, a car made a left turn into the intersection, and I leapt forward as it sped past me, honking.

"Jesus," shouted Gabe, running across the street to meet me. "You trying to get yourself killed?"

"Just trying to get home."

"Listen," he said more frantically. "Is this really what you want? Chatting with girls in the lunch line, doing your physics homework at night? Sitting in your boyfriend's nice little apartment, reading—*I* don't know—reading poetry? That satisfies you?"

"What's wrong with reading poetry? What's weak about it?"

"All right. Maybe it does satisfy you, for now. But what about later? You don't think you'll wonder what would have happened if you'd come with me? Here"—he gestured to the shops, the students shuffling down the street in groups, the lit windows of upper-story apartments—"you have a perfectly decent life, I can see that. You could marry this—*David*, and maybe you'll become a professor. I can imagine how your life might go from here, and I bet you can, too."

I was quiet as we turned onto my block. I could see the square window in the galley kitchen lit up; David was there, cooking dinner, and all I had to do was return to him.

"There's another thing, Sylvie. Keller's patients—they're not like most of us. They've got disorders that make them do things in their sleep. Dangerous things. They walk and talk—"

"I talk, apparently."

"But they do other things, too. They can act out their dreams, like Stu. Sometimes they hurt people—people they love."

"What do you mean?"

"I can't say much more now. But I can tell you that it's good work. We give these people a way to protect themselves, control their demons. Keller helps them to turn their disorders into something useful—something powerful. C'mon, Sylvie." Gabe grinned. "I know you're intrigued."

"But why me?" That question had been nagging at me. "I haven't studied neurology. There must be people better suited for this."

"You're studying psych."

"But you just learned that. It couldn't have been why you came."

Gabe looked down. We were steps away from my apartment now; David could have seen us if he'd looked out of the window.

"You're right," he said. "There were other people suited for the job. It was no small feat to convince Keller to let me try for you. But I lobbied for it, said you wouldn't let us down. He remembered you from school. He likes using people from Mills, giving us a chance out in the real world. I know it sounds hokey, Sylve, but I think he feels like a kind of father to us."

"To you," I said. I could still call up the image of Gabe in the mailroom at Mills, how he would go up to the counter and ask if anything had come for him from Florida, keeping his voice low so no one else in line would listen in. In the weeks around his birthday, he made us take a detour to the mailroom twice a day, after lunch and before dinner, and I always knew whose letters he was waiting for.

Night was falling fast, the sky shedding blue, and it was difficult to see Gabe's eyes. But with his hair so short, the structure of his jaw was more visible, and that made me remember something.

"When I saw you at the lamppost, in my dream. How could I have pictured you with short hair if you weren't really there? If I was dreaming, why didn't you look the way you did at Mills?"

"Hmm," said Gabe, his head cocked. "You might have seen me in town, even if it didn't register. I've been lurking around here for a few weeks, you know. Keller wanted me to make sure you were ready before I approached you. See how you were, what you were up to."

"Some people would call that stalking. I could probably have you arrested."

"Oh, that's a little harsh, don't you think?" Gabe grinned. "I was observing. I was coming to see an old friend."

I squinted up at the window again. Where was David? On the couch, probably, where he spread out with papers and poster board each night. Sometimes I liked to work in bed with the pillows propped behind me, but for David it was always the couch, never the bed. He only used the bed to sleep.

"I would have to leave school, wouldn't I?" I asked.

Gabe nodded.

"I'm sorry, Sylvie, but now's when we have the opening. I'll understand if it isn't worth it to you, and Keller will, too. But think of it this way—you'd already have a job. A real, paying job, with benefits and a place to stay. Keller puts me up in Fort Bragg. It's not a bad life."

"Do you have friends?"

It sounded small, and Gabe laughed.

"Friends? No, not many. But I don't need many friends. I have my research, which satisfies me, and Keller's been a sort of mentor. I keep in touch with my gran; she's still alive. And if you came with me, I'd have you."

It was thrilling to hear him say those words. Still, I told him I needed the week to think about it and that I didn't want him to come find me in the interim. He kept his promise. Whenever I sat down in a coffee shop or walked into a bookstore, I scanned it for him. But he was never there, and by the end of the week, I almost missed the feeling I got when

I sensed he was nearby. Perhaps I was honored, or foolishly curious, or maybe I was still in love; it was probably some combination of the three that fated my decision long before it actually came time for me to make it.

It was the way I had felt when deciding whether to go to Mills. In middle school, I became resistant—I wanted to go to the public high school where my friends were going—but somehow I knew that my resistance was little more than a show. I had worn my dad's old Mills sweatshirt since the age of eight, and I'd been hearing about the school for longer than that. The choice was mine to make, my parents said, but when I chose to go the route my father had, it seemed a choice made not by my rational mind but by the collective momentum of past experience. Later, in Keller's psychology class at Mills—a subject I certainly wouldn't have been able to take at the local high school, which adhered to a more limited state curriculum—I learned that Carl Jung had seen intuition as an irrational process, perception via the unconscious. I imagined intuition as an internal North Star, one that would lead me away from fairer climates of reason—if I chose to follow it.

In putting on a show of resistance, then, what had I been showing? Perhaps I meant to exert what I thought was my will, to prove I was governed by forces more logical, more solitary, than gravity or magnetism—the earth's magic tricks. My friends would be attending the public school; therefore, I would be happy there. It was a simple equation, and like most simple equations, it probably would have been true. It would have fulfilled me, I think. But I made the decision to fulfill something else; or, as it happened, the decision made me.

When I told David that I was leaving—leaving both him and the university—he blinked at me not with sadness or anger but with absolute surprise. For a moment, I was disappointed that he didn't react more strongly. Perhaps he had intended to break up with me, too, and was startled when I beat him to it. But if that were true, wouldn't he have also looked relieved? There was such wonder in his face, such astonishment; it was as though I had vanished, and in my place was someone he had never seen before.

# 8

MADISON, WISCONSIN, 2004

The morning after Jamie's session, I woke to thick, aggressive rain. It was nine o'clock, but it felt much earlier. The sky was a matte, slate blue, and I knew I hadn't slept enough. Gabe was dozing with a peacefulness that irritated me, his arms curled to his chest. I pulled on an old pair of sweats and went downstairs to work in what he had dubbed my Oval Office. I couldn't concentrate: I was still disturbed by what had happened the night before and angry that Gabe hadn't stood up for me in front of Keller. When he woke, I wanted to talk about it again. But when I checked on him at eleven, he was still in bed. I decided I would wake him at noon, and in the meantime, I went outside to the porch.

The rain had stopped. Instead, a faint mist hung in the air. It made the world look static and grainy, like an old photograph. I sat down on the couch the former tenants had left. Time had softened the nubbly fabric, and its deep brown color hid any stains. I must have closed my eyes, because I felt myself wafting in and out of consciousness. Every so often, I came to, feeling the couch beneath me, and then I slipped away again.

"Sleepy Sylvie," said a voice, too high to be Gabe's. The couch gathered substance beneath me. When I opened my eyes, I saw a shadowy figure on the other side of the porch screen. Thom.

Though I knew I was awake, the quality of the light made him look like an old movie actor. I thought he was smiling at me, but I couldn't be sure.

"Hello, you." Thom poked his head in the door, and his features sharpened. "Didn't mean to wake you—my apologies. Mind if I come in?"

"Sure," I said, pushing myself into a seated position. He ducked his head beneath the door frame and dropped two large bundles on the wooden floor.

"Got caught in the rain," he said, leaning against the screen. "I was picking up laundry. I'll just take a moment— my arms need a rest. Not working today?"

"We had a lab last night, so I'm working from home."

"Nice job."

He lifted his head and grinned. His eyes were bright and owl-like behind the thick rims of his glasses, and his bangs were slicked to his forehead.

"And what are you doing today," I asked, "besides laundry?"

"I teach a freshman composition course in the evening. And I'll work on my dissertation."

He hoisted one of the bags of laundry up on his back and straightened, tilting his head toward the door.

"Why don't you come with? You can help me carry the laundry, have something to eat at our place. More fun than sleeping, I'd hope."

"That sounds like free labor." I grinned. "What's in it for me?"

"The pure and stirring pleasure," said Thom, "of hearing about my dissertation. Lots of people vying to hear more about this project, you know. It's sure to make me a very attractive job candidate."

Now I almost felt sorry for him. "What time is it?"

"Noonish." Thom shook his shirtsleeve back and checked his watch. "Quarter after."

I craned my head to look in the kitchen, but Gabe still hadn't come downstairs. I wondered what he would think if he woke up while I was next door, but I wasn't doing anything wrong. Besides, it would be nice to spend time with another person. So I took one of the bundles and followed Thom from my front porch to his, where hanging chimes made frantic, high-pitched music in the wind.

"Is Janna home?" I asked as we crossed through the kitchen. I hadn't been to other parts of their house before, but now I saw it was the mirror image of the one I shared with Gabe—the rooms were identically shaped but laid out in opposite formation. In the living room, there were two wooden rocking chairs, a low table stacked with books, and an oval-shaped rug, knit in spiraling shades of pastel yarn. In front of a boarded-up fireplace, someone had set a row of candles on a tray. Along the wall were stencils in colored pencil, framed behind glass. The images were abstract, and they seemed to have been drawn in a quick, jittery hand; the thin lines had a sense of impulse and movement, and I had a strange feeling that the walls were quivering.

"She's at work," said Thom. "She has a new pair of clients, filthy rich, who founded some sort of artists' colony in the Driftless Area. Janna takes care of the grounds, so I take care of the laundry."

We set the laundry bags, the sort of drawstring sacks that may have once held a tent or a sleeping bag, down on the floor. They wavered, tubular and soft-bodied as dummies, before tipping over. A piece of Janna's underwear, silky and magenta, sprouted from the mouth of the bag I'd carried.

I took a seat in the smaller rocking chair and crossed my legs on its salmon-colored cushion. In the wall closest to me was a small door that our apartment didn't have.

"Where does that door lead?"

"The basement," said Thom, sitting down.

"Funny," I said. "You have a basement, and we have an attic."

Our attic was a small, cobwebby space accessible only by way of a rickety staircase. Probably it could have been an airy haven of some sort, if we'd put time into cleaning it, but we'd opted to use it for storage. There were piles of canvases and paints, boxes filled with winter clothing and Christmas ornaments.

"It's where I go to write," said Thom. "Clears my head to be underground. Nothing to look at, nothing to hear."

"It isn't depressing?"

Thom extended his legs and crossed one over the other. He wore a ragged sweater over a starched button-up shirt and a pair of beige slacks, which rode up around his ankles to reveal bones both large and delicate. His legs had the awkward grace of a giraffe, an unwieldy nobility, which made me want to pause in deference as he arranged himself.

"Depressing?" he asked. "It can be, but it also has the opposite effect. Sometimes I have to go to a place where there's nothing to look at in order to see clearly. The more attractive the outside world, the more difficult it is for me to retreat into my head."

"And what do you do there? What's your book about?"

"Keats," he said. "The poet who wrote the piece I quoted the other night—'yes, in spite of all, some shape of beauty . . .' You remember? He died at twenty-five, but he got more done in those years than most of us could hope to do by eighty. Keats was obsessed with beauty, thought it was the highest form of truth—he was a Romantic, so we can't blame him—and he rejected the rationalism that was taking hold at the time. Other artists tried to analyze the world, pin it down like a butterfly staked to a board, but old Johnny just wanted to stare. He got itchy around people like Coleridge, who sought knowledge over beauty—people who were incapable, as Keats put it, of being content with half knowledge. In 1817, he wrote to his brothers about it, and he came up with this phrase called *negative capability*."

"Negative capability?"

"'When man is capable of being in uncertainties. Mysteries, doubts, without any irritable reaching after fact and reason'—his words, not mine. What I want to figure out is how this *not knowing* can be productive—how it isn't a purely negative capability after all."

"But isn't that the point? That it isn't productive?"

"That's certainly the point a lot of people are making," said Thom. "Most of them are economists or scientists, some of them are educators, and plenty of them are ordinary, practically-minded people. People who chase facts like they're drilling for oil. People who don't believe in the value of poetry and who think the study of the humanities is a luxury. A part of me believes they're right. But I still chose to pursue this life, and now I'm trying to figure out why. If I can't defend myself—even if it's only *to* myself—then I don't want to finish the degree. I want to know why we bother with mystery and what leaving it alone has to offer us."

He leaned forward, resting his elbows on his knees.

"You probably don't find much use for it, do you, being in the sciences?" he asked. "Probably think it's a lot of hot air, poetry?"

"I read fiction. I can understand the value of escape."

But I couldn't remember the last time I had read a novel; it must have been in college. Mostly, I didn't want to prove whatever theory he had about me right.

"But that's precisely my point," said Thom. "Reading, writing—engaging in this kind of negative capability—I don't think it's an escape. I mean to argue that the real world, our world, *is* negative capability. Not knowing is the only reality, and our escape is the unreality of knowledge."

"So what you're saying," I said, "is that the world of poetry is the only reality, and whatever else we're doing besides reading it—like building irrigation canals, or improving electrical systems, or, I don't know, searching for a cure to HIV—all of that's just escapism?"

"So says the scientist."

"I don't consider myself a scientist. I'm a researcher. And all right, it's true—researchers pursue facts—but the facts I'm researching are a lot closer to your world than you give them credit for. We're looking at the mind and what lies underneath it. We're investigating mystery—and doesn't poetry do the same thing?"

Thom leaned back in his chair and brought his hands together so that the fingers were slightly bent, the pads touching, as if he were holding a large glass ball.

"It's different," he said. "Poets question mysteries: they observe, they stand witness but they don't necessarily try to solve them. What you're doing is much more dangerous. You're trying to put a face to the subconscious—something that should, in my opinion, remain faceless. You're dragging it out of its cave, shining a flashlight in its eyes."

I could tell that Thom was enjoying the debate, but after Jamie's session, I was squirming with discomfort. I was irritated, too, for being so susceptible to doubt. It was as though I'd discovered that the elegant system of rationale I'd built around our research was actually made of cards—as though I'd seen how very little it took for it to fall apart. Why I put so much stock in Thom's opinion, and so early, I wasn't sure; perhaps it was that he was the only person with whom I'd shared so much about our research, and his judgment, now, was the only one I could receive. But I had too much pride to tell him any of this. I raised my eyebrows, leaned back in my chair.

"Well, good luck writing a dissertation without answering any questions."

"Thank you," said Thom, with no trace of irony.

"Just because we seek answers doesn't mean we're being invasive or turning over rocks that would be better left alone," I said, gaining momentum. "I think your argument's too simple. Ignorance isn't always so noble, you know. We're meant to ask questions—that's what makes us human. And answers proceed naturally from questions."

"Do they? Naturally?" he asked. I paused, and he smiled, more gently this time. "Look at us. Put two academics in a room and all they can talk about is work. Tell me something else about yourself. Do you have a hobby?"

"I used to paint," I said. "But I haven't in years."

"Why not?"

"No time."

"No?"

I shook my head, my eyes level with his. I felt exposed, plucked from my usual habitat. Here the ground was flat, without boulders to hide behind, and there was no wind to make noise of the air.

"Do you have a hobby?" I asked.

"I do," he said. "I like to cook, and I make a damn good sandwich. Chicken salad's my specialty, and I've got some fresh in the fridge I made yesterday. Would you like one?"

"A sandwich would be great," I said. Thom stood and left.

"Anyhow," he said, shouting from the kitchen, "I didn't mean to push too hard on your research. I'm a poetry scholar, for God's sake. What do I know? I'll have to ask Janna—see how she feels about having her rocks turned over. Was she approved, by the way?"

"Approved for what?"

"For your research. She told me she stopped by your place a few days ago to ask about getting involved."

"Are you sure?"

I'd seen Janna at our house the day before, when she and Gabe were planting trees, but he hadn't mentioned that she'd come over before that. I remembered the remark she'd made about wanting to be hooked up to our machines. I just never imagined she'd try to go through with it.

"I'm positive," said Thom. "This must have been about a week ago. She said she spoke with Gabe, but I assumed you were home."

He came back into the room with a halved sandwich on a yellow plate. Each half had a generous helping of chicken salad held together with thick mayonnaise, bits of grapes and chopped-up apple visible throughout.

"Does she have any kind of sleep disorder?" I asked. I took a bite and licked the mayonnaise that spread to the side of my mouth.

"Not that I know of."

"You'd know."

"How?"

"Trust me." I shoved another bite in my mouth, and two grapes plopped onto the plate. "You'd know if she was violent, if she screamed in her sleep or kicked and thrashed. You'd know if she tried to hurt you—"

"Jesus, Sylvie." The amusement on Thom's face was gone, and he looked uneasy. "Is that what your patients do?"

"Like I said. You'd know."

Thom was silent as I finished the sandwich. I wiped the sides of my face with my hands and brought the plate to the kitchen. As I washed it at the sink, I noticed that the lights in the downstairs level of our house were on. It was still misty, but when I brought my face closer to the window, I could see

Gabe's shape moving from room to room. I put my plate in the drying rack and went back to the living room to tell Thom I had to leave, but the room was empty.

"Thom?"

Was he upstairs in the bathroom? I walked to the stairs and called again, but there was no reply. I decided to explain myself the next time I saw him; I was anxious to get home and ask Gabe about Janna. I was crossing through the kitchen when I heard Thom's voice behind me.

"Going so soon?"

He stood in the doorway of the living room wall, the one that led to the basement. He held a battered, ancient book, its cover soft and green as moss.

"I wanted to show you this," he said.

He held the book toward me. It smelled sweet and intoxicating, like rotting wood. I tensed, ready to tell him I was leaving, but something in his face made me swallow the words. In it I saw the same vulnerability, the same tentative desire to share, that I'd felt while discussing my research.

"What is it?" I asked.

"*The Poetical Works of John Keats*. Original edition, 1884. I thought I'd read the rest of the poem you liked. 'Endymion,' it's called. The Greeks believed he was a shepherd or an astronomer who fell in love with the goddess of the moon—some say the moon itself. But Endymion was just a man; unlike the moon, he could age and weaken and die. So the goddess cast a spell on Endymion—one that made him sleep forever, immortal. That way, they could always be together."

"That's incredibly depressing."

"It's not." Thom tucked his chin and pulled away, as though I'd insulted him.

"It is," I said, laughing. "The guy gives up his humanity, just to sleep for all time? I mean, granted, I haven't met her, but I don't get the sense that the moon makes a very good girlfriend."

"She certainly does," said Thom. "First of all, she's ridiculously prompt."

"She knows how to keep her distance," I added.

"She's like, four billion years old, so she's got a shit-ton of life experience."

"Her face is a little scarred, but hey, whose isn't?"

"According to the myth, they also had about fifty daughters."

"Good lord," I said. "That's nightmarish."

We were both laughing now, the book almost forgotten. When we became quiet again, Thom smiled, looking down at it, before putting it inside the open basement door.

"Well," he said. "Maybe another time."

I left through the porch, pulling the screen shut behind me. Wet grass squealed under my feet as I crossed to our house. When I stepped inside, Gabe was eating a peanut-butter sandwich over the sink.

"Hey," he said. "What were you doing at Thom's?"

I wondered how long he had been standing there. From the window above the sink, it was possible to see straight into Thom's living room.

"He invited me for lunch," I said. "You were still asleep."

"No, I left hours ago. Keller called—said they were under-staffed at the clinic and he needed me to take the place of one of the receptionists. I was going to tell you, but then I saw you on the porch, out like a light. So I left a note."

He gestured to the counter, where there was a small slip of yellow paper.

"You should have woken me," I said. "I could have helped."

"But you had such a rough night. I wanted to let you sleep. Besides, I was only answering phones. I thought I was doing you a favor by letting you nap."

It was true—there was nothing very exciting about answering phones at the sleep clinic. So why did I feel betrayed?

"Thom told me that Janna came by a few days ago," I said. "He said she wanted to be a participant in one of our experiments."

Gabe blinked.

"Right," he said. "It was over the weekend. You had gone to the bank, I think. Janna knocked on the door. We sat on the porch. We made small talk for a few minutes, mostly about gardening, and then she asked what she would have to do to qualify for one of our studies."

"But why? Why would she even want to qualify?"

"I think she liked the concept. Said she's been keeping a dream journal since her teens—one of those types." Gabe grinned easily. "She wanted to talk about this recurring dream where her teeth fall out. She said sometimes they rot or grow in crooked, and other times they fall out one by one with a light tap."

He took his index finger and tapped his two front teeth in demonstration.

"Did you give her Freud's interpretation?" I asked.

"What?" asked Gabe, amused. "That the loss of teeth is a symbol of castration? A punishment for masturbation? No, Sylve, I didn't tell her that."

"Regardless," I said, "we couldn't use her. We *know* her. It wouldn't be ethical."

"But what's more ethical than helping the people you know? Why should the process be so quarantined, so sterilized? I mean, science should be applicable to real life—so why should we divorce it from love?"

I stared at him. He washed his plate and dried it, then shook his hands of water. Little droplets sprayed my chest.

"Love?"

"Oh, come on," he said. "I meant on principle."

So Janna wanted to do exactly what Thom had warned against—to answer her questions, to crawl down her own rabbit hole. Thom believed it was wrong, and yet he hadn't tried to dissuade her. Did he respect her freedom to do as she chose, or didn't he care? Perhaps it was that he didn't think our research would work, dangerous as it was in theory. I thought about our patients. Was it true that their dreams felt more real than anything tangible, whether or not they were lucid? That the people they dreamed of—partners, children, even people they'd created—were more vivid to them than those who were alive?

But I quickly shook off the idea. If these dream characters *were* more vivid to our patients, it was because they were disturbed. That was why they'd come to us. And it was exactly why I was so angry that Janna had gone to Gabe. She didn't have a sleep disorder. She only wanted attention, and it seemed she wanted it from him.

• • •

That evening, Gabe left to work in the university library. He wasn't home by dinner, so I made cream of mushroom soup from the can and ate while I worked in the office. But soon I became restless, and I climbed the stairs to the attic.

I hadn't been there since we first moved in. It was a small, slanted space, the floors splintered and covered in a soft down of dust. There was one window, cracked open; each draft shook the pane. We'd thrown our boxes up here haphazardly in August, glad to be done with them, and they covered most of the floor. An extra pair of eclipse curtains was crumpled darkly in one corner. Foam peanuts were strewn across the ground, shining like plastic snow. My canvases leaned against the back wall, and my paint boxes were piled beneath an old exercise ball.

Maybe I was only looking for something to do with my hands, but I started to clean. Before long, I sank into a state that felt as close as I'd ever come to meditation. I began by nesting the smaller boxes inside each other and stacking them in towers. With the ground partially cleared, the room doubled in size. I mopped the floors and wiped the molding, cobwebs tangling around my hands like hair. I found an area rug in one of Gabe's boxes and set it in front of the window. I took a brass standing lamp from the living room—we never used it—and put it next to the rug. I collected the foam and bubble wrap in a trash bag. Then I brought a rag up from the kitchen and scrubbed the windowpane until it gleamed.

As dusk fell, I leaned against the window frame. I could see the fence that separated our yard from Thomas and Janna's. The maple trees, scarlet with fall, quivered like flame. A rabbit scampered over our porch and disappeared under the fence. I had not felt so peaceful, so hidden, in years.

Before I left, I tidied my paint supplies. It pleased me to see the canvases in neat rows, the paints organized and boxed by color. Ringing with accomplishment, I returned to the office, where I worked more efficiently than I had in months.

# 9

In June of 2002, I boarded a plane in San Francisco bound for Martha's Vineyard. This was where Keller had a research and training compound, and it was where Gabe and I would spend the summer so I could be brought up to speed before we left for Fort Bragg that fall. I had yet to learn about Keller's simultaneous potentialities theory of the subconscious mind, but Gabe told me it was mainstream enough to have earned him a tenured professorship at the University of San Francisco in the mideighties. Its fringier elements, though, had also attracted a cultish following of experimental academics, conspiracy theorists, and members of the artistic and political avant-garde.

While at USF, Keller founded an interdisciplinary philosophy-neuroscience-psychology program, commonly known as PNP. But in 1995, he left to become the headmaster at our small, private boarding school, hidden in the fog and black walnut trees and upside-down rivers of Humboldt County, California. While at Mills, I'd known that Keller was a psychologist with some degree of prestige, but I hadn't bothered to learn more than that. Gabe shared the rest of this with me in the weeks before we left Berkeley. When David wasn't home, he helped me pack and mail boxes. During work breaks, we spread out on the empty floor and ate pizza out of the delivery box as he told me about Keller. Gabe soon gave up trying to teach me about simultaneous potentialities, but it wasn't only the theory that confused me.

"So Keller was fully set up at USF," I said. "A tenured professor, the founder of this groundbreaking lucidity program, and he left to head up a high school? It doesn't make any sense. It's like he was regressing."

By now, we were on the plane from SFO, sitting in the seats Keller had purchased for us. These were the days when planes still served meals—something we dreaded at the time but later came to regard as a bygone luxury. We prodded the lemon chicken breast, set deep in a gelatinous yellow glaze. We unwrapped our twin bread rolls from aluminum foil and were surprised to find them still warm.

"It's strange, I know," said Gabe. He speared a piece of chicken with his plastic spork and swallowed it, making a face. "Almost like he needed a vacation. All I know is that he came to Mills in '95, just like us, and stayed for five years. Then he moved to Fort Bragg to do his own research."

"And you don't know why?"

Gabe shrugged. "There are some things I can ask him and some things I can't. My guess is that he started off within the university system because he had to, and over time he wanted more freedom. I know he's still connected to the university in a tangential way—he's sort of a grandfather to the PNP program—but other than that, they seem to leave him alone."

Keller spent each summer on Martha's Vineyard. The house was an inheritance, though Gabe didn't know from whom. All he knew about Keller's family was that his mother was a German immigrant while his father, a New York Jew with Eastern European roots, sold hats. Neither one seemed to have been particularly well-off, so I couldn't shake the sense that the house had been given to Keller by a third party.

We took a cab from the airport in Vineyard Haven, and as Gabe paid the driver—a tall, sweating boy in a limp polo shirt who couldn't have been any older than us—I stared at the wide expanse of the compound. It looked like three original houses, descending in size, had been pressed up against each other and were now linked. Gabe told me they were constructed in the late 1870s. Like many of the homes in Vineyard Haven, which had been built in the same neocolonial, Cape Cod style, Keller's compound had a symmetry and stately sense of proportion that seemed to me impenetrably masculine. Each house was sided with unpainted cedar shingles, which had originally been a rosy tan; over time, they took on the silver-gray sheen of moth wings. In front of the houses curved a crushed-shell driveway, long enough to hold three or four cars, though only one was parked there.

The entire compound was surrounded by dense, shade-giving trees, which keeled toward the house as if obligated to protect what was inside it. The landscape was new to me— the vicious storms of greenflies; the tall grasses that swayed with the airy fullness, the intention, of ghostly bodies—and I rarely ventured off alone. Fog curtained the beginning and end of each day like an ongoing play, and I feared that I would get lost inside it—that I would disappear into the gauze like the beetlebung trees and the vast, pale ocean. It didn't help that I couldn't find the house on any Vineyard Haven map. It lay at the end of an unpaved, dead-end road called Snake Hollow. Whenever Gabe and I talked about it afterward, we referred to the houses not as "Keller's compound" or "the place on Martha's Vineyard" but as Snake Hollow itself.

The day of our arrival was muggy and overcast. Every so

often, the sun broke through, brief and dazzling. As our cab driver backed out of the narrow road—off to pick up another batch of tourists, no doubt—a young woman came out of the house and walked toward the car parked in the driveway. She wore a cut-off pair of jean shorts with Birkenstocks and a baggy, short-sleeved T-shirt. When she came closer, I saw that she was pretty: African-American, with round, long-lashed eyes and hair that coiled up and out. She carried a bundle of clothing and a worn denim backpack over one shoulder, both of which she chucked in the open trunk of the car.

"What's up?" she called to Gabe as we walked toward the front door. Gabe carried his bags easily, but I had fallen behind, dragging my wheeled suitcase choppily over the shells. "This the new one?"

Gabe nodded. "This is Cassidy," he said as I caught up. "Cass, meet Sylvie—your replacement."

"You're such a dick," said the girl. But she was laughing, shaking her head. She leaned on the open car door, one knee bent. "Take care, okay?"

"I will," said Gabe. He hugged her briefly and slapped the roof of the car. "You say hi to San Francisco for me."

"Yeah, yeah," said Cass, slinging her body into the driver's seat. "Your old stomping grounds."

She flashed another smile, small white squares of teeth like Chiclets, and pulled out of the driveway.

"Who was that?" I asked as Gabe took out a ring full of keys and wedged one of them in the lock of the front door.

"Summer assistant—one of the kids in the PNP program. They come here on fellowships, stay for a few weeks, a month." The lock gave, and he pushed the door open with his shoulder. "You're taking her place. Come on in."

The house was filled with pastel light, as it often was that summer: the sun slanting through the kitchen blinds in lemony streaks or filling the library, while setting, with the orange sherbet of evening. Keller's old lamps emitted a warm glow, more heat than color. At night, they lent the house a dreamy haze, a sense that things were not quite what they seemed. Although the house was Keller's, it seemed to both obey and resist his mastery. Like a double agent, it dropped clues: an open window; thin walls that allowed sound to pass; a piece of softened yellow paper with blue handwriting, fluttering out of an opened book like a leaf from a late fall tree.

"Make yourself at home," said Gabe, leading me into a small, white kitchen from which the Atlantic Ocean could be seen. "Keller gets back on Monday."

"He isn't here?"

"He decided to go to a conference in Boston—sort of a last-minute thing. So I told him you'd spend the weekend getting acquainted with the place. And you can start your reading."

Gabe took two glasses from the cabinet above the sink, filled both with water, and brought one to me. The water was milky with bubbles. I swallowed.

"Hey," Gabe said, more gently. "Let's put your things away in the bedroom."

He must have detected my disorientation. I nodded and followed him down the hall, which gave off the sweet, musty odor of old wood. I knew, of course, that there would be long days of study here. But my memories of life in Berkeley were still so fresh that I wondered whether I'd made the right choice. My withdrawal from the university had been unsettlingly easy: I only had to go to the registrar's office and request a cancellation form. I'd imagined there would be someone who'd try to convince me to stay—a final test to be passed, like the spry, hopping creature at the final level of a video game. But the registrar was an ancient-looking woman who barely looked up before sliding a white form across the desk.

"This is all I need?" I asked.

"We'll see," said the woman, staring at her computer screen. "Are you an athlete?"

"No."

"An international student?"

"No."

"Have you been issued a call to active military duty?"

"Nope."

"Are you withdrawing for medical reasons?"

I shook my head.

Finally, the woman looked at me with brief appraisal, like an experienced doctor who could issue a diagnosis after a cursory glance at a wound, a rash, a swollen knee.

"Then all you need is this," she said, passing me a second form, an application for readmission, across the table.

I brought the application for readmission to Snake Hollow like a talisman, a reminder that I had not traveled too far into my decision for it to be undone. I hadn't even told my parents I'd pulled out of college. I just said I was taking the summer to "reassess my options," that a job had materialized and I wanted to see if it had any staying power before committing to the fall semester. They were alarmed, as I knew they would be. Minutes after I wrote by e-mail, I received a phone call from New Jersey with both of them on the line.

"Have you considered what you'll do if it doesn't work out?" my father asked, his voice booming through the receiver with more volume than it ever had in person. "Really picture what we're talking about here. You're twenty-two, twenty-three, you get bored or you get fired—"

"I mean, God forbid, it could be later than that," said my mother. I pictured her face, which must have acquired the look of valiant determination it did whenever she was fighting a losing battle with one of her children: her forehead creased, her eyebrows inching toward one another—eyebrows that, in their persistent, wiry growth, always seemed a bit too long for a woman.

"She could be twenty-eight," my mother said, continuing. "She could be in her thirties. You could be in your thirties, Sylvie, without a job or a college education, and what do you do then? You go back to school at thirty-five, that's a very big undertaking. My God, I couldn't go back to college now. I can teach college, but I couldn't go *back* to college."

"So maybe I'll teach college," I said. I felt raw and loose and panicked.

"Listen, honey, nobody's laughing," said my mother.

"But I have what every college graduate wants," I said. "A place to stay, a steady income, a job with one of the biggest researchers in my field. Besides, it's Mr. Keller. You guys love Mr. Keller."

"I wouldn't say we love him," said my father. "We like him just fine. But we like the idea of you staying in school a lot more."

When Gabe returned, rubbing vigorously at his head with a towel, I was sitting on the bunk bed that was mine for the summer. The room had eight bunks in all, so we called it the Bunk Room. It had been created to accommodate larger groups of visiting researchers, but now Keller used the room to house a few assistants at a time, which meant that most of the beds remained empty. The compound's original bedrooms functioned as guest rooms for people moneyed enough to come to the Vineyard for consultations and training sessions. Keller couldn't perform the sleep assessments that we would later do in Fort Bragg and Madison—the compound didn't have the equipment—but he often led seminars and retreats on lucid dreaming.

The people who came to these workshops weren't patients; their sleep was entirely normal. Lured by the novelty of lucid dreaming and the spectacular promises made by Keller's promotional materials (*WORLD SIMULATION*, read one pamphlet: *Just as a flight simulator enables people to safely fly, lucid dreaming can allow you to experience any imaginable world*), they came in droves on weekends: coiffed East Coast housewives, UMass undergrads in Teva sandals, eccentric elderly couples, even the rare celebrity. Itching at the limits of their own lives, they longed to try on new worlds like T-shirts, to slip easily into their fantasies and discard them before the plane ride home.

Did they do it? It was difficult to tell. There were always a few who left dissatisfied, Gabe said, but many people had been coming for years. Each month, we received testimonials: *For me, learning the truth of my feelings, however painful, has opened me to my heart and to my capacity to know love*, wrote Juanita Diaz, fifty-six, from Florida. And from John Simpson, thirty-four, an Afghanistan veteran from Colorado: *I know that I can change a frightening situation in a lucid dream, so I don't panic or get scared. And the strange thing is that in waking life I don't run away either anymore. People think I've changed through the years, but the fact is that this is the real me coming out.*

Later that summer, we watched as a seminar group napped on blue mats spaced throughout the living room. Gabe and I were standing on the beach, fifty yards from the house, but we could see through the room's French doors. Inside, twelve adults lay curled like fetuses, or like the pink shrimp that sometimes washed up onto the beach. Keller used yogic breathing and Eastern meditation techniques to help his guests nap during the day—it was easier and less expensive than hosting an overnight study—but I still wondered if any of them were faking it. Keller himself sat a small table, making longhand notes on one of his yellow pads as he scanned the sleepers. Beside each mat, there was a mini notebook and pen; to enhance dream recall—the first step in lucid dreaming—each patient would be asked to write down whatever they remembered as soon as the alarm went off.

"So you believe this stuff?" I asked Gabe. The ocean slid over my feet, frothy and white as steamed milk, and I wriggled my toes into the sand.

"Of course."

He picked up a piece of driftwood and chucked it into the spray. I squinted at the living room. The adults looked eerie: coiled into themselves and vulnerable with belief as Keller watched from his post in the corner. How invested could he be in these workshops, I wondered, in people he might only see once? That evening, after all the guests had left, I was rolling up the blue mats in the living room when I came across a stack of receipts. Keller had left them on the round table where he'd been sitting, and each one showed a charge of $425.

It was a four-hour workshop with a break for lunch—local lobster rolls, tasting mostly of mayonnaise, which Keller ordered by the trough. I did the math: slightly over $100 per hour—certainly less than the hourly rate of most psychologists. Still, Keller's workshops weren't therapy sessions, not exactly; for at least one of those hours, he was watching them sleep. Something about it didn't seem right. But it was true, I reminded myself, that Keller was in need of funding, and nobody expected him to give his research away for free.

I didn't ask him about it. As the summer went on, I would unlearn some of the nervousness I felt around Keller—a holdover from high school—but it was acute in the beginning. Though he was gone the weekend we arrived, it felt like he was right there with us. All through the house, discreet, typed signs hung from doorknobs or delicate nails. PLEASE DO NOT TOUCH was suspended beneath a framed handkerchief, the fabric yellowed and embroidered with a tiny *C.G.J.* (Carl Jung's, Gabe told me, though he didn't know how Keller had acquired it). DOOR CLOSED WHEN IN SESSION fluttered from the doorknobs down the hall. We knew there were no sessions when Keller wasn't there, but neither one of us ever tried to open them.

What struck me most of all, that first weekend, was how hard Gabe worked. He woke before dawn and spent the early hours reading in a rocking chair that looked out over the back porch. When I fumbled out of bed around eight or nine, I found him entirely absorbed: his back bent over the pages, a pen in hand, glasses pushed up on the bridge of his nose. I couldn't help but follow suit. Keller had assigned me a tall stack of thick, pungent books, the pages yellowed and tissue-soft. There were the seminal texts by Freud and Jung, along with more recent research on a range of sleep skills and disorders: Robert Stickgold's *Sleep and Brain Plasticity*, Rosalind Cartwright's *The Twenty-Four Hour Mind*, *Trauma and Dreams* by Deirdre Barrett, and Stephen LaBerge's full canon on lucid dreaming. Then there were the studies: academic papers with minuscule print and references so obscure that each one sent me on a fact-finding goose chase. In this way I slowly spun myself a web of knowledge, painstakingly linking one idea to the next, my purview widening strand by strand.

All this didn't even include the ancillary texts. Keller also left me a pile of photocopied nursery rhymes, fairy tales, and biblical passages. A note was paper-clipped on top: *Consider the cultural role that night has played throughout history.*

"Sure thing," I muttered, staring at the two-inch stack. "What does he want, an essay?"

I expected Gabe to fire off a snarky comment, but he only smiled.

"It's interesting," he said. "You'll see."

He was right. After a morning spent with the *Journal of Experimental Psychology: Human Perception and Performance*, this stuff was practically a guilty pleasure, as entrancing as it was unsettling. The Bible spoke of the lunacy that consumed those who worshipped the moon over God. But I was most disturbed by the nursery rhymes; the fact that these poems were written for children belied their currents of temptation and darkness:

> Boys and girls,
> rise from your beds
> and join the moon
> above your heads.
> Leave your sleep
> and heed the call
> out the door
> and o'er the wall.
> The wind awaits,
> the sky so bright:
> come and play
> all through the night.

We felt Keller's presence in the Bunk Room, too. Gabe and I slept like guests in a hostel, politely compartmentalizing the shared space. It wasn't that I'd expected us to fall all over each other as soon as we got a minute alone, but this civil distance still hurt. Hadn't Gabe suggested he'd recruited me in part because he felt something for me, something more than friendship, or had I been wrong? And if I had been wrong, then what was I doing here? Sure, I had also been tempted by the job security and the extraordinary opportunity, but it was clear to me now: I had come for Gabe. It was as if no time had passed at all, and I was sixteen again, excruciatingly aware of our bodies in space. When he left the room, my heart relaxed like the muscle it was, and when he came close to me—both of us chopping vegetables by the kitchen sink, our elbows inches apart—the space between us seemed to glow. We ate dinner together—bachelor's pasta sauces and kitchen sink salads—but even then, our topics were safe; whatever tunnel had opened up between us during our conversation in Berkeley seemed to have sealed off again.

Perhaps, I thought, Gabe felt responsible for me and my process of acclimation; perhaps it seemed best to professionalize our interactions now that we were on Keller's turf and not the floor of David's empty apartment. But my nerves were a lit city, buzzing with rush-hour traffic. It was Gabe—stocky, bullheaded, conspiracy-theorist Gabe, incorrigible smart-ass, organizer of dining-hall raids—who now went to bed at nine thirty, who brought me out to the back porch and pointed out with hushed solemnity the dark, oily leaflets of poison ivy that crawled across the Vineyard. The Gabe I knew would have trampled through the ivy in bare, callused feet, as if its consequences did not apply to him.

For distraction, I submerged myself in Keller's research. He was coming back on Monday, so that afternoon, I took the latest volume of *Health Psychology* and settled in a nook in the library. It was a gorgeous old room, with heavy mahogany furniture and French windows, separated by pillars, which let in great shafts of light. Shelves of old tomes stretched from the floor to the ceiling on one side of the room; against the opposite wall, a trio of leather couches had been arranged in a half hexagon. The wood floor was covered with a ruby-colored afghan, and several tattered leather footstools stood beside the higher bookshelves.

I loved its clarity. The other rooms were cluttered with kitschy, regional bric-a-brac: vases stuffed with seashells, porcelain fishermen, thin floral teacups that trembled hysterically on their shelves whenever somebody walked through the kitchen. More than once I came across a rusty pair of bird-watching binoculars, and on the back porch was a lobster trap, made of wood and netting, that the seminar guests reportedly went wild over. Keller thought the items were junky, but he still employed a live-and-let-live policy, as if they were an inherited nuisance—barnacles on the anchor of the house or native spiders who would, in the end, outlive him. I was not surprised when I learned that he preferred to work in the library.

That day, I was reading Jung's *Memories, Dreams, Reflections*—a mystical, ardent little book—while Gabe took a trip to the market. *Life has always seemed to me like a plant that lives on its rhizome*, Jung wrote. (Next to the world *rhizome*, someone had written *rootstalk* in tiny blue print.) *Its true life is invisible, hidden in the rhizome. The part that appears above the ground lasts only a single summer. Then it withers away—an ephemeral apparition. When we think of the unending growth and decay of life and civilizations, we cannot escape the impression of absolute nullity. Yet I have never lost the sense of something that lives and endures beneath the eternal flux. What we see is blossom, which passes. The rhizome remains.*

I turned the page and found that the text had been blotted out by a dark brown stain—coffee, perhaps—that bled straight through the next ten pages. I held the pages up to the light, but that made them even more indecipherable. I closed the book and walked to the shelves, which had been organized by author. Perhaps, I thought, Keller had additional copies of some of the more famous works, and I was right: there was another *Memories, Dreams, Reflections*, older but otherwise identical to the one I'd been reading. The book opened reluctantly, glue cracking in the spine. As I flipped through to find my place, three yellow pieces of paper shook out and floated to the ground.

I worried they were pages from the book itself. But when I picked them up, I saw that they came from an old notepad. They were frail and dry, covered in blue ink, and seemed to be part of a letter: each page was inscribed, in the upper right-hand corner, with *Zurich, 1978*, and one of the pages—the last, I presumed—was signed with Keller's name. I glanced at the driveway; Gabe had taken the car to the grocery store one town over. Still standing by the shelves, I began to read the last page:

> keep coming back to the idea that the subconscious is made up not only of the awareness of actual experience but also of the awareness of every experience that could have happened—simultaneous potentialities which, although near misses in real life, become fully realized in the life of the brain. It's my guess that the soul is made up of the sum of these simultaneous potentialities, that the soul has therefore an infinitely tiered or layered psychology and that it is only in traveling through these layers—which extend not up or down but inward—that self-knowledge can be achieved in any depth.
>
> I see this theory as being positioned at the intersection of Jungian psychology and the multiverse theories of William James and Max Tegmark, along with Alan Guth's more recent theory of parallel universes. I'm not a physicist or a cosmologist, of course, so I'm interested less in the notion of parallel physical universes than in the implications these theories may have for the brain. If we accept the idea that out of the original particles of our universe were created a vast number of identically particled other universes, and that these universes may have evolved differently but all possessed the same original matter and therefore a playing field of identical potential—could the same not be said of the mind?
>
> Jung's theory of the collective subconscious posits that in addition to the personal subconscious, each member of the human race has a subconscious of the species—a communal memory bank, an infinite vault of human instincts and experiences, which is at every moment expanding, much

*like the physical universe. If this is true, might the per-
sonal consciousness have too an infinite vault, not only of
realized individual experience, but of potential individual
experience?*

I felt a chill behind me. I turned around; the door to the
library was open, and Keller stood inside it. He wore a cuffed
white shirt and a pair of slacks, creased from the drive; in one
hand was a folded paper doggy bag that gave off the overripe,
saturated smell of food left in the sun.

"Sylvie," he said.

"I'm sorry." I fumbled with the papers, pressing them back
into the center of the book. "The other copy had a stain. I
didn't mean to pry."

Keller crossed to the desk and set the brown bag down.
Then he walked back to me and shook my hand.

"And what did you think?"

"Of the Jung? It's fascinating—I've only just started the
autobiography, but I read a bit more in college and I can see
why you're—"

"Not of the Jung. Of my letter."

Keller released my hand and smiled, his mouth closed. My
first test. Would it be better to pretend I hadn't read it? To
admit it and compliment him? Either way, it seemed worse
to lie.

"I only read part of it," I said. "So I don't have much to
go on."

"Well played." His eyebrows were raised with a boyish
kind of delight. "Our very own Pandora. *Always open the box.*
And?"

"I want to know more," I said haltingly. "I recognized
some of it—your theory of simultaneous potentialities—but
I didn't fully understand it."

"I'm not surprised. I wasn't much older than you when I

wrote that letter—my third year of graduate school. I suppose I've kept it for sentimental reasons. The theory itself was in its infancy and rather blurry—like one of those vast gaseous planets that takes shape only when seen from far away."

I had the strange feeling that he was being self-deprecating for my benefit—was it that he doubted I'd be able to understand and was trying to comfort me? But he was slyer than that; more likely, he was challenging me. I was transfixed by the sight of him. It had been years since I'd seen Keller, but my memories of his classes at Mills were sharp: straining for the answer as he stood stock-still before us, his expression impenetrable as a sphinx, his eyes glinting in the late-afternoon light.

"Can you explain it to me?" I asked. "Your theory?"

"Didn't Gabriel?"

Keller walked back to the desk and rummaged around inside the doggy bag. He came out with an apple, a compact and shiny Red Delicious, which he juggled absentmindedly in one hand.

"He thought it'd be better for me to learn it from you," I said.

A white lie, but I didn't want to tell Keller that I'd been totally unable to decipher Gabe's explanation. I hoped he wouldn't follow up with Gabe to ask—and this is what I was thinking about, whether or not Keller would find out how clueless I really was, when he raised his left arm and sent the apple hurtling directly for my head.

I made a pathetic gasping noise and ducked to the right; the apple sloped to the ground, hitting the floor of the hallway with a dull thud, and tumbled a few more feet before coming to a stop.

"What was that?" I asked, turning to look at the apple and then back at Keller, who was watching me with an utter lack of surprise.

"How do you feel?" he asked.

"I feel—what?" I sputtered. "I feel freaked."

"Your heart rate is up?"

"Of course."

"You're sweating?"

"A little."

"And you're angry with me."

"You almost hit me."

"But I didn't," said Keller pleasantly. "So why do you feel the way you do?"

I stared at him.

"Because you could have," I said. "You could have hit me."

"Ah. Precisely."

He walked out of the room to retrieve the apple, then brought it back inside, rubbing it on his shirt. It had caved in on one side.

"Forgive me," he said. "I knew you'd duck. I hoped you would, at least. But I was trying to make a point. When I threw this apple at you, I knew there were several likely outcomes. What were they?"

"You'd hit me," I said. "Or I'd duck before you could. Or the apple would miss me entirely."

"Good. The possibilities, of course, are infinite—I could have twisted my arm in swinging, sending the apple straight for one of these windows; Gabriel could have chosen to walk down the hall at that moment, in which case he would have been hit instead. But I chose to put my faith in probability. The apple would hit you, or it wouldn't. I'm pleased to say it didn't. But you're reacting as though it did. Not because it hit you—but because it *could* have."

"Right," I said. I was still wary, but my heart rate was beginning to steady.

"At the moment of decision," said Keller, "at the moment of action, an infinite array of possibilities are conceived in the mind—alternate but parallel psychological universes, each with its own set of outcomes and implications. Only one of these possibilities will be actualized. But what happens to the rest? If they folded neatly into submission, disappeared into the dust from whence they came, you would be, so to speak, single-minded. You would have felt no anxious residue, no fear or anger, when the apple was no longer a threat. And yet you *did* feel the threat of the outcomes that were not realized; indeed, you seemed to feel that threat more acutely than you did any sense of relief that the apple, as luck would have it, sailed right over your head."

"And those are your simultaneous potentialities?"

A part of me thought it made perfect sense; the other part wondered, with a flailing sense of alarm, just what I'd gotten myself into.

"Correct," said Keller. "I believe that these potential experiences are logged in the brain along with the actual one, that the mind processes potentialities and actualities simultaneously and that, therefore, an imagined nonevent—being hit by my apple, let's say—has as much cognitive power as the actual event."

"But wouldn't that be too much for our brains to handle at once?" I asked. "The possibilities would be infinite. How could we process all of them?"

"You're quite right. Thankfully, the brain is selective. We know that certain actual memories are encoded and stored long-term while others are discarded. This is true, too, for potential memories."

"But for memories to be stored, they have to be processed," I said. "How can they be processed if they're never experienced?"

"Aren't they?"

"Subconsciously, maybe." I shook my head. "But I thought you were working on sleep. What does all this have to do with dreams?"

"I hope it has a great deal to do with dreams," said Keller with mock solemnity. "We'll be in a rather tight spot if it doesn't. We already know that sleep—REM sleep in particular—plays an important role in long-term memory formation and mental health. If simultaneous potentialities are sufficiently processed and resolved in REM sleep, we find ourselves better able to focus on the reality of waking life. But what happens to patients whose sleep isn't normative and whose emotional processes are, therefore, disrupted? Patients like the ones I see, who suffer from REM disorders?"

"They can't resolve them," I guessed. "The simultaneous potentialities aren't processed. They keep looping, and the dreamers continue to act them out, these things they're afraid of—things that haven't happened yet, or things that happened a long time ago. Things that aren't real now—at least, not outside of their dreams."

I was babbling, spitting his words back at him less articulately than I'd been able to do in high school.

"It's a start," Keller said.

Through the open windows, I heard the crunch of shells that signaled Gabe's arrival. The two orbs of his headlights grew brighter, spilling into the library, before the car came to a halt and the power was turned off.

"That'll be Gabriel," said Keller, cocking his head at the noise. He turned back to me and smiled, but I could see he was distracted; it was as if he'd just remembered his unpacked suitcases, dinner to be made, whatever ends had to be tidied up after the previous assistant's departure.

"Mr. Keller?" I asked.

He raised his eyebrows.

"The letter," I said. "Who were you writing to?"

If I had crossed some line, he didn't blink.

"My thesis adviser," he said. "Meredith."

As I lay in bed that night, tossing in my UC-Berkeley

boxers, his ideas seemed to me frightening and revolutionary. And they were, I discovered—though PNP was revolutionary less for its novelty than for its return to so-called archaic notions of the mind as murky, spiritual terrain, terrain whose geography was better understood by folklore and poetry than it was by pharmacology. In hindsight, I can see that Keller's scholarly path was always one of upstream travel: the absorption of modern-day psychology into medicine and the hard sciences stranded him in murky terrain of his own, and though he had made use of his marginalization—there seemed to be a continual stream of people swimming to his rock, shaking the water off their backs, and clambering up to admire the view from the island—I know now that he worked always in fear of being delegitimized.

If I had known then what I do now, perhaps I would have been able to see Keller as he was: an aging, proud, and anxious man, unwavering in his convictions, persuasive in speech, but prone to paranoia and hermeticism. It should come as no surprise that someone so convinced of the mystery and idiosyncratic depth of the human mind should be self-isolating. But I could not help but see him, through the years, as a kind of martyr: brilliant, exiled, and lonely as a god.

# 10

As October gave way to the stark skies of November, its spindly, barren trees, I was surprised to find a cream envelope beneath the porch door of our house: perfectly square, licked shut, with a calligraphic scrawl—*G + S*—in black ink. I opened it in the kitchen while Gabe slept off the late study we'd monitored the night before.

> *Greetings, pals—*
> *Janna and I'd be delighted if you'd treat us to your presence(s) on the eve of 25 November. We'll give thanks, we'll drink copious amounts of liquor, and, Janna willing, we'll eat the appropriate troughs of food, American and otherwise. Come in your finest around the hour of five, post meridiem—and bring something to contribute, you lazy fucks.*
>
> > *Hugs—*
> > *T.*

I read the letter twice in a row with a seeping feeling of delight. It had been years since I'd had a proper Thanksgiving meal—not since I lived with my family. Gabe and I had a halfhearted tradition of eating dinner at an ethnic restaurant, though I'd never really been sure whether we did it out of protest or laziness. Thom's letter made me feel normal. We were the sort of young people who had neighbors, had friends; we would go to their house for Thanksgiving, and we would fall asleep, along with the bulk of the country, at the pathetic hour of seven thirty or eight, bloated and sewn-in as stuffed animals.

I decided to make a sweet potato dish, something roasted that I was sure I couldn't mess up. After picking up the ingredients in town, I stopped at the Goodwill on State Street. Keller paid us fairly well—even better now that we worked for the university—but I was my mother's daughter, and most of it went into savings. Usually, I was attracted to clothes in muted colors, though perhaps *attracted* is the wrong word; it was more that I knew these were the styles that suited me and I had resigned myself to our partnership. Today, though, I wanted something different. I brought home a suede skirt in a rich and dusty orange and paired it with a low-backed black top; as I closed the bedroom window, cool air brushed my spine. When I added the little gold hoops Gabe had given me for my twenty-third birthday and a pair of bronze heels, I felt almost unlike myself.

"You look great," said Gabe, in a tone I tried not to take for surprise, as he came downstairs to meet me. He had dressed up, too: he wore a starched navy shirt and a skinny green tie with his Chucks.

"So do you," I said. Had he gotten a haircut, or was the structure of his face always so clear—the sharp jaw, the deep-set and crinkled hazel eyes?

As we crossed the lawn to Thomas and Janna's house—a bottle of wine in Gabe's hand, the sweet potato dish in mine— we could have been any young couple. We rang the doorbell and waited on the porch, Gabe's sneaker tapping the planks.

Janna opened it. Her hair was newly streaked with purple and pulled into a bun, so that the stripes collected in a clean knot at her crown. She wore an orange dress, too, but hers was the neon color of construction signs. It ended in a feathery skirt at her hips. Beneath it she wore sheer brown tights and no shoes.

"Oh, look!" she said, clapping. "You're the same color as your potatoes!"

I looked down; it was true. She kissed Gabe twice, once on each cheek.

"Come in, come in," she said. "I've got to attend to the table, but Thomas will get you a drink."

With this she whirled out of the kitchen, and Thom sauntered in from the living room. The oven was releasing small curls of smoke. Thom paused in front of it and stared quizzically at its dials before turning to us.

"Hello, friends," he said. "What can I get you? Wine? Martini? Gin and tonic?"

"Gin and tonic, please, sir," said Gabe.

"Sylvie." Thom grinned, putting a warm hand on my shoulder. "You match your potatoes."

"I know," I said. "Janna mentioned—"

"Extra," said Janna, sweeping back into the kitchen, a butter knife in one hand. "Silly me—I set the table for five."

She sniffed and turned, with razorlike precision, to the oven.

"The *oven*, Thomas," she said. "The oven is *smoking*, darling."

She turned off the heat at the same time as she opened the silverware drawer next to it. After dropping the extra knife, she slid her hand into a bright blue mitt and pulled out a tray of beautiful, scallop-edged orange cups with little mounds of sweet potato inside.

"Oh," I said. "If I'd known you were making sweet potatoes, I wouldn't have brought them. But yours are gorgeous. How did you make them?"

"Easy," said Janna, licking a bit of potato off her ring finger. "You cut the oranges in half and scrape out the insides. Fill them with mashed potatoes, throw the pulp in the trash."

She wiped her hands on a towel and looked at us brightly. "Hungry?" she asked.

. . .

I don't remember much about dinner, only that we were woozy with drink by the end of it: first the gin and tonics, then two bottles of rich red wine, a post-dinner espresso splashed with bourbon. The moon rose baldly into the sky; Gabe took off one of his shoes and threw it behind his head, where it collided with an antique mirror that cracked into a delicate, spidery web and, Janna claimed, looked better now than it had before. At some point, we collapsed on the couch in their living room, a tangle of legs. I looked for the Keats book, the mossy old tome that Thom had shown me weeks before, but it was gone. Thom was singing something—*Oh my darling, oh my darling, oh my darling Clementine. You are lost and gone forever* . . . Did I imagine that at some point, Janna's head rested against my chest? I don't know how or why it would have happened, but I remember the warm sun of her skull, the streaks of hair that spread across my shoulders like purple kelp, her spindly fingers picking at the fabric of the couch.

It must have been one or two in the morning when we stumbled out the back door to their yard. It was a gorgeous night, unexpectedly warm. I can still see Thom running back to us, gazelle-like, all legs—he'd gone somewhere and returned with boxes of bang snaps. We threw them at the ground and yelped when they exploded too close to our feet. Gabe and I kissed pressed against the fence, dense and urgent, his hands beneath my shirt. How long had it been since we had kissed like that? And then he was gone, and I was sitting with Thom beneath the juniper tree in their backyard, a tree with a thick, warped trunk like a dish towel being wrung.

If my memories up until this point are imagistic and uncertain, here they sharpen. Here I remember not only sensory details—the leathery leaves and sharp little sticks beneath my legs; grass stains on the lap of my dress; Thom's sweet alcoholic scent—but whole stretches of conversation. Where were Gabe and Janna? I don't remember caring; I leaned against the juniper, its trunk kneading my back.

". . . the first man I ever loved," Thom said, his nose bulbous and jagged in the blue light. "Platonically, I mean—but I did love him. I admired him so much I felt my identity bleeding into his, little by little. Have you ever had a teacher like that?"

"No," I said, whether or not it was true. An owl cooed in the distance.

"No? Ah," said Thom. "Well, he was my first poetry professor. My first *real* professor. And Janna was his pet."

"He liked her poetry?"

"He liked— Well." He laughed, high and breathless. "You're a dear, Sylvie—you know that, don't you? You're a very sweet girl. But inside you there's a sour center. And that's why I like you."

Why that flattered me I can't say now. It was the alcohol, I think—the scent of the muddied leaves, Thom's voice sure as an incantation.

"Not that I'm exempt," he said. "I'm as dirty as they come. And I'm disgusted by it now. But, you know—I was so damn *idealistic* then. The art! That's what I thought was most important. He was the writer-in-residence at our college. I'd never met a man who was brilliant in the ways he was brilliant. And I thought I could *access* him, if I was with her."

"You only started dating Janna to get close to—your professor?" It struck me as funny; I laughed, and soon Thom was wheezing with me, knocking his head against the fence. But like a summer storm, Thom's laughter passed as suddenly as it had arrived, and once more he was confidential, solemn.

"Yes," he said. "I'll say it. I wanted to get to him. But when I stopped thinking that way—when I fell for *her*, and her only, nothing more—I experienced the most incredible purity. Do you believe in purity?"

I felt a tickle on my arm. Two ants were crawling toward the inside of my elbow. I brushed them to one side; they landed on Thom's pant leg, though he didn't notice.

"I'm a changed man, Sylvie." He ran a hand through his messy reddish hair, swift and shaky. "I've repented, believe me. I've changed"—and we both took swigs of our drinks, the dark sky ringing with stars. The wineglasses had all been dirtied, and we were drinking out of jam jars. I had never been so drunk. My mind spun and spun, a top inside my skull. The next thing I remember, I was waking up in bed, still in my orange dress, Gabe's heavy thigh cast over mine; I was peeling back the curtains by our bed, a white November sun high in the sky.

The conversation was so peculiar I almost wondered if I had remembered it wrong. But from the window I could see the juniper tree, wrenched, and when I looked at the lap of my skirt, there were the grass stains, there were the little lines where twigs had scraped the fabric.

· · ·

The next night, I dreamed I stood alone at an abandoned intersection in a small, plain town. To my left, wheat fields stretched fuzzy and golden; to the right was a boarded-up ice cream shop. The wind lifted my hair, blond and streaked with black. In one hand I held a whirligig that turned with the wind, spinning light. The wind stilled as if in wait, and the whirligig stopped moving. Then a flush of blackbirds rose from the field, arcing through the sky with a thick flapping noise, like the pages of a thousand books being turned. When they cleared, I saw a hot air balloon.

It moved through the sky with a stately elegance, unhurried as a mayor at a small-town parade. Its progress was so slow that I didn't know it was manned until a figure no bigger than an insect clambered to the rim of the basket and tumbled, flailing, over one side.

It was the first dream I had fully remembered in years. I woke slick with sweat, gasping, and looked for Gabe. He lay on his back with his hands behind his head, arms two pointed wings. The clock on my bedside table shone 4:23, but I knew I wouldn't be able to fall back to sleep. So I stepped out into the hall, closing the bedroom door quietly behind me.

My mind was dizzy, caught in the groggy purgatory between sleep and wakefulness, and I was still half-drunk. But I climbed the stairs to the attic and dusted off a clean canvas. Then I carried my paint boxes to the rug in front of the window. Kneeling, I began to mix black and white until I found something that matched the tenor of that pale gray sky.

The dream began to sharpen as I painted it. In shaping the great rainbow bulb of the balloon and its brown thatched basket, I saw the way the figure inside had first leaned out of it, looking down, as if gauging where to land. Why? Because he was harnessed to a parachute, and I remembered it now: a pillowy lavender arc that looked quilted from below, floating toward the ground at the same leisurely pace as the balloon.

I wasn't paying attention to the way the painting looked. My goal was not the finished product but the accuracy of my recollection. I was painting what I remembered as I remembered it, and the only way to do that was to paint right on top of what I had done only moments before. And so, as the flyer came nearer and nearer to the intersection where I waited with my whirligig, I painted him again and again—because now I was sure that it *was* a him, that the gangly legs hung from a pale torso brushed with hair as rough and golden as wheat; that up close, he smelled like alcohol and juniper, and if I were to pull up his shirtsleeve—which I would do as soon as he landed—I would find two ants crawling down one arm in slow procession.

I stepped away from the canvas and stared at it for the first time as a whole. It was cluttered, kaleidoscopic: the balloon traced over and over, the man's insect legs stretching toward the ground like an alien craft. My face was messily drawn and stretching apart, covered in whirligigs.

It was nothing I wanted to see again. I took a tube of black paint and squirted it across the canvas. With my widest brush, I swiped the paint from left to right, top to bottom. Light was beginning to inch up the sky, darkness drawing back like a tarp, but I was exhausted. When I returned to bed, Gabe was right where I had left him, as if no time had passed at all. I fell with surprising ease into a simple, passive sleep that must have lasted for hours. The next thing I remember was a soft rapping noise at the door, Gabe's broad nose poking through, the snuffling noise of his laughter.

"Sylvie," he whispered. "Sylvie, my God, wake up. It's already one o'clock."

. . .

I spent the next week in a haze. My sleep was fitful and uneven: too much, or not enough. During the day, it was all I could do to stay awake. I told Gabe and Keller I thought I was coming down with a cold. Keller had me cover shifts at the sleep clinic, where all I had to do was sit bleary eyed at the front desk. At night, I fell asleep immediately, and I woke blank as a baby.

I thought I was back to my old patterns until a cold Tuesday morning in the beginning of December. I dreamed of Thom; this time, there was no mistaking it. We were in an enclosed, dimly lit space with a desk and one chair, but we huddled on the floor as if in a bunker. Spread across the floor in front of us were old photographs that Thom showed me one by one. A dull, dusty-chained bulb provided a dim shaft of light. An orange cat slipped between us, purring.

I could see myself, but I was apart from myself. Like a ghost, I watched the dream me sitting with Thom on the floor—watched as he lifted the next photograph into the light, which showed a grand brick building on a hill. Below the building was a dusty path, flanked by tree trunks and globe lamps that glowed whitely as moons.

"Alumni House," said Thom. "It's this fancy building that was gifted to the college by two filthy-rich sisters—Rose and Blanche something. All the rich alumni could sleep there whenever they were in town, and the place had a restaurant that hosted all sorts of schmoozy, hobnobby events. He used to take Janna there. I wanted so badly to get inside. I used to stand at the bottom of the hill, just taking pictures of the damn thing."

His face floated toward me with the 3D transparency of a hologram. He reached for me with one hand. I ducked, but I wasn't fast enough, and he plucked something from my ear. I felt a *pock*, the hollow release of suction, and he held out his palm. Something fuzzy, black and yellow-spotted, wriggled inside it: a caterpillar. Suddenly, the hand was Gabe's—I saw his broad, callused palms, his long lifeline. The caterpillar inched its way across his wrist, and I felt nauseous.

"That came—out of me?" I asked. I put my finger in my ear. Empty as a whistle.

"Dreadful sorry, Clementine," sang Gabe.

I woke at five thirty, my chest heaving, my collarbone

slick with sweat. The windows rattled, our curtains slivered apart by the cold air that came through a crack in the pane. I looked at the window, my body turned away from Gabe, as my heart rate came down. Snowflakes clung to the glass like tiny skeletons.

When I turned around, Gabe was propped up on one elbow, staring at me. We looked at each other in silence.

"Bad dream," I said finally.

Gabe shook his head. "But you never remember your dreams."

"I know," I said. "It's odd."

Gabe was staring at me with a bare kind of exhaustion— or was it resignation? He opened his mouth, then seemed to think better of it.

"Sleepy Sylvie," he said, inching across the space between us, collecting me into his arms.

PART TWO

# NIGHT

# 11

When I look back at the rest of that first summer in Snake Hollow, I am tempted to say—as much as I resist this sort of statement—that it was the best time in my life. The thrown-together dinners, Gabe chopping zucchini and eggplant, Keller pouring salt crystals into a pot of bubbling water while flipping strips of pancetta with the many-armed grace of a Hindu god; Keller taking us out to the glass-littered beach at night, striding through the dune grass and salt-marsh hay with boyish enthusiasm—"Look!" he said, "feel something, for God's sake—get out of yourselves"; or sitting with Gabe on the floor of the library as Keller strode between us—spun through the room, it seemed to me, in my three A.M. haze (*When does he sleep?* I often wondered)—his voice ricocheting off the walls, the dim lights of the library flickering in his wake.

"We are living in a *twenty*-four/seven culture," he said. "Convenience stores are open at all hours of the day. Twenty percent of the working population in developed countries works the night shift. Planes take off and land, universities hold classes, hospitals are staffed, all during the night hours traditionally reserved for sleep. Human beings are more productive than ever before, but they're also unhappier. They feel oppressed by the limits of their lives: the boredom, the repetition, the fatigue. What if you could use your sleep to do *more*—to receive all of the traditional regenerative benefits while problem solving, healing, even experiencing alternate worlds?"

He was jittery with enthusiasm, pacing the library like a teenager. Earlier that day, Gabe and I had traveled to Boston to watch Keller give a talk on lucid dreaming. He was even more dynamic than he'd been at Mills, his voice carrying through the auditorium, his limbs shot through with energy; it was as though, like Benjamin Button, he was aging in reverse. "This freedom, hard to imagine within the constraints of waking life," he boomed, "is astounding, exhilarating, and inspiring. The laws of science and society are abolished. The possibilities are boundless, and the choices are yours. Wouldn't you be capable of extraordinary things?"

A college student with a bushel of red hair raised her hand. She stood when Keller called on her.

"Okay," she said, "but people are capable of terrible things, too. What if somebody wanted to dream about hurting someone? Or killing them?"

"You're right: violence is a part of human nature," said Keller. "But if those urges can be experienced and processed safely, within the construct of a dream, they can be put to rest."

"And if they aren't put to rest?" shouted a man in the front row. "What if it doesn't work?"

"There will always be people who aren't helped by our research. Successfully matching patient to treatment is as complex as any marriage, and it does require trial and error. But most of the patients I see are capable, while dreaming, of being at their best: their *most* resourceful, their most creative, their most intuitive."

Gabe and I had similar conversations with Keller at Snake Hollow, sitting around the dinner table or sprawled on the leather couches in the library. At these moments, Snake Hollow felt almost like Mills—or some bare-bones version of Mills, the school stripped of its landscape and buildings and students until all that was left was Gabe and Keller and me. Keller taught us his theory of interactive lucid dreaming, the same theory that would later bring us to Madison. His research participants were what he termed interactives: people who, due to a medley of possible disorders, exhibited unusual activity in sleep.

Keller's participant criteria were so specific that his applicants were few in number but generally ideal in demographic. They had to have vivid dreams that they could at least partially recall; they had to have been aware of at least two episodes of sleep activity in the past six months, whether through their own report or that of a partner; they could not be taking any pharmaceutical or recreational drugs; and they could not have been diagnosed with any psychiatric illness unrelated to sleep. Most of the patients who came to us had struggled for years to control themselves. Some had resorted to sleeping zipped-up in sleeping bags; others tied themselves to their bedposts and cleared their rooms of breakable objects before sleep.

Our patients were usually diagnosed with one of two disorders: REM behavior disorder, also known as RBD; and parasomnia overlap disorder, a dysfunction that incorporates symptoms of both RBD and sleepwalking. Both cause the loss of muscle atonia, the physical paralysis that normally occurs during REM sleep. As a result, these patients—who often suffer from trauma-related nightmares—are able to rise from bed and act out their dreams. The differences between the two disorders may have seemed small to an outsider, but they were significant to us. Patients with RBD rarely open their eyes or leave their bedrooms, but they have nightmares that cause them to violently, clumsily defend themselves. As a result, they're prone to injury and unintentional destruction: an RBD patient might topple a table, slam into a dresser, or hurt the very real body of the partner lying beside them. Sleepwalkers are more dexterous, capable of complicated motor skills, sexual activity, and conversation; many can even drive. Most of the time, sleepwalking takes place during non-REM sleep, separate from dreams. But patients with parasomnia overlap disorder—the ones Keller studied—sleepwalk during REM sleep, when dreaming occurs.

And what were the dreams that Keller's patients were compelled to act out? Usually, they were horrifying, trauma processing and self-protection gone terribly awry. Keller saw this as evidence of the mind's obsession with safety and defense. He believed that nonparalyzed REM sleep was the site at which dysfunctional dreamers experienced the unresolved simultaneous potentialities of their waking lives, like alternate tapes that played on a loop. He believed, too, that training in lucid dreaming would give patients much-needed self-knowledge—and the capacity for intervention.

But earlier research in lucid dreaming had proved the technique also offered a myriad of benefits to normative sleepers: adventure and fantasy, nightmare resolution, problem solving, even physical healing. The term *lucid dreaming* was coined in 1913 by Dutch psychiatrist Frederik van Eeden, an acquaintance of Freud, who discovered that lucid dreamers were able to think clearly, act intentionally, and remain cognizant of the circumstances of waking life—all while experiencing a dream world that felt equally real. Interest in lucid dreaming flagged until the late 1960s, when van Eeden's paper was reprinted in books by dream scholars Celia Green and Charles Tart. In 1987, Stephen LaBerge—a psychophysiologist with a bachelor's degree in mathematics—founded the Lucidity Institute. LaBerge did more than validate the study of lucidity in academia: he also created the first technique for lucidity induction and developed a series of light-emitting devices that made lucid dreaming available to an increasingly curious public. Some of Keller's funding came from the normative dreamers who attended his classes and retreats— people who wondered, as he did, what the mind had to offer when exercised to its full potential.

Keller's timing was impeccable: his research also emerged in the midst of a cultural fascination with the unconscious mind and its capacity for violence. As part of my reading that summer, I was expected to familiarize myself with two watershed trials. In 1988, a person was acquitted, for the first time, of murder while sleepwalking. Ken Parks, an unemployed high school dropout in his midtwenties, had risen from sleep and driven fourteen miles to the home of his in-laws. He nearly killed his father-in-law, and he stabbed his mother-in-law to death. He woke several hours later to find himself standing above her body, with no memory of the event and a faint feeling of pain in his hands. He was acquitted on the basis of sleepwalking at a trial whose verdict was later upheld by the Canadian supreme court, which declared that his actions were due to a noninsane automatism. The supreme court believed that Parks's actions were so rare, so anomalous, that they would never be repeated; but the Parks case, it turned out, would set a controversial precedent.

In 1999, the year I left for college, Keller testified as an expert witness at the trial of Scott Falater, a Mormon and father of two. That night, Falater attempted to fix the pump that filtered water for his backyard pool, but he went to bed when it became dark around nine thirty. About half an hour later, Falater rose, just like Ken Parks, and returned to the pump. What happened next is the product of expert conjecture and the eyewitness account of Greg Koons, Falater's neighbor, who saw Falater drag the stabbed body of his wife,

Yarmila, into the pool and drown her. Falater then changed into his pajamas, tucked his bloody knife and work clothes into the wheel well of his car, and returned to bed. He woke, along with his children, to the sound of police dogs. Yarmila had been stabbed forty-four times, and though the evidence proved resolutely that Falater had killed his wife, he never regained any memory of the event.

The court ordered an array of psychological tests, but the murder could not be tied to a psychotic episode, a seizure, or a dissociation disorder. The psychiatrist could not diagnose him with any psychiatric illness, and Falater's scores on the Minnesota Multiphasic Personality Inventory showed him to be almost ideally normal, with no psychopathic tendencies. They found only that Falater had been anxious about an ongoing struggle at work, which had left him feeling insecure and emasculated, and that his sleep had suffered. Falater had begun to use caffeine pills during the day, and at night, his rest was difficult and uneven.

Unlike Ken Parks, Scott Falater was pronounced guilty. The prosecution argued that Yarmila's murder had been consciously planned and executed, and the jury was not ready to believe something as outlandish as the idea that Falater had been sleepwalking. But the case became a point of contention in an ongoing debate about the role of sleep in emotional regulation—and what happens when the regulation process is disturbed. Keller saw a disordered dream life as a critical indication of unrest in the patient's waking life—a place of uninhibited, instinctive emotionality, and therefore, a site of both great danger and great healing.

"For dreamers to return to a state of mental health," he said, "they must understand their dreams, not erase them. The patients I see keep cycling through the same nightmares for a reason. And until they discover *what* that reason is, they'll never be safe—and neither will their bedmates."

Keller wanted Gabe and me to be able to dream lucidly before we helped him to train others. He taught us the MILD technique, Mnemonic Induction of Lucid Dreams, developed by Stephen LaBerge. It was a four-step process that Gabe picked up with relative ease, but I was never really able to access it, as much as I understood it conceptually. The first step was dream recall. Like Keller's workshop participants, we slept with notebooks beside us, writing down whatever we could remember as soon as the alarm went off. Next came reality checks: in order to recognize a dream state, Keller taught his patients to look for certain common markers. I *knew* the signs: difficulty reading words, flashing lights or ill-defined light sources, problems with mechanical objects, and, of course, the dead. I knew to meditate before bed—my body soft and relaxed until the edges of the waking world began to smudge and dissolve—but as soon as I sank into sleep, my mind went dark until I woke, disoriented and increasingly frustrated. Step three, lucid affirmations—commands programmed into memory and recalled later, while dreaming—was even more hopeless. Keller had me focus on my hand—*When I see my hand in my dream*, I was to repeat to myself, *I will know I am dreaming*—but whether I saw my hand in my dream or not, I never remembered it. The final step was to visualize a recent dream while awake, but since I couldn't remember my dreams, I spent most of these sessions lying irritably on my blue mat.

Finally, Keller encouraged me to wake myself out of REM sleep with an alarm clock and immediately write down whatever I could remember. I still couldn't grasp whole narratives, but this method allowed me to piece together the recurring dream that occupied my mind that summer. Perhaps I would have been able to remember even more if I had not stopped the alarm clock system. I didn't want to know any more of the dream, and I didn't want there to be a document that preserved it. I destroyed what I had, feeding it into the shredder when Gabe and Keller were out, and I never brought it up with Keller again.

In the dream, I stood before a mirror in an old public bathroom, which seemed to be part of a previously grand hotel that had fallen into disrepair. The bathroom had beautiful details: crown molding, tarnished gold faucets, turquoise-and-black-tiled walls. The mirror was so foggy and stained that I couldn't see myself clearly. I turned on the faucet, but no water came out, though I could hear it running in the pipes.

At some point an elderly woman came into the bathroom. She was unremarkable—of medium build, white-haired, dressed in a dignified, old-fashioned way. The only exotic thing about her was the purse she carried: large and rectangular, like an antique doctor's bag, with a giant metal buckle. It was made of a gleaming purple material that appeared, upon closer inspection, to be snakeskin. I observed the purse with interest but was otherwise indifferent to the woman. She walked into a stall; I heard a muffled drop as the purse was set down on the floor. I tried the faucet again, and this time, water rushed out.

I stared at the water before turning the faucet off again. The woman emerged from the bathroom stall. She was naked from the waist down. She still wore a silk blouse and cardigan, but her pressed pants and heels, even her underwear, had been removed. Between her legs was a rough gray pelt. She did not seem to notice me; she washed her hands in the water—there was no soap—and glanced briefly in the mirror. Then she walked out of the bathroom as perfunctorily as she had arrived.

The door of the stall she had used swung open with a slow, rusty whine. It was empty except for the purple snakeskin purse. Loud noises came from outside the bathroom, and I knew that others would soon come in search of the purse, that

I would be implicated as its new owner. I needed to move the purse, but first I had to see what was inside it. I went into the bathroom and pressed on the buckle. There was a click like the sound of a gun's safety being switched off. The lid of the purse opened automatically, willingly. And then I woke.

I told Gabe about the dream, late at night in the Bunk Room when we knew Keller had already gone to sleep. He listened with the knit-browed interest of a psychiatrist, and though there was no judgment on his face, he couldn't unlock the dream any better than I could. We still slept in our own beds—still barely touched, aside from the brief brush of arms as he sidled past me in the kitchen—but we had begun to talk late into the evening, Gabe leaning over the ledge of his top bunk and I looking up from below. Sometimes we talked about our dreams. Other times, we talked about Keller.

"I just don't believe that he's lived here, all these years, alone," I said one warm, sticky night in July, my legs on top of the sheets. "He never had a family of his own?"

"He had a wife," said Gabe.

I rolled to the side of the bed and craned my neck to look at him.

"You're kidding. He was married? When?"

"Years ago," said Gabe. "Before he came to Mills."

"What happened to her?"

Gabe glanced at the door. The floor was so old that if Keller was still padding around, we could generally hear him.

"She died," he said in an undertone.

"How?"

"Beats me. That's all I know, and I'm not even sure how I know it. Keller never mentioned her to me, that's for sure. I think it was someone at Mills who told me—maybe Mr. Cooke."

Gabe scrunched up his nose in the way he did when he was trying to recall some fact. Then he shook his head.

"Do you think that had something to do with it?" I asked. "With why he left USF, started teaching in a high school?"

"Who knows?" Gabe shrugged, the twin curves of his shadow shoulders rising against the opposite wall. "Anyway, there's a picture of her in Keller's bedroom. I stumbled in there one day, thinking it was one of the studies. It's on his bedside table. Have a look, if you want, but make sure you don't do it when he's around."

It was my first glimpse of the old Gabe. And though I knew he couldn't see me, I was grinning in the dark.

I was eager to see the photo, if only to satisfy my curiosity about the kind of woman Keller would go for. For the next few days, I glanced in his room whenever I walked down the hall, hoping I wouldn't have to go inside to see the photo. But the door was only ever open a crack, if at all, and soon I realized I would have to be ballsier if I really wanted to go through with it.

Keller kept to a strict schedule: he went to the grocery in Edgartown on Tuesdays and Fridays, he ate dinner no later than six thirty P.M., and he took a walk to the water each day from four thirty to five fifteen. One Thursday afternoon in late July, Gabe was out, too—Keller had sent him to the Vineyard library to find a book on Jewish mysticism. At five P.M., seized with the fear that one of them would come home early, I opened Keller's bedroom door.

I scanned the room, which was small and spare. Most of it was taken up by a queen bed with one pillow, white sheets precisely flattened and tucked. A painting of a battered canoe hung above the bed. Beside it was a small wooden table upon which there was a pen, a few scattered sheets of paper, and a square photograph in a gold frame.

I stole closer, making sure not to disturb the books that had been set in stacks on the floor, and picked up the frame. The photo showed a woman from the waist up. She looked to be at least in her forties, older than I expected. She had a small, fervent face, her features angular and catlike and held in place by a tight network of bones. There was something severe in her expression: the sharp little nose; the lifted chin; the pursed lips, less a smile than a contraction. But in her eyes I saw a swallowed depth and vulnerability that startled me. It's possible I'm remembering the photo incorrectly, that I've ascribed this vulnerability to her in hindsight. But I remember being struck by her unusual mix of challenge and urgent appeal. Her most striking feature was a helmet of bright strawberry-red hair, which had been cropped to her chin and smoothed into a bob.

At dinner that night, I realized I hadn't noticed the angle at which the photo had been placed before I picked it up. My body grew hot, and my heart began to pound. Gabe was telling some joke, his mouth full of pasta, Keller glancing at him with amusement. I could excuse myself from the table and go fix the photo, if I only knew how it had originally been positioned. No; it was useless. I could only pray he didn't look at it too closely.

Years later, I found myself in the main branch of the San Francisco Public Library, and I decided to look through their archives of the *Chronicle* in the hopes of finding a particular article about Keller's Snake Hollow compound. After a few hours of searching, I found it in the style section of the Sunday paper on June 18, 2000—Father's Day of that year. "Space to Dream," it was titled: "The Prodigal Father of Experimental Dream Psychology on His Vineyard Escape." The text itself was not very interesting: cursory details about Keller's approach, some of which the author had gotten wrong ("Mr. Keller is most well-known for his polarizing theory of potential simultaneities"); he was clearly more interested in the Snake Hollow property, and most of the article's space was taken up by large, full-color photos of its interior.

June of 2000 was the summer after my freshman year of college, just before Gabe returned to work with Keller, but the house looked the way it did when we stayed there together. There was the library, vast and secretive; there was the kitchen, its white cabinets and fragile china. But something about the photo of Keller's bedroom gave me pause. The bed was the same—even the bedding had not changed—and the canoe painting still hung above it. His night table was cluttered with papers and pens that the photographer had not moved, preferring a naturalistic effect. But the picture of Keller's wife was gone.

There are explanations for this, of course. Perhaps Keller had moved the photo, not wanting such a personal item to be included in the article; perhaps he had simply put it on his night table sometime after the article was written. But for reasons I still can't fully articulate, the absence of the photo confirmed my suspicion that it had been placed there for my benefit, shortly before my arrival in June of 2002. I've never been able to prove that Keller wanted me to see it, and I doubt I ever will. But the question has stayed with me—pesky, cobwebbed—something I come back to on nights when I can't sleep or while on a drive that doesn't demand much of my attention. If there are no other cars, or if the road is long and flat, dotted black and white and brown by cows and dry grass—in moments like this, I let my mind float away from my body and return to the dusty attic space in me that Keller still occupies, a place with ashy shapes and sunken goods like the ruins of an old city, a place I have never really been able to leave behind.

# 12

December crawled on, and I got my first taste of winter in Wisconsin, the snow and rain that alternated like dueling lawyers in a courtroom battle. First came the soft flakes, demure in their quietude, which settled gently on cars and trash bins so that they swelled like marshmallows; then the balls of hail as big as eyes, spraying branches until they were bony and shivering. On a particularly frigid day midmonth, Gabe and I inexpertly scraped the car of snow and drove to the Walmart in Waukesha County to buy the sleeping-bag coats everyone else owned. We invested, too, in real snow boots: fur-lined, insulated monster shoes that could protect the feet in temperatures as terrible as forty degrees below zero.

If we felt isolated in the summer, that humid haze was nothing when compared to the stark, icy quarantine of winter. I couldn't have stopped to say hello to a familiar face if I'd wanted to; I was focused only on survival, my face raw with cold, hands frozen in a rigor mortis grip around laundry bags or library books. When I stepped inside our house, gasping, I had to sit pressed up against the heating vents until my skin began to thaw. Once, Gabe and I saw a man waiting for the bus in a bank robber's ski mask, with tiny holes for his eyes and nostrils, and though we laughed at the time, I can't say we weren't tempted to get our own.

We saw Thom and Janna less and less. Every so often, they invited us over for a game of Scrabble or Charades, and though Gabe showed interest, I was filled with an aversion that confused me. ("Go yourself, then," I snapped during a hailstorm, pulling a blanket tighter around me.) Since Thanksgiving, I had dreamed of Thom: frenzied, consuming dreams that I found myself unable to shake the next day. I could never remember how they began. My consciousness picked up somewhere in the middle, in the underground room with the golden light. I realized it was Thom's basement. A clock hung on a cord on the wall behind Thom's head, and the hour was four, or two. Thom leaned against the wall, his legs spread in a wide V, a jam jar between them. In the jar was a honey-colored liquid without ice. He played with the glass, stirring the liquid with the tip of his ring fingernail.

Or we were sitting beneath the juniper tree of his backyard, Thom listening attentively—leaning in with his whole body, his chest curved toward me like a cave I could speak into. We sat on the ice, but neither one of us was cold.

"You're wet," he said. "Your hands—they're wet"—and he nuzzled me, the soft fuzz of his chin on my cheek, his skin blessedly warm, as an orange cat purred its motorized hum and the moon shed light like a second skin.

I always woke from these dreams sweating, the blankets soaked and tangled, my muscles throbbing with strain. I had never remembered this much of my dreams. Now they were so vivid that I was terrified I'd spoken out loud, but whenever I looked over at Gabe, he was shut-eyed and still.

And so I left him. I climbed the stairs to the attic and turned on the lamp by the window. My canvases appeared suddenly, like a television turned on in a dark room. I painted my dreams to get rid of them, to exorcise the shame and betrayal they brought up in me. I wanted to remember them and let them go, as if the act of memory would give me control. I had only brought five canvases to Madison, but I didn't buy more for fear that Gabe would wonder what I was doing. Instead, I painted over and over those same five canvases, sweeping each one black when I was done.

Sometimes, when Gabe and I returned home in the early morning after a session at the lab, we saw Thom striding to the garage in his corduroy pants and dress shoes, an arm held over his head to block the snow. In these moments, Gabe raised a hand in salute, but I ducked my head and climbed into the car. The dream Thom had become so vivid that the sight of the real one gave me a crawling feeling of guilt. When Gabe shut the car door and turned to me—"That was Thom; did you notice?"—I always feigned surprise, said I hadn't seen him through the snow.

Besides, we had bigger things to worry about that winter—and perhaps that's why my dream life took on its own menace. Five days before Christmas, Keller called and told us to meet him at the lab. A fuse had blown in the living room furnace, and we were cranky, sore with cold. Besides, it was Sunday, a day we were supposed to have off. But Keller spoke in the stiff tone that indicated he was not open to debate, so we grudgingly trudged outside to scrape the car in our new boots.

We never made it to the lab. A storm was dumping buckets of nasty slush on the roads, and the ground was so wet that we skidded twice before we pulled into somebody's driveway and called Keller to say we'd have to meet him somewhere else. We wound up at the Starbucks on State Street—the kind of place Keller abhorred, but it was the coffee shop closest to our car.

It was the last day of finals at the university, and it seemed that every undergrad had fled their dorm for the heat and cloying music and sweet whipped drinks at Starbucks. The chairs were covered in down coats in shades of pink and red and blue; scattered across the floor were backpacks splayed like fallen soldiers, squashed Ugg boots, pom-pom hats, fat little gloves. Mariah Carey's Christmas album played over the speakers. We took the stairs to the second level, where there were more tables and leather armchairs ("Sorry," said Gabe as he brushed past a girl who had fallen asleep with a chemistry book open on her lap, her mouth agape).

We found Keller standing in a back corner, hands linked behind his back as he scanned the room for us. He'd staked out a trio of tables, not because we needed to spread out but because we needed the privacy. He hadn't purchased anything, and a huddled group of underclassmen searching for a place to sit stared at his three empty tables with undisguised irritation.

"Have a seat," he said, oblivious. Gabe and I sat down, each at our own table, and pulled off our hats. A flurry of snow settled on our eyelashes and hair; we brushed it off, staring at him. Keller reached into his briefcase—black leather, tattered now, the same one he'd carried around at Mills—and put a thick newspaper in front of us. It was a copy of the *San Francisco Chronicle*, dated that same day.

"I didn't know you still get the *Chronicle*," said Gabe, his brows raised. "Homesick?"

"That's beside the point," said Keller, jabbing a finger at the paper. He had opened it to the crime section of the "Bay Area and State" page. Below his finger was the mug shot of a woman with scraggly blond hair—yellowed at the ends, brown at the roots—and sallow, deep-set eyes. I immediately recognized her cleft chin and widow's peak, the pocked scars along her temples—remnants of a bad childhood bout with chicken pox, she'd told us, though we always suspected otherwise.

### MURDER ARREST MADE IN OAKLAND CASE

*(20-12) 06:51 PDT Rockridge—A suspect has been taken into custody in connection with the deaths of James, Leslie and Charlotte March, the Rockridge family found dead in September, authorities said Saturday.*

*Anne March, 26, of San Francisco, was arrested on suspicion of murder after an extensive statewide search. March, who worked as a pediatric nurse at Kaiser Permanente, was first reported missing in early October. The turning point came last Tuesday, when an anonymous tip directed city police to an abandoned house in San Francisco where Ms. March was found squatting.*

*"We have probable cause to believe Ms. March committed the murders of James, Leslie and Charlotte March," said Sheriff's Sergeant Jose Mendoza. Mendoza declined further comment, saying a press conference was scheduled for Monday morning. Other members of the March family are expected to attend.*

*The suspect attended Oakland High School and college at California State–Long Beach. She has no prior criminal history, and public defender Linda Meyers has implied that the state might consider an insanity defense. Though prosecutor Kevin van Dyke called this "ludicrous," citing Ms. March's passing scores on the psychological exams required of all licensed nurses, Meyers maintained that "mental health cannot be reduced to a numerical score, a true-or-false question, a pass or fail." Meyers alluded to Ms. March's participation in a 2002 psychological research study as possible evidence of past instability, though she declined additional comment. Efforts by the* Chronicle *to contact the study's director were unsuccessful.*

*March was transported to the Central California Women's Facility, where she faces a sentence of 50 years to life for the murders of her parents, James and Leslie, both 52, and her younger sister Charlotte, age 11. The* San Francisco Chronicle *first reported on the March case on September 12, when James March's employer called city police to report his absence at work. The three victims were found in bed, dead due to fatal doses of morphine, administered intravenously. Their time of death was estimated to be ten days prior.*

*CCWF is the largest female correctional facility in the United States. It houses the state of California's death row for women.*

"Jesus Christ," said Gabe. He set the paper down and stared at it for a beat before looking up at Keller.

"I knew this would happen," I said. "I knew it."

We were quiet. Something seemed to rise and spread between us like toxic gas. In the hall behind us, a toilet flushed, and two girls came out of the bathroom, their arms linked. The taste of bile climbed my throat.

"Well, what do we do?" asked Gabe. "What the fuck do you suggest we do?"

It took a moment for me to realize he was talking to Keller. I'd known Gabe to quibble with Keller, tease him, even, but I'd never heard him use this kind of language. Keller looked at him evenly, his head slightly bowed.

"I suggest," he said in a low tone, "that you don't pick up the phone unless you're sure the call is from one of us. Let everything else go to voice mail. If you're contacted by anyone you don't know—a reporter, a stranger, anyone—come to me immediately. I don't care how innocuous it seems."

"Jesus *Christ*," said Gabe. He ran his hands through his hair. "Okay, let's think about this. Maybe it's not so bad. It's possible she wasn't asleep, right? And even if she was, how could they possibly prove it?"

"She definitely wasn't asleep," said Keller.

"How do you know?" I asked.

"She couldn't be. If you remember anything about Anne's case, you'll know that she was never a sleepwalker—her disorder most closely resembled RBD. She never left her bedroom. Her eyes were always closed. She was violent but clumsy. She had none of the fine motor skills required to operate a car or fill a vial of morphine."

"That's a good thing, right?" asked Gabe. "That she wasn't sleeping? I mean, if she was awake when she committed those murders, how could our study have had anything to do with them?"

"It isn't a good thing," I said. "My God—do you really think we had no part in this? We knew exactly how violent she was. We gave her knowledge of her deepest impulses, and then we left her. We trusted her to know what to do with it."

"We aim to help patients resolve their sleep disorders. But we're not responsible for the knowledge they receive in lucidity training, nor the actions they take as a result of it," said Keller tightly. "You know this as well as I do—it's in our release."

"Legally, maybe, but what about morally?" I asked. "I mean, isn't that why we're sitting here, freaking out? That disclaimer's all well and good until somebody gets *killed*."

"We were operating within the constraints of client-patient confidentiality," said Keller. "Besides, RBD is characterized by unconscious outbursts of violence and self-defense. Nearly every patient we see shows these symptoms."

"Yeah, but Anne was different," said Gabe. "She was cagier. Manipulative. We all knew it."

"Exactly," I said. "We should have told somebody. We should have turned her in."

"And what should have happened then?" asked Keller. "Should she have been arrested for dreaming of murder?

Charged? Where would it stop? Imagine—people being rounded up and accused, not for what they've done, but what they *dreamed* of doing. It's thoughtcrime, and we would have been the policemen."

"Fine—but that still doesn't mean we aren't culpable. We held a mirror up to her mind and showed her what was inside it." I felt nauseous, my head thick. "We gave her the idea."

"That's impossible to prove," Keller said.

"But are you denying it?" asked Gabe.

A strange, new dynamic uncoiled itself between us: Keller leaning slightly back, Gabe and I staring at him hungrily. Hungry for what? For him to admit some wrongdoing? For him to crack?

Keller was silent, staring at a spot behind our heads, either lost in thought or ignoring us completely. For a moment, I thought he wasn't going to reply; then he opened his mouth and exhaled, a rattle of a sound.

"I don't know," he said, articulating each word carefully, and somehow this was worse, more humiliating, than a denial.

I thought of Jamie: his tufted hair, his limbs straining against our straps, his shoes blinking red as he walked away from us. And I remembered something else: a warm night in September, a locket hanging from an index finger. My first conversation with Thom.

*Couldn't what begins as an exercise in self-knowledge actually reveal our darkest impulses?* he'd asked. *Once we experience our dreams—not via recollection, but right there in the moment— how long is it before we start to believe that this is who we really are, what we really want, how we really feel? When does one's dream consciousness become their consciousness, I mean? Maybe the dreams themselves aren't dangerous. Maybe what's dangerous is putting people in contact with them.*

"Oh my God," I said, leaning back in my chair. "Thom was right."

Gabe had been staring at the wall, dazed, but now his eyes narrowed.

"Thom was right?" he repeated. "You talked to Thom about our research?"

"Well, you talked to Janna."

"She *asked* me about it. That's different. I didn't tell her shit."

"What's going on?" asked Keller. "Who's Thom? Who's Janna?"

Neither one of us answered immediately. But Keller looked stricken, as if we had betrayed him, and Gabe caved first.

"Our neighbors," he said.

"I have told you," said Keller, "countless times—"

"Yeah, we know." Gabe's voice was tired, flat. "The first rule of Fight Club is that you don't talk about Fight Club."

Keller was rigid. "This is hardly the time to joke, Gabriel."

"Who's joking?" said Gabe. "If they subpoena our files— if they find out what we knew—we're fucked. We could be implicated."

He slammed the heel of his hand on the table. The students sitting closest to us looked up, but nobody else paid much attention. They probably mistook Gabe and me for siblings, undergrads, and Keller for our father. A family tiff, they would think—our father come to pick us up after finals, Gabe edgy from that morning's exam.

"They won't subpoena her file," said Keller.

"Why not?" asked Gabe.

"Because I've gotten rid of it."

He was very calm. We stared at him.

"That's just great," said Gabe. "That's really great, Adrian. And what's our excuse?"

"A fire at the lab in Fort Bragg. Some combustible substance—kerosene, naphthalene, one of the pyrophorics. An act of carelessness, to be sure, but an ordinary accident."

Keller took off his glasses and set them down on the table on their delicate, spidery legs. He rubbed the bridge of his nose. "Though I'm open to other ideas, if you have them."

"What if you have to testify?" I asked.

"Then I will," said Keller. "The publicity is not necessarily the issue—it's what *kind* of publicity it is. I have no problem speaking on behalf of our research. And if you find yourself in a similar situation, be sure to make it clear that the March case was entirely ordinary. Underwhelming, even. We worked with her for eight weeks, during which she couldn't attain a lucid dream state. Because she was unable to meet the demands of the study, we released her."

"And what if she tells them otherwise?" I asked. "She *was* lucid."

"A little too lucid," muttered Gabe.

"With an insanity defense," said Keller, "I can't see that sort of inconsistency as being much of a problem."

We were quiet as the music—a rousing hip-hop version of "God Bless Ye Merry Gentlemen"—came to an Auto-Tuned crescendo. When the next song began, Keller shook his head.

"It's a tragedy," he said. "She's exactly the kind of patient we could have helped."

. . .

On Christmas Eve, I dreamed of lying with Thom on the floor of the basement. Our bodies were slick and pressed together, pulsing against the floor's wooden planks. Thom held my hips, easing me back and forth. Afterward, I climbed off of him, warm and light-headed, and he put his hand between my legs. When I came, sliding down the planks with my face pressed to his neck, the feeling was as strong as it had ever been when I was awake.

A thin woman with a sliced red bob sat on the desk chair, watching us. It was Keller's wife. She beckoned to me, and I rose. Gently, she tugged on the dangling chain of the bulb, but before the light came on, I woke up.

I blinked in the darkness, my heart thumping, Gabe beside me. Sleeping with Thom—this was what I had been dreading and what a part of me wanted, too. But just as unnerving was the fact that the lightbulb—a dream bulb, and therefore, according to Keller's rules, impossible to turn on—had almost worked.

It was five in the morning now, Christmas Day. Gabe stirred heavily, sighing, and sat up; then he pushed out of bed and trudged into the hall. I heard the bathroom door close, the light turn on, the rushing noise of Gabe peeing. Full with the memory of Thom's slack, open face—the way the lines on his forehead erased themselves as we rocked together—I slid my hand beneath my pajamas. Inside, I was slick, the flesh molding snugly around my finger. When Gabe stopped peeing, it was silent again, and I froze. After a pause, the toilet flushed and I pulled my thumb downward, my body beginning to shake.

• • •

Christmas Day seemed to yawn on infinitely: the practical gifts, the rigid appreciation, walking around in our sleeping-bag coats because the living room furnace still hadn't been fixed. Every half hour we refreshed the major news websites, scanning them for news of the March case. So far, there had only been a brief addendum in the *San Francisco Chronicle* about the press conference, which devoted more space to the speeches of Anne's relatives than to the insanity defense. Neither of us was very hungry, but the thought of the year-old cans of chicken soup in the pantry made me feel sick, so I left for the market with two layers of sweatpants beneath my coat. I brought home a rotisserie chicken for dinner, and because we'd eaten so little all day, our appetites surged: we picked it clean to the bone.

That night, I felt too guilty to sleep. I lay awake until the clock on my night table read two thirty, then three thirty, then four. At four thirty, as the sky turned from black to charcoal, I pushed out of bed and went downstairs for a glass of water. I turned on the tap and let it run until the water turned from reddish-brown to clear. Outside, our car was a great white beast, magnified with snow. After drinking, I climbed the stairs to the attic.

I opened the door slowly, so that it didn't creak, and sank to my knees in front of the window. The moon glared outside the window like a policeman on night watch. As the rug printed my legs with the nubbly pattern of its yarn, I sketched my transgressions: Thom's hips pressed to mine, the red-haired woman watching us. Angel or prison guard, I painted her in angles: the sharp points of her bob, the slice of nose, the eyebrows arced in expectation. She was orange, the floor mahogany, and I was red as pleasure.

When it came time to paint the canvas black again, I paused. This time, I wasn't ready to return to bed, but I forced myself to open the lid of the black tube. As I did, the phone began to ring.

I froze for only a second before running down both flights of stairs. We had two landlines, one at the first-floor landing and one in the bedroom. Gabe was out cold, but I knew he'd wake up if the phone kept ringing. I picked it up downstairs, the tube of black paint still in my hand.

"Hello, neighbor," said the voice on the other end.

It was Thom. His characteristic lilt made me grow warm.

"Thom." I was stunned. It came out as a whisper, almost a question.

"Don't wear it out." Thom was whispering, too; we had dropped into a low tone of intimacy that was as confusing as it was electric.

"You shouldn't call at this time of night," I said.

"Why not?"

"Because I was sleeping."

"You were not."

"How do you know?"

"You answered the phone." He paused. "Plus, your light is on."

I turned. Faint light spilled into the stairwell—one of the lamps in the bedroom. My stomach clenched. Had I turned my lamp on before getting out of bed without realizing it, or had Gabe woken up?

"Anyway," said Thom, "I only called to see if you'd be interested in a nightcap. Fellow owls and all that."

"I was sleeping," I said, more sharply than I'd meant to. Suddenly I felt guilty; he couldn't know why he made me so uncomfortable. "Maybe another time."

"Strange," said Thom. "I thought I saw you go downstairs for a glass of water."

"You were watching me? That's harassment."

"I didn't mean to." The playful edge of his voice was gone; he sounded affronted. "I was sitting in my living room—couldn't sleep, like I said—and I saw a shadow at your kitchen sink. Slight, so I figured it was you. Anyway, it was your shades that were up. Don't leave your shades up if you don't want to be seen."

I had stiffened, but not because of what Thom had said. It was because I'd heard the quietest click, the sound of a receiver being picked up.

"Please don't call again," I said.

I hung up. The phone rattled in its cradle, a smear of red paint across the back. Upstairs, I heard a louder click—a door being closed. I cursed, licking my finger, wiping at the red paint until it was clear. When I went upstairs, there was a sliver of light beneath the door of the bathroom. I padded to the bedroom and climbed back under the covers, my pulse thumping. The lamp on Gabe's side of the bed was on. I was terrified he'd be angry with me, but when he came back into the room—adjusting himself through his boxers, his hair sticking up on one side—he looked at me with groggy surprise.

"Hey," he said. "Had to pee. I turned my light on and you weren't here."

"I went for a glass of water."

"I figured."

He looked at me for a moment, as if waiting to see if I'd say anything else. Then he climbed in bed, pressing his chest to my back. I could feel him growing hard through the seat of my cotton pants.

"Hey," he said again, more quietly this time. He burrowed his face in the back of my neck; a train howled its hoarse approach outside our window.

It was the first time in years that we slept together the way we had at Mills. *Slept together*—a funny phrase for sex, though perhaps it's not so unlike sleep after all: the mindless force of it, the slick grasp, the wild and glassy-eyed awareness. My shins rubbed to a burn against the sheets. Gabe rose and fell above me with rhythmic, tidal sway. I had forgotten how it felt, this closeness. I floated with relief, the old love bounding back to me like a dog.

When we woke the next day, it was already eleven, winter's bright cold sun washing the room. Gabe went downstairs to start the coffee, and I began to make the bed, but as I pulled back the down blanket, I saw a streak of red paint in the center of the white sheets. I stared for a moment before stripping them, my heart pattering in its cage.

I had almost made it to the laundry machine when Gabe came upstairs, a mug of coffee in each hand. He glanced at me with surprise.

"We washed the sheets last week," he said.

I had bundled them in my arms, but the red was too loud to hide. I could see his eyes find the bright spot.

"I bled," I said, edging past, leaving him alone at the top of the stairs.

Like a plane blinking in the night, my progress away from Gabe was steady. Perhaps if I had told the truth that morning, I could have changed the course of that dark machine, wrenched it around by the wings. But blood had already become less threatening than paint, reality the fair sister of illusion; and so, pouring bleach into the mouth of the washing machine, I continued.

# 13

When August came in Snake Hollow, we began to prepare for our departure to Fort Bragg. After leaving Mills, Keller had settled in this small coastal city, a Civil War military garrison about two and a half hours south of Eureka. In the summer, tourists came to visit the remains of the fort and walk Mendocino's rocky, glass-strewn beaches. The entire city smelled like salt water. It was quiet enough for Keller to afford an abandoned redbrick storefront at the edge of town, which he converted into a small laboratory and research center. Many of our patients drove from other parts of California—Fort Bragg is three hours from San Francisco by car—but those who flew in were offered lodging in a studio apartment above the lab, which Keller had renovated to accommodate overnight sleep studies.

It may have been picturesque, but it was an odd place to plop a research facility. Martha's Vineyard was no academic stronghold, but Fort Bragg was practically barren in that respect. It was fortressed by the toothy cliffs of Mendocino County, and its main industries were logging and construction. The closest universities were two hours north and south. But Keller did nothing unintentionally; he was as fearful as he was crafty, and I began to suspect that Fort Bragg's isolation was part of its appeal. After five years at Mills, after leaving higher education entirely, he chose to build himself up again in relative secret.

Keller's house was small and shingled, several blocks away from the lab. When he was being self-deprecating, he called it his cottage, but it was clear he took pride in it: he'd refinished the wood floors, installed new windows, and painted the exterior himself—robin's egg blue with white trim. Gabe offered to share his basement apartment with me—he could sleep on the fold-out couch in the living room, he said, chivalrously offering me the bedroom—and I agreed. The distance between us filled me with a pained, nostalgic longing for the way we used to be, but I still thought I'd be happier living with Gabe than being on my own. Besides, his place was fully furnished, so there was nothing I had to bring or buy.

We lived a block away from Keller. That fall, we spent most of our dinners at his place. We made many of the same meals we had in Snake Hollow, but the frenzied electricity of the summer was soon replaced by a lower frequency, a worker-bee's hum. Though our small group hadn't shrunk in size, I experienced small moments of loneliness. They came like chills as we sat at Keller's round table with the windows open: rain tapping the sidewalk, the sky a lunar indigo. We ate in new silence, interrupted only by the clink of a knife on the butter dish or the dull ring of a water glass set down. There were only so many things for us to talk about, given how often we saw each other. Still, I was reminded of dinners with my family in New Jersey, when we'd exhausted the usual topics and the day's fatigue set in—how disappointing it was to discover that even my closest relationships were not immune to distance.

Sometimes, though, our patter was as quick and engaged as it had been that summer. In early September, Keller briefed us on the case we would begin midmonth. We cleared the round table of place settings, replacing them with a corked bottle of wine and a stack of files. I was excited: it was the first time I would see an actual patient, take part in a real experiment.

Keller pushed his glasses up on his nose and opened the manila file in front of him.

"She's younger than I usually see for RBD," he said. "But she shows all of the signs."

We looked at the photograph on the top. It showed a woman with light blond hair pulled into a slick bun and pale, powdered skin; she looked like the sort of person who never left the house without sunscreen, even in winter. There were two bluish half-moons beneath her eyes, shadows of fatigue that she had tried to disguise with yellow foundation. Keller publicized his research through various channels, including state universities throughout California, and this woman had seen an ad for his study on the bulletin board of the nursing building at Humboldt State. Her name was Anne March, and she was twenty-four years old. In our research, she would be called patient 222.

Two weeks later, I met Anne for the first time at the lab. She hesitated before speaking, and when she did, her voice was halting; she could barely finish a sentence without encouragement. Because this was my first study, Keller asked me to observe her interview without interfering. He told Anne that I was a new trainee, a student, but her eyes still flickered at me with distrust.

For six months she had been living with disturbing, daily nightmares—nightmares she described as having a hallucinogenic quality, which compelled her to get out of bed to protect herself. When she woke, she found herself standing in another part of the house—once in the shower with the water off, another time in front of the living room window, her hands against the glass. Her heart was always racing, and she was so drenched in sweat that she had to bathe or change clothes (she said this in a voice so quiet that Keller had to ask her to speak up). The dreams, she said, were horrific, but she could not remember their specifics, only the lingering sense of fear and revulsion that was present when she woke up. That, she said, was why she'd come to us—so she could figure out what she'd been dreaming and why.

She was also newly engaged. She and her fiancé shared an apartment, but now they slept alone. Three months before, Anne had been forcibly woken by her fiancé, who'd opened his eyes to find Anne's hands around his neck. As a nursing student, Anne knew the importance of documented evidence. She brought him to the laundry room in her apartment complex, where the fluorescent lights were brightest, and took photos of the scratches along his neck, the crescent imprints made by her nails.

As she showed us the photos, copies of which we'd already seen in her file in Snake Hollow, Anne was not emotional. In fact, whenever I saw her awake, she was restrained—delicate, perhaps, but with an inscrutable comportment that veiled whatever was going on inside her like the mess of a teenager's room shoved underneath the bed: a haphazard method, but one that did make the floors look temporarily clean.

Gabe told me this was normal. "Most of our patients seem entirely sane when they're awake," he said as we packed up one day after a lucidity training session. "They're mild mannered, sort of embarrassed—and they're a lot more pleasant than she is, to be honest."

The night before, Anne had slept at the lab during her first lucidity study. She seemed on edge when she arrived, and her mood worsened as we prepared her. She complained that the lab was too cold and then, when we turned the heat up, too warm; she had forgotten her usual Colgate toothpaste and refused to use the Crest we had in the lab, so I drove to the closest twenty-four-hour pharmacy. Because I was new, Gabe took Anne's vitals and set up the video camera while Keller readied the EEG. I scarfed my dinner in Keller's office. Minutes later, Gabe burst through the door.

"It's bullshit," he said. "Absolute bullshit. She said I *touched* her—inappropriately, that is. I was only trying to take her goddamn pulse."

"What?" I put down my fork. "Did she know that was part of the procedure?"

"Of course she did. Keller briefed her on the whole thing, just like usual. Thank God I already had the video running."

That tape was enough to clear Gabe of any wrongdoing— it was obvious that he had affixed the straps exactly as we had been trained to do. But Anne's accusation was enough to hint at what she would soon discover herself. She was a fantastically quick learner; participants were required to show signs of lucidity within eight weeks if they were to continue in the study, but Anne was dreaming lucidly within the first three nights. She responded with the necessary left-right eye movements to our LEDs, though it was days before she would tell us what she'd seen.

"I think a part of me has always known," she said. "But I never let myself think about it."

We were in Keller's office. Anne sat across from Keller, rigid-backed as a vigilant cat, one crossed leg twitching; I sat to Keller's right, scribbling notes. Later, I would edit them for accuracy, sitting at the kitchen table with a tape recorder, pausing it every few seconds. When Keller told us, that day in Starbucks, that he had gotten rid of the files, this is what came to mind—not Anne, not her parents or sister, but those hours of meticulous work beneath the kitchen's low bulb. The research was Keller's, and Gabe assisted him during the trials. But it was my job to write our patients' stories, and that work made me feel valuable. Even my parents could not deny that Keller's research was intriguingly cutting-edge, and they slowly came to see my decision to leave Berkeley as evidence of my skill. It was a fib I told myself, too—that I had been chosen for my talent and not something else—but it kept me going.

It was easiest for me to do this transcription work alone. At night, after Gabe went to sleep, I sat at our rickety kitchen table with my headphones in and Keller's tape recorder in my lap. Anne's voice filled the room, ghostly and delicate as a night-blooming flower. When the interviews began, her tone was flat, but over the course of the session it became wispy and faltering. Always, though, there was an undercurrent of challenge, sharp and glinting like steel.

"Do you believe your sister to be at risk?" Keller asked once. His voice was clinical, impartial.

"Tell me, Doctor," said Anne, pronouncing the consonants with particular relish. "Do you?"

The dreams were not always the same, but they followed a reliable pattern. First, there was an image of trespass: a dog with hanging jowls pissing on a green lawn or a rat scurrying into a child's bedroom. Next, Anne became conscious of her body in space. Sometimes she huddled in pillows, her limbs pretzeled into tight shapes. Other times, she found herself on the lawn of her childhood home, the stench of urine thick in the air. She experienced a growing sensation of defilement. She stood, her movements blundering but determined—it was only after Anne that we started to strap patients to the bed. At that point, it was only moments until she struck. Once, she pummeled the wall with such force that the skin ripped across her knuckles before Keller could stop her. After that, we had her wear thick, puffy gloves. Though she spoke of seeing a rat or a dog while dreaming, she always reported, upon waking, that she'd believed the animal to be her father. She reported, too, that she had gotten rid of him.

Within weeks, we learned to estimate the moment of her attack and flash the light stimulus right before it happened. If we could remind her that she was dreaming, we reasoned, we could help her intervene in her behavior before it turned violent. We were right: Anne paused in the room, dazed, and responded to the stimulus with the eye-movement signal we'd taught her. Then she returned to bed and woke out of slow-wave sleep about twenty minutes later.

It took months for Anne to reveal that she had suffered sexual abuse, that it had been at the hands of her father, and that she was worried for the life of her younger sister. Keller believed our study was giving her an opportunity to safely express her anger and process her impulses. He was electric: Anne became lucid more quickly than we'd ever seen before, and her reaction to the light stimulus was perfectly in line with his theory. He saw her as a landmark case, one that could be used to lobby for grant money and legitimize interactive lucid dreaming.

But we never saw Anne again. One day in late October, Gabe and I arrived at the lab to find Keller in his office, dazed and blinking, as if he'd just woken up.

"She's pulled out," he said. He nodded at the phone, its voice mail button red. "Listen."

Anne rambled. She appreciated our time; she felt she had attained her goal, having seen what she'd been dreaming; and, having said as much, she felt no need to continue to participate in our study. She meandered for another minute or so—she could no longer afford the three-hour drive to Fort Bragg from San Francisco; gas prices being what they were; we understood, she was sure; and that wasn't counting the *traffic*—until Keller stopped the message.

I had never seen him so dejected; it was as if someone had died. Gabe, with characteristic brazenness, began to tease him.

"Cheer up, old chap," he said, slapping Keller's shoulder. "She's just not the one for you. There'll be other fish in the sea."

Gabe and I were disappointed, too, but deep down we were grateful to be rid of Anne. She was crafty, unpredictable, and she had made us both uneasy. When I thought of her later, I felt a retrospective squirminess. It was like the memory of having accidentally eaten an insect: an ant on a bread roll, a spider in the salad.

That night, when we returned to the apartment, we buzzed with the wild, uninhibited energy of guests at a late-night wake. Our nervousness hung in the room, sparking like power lines. Gabe rummaged around in the pantry until he found an old bottle of red wine. We drank, splayed on the couch, until we were more woozy than anxious.

"To Anne," said Gabe.

"To Anne. May she sleep in peace."

We clinked, then quieted. Had we let Anne down, or had she done that to us? She had weaseled out of our hands, disappeared through a crack in the wall. Though she had been the patient, we were the ones who felt exposed.

Gabe took another gulp of wine.

"I won't miss her," he said.

"No. Me neither."

Gabe put his glass on the ground. Then he placed his hand on my knee. He kept it there as I looked at him, then began to move it up my thigh. He undid the button at the top of my jeans and slid the zipper down, resting his hand on the soft, tender skin below my belly. For seconds, we eyed each other.

Then one of us moved, and we stopped thinking. Perhaps this was what we had wanted—the end of thinking—and what suspension: it was as if we shared one set of lungs, one pulse, one thick and muscular heart. His body, older now, was only half-familiar. It *felt* more, I could tell; like my body, his was somehow both more confident and more vulnerable than it used to be. After, we lay on the living room rug, warm and panting. Rain flicked through the open window. Otherwise, the block was silent; it felt like nobody lived in Fort Bragg but us. But I wasn't lonely anymore.

"What took you so long?" I whispered.

"Me?" asked Gabe. "I've been waiting for you this whole time."

• • •

We spent two years in Fort Bragg: biding our time, building our arguments, feeding our research until it grew strong like an organism. Keller may have been skittish, but he still craved institutional validation. After we had enough material to make a convincing case, he applied for a position as a visiting researcher at the University of Wisconsin–Madison. Gabe and I were at his house, cleaning up after a late dinner, when news of his acceptance came by e-mail. Keller laughed, in surprise or in vindication, his face an inch from the computer screen and filled with undisguised glee. For years he had kept his research protected, whittling it little by little. Now he could strip the tarp off the statue, leaving the Pacific Ocean and the salt air and the little blue cottage as if he had never really loved them to begin with.

# 14

Like all good liars, I took pride in my ability to deceive and thought it seamless. I painted my canvases black with a zealous attention to detail, allowing no trace of the original painting to shine through. Those covered-up paintings were works in themselves, as layered and intentional as what was underneath. There was only one painting I'd forgotten to black out: the one I had been working on when Thom called, on Christmas night. I'd shoved it behind the other four dark canvases and left it there.

One afternoon in January, I came inside after scraping ice off the porch, an old shovel in hand, when I noticed that Gabe wasn't in the kitchen where I'd left him. With the specialized intuition of the paranoid, which told me that the only possible outcome was the one I most feared, I knew he was in the attic.

I pounded up the stairs and pushed open the door. He stood at the window, light striking his cheekbones. The four black paintings were scattered on the ground like fallen soldiers. In Gabe's hands was the painting of Thom.

"You didn't tell me you were doing this," he said without looking up at me.

"It's a new project."

"I see."

He held the painting up to the light. My stomach tumbled, for I knew what it showed: Thom and me on the floor of the attic, our bodies making angles as we rocked together. But I had painted it the way I always did my dreams—narrative on top of narrative, the same scene sketched over as more of it came back to me—and now the lines were dizzying, almost indecipherable. Gabe squinted at it, straining to tease out the piece's meaning. A test: how well had I hidden it away?

"What is it?" he asked, finally.

"I don't know. I was just messing around. Playing with color and lines."

But maybe I had wanted him to find the painting; maybe it was I who was testing him. *How much do you know about me, Gabe? How far will you go to know it?* He hadn't put the painting down; he was staring at the lower left corner, where I had painted Thom's cast-off glasses. The glinting little lenses, the black temples folded shut.

"Those glasses look familiar," he said.

"Really?" I blinked. "Huh."

He put the painting down on the ground and brushed his hands on his pants. When he looked up again, his face was fixed.

"They're Thom's," he said. "Funny, isn't it?"

I thought I had won, but now I saw I was wrong. Gabe was feigning disinterest, something he only bothered to do when he was supremely, painfully interested. He wouldn't give up without a fight.

"Why funny?"

Gabe ignored this. I crouched and began to clean up the foam peanuts that had fallen out of a large, tipped-over box. He was silent, watching me.

"Is Thom really that interesting to you?"

"That's a ridiculous question. First of all, Thom doesn't have a monopoly on black-rimmed glasses. And secondly, they're only a small part of the painting."

"Right. I forgot to mention the crazy lines zigzagging all over the place. And the two naked bodies." He laughed hollowly. "I'm not blind."

"Gabe." I released a long breath. "It was a dream, okay? I had this weird dream about Thom, and it freaked me out. I came up here to process it."

"A dream. So you're still remembering them."

"I guess so. Parts of them, anyway." I crossed my arms. "I thought you'd be happy I'm painting again."

"You're changing the subject. And you're defensive."

"Of course I'm defensive. You're acting like I've done something wrong, like I've betrayed you, but I can't help what I dream. And don't I have the right to—to artistic freedom?"

I was bluffing; in truth, I felt just as guilty as Gabe thought I was. But he believed me, or he wanted to—I could see it in his face. His jaw softened, and he exhaled.

"I'm sorry." He shook his head, ran a hand through his thick brown hair. "I don't know what's wrong with me. I know you can't help it."

He walked out of the attic; his shoulder brushed mine as he passed me, and then I heard his heavy, quick footsteps on the stairs. A moment later, the screen door gasped open, rattled shut. He had left.

In my first year at Berkeley, I took a psychology course that focused on love. Most interesting to me was the section on communication between couples. I learned that even the slightest change of facial expression in one partner, a raised eyebrow or a curled lip, can be enough to trigger an increase in the heart rate and adrenaline of the other. Even more striking was the fact that couples begin to look alike as they age: their faces are quite literally shaped by shared experience. It was clear that couples speak with their bodies, not just their voices; that the body is confused in its allegiances; and that, sometimes, the body betrays the mind of its owner in order to communicate something to the partner—an insurgent rushing across party lines with a letter in hand.

I should have been relieved when the conversation was over, but I wasn't. Gabe's unease had amplified my own alarm, for I could no longer deny that my dreams were beginning to bulge into my days. Time was no longer fastened to my life; it had become unsewn, a hanging hem, a sibling whose days had once been braided with mine but had since moved on. I tumbled into morning feeling disoriented and incongruous, like a nocturnal creature blinking in the harsh, wrong light of dawn. Sometimes my muscles were sore, my breath short, as if I'd clenched them through the night. At other times, a faint, ebbing pleasure washed through my body.

My dreams of Thom had grown richer and more detailed, and they had a sensory, physical weight that stayed with me when I woke up: Thom's scissored legs around me, warm and long, sparsely patched with hair; the knobs and hollows of his face pressed against mine, soft eye sockets, ridge of nose, as he whispered something to me—a song—*For there's a change in the weather, a change in the sea. My walk will be diff'rent, my talk and my name* . . . It was an old big-band song from the 1940s, a Benny Goodman song, and where had I heard it before? For it to occur in my dream, I knew, I had to have heard it somewhere. But when I played the song online, in the office with the door shut, it reminded me of Thom, only Thom, nothing more.

Until now, I had felt helpless, resigned to the dreams as they came. Years ago, I had given up on the lucidity exercises Keller taught us in Snake Hollow. But what if I tried again? If I could train myself to be lucid—if I could watch the old machinery of my subconscious creak to life while standing apart from it—perhaps the dreams would lose their power. If I could name them, I might be able to disarm them. Maybe I could even control them.

That night, lying in bed, I took inventory of the things around me: the bedroom door, slightly ajar; outside my window, a yawn of moon; hanging from my nightstand, the cotton skirt from which I'd scrubbed a stain the night before. *When I see my hand in my dream, I will know I am dreaming,* I thought as Gabe snored lightly next to me. I reminded myself of the dream signs: broken electronics, impossible feats of physics, the dead. And when I emerged in a dream, minutes or hours later, I looked for them.

I was never aware of how the dreams began. Instead, I became conscious partway through, and it was almost like waking—slowly my eyes would seem to open and that musty, subterranean world materialized again, always the basement, its cracked floorboards and dusty bulb. Lights didn't turn on in dreams, and so it was light I would start with. But when I reached for the bulb's dangling chain one night, Thom stopped me.

"Are you crazy?" He batted my hand down like a fly. "Gabe might see."

The threat was enough to freeze me in place. I was distracted, too, for Keller's wife had appeared. She never spoke, but she watched us. She wore a red suit jacket and skirt, her expression impassively appraising: she was either fascinated by us or very, very bored. Sometimes, she sat in a chair across from me and trimmed her hair, staring into my face as if it were a mirror. Other times, she ignored us entirely: she inspected the room or leaned against the wall, humming like a teenager waiting for a train to arrive. Another time, Keller's orange cat wound between us before settling on her lap.

Thom followed my gaze.

"What are you looking at?" he asked, his voice low.

The woman caught my eye, one brow raised in an elegant, sideways S.

"I don't know," I lied.

"Sure you do," said Thom, wheedling me.

Thinking felt like swimming through sludge. I had mastered one task, at least: I knew I was dreaming. But what was I supposed to do now?

"Don't know how to," I said. "How to wake myself up."

"Then don't bother."

"You're no help."

"You don't need my help." Thom scooted over toward me and laid his head on my lap, crossing one leg over the other. His feet were long and wide, the bones raying out like fans. "You'll wake up in the morning."

"But what do I do until then?"

The cat slinked by, and Thom grabbed it. He held her above his head, his large palm beneath her stomach. The cat bristled, her back arching, before relaxing in his grip. Her legs, dangling toward the ground, twitched and went limp.

"A thousand things," he said. "We could have a staring contest. A wrestling match. Play blackjack. Run away. Though there are plenty of fun things we can do right here."

He wiggled his eyebrows.

"Don't be disgusting," I said, but as if watching a film I couldn't stop, I kissed him. He tasted muddy and sweet, and I did it again.

"Stay awhile," murmured Thom.

With his hand behind my neck, he held me close. Why did it feel so good to kiss him? He had none of Gabe's forceful need, his blunt charisma; Thom was coy and languid, drawing me to him before pulling back again. His body lacked the tight density of Gabe's—the hard chest or thickly muscled arms. When I pressed my fingers into Thom's skin, it was responsive, but through it I could feel bone.

He lit a candle. It made his face glow gold, then red. Light played other tricks on me, too. Sometimes, I climbed the stairs to look out of a small window set in the basement door. The sky was an inky black, unnaturally matte, like dried paint. I could see nothing else—no shapes, no garden, no stars.

"Why can't I see stars?" I once asked Thom. I shook him by the shoulders, and his head bobbled, moving from shoulder to shoulder like a scarecrow's.

And then I was in bed with Gabe, and it was his shoulders I was shaking, though his head remained fixed in place, his sturdy rottweiler's neck unmoving. His eyes were wide and focused.

"Because we live in a city," he said. "There are streetlamps. Light pollution. We aren't in the middle of nowhere anymore."

Could it be possible that something about the winter— the light pollution, the atmospheric density—had blotted out the stars? One night, I stayed up to see. I sat on the side of our bed with a glass of water. We had returned at three P.M. after a long session at the lab, and now it was evening. I was exhausted, and the urge to sleep tugged at me like a riptide— the strongest urge we have, I've often thought, greater than hunger or sex. But I waited as the digital clock beside the bed shone six thirty, then seven, then eight.

It was eight thirty when they began to appear. Like guests at a lavish party, some were early, others fashionably late, but one by one they filled the sky. Hyades, Cygnus, Pleiades. The Seven Sisters with their assigned seats at the table. Assured that I had indeed been dreaming, I fell asleep as if taking my rightful place below them—Gabe and I clustered in bed, assigned to our roles: in the mind as on earth, on earth as in the heavens.

* * *

A door had sealed off between Gabe and me, and we squinted at each other through the peephole. I couldn't tell him that I was afraid of the dreams that still took me at night, or how much Anne's reentrance into our lives had disturbed me. It was difficult to tell where his loyalties lay, and we were spending less time alone. Keller, so rarely a presence in our house, had begun to stop by unannounced; or at least it seemed unannounced to me, as I was never there when he arrived. I pushed through the door with grocery bags or library books, my face flushed and muscles rigid from the cold, and there he was—sitting with Gabe at our kitchen table or washing a glass at the sink.

"Sylvie," Keller would say, nodding, and Gabe would jump in: "Adrian was in the neighborhood." Or, gesturing to the newspaper spread out on the counter: "Another article about Anne's case. Have a look. Where've you been, by the way?"

Keller didn't live nearby, and he had no reason to be there unless he was coming to see us. I suspected he wanted to make us feel he was there during an obviously disturbing time—though I wasn't sure whether he meant to comfort us or keep tabs on us.

Gabe thought he was lonely.

"You know what Anne meant to him," he said after Keller had stayed over for dinner and two drinks before finally shuffling out the door around eleven.

I eyed him from the sink, drying my hands on a dish towel.

"To his work, you mean," I said.

"You know Adrian. For him, there's not much difference between the two." Gabe sighed and leaned back in his chair, wincing, until his back cracked. "He's never claimed to be perfect, Sylvie. He's dealing with a lot, and the least we can do is be there for him."

"Why are you going so easy on him?" I remembered Gabe's anger that day at Starbucks—how good it felt to be on the same side. "He screwed up, remember?"

"Maybe." Gabe sighed. "Maybe not. It's a shitty situation all around, but I think we might have jumped the gun in blaming him. If it's anyone's fault, it's Anne's."

His defection made me feel bewildered and abandoned. And it brought me back to a hazy night in October of 2002, shortly after we moved to Fort Bragg. Gabe and I were cleaning the kitchen after a roast chicken dinner, raising the windows to let the smoke out, when I brought up the fact that Anne took direction only from Keller. That morning, we had finished another frustrating session in which she refused to let Gabe or me prepare her; it was Keller she trusted, and Keller was the only person she allowed near.

"He's reinforcing her bad behavior," I said. "He's coddling her. If she's going to be a part of our research, she's got to accept the fact that she also has to deal with the underlings."

"It's still early." Gabe wiped the plate I'd just washed with a dish towel and slung the towel back over his shoulder. "She's clearly pretty damaged. And that's just how Keller is."

"An enabler?" I asked. I was braver then; it still wasn't too late for me to reenroll at Berkeley for the spring semester.

"If you want to put it that way." Gabe shrugged. "But there's no reason to villainize him. Keller's always wanted to help the people who need him most. I don't think there's anything wrong with that."

"Maybe he's the one who should be in therapy."

"He has been."

I laughed in surprise.

"How do you know?"

"He's mentioned it," said Gabe. "I don't know what about—maybe Meredith."

"Meredith?"

"His wife. She died, for Chrissake, and young—how are you supposed to get over that?"

That night, I lay awake for hours in the bed that Gabe and I had shyly begun to share. Meredith: the name sounded familiar, but I couldn't place it. Gabe was snoring beside me, a peaceful mound. I climbed out of bed and started up the computer, waiting as it sputtered and groaned. I pulled up Google and searched for some combination of Meredith and Keller. Why I felt the need to do so privately I wasn't sure; I only knew that I was betraying Keller, and somehow, Gabe, too.

What came up was the 1993 obituaries page of the *Vineyard Gazette*. I had to scroll down through a long list of other names—"Mary Lu Jensen, 78, Cared Lovingly for People, Plants"; "Kenneth Bryors, 94, Enjoyed Island Life, Family Visits"—before I found hers.

## RENOWNED SCIENTIST AND PROFESSOR MEREDITH KELLER DEAD AT 43

*A graveside service at Crossways Cemetery will be held on Saturday, December 4, to honor the life of Meredith Keller, née Meredith White. Born in 1950 to Mary and Lewis White in Oak Bluffs, Meredith received her MA in psychology at the University of Tennessee and her PhD in neurobiology at Yale School of Medicine. Shortly after graduating, Meredith became a teacher in the US military school system, educating children in Vietnam, Germany and Japan before accepting an assistant professorship at the University of San Francisco in 1979. It was there that she met her husband, researcher Adrian Keller, a PhD student who later joined Meredith on the faculty. They were married in 1985.*

*Meredith took her own life on November 26, 1993. She*

*is survived by her widower, Adrian Keller, and her mother, Mary White. She had no children.*

*Donations in her memory may be made to the Meredith Keller Foundation for Interactive Lucid Dreaming through the philosophy-neuroscience-psychology program at the University of San Francisco.*

"You don't find that a little unethical?" I demanded of Gabe the next morning. As surreptitiously as I had found the information, I couldn't keep quiet now that I had it. "I mean, Jesus—Keller's wife commits suicide, and he funnels all of her donations into his own research?"

"The research was both of theirs," said Gabe. His face was rigid with a defensiveness that surprised me. "They were partners."

"I thought you said you didn't know anything about her," I said. "Nothing but the fact that she died."

"I knew they were colleagues."

"Hardly," I said. "He was her student."

Gabe paused in surprise.

"How do you know that?" he asked.

I had put it together that morning, lying in bed as the perimeter of our eclipse curtains glowed with apricot light. The letter tucked in Jung's *Memories, Dreams, Reflections*—the three delicate pieces of paper, falling to the floor as if in invitation. *Who were you writing to?* I'd asked. *My thesis adviser,* he'd said. *Meredith.*

"He told me."

"Why?" asked Gabe. "In what context?"

He was standing across from me in the bedroom, his chest lifted in a proud sort of hurt.

"I found a letter he wrote her. I stumbled upon it in the library at Snake Hollow, and I asked him who it was for."

"That's a little invasive, don't you think?"

"Maybe he wanted me to see it."

"What do you mean by that?" He looked genuinely bewildered.

"Nothing," I said.

I felt ashamed; I had scribbled too far outside of the lines. What did I know of Keller's life, his marriage? I had never lost someone I loved. But the realization that I'd learned something of Keller that Gabe didn't know made me uneasy. I still had the nagging feeling that I had not discovered the letter to Meredith and the details of her death entirely of my own accord. I even realized that the photograph above her obituary was the same one I had found in Keller's bedroom, which could have been a coincidence but still gave me the eerie sense that I had unintentionally connected two dots. And although I found this impossible to prove—how could Keller have known I would search for a second copy of Jung's book or that I would care to find out more about his wife?—I still felt like I was following a path that someone else had set out before me.

Perhaps that's why I stepped off of the path entirely—or maybe I turned around and started walking the other way. Whether it was in fear or revolt, I didn't want to know more than I already did. I wanted to believe that I could choose not to learn more about Meredith. I would accept the ground I was standing on; I didn't always have to search for cracks. If knowledge was an offering, from Keller or somebody else, all I had to do was decline it.

# 15

There were times, of course, when it was impossible to avoid Janna and Thom. We bumped into them at the movie rental place, Janna clutching a silent film, or we saw Thom on campus—Gabe and I grabbing lunch during a daytime shift at the sleep lab, Thom running across the street with his gazelle's legs just as the light turned red. Each time, my reaction to Thom was visceral, equal parts magnetism and repulsion. Gabe watched me; how couldn't he? I tried to seem unconcerned. But that shift was seismic, governed by laws outside my control, with a lure as powerful and bewildering as déjà vu.

One sleepy, sunny morning at the beginning of February, the phone rang while Gabe and I ate breakfast—hard-boiled eggs with a piece of fruit on the side. Gabe nodded at me with half an egg in his mouth.

"You gonna get it?"

"Let's not," I said.

There was a cut-open blood orange on each of our plates. Several days ago, we returned from the market with a bag of the swollen, thick-skinned fruit. Each was so juicy it dyed our napkins purple.

How was it possible that the phone was still ringing? Gabe paused with his fork in the air.

"It could be Keller," he said.

"He'll leave a message."

Gabe pushed his chair back and wiped his hands on his pants, which stained.

"There's no need," he muttered, crossing the room, "to play games. Might as well find out what he wants."

But before he could pick up the receiver, the ringing stopped, and there was a sharp rapping noise at the door.

"Jesus," I said. "Can't leave us alone for one morning, can he?"

I salted my last egg as Gabe strode to the door. I was already sick of the fleshy whites, their Jell-O texture.

"Thom," said Gabe.

The sound of his name made me want to run. I was ashamed of myself; I had done harder things than this. But I waited at the kitchen table while Gabe and Thom conferred outside, hoping that Thom had only come with a quick question about road closures.

There was a jagged peak of a laugh—Janna's.

"Sounds like fun," said Gabe.

He let the door swing open. Thom and Janna stood in their winter regalia: Thom in a long houndstooth overcoat, Janna in a satiny turquoise jacket. Its exaggerated, stand-up collar rose as high as her nose.

"Bocce," said Gabe. "Want to play?"

His voice was bright, seemingly transparent, but sharp-edged—a tone that reminded me of Janna. It seemed like a dare.

"I'm not dressed," I said. This was not exactly true; I was wearing a drab combination of sweats, but the sight of Janna made me feel as though I might as well have been in my pajamas.

"It's such a lovely day," Janna said. "Warm in the sun."

"Warmish," said Thom.

"Warmish," Janna repeated.

"Come as you are," Thom said.

He was looking at me in a peculiar way—questioning, hesitant, as though I'd hurt him. His nose was pink with cold, his eyes searching my face. It would be a victory of my dream life over my real one if I said no, I thought—so I stepped into my boots and met them on the porch, where Janna was swinging a blue and red bag, the lumpy shapes inside shifting like an irritable cat.

We walked down a strip of land beside the Yahara River and set up camp near a clump of picnic tables. It was the first day in the forties we'd had all year. Small, slushy puddles pooled in the grass.

"I don't know anything about bocce," I said, holding a hand over my eyes as Janna opened the large bag. I was keeping close to Gabe, my fingers wound with his; I felt desperate as a schoolgirl with a first boyfriend.

"It belongs to the *boules* sports family," she said. "Closely related to *pétanque* and bowls, with a common ancestry that dates back to ancient games played during the Roman Empire."

She turned the bag upside down and a group of heavy-looking, brightly colored balls fell out in a heap. I stared at her dumbly.

"All you really need to know," said Thom, picking one of them up, "is how to throw a ball."

Thom suggested ladies and gents teams, not couples, so I found myself standing with Janna as Gabe threw the jack across the field. I was relieved I hadn't been paired with Thom, but I was nervous around Janna, the way some people are with big dogs; if she were in a toothy mood, it seemed, she could drag me around by the hair. The boys were blue and we red. We took turns heaving our bocce balls toward the jack. I thought I'd struggle to throw mine more than a few feet, but as it turned out, Janna and I were evenly matched. By noon, each team had bowled five times, and we were one point ahead of the boys. If they'd been more focused, they might have played better, but Thom and Gabe were horsing around in a way that reminded me of the boys at Mills. It was part play, part viciousness: Gabe cutting Thom off with a swift kick to the shins or racing him to the farthest tree, their pants splattering with sludge.

Janna leaned against one hip as we waited for them to return. Her thin legs were encased in thick brown tights and dwarfed by a pair of quilted snow boots.

"Sometimes," she said, "I think Thomas has homosexual tendencies."

Thom and Gabe careened toward us. They seemed to be racing, but then Gabe dropped behind Thom. In a swift, subtle movement that only I saw, he hooked his ankle beneath Thom's right leg. Thom skidded forward, his legs splayed, before tumbling to the ground like a calf.

"Fucking hell," said Thom, unharmed but irritated. He clambered up to a standing position, a clump of mud on his chin, as Gabe ran ahead. "What was that for?"

"Well," said Janna. "Not so much anymore."

Why was it impossible for me to see her as she was? Whenever I came close to Janna, she seemed to change form with the ease of an optical illusion. Even now, I see her in the girls who attend the private school near my apartment—in the Cheshire flash of their smiles or the legs that begin at their waists. Janna had once been a girl, and what kind of girl had she been? I assumed she'd been the kind I'd always feared: slippery, shrewd, one who would tie your shoelaces together if you weren't looking or poke you with tweezers and hairpins. But what if she had been a girl who sat pressed up against the whir of the laundry machine in her parents' basement reading books about plants? If I'd known her as that girl, perhaps I wouldn't have been able to do what I did. The more I made Janna a hologram, the more she seemed to haunt me, and the less it seemed possible that things could be the other way around.

As we walked home, Janna asked Gabe about the state of the dogwood trees they'd planted. The trunks had become withered and stunted, and neither of us knew whether they would survive the winter. Thom slowed, falling in step with me. There were ten feet or so between us and the others.

"Good game," he said, looking ahead.

I nodded. Something fluttered in my chest with the crazed helplessness of a brochure caught under a windshield wiper. He swayed closer to me, and our arms brushed. I wondered if he had been drinking: his breath had the metallic tang of alcohol.

"I finished the next section of my dissertation," said Thom. "The second chapter. I'll tell you, it feels good to be getting some traction. Like I'm wearing cleats now, and not slippers. The big questions start to quiet down, and the difficulties are more procedural. Where to insert this piece of evidence, that citation. What will convince you. Though perhaps I shouldn't be so confident. I'm only halfway there."

He chuckled, a tinny sound. His little monologue had taken up most of the block, and I was both grateful and flabbergasted. The abrupt lead-in, his assumption of my interest, seemed to suggest we had talked about this before.

"So we aren't speaking?" he asked.

I froze. What he said had jogged my memory of our phone conversation on Christmas. How he had rung late in the night, and I had told him not to call again.

Janna and Gabe had reached the driveway between our houses. They turned and waited—Janna leaning on the skinny pole of one leg, Gabe watching us with feigned disinterest.

"Fine," said Thom. He edged ahead of me, limping slightly from his fall. I was panicked, lockjawed. Thom's face was injured, but his back was bent with a weary, almost feminine nobility, like that of an old horse.

That night, I startled awake after another dream of him. This time, though, I hadn't been able to catch it; I remembered only Thom's face, golden and disembodied, his forehead drawn with the same wounded uncertainty I'd seen that morning. I swung my legs around the side of the bed and walked to the bathroom. The light above the sink wavered as I splashed cold water on my chest and dried off with a towel. When I went back to bed, Gabe was propped up on one side, waiting for me.

"What was that?" he asked.

"What do you think?" I was overheated and irritable. "Bad dream. Why? Did I wake you?"

Gabe didn't answer. He was staring at me with a queer expression, his head cocked to one side.

"Did you see your hand?" he asked.

"What?"

"You know. Did you see your hand?" He adopted Keller's throaty baritone. "*When I see my hand in my dream, I will know—*"

"Stop, Gabe. I'm not a patient."

"Might make 'em feel less real, is all."

He was smiling, but his eyes were cool and evaluative. It was a look I'd seen many times in Keller. I rolled over, away from him. For minutes, there was no movement from his side of the bed. Finally, he sighed and shifted, the old bedsprings squealing beneath him, and I was able to close my eyes.

• • •

The next morning, I woke to the sound of low voices downstairs, dulled by the bedroom door. When I walked into the kitchen, I saw Keller and Gabe at our round breakfast table, their heads bent toward each other.

"Sylve," said Gabe. He sat up.

I crossed to the coffeemaker. There was a fresh cup waiting for me.

"Run out of cereal?" I asked Keller.

He laughed, a surprise. Usually he would have tried to tell me off. He wore a ragged sweater, tattered around the wrists, and a pair of jeans. I had never seen him in jeans before.

"I made you coffee," said Gabe.

"Thank you. I saw."

"How'd you sleep?" Keller asked.

"Fine. Why?"

"Gabriel mentioned you've been having nightmares."

Keller's face was pleasant, but his body was still: his back stiff, his coffee cup in a firm grip.

"I'm fine." I poured my coffee and put the pot back on the burner, where it hissed. "Thanks for your concern."

As I reached for the sugar bowl, the phone began to ring.

"That goddamn phone," I said. "It rings and rings and there's never anyone there."

"Is that so?" asked Keller, frowning.

I strode to the phone and picked up the receiver. No noise. I hung it up again. It had happened three times in the past week.

"Do you think we should be concerned?" I sat down between them, crossed my arms. "I mean, if it's somebody calling about the case, why would they hang up? Wouldn't they ask for whatever they wanted when we pick up?"

"Maybe that's what they wanted," said Gabe.

"Just to know we're home? Why?"

I looked to Keller, but he was impassive.

"Listen," I said. "I'm sick of the conspiracy theories. Living with this kind of anxiety—it can't be worth it. Why don't we come out and say Anne was working with us? What's the worst that could happen? We could help the prosecution, maybe even gain a little publicity. That's what you believe, isn't it? That there's no such thing as bad publicity?"

"I didn't say that. Not exactly." Keller rubbed the back of his neck. His eyes were heavily lidded, and the skin of his cheeks seemed to hang. "We would have to think it through."

"You can't be serious," said Gabe. "That would be tantamount to turning ourselves in. The university wants a success story. Our money is tight as it is, and after the mess that happened with Jamie, we can't afford to tell them that one of our participants went off and killed someone."

"Well, maybe we need to face up to the fact that we don't have a success story," I said.

Gabe glared at me. *Not in front of Keller*—I knew that was what he was trying to tell me.

"We still might," Gabe said.

"We'd better hope so," said Keller, "for your sakes as well as mine. I can't pay you out of pocket."

"I can't imagine that things are already that dire," I said. "It's not like you have a team of twenty researchers. You've only got the two of us."

I didn't realize what I'd said until I saw Keller's reaction. To an outside observer, he would have looked just the same. But I saw the way his nose twitched—a sharp little rabbit's motion, as if he'd smelled something sour. He looked out of the window, where the sidewalk had been scraped of snow and doused in salt.

"You're right about that," he said. Then he stood, pulled on his coat, and walked outside to his car.

Gabe's fingertips were white against the table.

"What the hell do you think you're doing, bringing that up?" he asked. "The man lost his wife."

I was too surprised to be indignant. "I didn't mean it like that."

"Well, maybe you should think a little more before you open your mouth. Think about the implications of what you're saying. You can't *talk* to him that way."

"I talk to him like an equal."

"That's my point. He's our boss."

"Oh, he's a lot more than that, and you know it."

"So talk to him like he's more than that," said Gabe. "Not like he's some kind of failure."

"He's not your parent, Gabe. He's not your therapist. You can say whatever you want about yourself, but you had no right to tell him about my dreams."

I got up from the table and washed my coffee cup. I was already on edge, my anger fueling.

"I'm worried about you," said Gabe. "I confide in him because I trust him. Is that such a crime?"

"Christ, Gabe." I dropped the mug into the dish rack, where it clanged against a bowl. "How much is he paying you?"

"Same amount as you."

"Then you're working overtime."

Gabe was still sitting down, but his shoulders were clenched around his neck like a boxer ready for attack.

"Don't you have any faith?" he asked.

"Not blind faith. Not blind."

I turned toward the sink and wiped my hands, but I could feel Gabe staring at my back. When I turned, his jaw was tight, but his eyes were wide with misery.

"What's happened to you, Sylvie?"

I wanted to claw him. The sight of him in such pain—and worse, to be blamed for it—was more than I could stand.

"What happened to me?" I asked. "What happened to *you*? You used to be an insurgent, Gabe. A renegade."

"And now?" he asked. "What am I now?"

His fists rested on the table. Below, his legs were crossed

at the ankles, feet clad in the wool socks Keller had given him one Christmas.

"A lapdog," I said.

I walked to the screen door that led to the back porch; it wheezed open, coughed shut, and there was cold air in my face. My breath was rickety, my cheeks hot. When I blinked, I saw firecrackers. I went to the fence, where I knew Gabe couldn't see me, and ran my palms over the rough, papery surface. There was a loud snuffle behind me, and I jolted away from the wall, expecting to see one of the sly, fanged raccoons that ferreted through our trash bins at night. But nothing was there; the noise had to be coming from Thom and Janna's garden. I came close to the fence again and peered through the sliver between two planks.

Thom leaned against the juniper tree as we had done together on Thanksgiving. There was an open book on his lap; his head was bowed and unmoving. The snuffling noise came again, followed by a high whistle. Thom's head rose jaggedly, as if pulled by strings, before bobbing back to stillness. He was snoring. The pattern repeated every few seconds, familiar as a song I knew by heart.

"Gabe?" I called. My chest squeezed like a fist, tightness radiating up to my jaw and throat. I stayed where I was until my vision cleared, the shapes of our yard reassuming their positions like actors after intermission. There was the rhododendron shrub, its petals vivid and velvety as scraps of brilliant fabric; there were the dogwood trees, their branches growing horizontally, as if to reach out for each other.

There was a quick movement in the window of our bedroom—a flash of brown as someone's head withdrew.

Gabe had been watching me. The bedroom window was open, our eclipse drapes pushed to one side.

I walked back into the house, grabbed my coat from the closet and took my keys from the basket by the door. On second thought, I took Gabe's, too, shoving them deep into my pocket so he couldn't come after me.

• • •

The parking lot was empty when I arrived at the lab. The Hungarian researcher was with family in Eastern Europe; I didn't know about the other researcher. I flashed my ID card and stepped through when the doors opened for me. My footsteps made a flat rapping noise as I took the stairs to the basement, the fluorescent lights turning on automatically. *A migraine in a box*—that was what Keller called this building. I knew he had suffered from headaches for years, though he almost never mentioned them. Every few months, I saw him reach into his pocket for a small tin filled with flat, white rounds. If I didn't know any better, I'd have thought they were mints.

The lock on Keller's office door jammed for a moment before giving way. Inside, it was silent: the air boxed and windless, the computer waiting patiently to be woken.

I sat down in Keller's chair and slowly spun. Now that I was here, I didn't know what to do with myself. I'd come to look for something, but I didn't know what it was—all I knew was a rumbling, bone-deep feeling of unease, the *Madeline* sense that something was not right. Keller's new presence at our house. His hushed conversations with Gabe. It was as if there were a dark spot dancing at the edge of my vision, a jumping bean, slipping out of view whenever I looked at it directly.

I came to a stop in front of the file cabinets. Keller had asked me to reorganize all of our hard-copy files. Right now, they were arranged in alphabetical order by last name, but he wanted them ordered chronologically by case number. It wasn't difficult work, but it would take time—Keller had observed over three hundred subjects. I had been around for forty-eight of them, Gabe one hundred and twelve. The project afforded me unlimited access to Keller's hard-copy files.

The main filing cabinet was nearly six feet tall; I had to stand on the spinning chair, grabbing hold of the cabinet to steady myself, in order to reach the higher shelves. I took files out by the fistful, dropping them in stacks on the floor. There it was, our work: each patient reduced to a neat pile of papers in a pale folder, except Anne. I decided to start with the present and work backward. I knew 304—that was Jamie. I put a red label sticker on the edge of his file for the year and wrote the month on a white tab in a clear sleeve. Then I put it back in the first drawer, pressed against the back.

It was the kind of rhythmic work that Keller could rely on me to do well. *You're a machine, Sylvie*—that's what Keller said to me, once, as he watched me entering numbers. It was easy, I told him—you just couldn't get snagged. Each patient a number, each number an entry, each entry logged and saved in the automated depth of the computer's memory. Such elegant architecture, and I the architect! Chip by chip, I built whole mechanical cities, maps of human dysfunction, each node blinking in place: 298, Maura Sanchez, a cafeteria worker who came to us after waking to find herself standing at the edge of a seventh-story fire escape; 296, bus driver Daryl Evans, who had screamed at night with the shrill and enduring vibrato of a soprano.

By late afternoon I had worked my way down to participant 212. I'd filled an entire drawer with red-labeled folders, but I hadn't found anything out of the ordinary. I opened the bottom drawer and took out the folders inside it, five at a time. When I finished, one folder was left. Either it had dropped out of my hands, or it had been wedged horizontally beneath the others.

It was unmarked: no name, no number. Inside was a stack of old newspaper articles. An obituary in the *San Francisco*

*Chronicle*, March 21, 1985. An interview with a well-known neurologist—Alec Ivanov, since deceased—in *Time*. An article from the *Chicago Tribune*, November 23, '86: "The Fall of the Sexsomnia Defense: Delivery driver jailed for sexual assault, during which he claimed to be asleep . . ."

Beneath the articles was a stack of smaller, handwritten notes on beige lined paper, the edges uneven, as if ripped from a journal.

### SEPT 16 '91

*Another similar report. Twelve thirty—the second REM cycle, so far as we've been able to discern. I turned from back to stomach, reached for him. The testicles, as before. How humiliating it is to write this out. His report, of course, and it's all I can do to trust it. Have thought of installing a camera but I've no desire to see myself that way. Sticky in the morning—again, as before. But I must not blame him. Tomorrow we have an appointment with Alec, the only one I'll see. Adrian thinks it best to see someone who doesn't know me, but I disagreed, and he relented. Someone who knew me as I was, and not only as I've become: this, I believe, is true impartiality.*

### NOV 4 '91

*Woke again at four this morning after another night of the new system. I've got it down, you might say, to a science— forty-five minutes of sleep, then the alarm. I get out of bed, distract myself. Then another forty-five minutes, then the alarm, and this way I recuse myself from each REM cycle like an athlete pulling out of a match. It's my choice, though I can tell it hurts him. Perhaps he liked me better as I was:*

*all animal, brute instinct. But I'd rather it be controlled. The device I keep under the waistband of my pants, next to the skin. Ingenious, now that I've figured how to cut the noise. It only vibrates, and in doing so it wakes me while he sleeps.*

JAN 1 '92

*W 112*
*H 5 ft 6*
*T 98.6*
*BP 90/60*

*Six A.M. Exhausted. A happy New Year. I slept through the last two cycles this morning and I'm afraid to ask what happened. He'll sleep another hour, and then I'll do it. How much faith I had in that little toy! But it's stopped doing its job, just like me. I may have to use noise again, though the thought of it is terrible—a regression. And who will I be if I keep going backward?*

FEB 21 '92

*W 106*
*H 5 ft 6*
*T 98.7*
*BP 80/55*

*All nighttime things have taken on their otherworldly alternates. The moon, the stars, darkness and its shadows—all these are threatening for what they precede. My perceptions must be named as part of one of two camps. I am asleep, or I am awake. I am myself, or I am not. Each morning I take vital signs to see if my self has changed, mechanically speaking. Height is stable at 5 feet 6 inches. Ditto temperature, at 98.7. Weight has dropped and fluctuates weekly depending on my cycle, which I've managed to retain. Adrian says I shouldn't worry so much about control, but it's easy for him to say, who has it. He is eternally patient with me. I've no business asking why. Each morning we write our notes, compare them for holes and accuracy, and compile a cross-report. I must have faith that what we are doing will be of use to someone else, if not to me.*

The entries continued until October 5, 1993, with significant gaps between. Behind them was a patient intake report—an earlier version of what we used now. The boxes were supposed to be filled out by the patient, but I recognized Keller's tiny, slanted black script.

PATIENT: *Keller, Meredith*
DOB: *January 4, 1950*
ORDERING PHYSICIAN: *Ivanov, Alec*
REASON FOR TEST: A) SLEEP APNEA B) HYPERSOMNIA
    C) SNORING D) LEG JERKS (PLMS) E) INSOMNIA
    F) SEIZURE G) NARCOLEPSY H) OTHER: *RBD*
READING DOCTOR: *Keller, Adrian*

The bottom of the form was to be completed by the research team, then as now. In the line beside Patient Number, Keller had written, in his thin, recognizable handwriting: *1.*

• • •

When I returned home, the door was unlocked, and Gabe was gone. Perhaps he was on his way to the lab; he might have even rumbled past me on the bus as I drove by in the opposite lane.

I paced the living room while waiting for him. What did it mean that Keller's wife was his first patient? Maybe it meant nothing at all. Clearly, she had made herself a subject. So why did I feel a sour crunch of nausea?

I could do one of three things. I could tell Keller, but I would have to admit to snooping. I could tell no one, of course, but this knowledge was more than I could sort through alone. Despite my fight with Gabe and his loyalty to Keller—it was becoming clear to me that he saw not Keller but some kaleidoscopic version of him, a Keller whose bright particles could shift, protean, and rearrange to fit the shape of any answer—Gabe was still the person I trusted most, the only person I had.

From the table next to the stairs, the phone began to ring. I picked up the receiver and slammed it down again. Next to the phone was a list of numbers I'd laminated with packing tape. Cell numbers for Gabe, Keller, and me, landlines for my parents and Gabe's grandmother. The lab. The university sleep center. These were the numbers we dialed most often—really, the only numbers we dialed at all.

I lifted the receiver and began to call Gabe before I realized there was no dial tone. I hung up the phone, picked it up again. Nothing.

I put the receiver down and began to trace the wiring to the wall. I hadn't set up the landline, but I assumed it connected to the plug a foot or so behind the table. But it was strange; the phone's clear wiring, nearly invisible against the white wall, snaked around to the stairs. Then it began to travel upward, secured with plastic pins.

At the landing, it took a left and followed the hallway to our room. Another left. Inside the bedroom, it threaded down the wall next to Gabe's side of the bed, and then it disappeared behind his night table.

I crouched and tried to pull the table forward, but it was

too heavy to budge. What could he be keeping in those draw-ers? I opened them: scientific encyclopedias, a thick hardcover on rail transportation in the US. A large, knobbed fossil he had found on Martha's Vineyard and insisted on bringing home, lugging it through Boston Logan in his carry-on. I laid each item carefully on the bed. Then I lifted the table and knelt next to the wall, where the plug finally found its entrance.

The wire had been cut. About two inches from the wall was a tiny, rectangular black box, about half the size of a deck of playing cards. Two black probes extended from one end of the box, clipped to the ends of the severed wire.

I shook my head. Where had I seen something like this before? A movie? A television show? The sleek little bug with clips as sharply ridged as incisor teeth. The innocuous black box, deadpan, poker-faced. Downstairs, the door opened and closed with a bang.

"Sylve?"

I sat in front of the bug as if rooted while Gabe climbed the stairs. The door flew open—we were accustomed to barg-ing in with the heedless entitlement of college roommates. He stood in the doorway, panting, his hands braced in the frame.

"I just wanted . . ." He inhaled. "I wanted to say I'm sorry. For yelling at you. I shouldn't have. You don't need me to tell you how to talk to Keller. You can talk to him how—however you like."

It was then that he looked past me to the wall. He stared at the bug.

"Gabe?" I swallowed—a hard, scratchy knot. "What is this?"

He squatted next to me and picked it up in one hand. Shook it lightly, as if to test its weight.

"When did you find this?" he asked.

"Just now."

The sun was sinking its little mound below the horizon of the city. Pink light skimmed Gabe's cheek.

"Sylvie." His voice was low, steady. "Let's not jump to conclusions."

"How many conclusions can there be? Someone's been listening to our calls, and the only person who's been here is Keller. Keller, and you and me."

Gabe's hair was wild, his breathing labored. He looked at me a beat too long.

"Oh, Gabe," I said. "You can't think I had anything to do with this."

"I didn't say that."

"Why can't you admit that he's fallible, that something incredibly sketchy might be going on?"

"What do you mean, something sketchy?"

He was still squatting, and one of his knees cracked. I climbed over him, leaving the bug by the wall, and padded quickly downstairs for my backpack. I brought it up to the bedroom, tossed it on the bed, and rooted around for the manila folder I'd taken from the lab.

"I found this today," I said, handing it to him. "It was in the filing cabinet, wedged beneath the others."

Gabe opened it gingerly and sifted through the papers inside.

"Look." I leaned toward him, pointing. "It's Keller's wife, her intake form. She had some sort of RBD—sexsomnia, it sounds like, if that even exists. She was tracking herself, keeping a kind of diary. Look at the handwriting. You recognize it, don't you?"

Gabe was silent. His body was perfectly still, but his eyes shifted across each page with incredible speed.

"I don't trust him," I said. "He's never told us about this, never even alluded to it."

"But why should he have told us? It was personal."

"That's my point," I said. "Science is supposed to be impartial. It's supposed to be objective. And I'm starting to feel like Keller's mission isn't professional—it's personal. It's like he has a vendetta, Gabe—like he's trying to avenge her by curing other people of the same sickness."

"And what's so wrong with that?"

I remembered something Gabe said months ago, last fall—both of us standing in the kitchen at dusk as the hazy golden light of evening slanted through the window. *But what's more ethical than helping the people you know? Why should the process be so quarantined, so sterilized? Science should be applicable to real life—so why should we divorce it from love?*

Outside the window, a crow paused on the fence. It trained on us one dark, beady eye before sweeping away.

"How much do you know about this?" I asked.

"Nothing," said Gabe. "Nothing."

"Then why are you protecting him?"

"I'm trying to see the good."

"But what if you're wrong?"

My faith in Keller had begun to erode years earlier, I think. But my faith in Gabe was, until that moment, mostly intact. Who else did I have but him?

We looked at each other carefully. Then he sat next to me on the bed, kissed the line of my jaw.

"Everything I do," he said, "I do for you. For us. You know that, don't you?"

Was that romance? I had known no love but his. Rolling through the grass like wolves, limb for limb, scavenging for attention—the brute hunger, the desperate force—and then, days when we hunted alone, nosing our way through the brush and picking at stones, days when our tracks were parallel but far apart. That Christmas, my mother had called, her voice crackling with static, and asked if I thought I would marry him. I looked over at Gabe, who was making oatmeal at the stove, holding a copy of the *San Francisco Chronicle* in his non-stirring hand. What could I tell her—that we were caught in the purgatory of Anne's trial, a trial that would name her fate but seemed just as likely to direct our own?

I knew Gabe well enough to know when he was lying. Even so, the truth seemed elusive, as faint and faraway as half-hidden stars. I was afraid to look up. Why, I should have asked myself, did Gabe not suggest we dismantle the bug? As he walked to the bathroom to shower, I crouched on the floor and unclipped its teeth.

• • •

Psychologist Abraham Maslow's hierarchy of needs lists physiological needs—for breathing and food, for sex and sleep—as the most basic of all drives. Next comes the need for safety, followed by the need for belonging. But what about the need to forgive? There is no belonging without it, no safety, no love. And so I found myself climbing into bed with Gabe that night. I started to read my novel, but Gabe was fidgety: he rustled through the *Isthmus*, discarded it, futzed with his radio alarm clock. Music crackled to life: Jay Z, a classical crescendo, a mariachi band.

"Can you turn that off?" I put my book down. "I'm trying to read."

"Hold on."

He fiddled with the dials, and Diana Ross's "Ain't Nobody's Business If I Do" came through, rich and jazzy and clear. Gabe began to groove in his seat. A pillow bounced and fell off the bed. He got to his feet, still on the mattress, and extended his hand.

"Dance with me?" he asked.

"Gabe—"

"Come on, Sylve. We need a little music."

Diana's voice faded, and the Jackson 5 took her place. *I*

*want you back*, they crooned, and what could I do but take his hand? We jived down the mattress, jumped and rebounded; we spun and dipped and clung. Gabe knelt, playing air guitar, shaking his head until his eyes were masked by hair. For seconds, it was possible to forget everything we had ever done to each other. Hysterical with need, we yanked the curtains shut. As the furnace exhaled heat, we stripped off our clothes and climbed back onto the bed.

But something wasn't right, something had been lost, and we scrambled for it with increasing panic. We searched coolly at first—an arm adjusted, a shift in the hips—and then hastily, furious in our bafflement and so thorough that any desire turned to exhaustion, though we couldn't stop. We wouldn't. We tried positioning Gabe behind me and above me, my ankles on his shoulders or cast to the left. I lay on my back, on my stomach, on my side; I crouched on my knees with my elbows pointing into a pillow and my forehead bumping the bed frame. We sat up, my legs pretzeled around Gabe's waist, and rocked. The radio music faded; a commercial came on. Gabe braced himself against our comforter, his fists sinking into the down, and thrust with as much determination as I'd ever seen in him. It was no use: he was softening, his face twisted with humiliation.

"I'm sorry," said Gabe.

He lay back heavily, and our bodies came apart.

"It's okay," I said, disentangling my legs from around his waist. My knees popped, the skin rubbed pink.

It must have taken minutes for us to notice that the doorbell was ringing. By the time we scrambled into our clothes and turned off the radio, someone was rapping on the door. Who could it be but Keller? We slipped down the stairs in our sweatpants and socks. Neither of us bothered to look through the peephole before Gabe unlocked the door.

Two police officers stood on the porch. One was a stocky

younger man with ruddy skin and a brown mustache, precisely clipped; the other was a tall, lean woman with deep-set eyes and a tight bun, which tugged at her forehead.

"Dane County Police," said the man.

Both cops pulled out their ID badges and flipped open the leather card cases before putting them away again. The woman took a small notebook from her belt and flicked up the cover.

"Am I looking at Gabe and Sylvie Lennox?"

"I'm Patterson," I said. "Sylvie Patterson."

"Gabe Lennox and Syl-vie Patterson." The woman squinted at her notebook, writing quickly. "Lived here long?"

"Since August," said Gabe. "What is this about?"

The woman looked up at us. "Is that your car in the driveway?"

"We don't have to answer these questions," said Gabe.

I squeezed Gabe's arm. "It's our car," I said.

"Anyone else in the house?"

Gabe and I didn't flinch, but a current passed between us.

"Is this about Anne?" I asked before I had the sense to stop myself.

"Anne?" asked the man, taking a step forward. He was broad across the chest, and he strained in his belted jacket. He and his colleague exchanged looks, and she scribbled again on the small pad. "Is Anne in the house?"

"No one is in the house," said Gabe. "No one else is in the house."

"Mind if we confirm that?"

It was the woman this time, her eyebrows cocked.

"Yeah, I do mind if you confirm that." Gabe's face was fixed with tension. "I know my rights. Tell me what this is about and we'll go from there."

The two cops exchanged another glance. Then the man sighed, and the woman flipped her notebook closed.

"Listen." The man inclined his head confidentially. "You want to tell us what you were thinking making all that noise at twelve thirty on a Tuesday night?"

"That's all this is?" spluttered Gabe. "A—a noise complaint?"

"Hey, buddy, hey." The cop put his hands up. "We take noise complaints very seriously in this town."

"I bet you do. And I bet you think you're really fucking funny." Gabe's voice was rising, his neck veined. "Bet you thought it was hilarious, scaring us like that. You know what I think is fucking funny? Cops not doing their jobs. Cops coming to *my* front door, hassling me about a fucking *noise complaint*, when people are killing each other out there—"

"Not helping your case, my man," said the cop, taking another step forward.

"Stop it, Gabe." I took his wrists in mine, digging my nails into the thin underskin. "Let it go."

Gabe had stopped shouting, but his face shook. A drop of sweat quivered at the tip of his nose.

"We'll stop, I promise," I said, keeping hold of him. "We've already turned the music off. We were having fun, that's all. It was stupid."

The man crossed his arms. His partner stared at us over the bridge of her nose.

"Understand, you are this close"—she squinted—"from a misdemeanor. We get another call, things get more serious."

I nodded. Gabe wriggled out of my grasp and watched from the porch as the cops walked back to their car.

"Hey," he shouted, just before they opened the doors. "Who reported us?"

The man opened the driver's door and got inside without answering. The woman covered her eyes with one hand, as if trying to see us through the glare of the streetlights.

We didn't notice that the light in Thom and Janna's bedroom was also on until it abruptly went out, throwing the policewoman's face into shadow. She nodded slightly. Then she climbed into the car and yanked the door shut. The car began to move, blinking in the night.

I locked the door. Gabe turned away from me and headed for the stairs. But before he got there, he turned abruptly and slammed the heel of his palm into the living room wall.

"Gabe," I gasped.

"What kind of fucking business did they have reporting us?"

"Maybe we really were being loud."

"Bullshit. They were our friends."

His forehead was dented with anger, the folds around his eyes so deep a penny could have balanced inside them. He glared at me, waiting for a response. But I wanted to be back in our room, jumping on the bed with the radio on and my stomach in my throat. I wanted to see Gabe playing air guitar with as much vigor as any other twenty-four-year-old, his hair streaking the air. I wanted him to be blurry again.

PART THREE

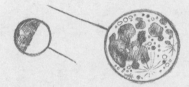

# MORNING

# 16

MARTHA'S VINEYARD, MASSACHUSETTS, 2010

This summer, I've had plenty of time to think about my years with Keller and what they meant to me. I could have taken a plane to the Vineyard, but Hannah insisted I drive. See the country, take my time. I've saved up a bit of money—enough for a motel room in Cheyenne and another outside Iowa City. The first thing I do, when I get to a new room, is stand in front of the air-conditioning with my arms spread out like plane wings. It's been a hot summer, and I've pitied the animals I've seen on the way: the thick-skinned sheep, horses swishing their tails like fans.

It isn't so awful, being alone, not when you get used to it. Every decision's my own. Whenever I like, I can stop at a gas station for cheap coffee or Slim Jims. If there's a fruit stand, I'll pull to the side of the highway—I keep the bags in the passenger seat, knotted to keep out flies—and sometimes I get out for a roadside attraction: the Angel Museum in Beloit, Wisconsin, or Amarillo's Cadillac Ranch. Mostly, though, I try to make good time. That way, when I touch down for the night, it feels deserved.

At each motel, after I stand in front of the air-conditioning—or, for the cheaper ones, the fan—I pull on my old Speedo one-piece and go out to the pool. Even the motels without air-conditioning have pools. The color is always the same: a too-bright, mouthwash aqua. Smallish and rectangular, lined by a curved ledge of concrete and rows of beach chairs in various stages of decline, the pools shine like beacons amid the surrounding mediocrity. I ease myself into the deep end—too tall to dive like the children holding life preservers, or too old.

It feels good to be surrounded by families, even if they aren't my own: the children chicken-fighting with a viciousness reserved for siblings while their wide-set mothers yell for leniency. After I swim, I set up on one of the folding chairs with a hotel towel and chip away at the twenty-seven books I loaded onto my e-reader before the trip. When I was studying for my preliminary exams, it was more—a hundred and sixty, give or take—but I'm now halfway through my dissertation, and my reading has become more focused.

How different it would have been if e-readers had been around when I worked with Keller! None of the fragrant, heavy books, their pages wilted as old dollar bills. The Kindle was too practical to resist—that sleek little machine, light as a paperback—but I miss the days when books were weighty and tangible. If all goes as planned, I'll graduate in a year, apply for jobs this fall. I'd hoped this trip would give me time to read the rest of my texts, and I think I'm on track. If I'm honest, it helps to have a distraction—to believe that my mission this summer is to finish my reading, and not something else.

I've been on the Vineyard for two days now. I'm staying in a little motel by the water—the most expensive one I've visited, but I've been frugal enough in the past six years to manage it. It's located across the island from our old haunts. I wanted to keep my distance, at least until I was ready. In the morning, I have breakfast on the deck: a piece of fruit and one of the boxes of cereal I filched from the continental breakfast in Iowa City. When it gets hot, I read inside my room—I can see the ocean through the window.

I don't know exactly what I'm waiting for. I guess I'm expecting to drop into a different state, one in which I feel meditative and unflappable. I get frustrated when I snag on things. The silvery color of the motel siding, for example. The fog and its familiar descent.

I planned my route so that I had to drive through Madison; I wanted to prove to myself I could do it. I hit the Wisconsin state line on the afternoon of July 4. I had planned to drive through the capital without stopping, but by evening, the holiday traffic had become unbearable. My muscles were rigid, and the air-conditioning in the car was less effective as the temperature rose outside. At nine o'clock, I pulled into a cul-de-sac on Rutledge and parked. I was ten minutes on foot from the old apartment in Atwood, two minutes by car. Through the window, I heard the high shrieks of the children who had gathered, with their parents, to watch the fireworks.

I unlocked the car door. I only meant to stretch my legs, but I found myself wandering down the stairs between two waterfront houses, which led to a grassy patch of land at the edge of the lake. Families sat on the grass and on the benches by the stairs, waiting.

We were bound by a congenial feeling of mutual anticipation. One of the children began to climb the fence; his father pulled him down, but not before the child pointed over the fence and hollered notice of the first explosion. It was a green shower of lights, shooting up in stalks to our right. The next one—red sparks, flaring and dissolving—came from the opposite direction. The land was so flat that we could see the fireworks of a succession of different towns. They burst one after another in all parts of the sky. The biggest explosions must have come from the closer towns, like Sun Prairie. The smaller ones followed like echoes.

We waited until the last town had sent up its final spark; the coda was a happy face, accidentally upside down. Watching the layered lights of these Wisconsin towns, many of which I'd driven through before, left me with a sore, vacant feeling. As parents collected their children and couples ambled back to the road, I found myself waiting by the fence, as if another show was soon to start or someone was coming to meet me. I could have been any other thirty-year-old woman—a well-lit apartment down the block, a partner at the stove. I look much the same as I did when I lived in Madison: the same slim, compact frame, skin beige and dotted with freckles in summertime. Two years ago, I changed my haircut, adding bangs—the feathery whim of a Berkeley hairdresser. I had hoped to be transformed, but when he spun me around to face the mirrors, it took only seconds for me to register myself. Like a child waking to a bedroom at first fuzzy and strange, the details soon sharpened into familiarity: the mole beneath my left eye, light eyebrows peeking out from behind a fuzzy shelf of hair.

When I'd spent several minutes alone and it was clear that the fireworks were over, I climbed the stairs and walked back to the car. I was already turning my mind to logistics. Accustomed as I was to working through the night, I started driving again. By the time dawn was peeling night from the landscape, returning color to the pastures and wetlands, I was in Ohio.

# 17

In March, Madison shook off its crust of snow. Tree branches and grass blades shivered baldly in the early spring air; the most adventurous undergrads began to wear shorts, their legs defiantly exposed and covered in goose bumps. I lived in a vigilant state of alert. After seeing the bug on our phone line and finding Meredith's file, I was determined to find out more. And if Gabe wouldn't help me, I'd do it alone.

I was distant from him, as if preparing myself, as if I already knew how our story would end. He was in charge of recruiting new participants, driving through the state to post flyers at satellite campuses of the university, and I continued the file reorganization project. We needed a success, and soon: our funding for the following year was not guaranteed. But we had no more than two new participants that spring, and I think a part of us had given up. Every morning, we read the *San Francisco Chronicle* online on separate computers, and at night we fell asleep in our clothes.

By the end of the month, I'd finished organizing Keller's patient files by case number. But one was missing: no matter how hard I searched, I couldn't find number 111. I paged through each file, checking to make sure it wasn't sandwiched inside a different folder. When I found nothing there, I turned on Keller's computer, but everything in the ancient Dell was protected. What would Keller's password be? I tried *mills, meredith, fortbragg, sanfrancisco*. No go. Next, I tried *snakehollow*, but the password box shuddered, as if shaking its head, and went blank again.

"Come on, Keller," I said. I pictured a ghost Keller standing inscrutably before me, a Keller hologram—his hands woven daintily together, his slight smile impassive. "Give it up."

Rolling my neck, I swung back to the keyboard and typed *hollowsnake*. The computer made a gurgling noise of happiness, and the password box sprang to one side. I laughed; could it really have been so easy? Each e-mail was now readable, each link clickable. But two hours later, I was even more alarmed: in Keller's documents folder, I found scans of every file but 111.

I could feel a headache coming on as the fluorescent lights flickered in the ceiling. It was three in the afternoon, though you'd never have known from inside the windowless office. I'd propped the office door open with a paperweight so I could hear if someone was coming, but the hallway was silent. It would be easy to lose your mind down there, I thought; maybe the three of us already had. The top of Keller's desk was devoid of personal items: there were only a couple of Post-its, a tiny dish of paper clips, and a Martha's Vineyard mug (HAPPY CHAPPY!) full of identical ballpoint pens.

I spun around in his desk chair, rubbing my eyes with the heels of my hands. If Keller wanted to hide something, where would he put it? His own computer was too risky, too obvious. The same went for his hard-copy files: he would never leave a paper trail. As the chair whirled, I passed the cabinets, the propped-open door, the mini refrigerator where Gabe and I kept our dinners. On top of the refrigerator was a slender laptop, closed like a mouth, its battery light blinking green. It was Gabe's. He often left it here overnight, especially if he decided to walk home from the lab. It was heavy, an early Dell he'd covered in band stickers—Led Zeppelin, Radiohead— and bandaged, over the years, with packing tape.

Gingerly, I opened it. Gabe had a password, too, but I knew that one without thinking: 33173, his dad's zip code in Florida. It had been the combination for his gym lock back at Mills. In Gabe's documents, I found electronic files that went back to patient 110: Stuart Cappleman, the dining hall worker at Mills.

It's strange; I don't remember my body heating up or my heart rate speeding—the marks of my old panic attacks, though they weren't diagnosed as such for another year— when I finally found file 111. In the storm's unblinking eye, all the training I'd done leapt to my defense: my practiced, even keel, my ability to stay calm when dealing with the most hysterical patients. I didn't read it yet. I wanted Gabe to be with me. So I tucked the laptop in my backpack, locked the office door, and drove home.

It was a bare, cool day at the end of March. The smallest leaves had budded with the cautiousness of all plants born in early spring. The heat was on as I came through the door and discarded my layers. A carnation Gabe had given me for Valentine's Day sat in a narrow vase next to the sink, its neck keeling elegantly toward the counter. I hung my sleeping-bag coat on the peg where it would sit, untouched, until I packed it haphazardly three weeks later. Gabe sat at the kitchen counter with a glass of milk. Abruptly, the heat shut off. The dust motes and down feathers that had been swirling in front of it swooped to the ground.

"You left your laptop at the lab," I said.

A blank haze came over his eyes like a passing cloud. Then they sharpened again.

"Oh?" he asked, but his voice was too flat, his shoulders too still.

"I found something in it," I said. "It's a file, number one eleven. We don't have it in hard copy—Keller must have destroyed it—and it isn't on his computer, either. But I found it on yours. I don't know whose it is, Gabe, but I know something's off."

The words spilled out of me with relief. Even as I walked to him, holding his computer in my arms, I was irrationally convinced of his innocence. I wanted to believe that Keller had uploaded the file, that Gabe had never seen it before. After all, if Keller wanted to keep something from me, there was no hiding place more brilliant than Gabe's computer— Gabe, the person I loved, the person I was least likely to suspect. I could finally prove to him that Keller had kept secrets from us, big ones; that he didn't trust us and we had no reason to trust him. It would be difficult for Gabe to accept, but I would help him. We could go anywhere in the country: find different jobs, spin ourselves new. I pictured us in the pocked, lunar deserts of Utah or a seaside town in Maine, eating toast with jam at a light-cast kitchen table. There would be moisture in the air. Buoyancy.

Gabe had frozen. But he did not seem to be in shock; he listened to me with the stoic commitment of someone carrying out orders. I opened the computer and double-clicked the file.

It took no more than a glance at the form for me to realize what it was. I had seen hundreds of them before. Now my heart began to knock against my ribs. I should have looked at the file by myself at the lab. How had I not looked at it?

"Did you know about this?" I asked.

"Sylvie," said Gabe. His hands found their way to my shoulders. "Let me explain."

The words on the page were startlingly clear. Weren't they

supposed to blur, change form and run away from me, at a time like this? Outside the kitchen window, there was a scrabble of feet and a rush of air. A clump of blackbirds rose from a tree and scattered like pebbles.

My shoulders shifted beneath his hands—the small, barely perceptible movement of an animal readying to strike.

"Read it to me," I said.

Gabe removed his hands.

"Sylvie."

"Read it."

He sat down beside me and took the laptop in his hands. Ordinary noises were amplified: the dull creak of the floorboards beneath his socks, the crack of his jaw as he opened and closed it.

"'Patient name.'" His voice was quiet and muffled. "'Sylvia Patterson. Female. Patient number—one eleven.'"

I had never seen him cry before, not like this. He was silent, his face rigid, each drop pooling at the side of his lower lid before beginning its own slow, meandering trajectory down his cheek.

"'Birth date—January fifth, 1980. Referring physician—Adrian Keller. Marital status—single. Chief complaint—trouble sleeping at night. Unwanted behaviors during sleep.'"

How many times had I seen this form, filled it out myself? I knew what question came next.

"For how many months or years?" I asked. I was biting down so hard that my teeth shook.

Gabe made a barely audible noise. It sounded more like his voice cracking than a single word.

"Seven years."

"I don't understand. Seven?"

I still had some hope that this was a mistake, that Gabe knew nothing of what he was reading. But he held my gaze.

"Seven," he said.

My voice came out as if dispatched by someone else.

"Typical amount of time it takes to fall asleep," I said.

"Twenty minutes."

"Typical number of awakenings per night?"

"None."

"Sleepwalking episodes, and how many?"

"Yes. One to two per night."

"Dream enactment?"

"Yes."

"Typical time patient gets out of bed."

"Between twelve thirty and two A.M."

Something had lodged in my chest like a bone. I could breathe only shallowly.

"Sleep habits," I said.

Even in the first weeks of my work with Keller, I could have uttered the list that followed on command. It measured almost a full page. It had been my job to check the applicable boxes for each participant.

"'Patient has nightmares as an adult,'" read Gabe. "'Patient sweats during sleep. Patient kicks or jerks arms and legs during sleep. Patient drinks alcohol during the night. Patient wakes up early in the morning, unable to return to sleep. Patient grinds teeth during sleep.'"

"I don't do that," I said. "I've never ground my teeth."

Gabe looked at me. Then his eyes returned to the form.

"'Patient grinds teeth during sleep,'" he said. "'Patient walks in sleep. Patient talks in sleep.'"

His head rolled forward. He supported it with his left palm, his elbow on the table.

"Sylvie," he said. "Please."

I had stood. I couldn't sit still next to him; I needed some leverage, a broader view.

"Keep going," I said.

"'Patient has had blackouts or periods when she is unable

to remember what has happened. Patient has fallen asleep during conversations. Patient has fallen asleep in sedentary situations. Patient has had injuries as a result of sleep. Patient has had hallucinations or dreamlike images while falling asleep or waking up.'"

I knew we had come to the end of the section.

"Past sleep evaluation and treatment," I whispered.

"'Patient has had a previous sleep disorder evaluation. Patient has had a previous overnight sleep study. Patient has had a daytime nap study. Patient has previously been treated for a sleep disorder.'"

"Social history."

"'Patient shares a bed with someone,'" said Gabe. "'Patient has a partner.'"

"That's enough."

It was not blood in my veins—it was something faster, hotter, and more slippery, a violent substance that gave me powers I did not normally have.

"Please, Sylvie," he said. His voice was urgent, rising in pitch. "I'm begging you. Let me explain."

We were a foot apart, maybe less. I waited until I could trust myself to speak steadily.

"You've been watching me," I said.

He was silent. He stared at the table, his eyes wide. Two small fire ants walked across the center plank, next to the salt and pepper shakers. Then they slid into the crack between two planks and were gone.

"How would you feel if you found out I'd been watching you?" I asked.

"I would feel grateful."

He spoke slowly, carefully, as if he had rehearsed this line before.

"For what?"

"That you loved me enough," he said. "Enough to help me."

"If you loved me, you wouldn't have done this. You couldn't have."

He reached out for me, but I sprang away. I wrenched my right arm back and struck him, the edge of my palm colliding with the hard bridge of his nose. I heard a soft pock, and then I felt the bones loosen.

Gabe opened his mouth in pain, the lips peeling back to the gums. Like mine, his blood seemed too bright for blood, too fast; it emerged from both nostrils and streamed into his mouth like paint. He tipped his head back, so that it hung over the chair, and moaned.

"That's not the full file, is it?" I asked. "How long is it?"

Gabe shook his head. He made small snuffling noises, his snot streaming red.

"How long, Gabe?"

"Oh, I don't know." He voice was nasal, pleading, his eyes squeezed shut.

"Estimate."

"A hundred forty-five pages," he said. "A hundred fifty."

The numbers were too large. I needed something to do with my hands. I walked to the sink, doused a towel in water.

I returned to him and wiped the blood from around his mouth, his teeth. Later, I would find this towel in a box filled with winter clothes. Somehow, in my haste, I had taken it with me.

"You don't need to take care of me," said Gabe.

"I'm only doing this so that you're well enough to talk," I said. "To start from the beginning."

With his nose clogged, Gabe sounded younger than he really was. I remembered him at seventeen, racing the other boys up the hill on the night of the eclipse. His strong, moist palms, the wide hooks of his shoulder blades. Dolphining through the water at Will Washburn's pool, bursting through the surface every few minutes—his head turning wildly, wet hair splattering the others, until he found me. The look on his face of bare pleasure and surprise, as if he could not believe I was still there, watching him.

"You must have realized by now that it started at Mills," he said. He closed his eyes as I pressed the cloth to his nose. "You know that I talked to you while you were sleeping, that I told you what I was doing with Keller. You were so damn *helpful*. You had ideas, good ones, and you weren't even awake. You weren't lucid; I knew that much. You didn't remember anything the next day—I asked these little probing questions, trying to find out—but when you fell asleep again, you remembered it all. It was as if you dropped into this other life at night, and your brain kept separate track of it. It was eerie. Impressive. But I was afraid for you."

"So you took me to Keller."

Gabe nodded. He lifted his head, winced as I wiped around the rims of his nostrils.

"He couldn't believe it. He'd never seen anything like you, even compared to other sleepwalkers. You could talk to us. You had impeccable control of your motor functions. You were *you*, I mean—an alternate version of yourself, a double."

"Were you training me?" I asked. "Trying to get me to be lucid?"

"At that point, no. All I did was take you to his house. Let you walk around—three times, maybe four. But you didn't like it there. You were freaked. And when I saw you that way, I wondered if I'd been wrong."

"The day I followed you," I said. "It was the last night of Thanksgiving break, our senior year. I was awake. You came out of Keller's house. He chastised you—he took away your night privileges. He made you write an essay."

"It was an act. We had been working. He'd told me what to say if it happened."

I jolted through the years. My senior fall at Mills—waking

up with the cuts and bruises that I thought were from sex. The strange sense of foreign landscapes, trees, new rooms, ebbing from my body. The brush of a small creature with a stiff bright tail.

"The cat."

Gabe stared.

"Keller's cat," I repeated. "Orange, with a long tail. I was always repulsed by it, and I never knew why."

He still looked ashamed. But is it possible that I saw something else in him? A curiosity, some thrill—and somewhere, faint pride, as if I had impressed him?

"You never liked that cat," he said. "You got spooked when it touched you, like a little kid. I can't believe you remember it."

I sat down opposite him, leaving the rag on the table.

"How could you do it?"

"It was awful, Sylvie. It felt wrong, and I knew it. So I left school."

"Without warning me? Without telling me what could happen when you were gone?"

"You don't understand. You wouldn't go to Keller's place without me. He could hardly go to the dorms to retrieve you. I had clearance to assist him, and if we got stopped by a hall monitor or one of the house fellows, you were okay so long as you were with me. I was the link. And if I took myself out of the equation entirely, I thought I could free you."

"How could this happen?" I asked. "Legally?"

"That was part of the problem. But we had you sign a research release, just to be sure."

"I must have been sleeping. I could sue you."

"But how could you prove you weren't conscious?"

"Because I was *sleeping*."

"Sleep and consciousness aren't mutually exclusive, Sylvie. You know that."

My brain was moving with remarkable speed. I was trying

to think of every possible question, as if I knew, even then, that I would go over and over Gabe's answers for years.

"Did the other teachers know?"

"Some knew more than others. Mr. Cooke left because of it."

How much easier it would have been if the room was swimming, as I've heard rooms do at times like this. Instead, it was clear as day: the shapes of the kitchen static and angular, the clock ticking evenly, as if everything inside the room had conspired to stay still enough for me to remember it.

"I know you'll want to know why I came back," said Gabe. "To Keller, and to you."

"I was in college," I said, to remind myself. "I had almost graduated. And I kept seeing you. That day I left the apartment, and I saw you by the lamppost—I thought I was dreaming. But you were really there, weren't you?"

Gabe nodded.

"It was me. When I saw that boyfriend of yours, I split. I took off down the block and hid behind a car. I knew then that I had to be more careful."

"But you also knew that I was still sleepwalking," I said. "Is that why you came to me? To see if you could make me into a lab rat again?"

"I've never thought of you that way." Gabe squeezed his eyes shut. "You're special, Sylvie. I didn't want you to hurt yourself. When I left Keller, left Mills, all I could think about was you. And what would happen to you, if you got into the wrong hands."

"And you don't think I did?"

I was seething. But some part of me still wanted desperately to be convinced.

"I know it feels that way," said Gabe. "But we had other motivations for recruiting you. Everything I said to you that day in the coffee shop—it was true. You were smart and resourceful, a psychology major. You knew Keller and me. And you'd understand our patients, however subconsciously. The fact that you were a sleepwalker—it was just an added bonus."

"An added bonus." The words were dry in my mouth. "So what did I do?"

I still imagine how it would be if I hadn't asked. Would I think of myself differently? Or would I still have known, somewhere deep in the recesses of my consciousness, as Keller and Gabe believed I did?

"In Fort Bragg," Gabe said, "you did little things. I'd wake up in the middle of the night and find you in the computer room, searching for something on Google, or sitting at the kitchen table doing your transcription work. Sometimes you even went up to the ground level, walked around in the grass. You never went very far. You just seemed to want a little air."

"And here?" I asked. "How far did I get here?"

"Do you know?"

His face had the same odd expression—that mixture of shame and curiosity, of pain and hunger.

"You tell me," I said.

Gabe inhaled, his breath uneven. He pushed himself to a standing position. The blood around his nose was still wet, and I could tell he was faint. But he walked slowly to the back door that led to the yard.

"You went outside," he said. "Through this door here. Took the stairs down to the yard. Come."

I followed him into the grass. Outside, it was dizzyingly bright, the sky the harsh gray-white specific to March. We stepped around the dogwood trees, which had managed to survive the winter; some had even sprouted fleshy little leaves, oily and lined like palms. Gabe led me to the back corner of the fence that separated our yard from Thom and Janna's. Three planks had been removed, leaving a jagged hole through which an animal or a small person could pass. The hole was mostly hidden from view by a weedy bush. I didn't remember seeing it before.

"Did I make this?" I asked.

"You or him," said Gabe. "I wasn't sure."

Thom. His calls in the night, the oddly familiar way he spoke to me after the bocce match.

"You egged me on," I said. I remembered the night of the match—how I had woken to find Gabe looking at me. "You asked me if I could see my hand—you said it made the dreams less real. You were trying to make me lucid."

"We've been trying for years. Keller thought it would be better if I worked with you—he obviously didn't have access to you at night, and we didn't want to make you suspicious. In Fort Bragg, I would talk to you in your sleep, but you didn't make much progress until we came to Madison. These past few months, you got so close. I could tell you were remembering more—you were becoming lucid, Sylvie. I couldn't help but nudge you when you were conscious. I felt like I was helping you do something extraordinary."

"Why didn't you just tell me?"

"Do you really think you would have stayed? We should have told you at the very beginning, back at Mills, but we didn't. We couldn't tell you now." Gabe's eyes were swollen, his nose already bruising blue. "I didn't want to lose you, Sylve. I still don't."

"But you *were* losing me. That's exactly what you were doing—you sat there and watched me leave. It didn't bother you? It didn't hurt you, when you saw me go into his house?"

"Of course it did. It was excruciating." Gabe eyed the house next door and lowered his voice, though the rooms were dark and the shutters closed. "But we were doing something that had never been done before: we observed the subconscious mind in a totally uninhibited state over the course of almost seven years. You gave us the opportunity to watch a sleep disorder evolve in real time, to see how it was affected by lucidity. Keller was convinced you'd change the way parasomnias are understood. If it was the other way around—if it had been me—would you have been able to resist?"

Gabe had gathered energy. He looked entreating and cautiously optimistic, as if convinced of a truth that I would come to see myself.

"You're sick," I said. "You are verifiably fucking insane. This isn't my achievement. You forced me into it—you took away any freedom of choice I had."

I was walking back to the house, stumbling over steppingstones and tangled plants, winding my way around the dogwood trees.

"Do you really believe that?" asked Gabe from behind me. "You *knew*, I'm sure of it—at some level, even if it wasn't conscious, you had to have known."

"Don't tell me what I knew. I didn't know a goddamn thing."

But I wondered if it was true. Had I wanted this? Had I been complicit? And, in some way, had I already figured it out myself?

We walked into the kitchen again, and I pulled the glass door shut. All outside noises were sucked from the room. The hum of the refrigerator, now, the click of the clock. The slight buzz of the overhead lighting.

Gabe held his hands up like a camper trying to calm a bear.

"If that's what you think, fine. But I think that, with time, you'll come to see a picture that's more complicated."

"Did you bug the phone, or was it Keller?"

"We did it together."

"To listen to my conversations with Thom."

"Partly, yes. We had no way to know what was going on otherwise. We didn't have anything set up at his place. And then there was the business with Anne."

"So Anne March is on trial."

"Of course she's on trial."

"She killed her parents, and her sister, too."

"You know that, Sylvie."

He was looking at me quizzically, the space between his brows furrowed. I felt reality as a whole slipping away from me like an enormous tide. I had to reconstruct it by hand, to verify the simplest details.

"It isn't fair." I felt frail and cold. "You saw sides of me I didn't see myself."

"But isn't that incredible?" His eyes were slick. "We *know* each other, Sylvie, in ways other couples can only dream of."

"People shouldn't know each other this well. You watched me behave like an animal."

"No," said Gabe more forcefully, shaking his head. "That's not true. I saw you behave honestly. You have nothing to be ashamed of."

"You know me, but I don't know you."

"I know it seems that way. But you will, I promise you. Now that you know about all this—and believe me, my God, I've wanted you to know so badly—we don't have to have any more secrets. We can be totally open."

"And what about Thom?"

"I don't care about Thom. It was all my fault."

"But what does he know?"

"I have no idea. I haven't spoken to him."

"No? You haven't filled him in?"

"I told you," Gabe said. "We had no way to know what happened when you got there. We couldn't figure out much with the phone bug; whenever you picked up, you seemed to want nothing to do with him. All I could do was take down the time when you got out of bed. Then watch as you walked through the fence."

"You were pretending to sleep."

He nodded.

"I don't understand," I said. "I don't understand which side you were on."

"There aren't sides," said Gabe. "We're all on the same side."

He caught hold of my forearm and tried to draw me to him. But I pulled away, twisting until his arm wrenched behind his back. He let go of me with a gritted noise of anguish. Panting, he dropped forward, his hands meeting his knees.

"Jesus, Sylvie," he said. "I just wanted to—"

But I barely heard him. I was running for the door, and then I was outside, lurching down the porch steps to the sidewalk. Across the street, a young couple walked two golden retrievers, wheat-gold and wily; the woman spoke sharply as they strained at their collars. Nausea came over me, sudden and boiling. I turned away and retched over a storm drain, vomit tumbling colorfully through the slats. One of the dogs barked, and the woman clicked her tongue, glancing at me with alarm as she ushered them forward. When they turned onto Atwood, the block was empty. I stumbled ahead.

The wire fence that separated the train tracks from our house was overrun with ivy and backed by spindly trees. I stepped around it and began to walk down the length of the tracks, my feet inches from those gleaming steel bars. The air was cool and soft. I walked until I couldn't see our house anymore; then I hooked my fingers in the open diamonds of the fence, leaned back, and closed my eyes. When I opened them again—how much later, I wasn't sure—I heard a whinnying noise, grievous and faraway as a ghostly animal. The sound increased in urgency, accompanied by a bellowed horn and the ghastly screech of wheels on steel.

Though I had heard plenty of trains in Madison, I rarely saw one; at home, the dark lacework of the trees blotted the tracks from view. Electricity whipped through the air. As the train came closer, my whole body shook, and I wound my hands deeper into the fence. I pictured the flash of a searchlight, a thunderous rush of air, my body whisked like a leaf. It would be so easy, so quick. The tracks were squealing, now, the ground rumbling with energy. Fear roared inside me, and I tried to yank my hands free. But my knuckles had swollen, and the sharp pull did nothing. The first car loomed into view, round nosed and gleaming, and I screamed.

In one brutal movement, I ripped my hands from the fence and leapt to the other side of the tracks. The first car barreled past me, and the force of its trajectory knocked me to my knees. I crouched in the pebbled dirt—candy wrappers and soda cans, beer bottles rolling in the wind—as the other cars came into view.

I had pictured the majestic ferocity of old freight trains, the coal-black engine and husk of white steam. But this train was ramshackle and tired, with a child's crude design: blunt wheels, wagons in sallow shades of orange and yellow and brown. The sides were sprayed with graffiti. The train itself seemed to howl in protest, condemned to carry these stories, for how to clean a train—a pressure washer, a sandblaster?—and what would be the point, if the next night someone new came, spray paint in hand, to find the train's canvas cleaned and ready?

I coughed dust as the last car passed. This was no brick-red caboose: those had been phased out in the 1980s and '90s to cut costs, Gabe once told me—one of the random bits of knowledge I was no longer surprised he had. The manned caboose and its crew were deemed unnecessary, he said, the rails safe enough. The caboose conductor was replaced by an end-of-train device: a small electronic unit with a flashing red taillight.

But someone stood on the back of this car, his feet on the small aluminum platform, hands gripping the railing.

He wore layers of dark clothes and studded boots, a knit cap pulled low; a heavy beard hung down to his shoulders. A train hopper. I had heard they rode in open boxcars or in the wells behind cargo containers. With night falling, the man blended into the charcoal-colored car and the dusky sky. Perhaps this had emboldened him, or maybe he just wanted air. Every few seconds, the flashing red light illuminated his swan-shaped cheekbones and the tube clutched in one hand—a map? A newspaper? I couldn't tell.

As the engine pulled away, our eyes met, and sparks ran down my spine. He raised a hand in salute, and I did the same. Then the train sank into the darkness, swallowed like a stone in water, and just as unexpectedly as he had appeared, the man was gone.

# 18

The Vineyard feels much more benign than it used to. It's sunnier than it was in the summer of 2002, the product of a world hell-bent on heat. This year, seventy-degree days have been replaced by scorching stretches of drought, and the fertile plains of the Midwest are unable to bear food. The fog is a relief. Was it ever as foreboding, as secretive, as I once made it out to be? I'm eight years older now than I was that summer—in August, I'll turn thirty—and my anxiety about the fog, its powers of concealment, has slipped away from me. It's better that way, though I suppose the world has lost some of its glitter. It's as though I've peeled away some holographic veneer, and the world is stark, actual. Night fits obediently into its little box. And I, perhaps, fit obediently into mine.

It's been years since I dreamed the way I did in Madison. I don't walk in my sleep anymore—two nightly medications and four years of careful calibration have seen to that. It's strange; actually, the medications make my dreams easier to remember. I set up a video camera at the foot of the bed—an extreme measure, I know, which made me feel both protected and marginally insane—and each morning, I reeled through the previous night's videotape. Aside from the occasional twitch, I was slack as a sack of flour. This calmed me, and soon I came to enjoy my dreams. Other people dropped into a state as blank and idle as a sleeping computer. But every night, I got to go to the movies—my one concession to the way I used to be.

Or maybe that's just what I tell myself. There's a crack in that floor, and I stay as far away from it as possible. The truth is that there will always be a fault line in me, and fault lines are never a single, clean fracture; when the surface of your world is displaced, the plates shuffled and broken like china, you can never step as carelessly as you used to. The medications keep me asleep, and trying to find some pleasure in my dreams keeps me from hating them—or the place in me they come from. How can I explain how it feels to be constantly on guard, afraid not of what someone else could do to you but of what you might do to yourself? It's like owning a rottweiler: no matter how sweet she is at home, she'll speak for herself once she's off-leash in the dog park, and there's not a thing you can do to control the way she tears through the grass, the way she howls like sin; you can only smile with embarrassed apology at the other owners and mutter thinly, "She thinks she's a wolf."

Once I got to the Vineyard, I couldn't resist the urge to drive past the Snake Hollow compound, even though—or perhaps because—I knew it would look nothing like it used to. In the fall of 2008, a developer bought the compound, gutted the insides of the buildings, and began work on a two-year project that turned each one into a cluster of vacation condominiums. He kept the name—Snake Hollow, sure to attract couples in search of a storied, moody island escape—but to me it felt terribly wrong. I pulled smoothly into the driveway, which had been dug out and paved, and there they were: the three original structures, shingles painted the impeccable white of veneers.

Each building was roughly the same shape and size, but there were new appendages here and there: another porch, an extra wing. Each condominium had its own entrance, so that walkways jutted out of the building in various directions, crawling with guests. A family of five emerged from what was once the bunk room, clutching noodles and boogie boards and a giant yellow float in the shape of a slug; a child stood inside one of the windows of the old library, testing the air with her foot before being sucked into the room by an invisible parent. In front of the driveway, on a newly planted stretch of bright green grass, a young couple sat knock-kneed in sunglasses, sharing a peach. They looked at me with casual interest as I reversed out of the driveway.

On the side of the road, stalks of dune grass waved in salute or farewell. Twenty yards away was the beach, where a group of teenage boys stood with fishing poles. I slowed to watch them: their slender, eager bodies, the round whip of the lines. Every so often, a lone holler signaled a tug from the water. I still remember the night Keller returned to the compound from one of his afternoon walks with the gasping, sparkling body of a striped bass. Its jaw gaped, lips wide enough to hold a grapefruit. It wasn't even bloody. Silver-green, round-bellied and pulsing, the fish was so robustly itself that it was hard to believe it would soon be split, skin slipped off like a dress, and reincarnated on Keller's floral china plates, the meat buttered and fried to a crisp.

The sunset that night was startlingly neon—searing orange and highlighter pink as Keller paused in front of the French doors and the fish stilled. I wondered why it didn't resist him. I'd heard about the power of striped bass. They weighed as much as sixty pounds; mature, they had few enemies. But the one in Keller's hands was docile, resigned. Its eyes—even larger than a human's, the black irises pits in pools of yellow—stared out at the room with what seemed like attention, as if Keller were offering not death but a privilege. Here, he seemed to say, was life on land.

# 19

My mind wanted to forgive Gabe. But my body couldn't. I kept expecting to return to bed with him, but as the days passed, the charge around that room only gathered strength. I went upstairs to grab clothes or a book when he was out, and when I returned downstairs, I felt contaminated. Only one thing made me feel better: that Gabe didn't know—or wasn't sure about—what had happened at Thom's. At the time, it was my only, meager stitch of power. That knowledge, knowledge of how far I had gone, was what Keller and Gabe most desperately wanted. It was what they had spent years fishing for, what they were betting their careers on. And in the terrible weeks that followed, weeks I spent in a hazy state of limbo, I guarded it with everything I had left.

I slept on the couch and adopted Meredith Keller's method of RBD intervention, waking myself with a cell phone alarm before I could sink into REM sleep. It had never been so difficult to deny myself that most basic instinct. I was pulled toward sleep's depth and what awaited me there. Was Thom expecting me? Twice, the phone rang—once while Gabe was at the lab, and another time when he was home, though it stopped after the first ring—but I never picked up.

My memories of those final weeks are few, but static images, like postcards, surface now and then. Lying on the couch before dawn, half-asleep and wrapped in my coat. Standing before the bathroom mirror in the darkness of very early morning, turning the fluorescent lights on and off so that the bright shock kept me awake. Sitting at the kitchen table with a bowl of cereal and Gabe in the chair across, his eyes bleary but focused on me.

"Say something, Sylvie. Anything."

I didn't answer. Mostly, he knew enough to let me alone. I made the living room into a haven, for I was afraid to venture very far outside; the thought of seeing Thom was even worse than seeing Gabe. But it was not long before the outside came to me.

It was the beginning of April, one week after I found my file at the lab, and I had spent it indoors. I'd sent Keller a brief e-mail saying that I had come down with the flu to buy time while I thought through what to do—whether and how to confront him, whether and how to leave. But my brain was foggy, and I was spending less and less time conscious. While Gabe was at the lab, I dozed in my coat on the living room couch. My sleep was never deep enough to be satisfying, which made it easy to fall in and out of it. So when I heard a sharp rapping at the door, I rose.

I expected to see Keller, but it was Janna. She stood barefoot on the porch in a pink silk pajama top and what looked like Thom's jeans. They sank into folds around her knees and ankles. She had dyed her hair an unnatural, all-over red. And she was staring at me expectantly, as if it was I who was on her porch and not the other way around.

"May I come in?" she asked finally.

I nodded. She stepped lightly through the door. I became conscious of the living room and its air of agoraphobia: the windows covered with black sheets, coats crumpled on the couch and floor. In the air was the damp, close smell of bodies. She looked at the video camera I'd set up at the foot of the couch and averted her eyes.

"Can I get you something to drink?" I asked.

"Anything with alcohol."

Her tone was almost flirtatious. But beneath it was a stale tone of affect, of attempt.

"All right," I said. I walked to the refrigerator and opened it: eggs, a scattering of leftovers, old cold cuts for lab lunches. Nestled in the back was a half-full bottle of old white wine. I sniffed it and poured a glass.

"Actually," said Janna, "don't bother."

She had seated herself at the kitchen table. Her silk top, oversized, pooled on the chair.

Not knowing what else to do with it, I kept the glass for myself. I sat down across from her. She was silent. Months earlier, I would have tried to make conversation, but now I was exhausted. I stared at my wineglass, fingered the thin flute. Slowly, my nervous system was waking up, pawing its way through the grogginess of afternoon. It was minutes before I noticed Janna staring at me.

"You don't look well," she said.

It would have been less painful if I had detected a tone of insult. But her voice was bare of its playful filigree, its musical lilt. Even the nasal clip of her Finnish accent had softened.

I'm not sure how long we sat like that together. It felt to me like hours, but in reality it must have been no more than a few minutes.

Abruptly, Janna stood. "It smells in here."

When I call up that memory now, I see her in the loose pajama top, her nostrils flared and her stomach already pushing against the waistband of Thom's jeans. But I think I've added that detail in hindsight; at the time, I later learned, she was no more than four months along.

I followed Janna to the door and out onto the porch. She began to lean toward me, as if to lay her head on my shoulder. Her cheek brushed mine. I don't know why I didn't pull away.

"If you come into my house again," she hissed, "I'll call the police."

Without meeting my eyes, she turned toward the screen door. There was a quick flutter of air as it opened and closed, and then she was gone.

• • •

At that time, I could count on one hand the people whose phone numbers I knew and whom I spoke to with any intimacy. I had long since lost touch with any of my college friends. I called my mother.

I still marvel at the speed and efficiency with which she extricated me from life in Madison. I didn't tell her about my participation in Keller's experiments, and whatever her suspicions, she took me at my word: it was only a bad breakup. Like most young people, I'd convinced myself that her romantic life had begun and would end with my father. But as we flew from Madison to Cleveland, then from Cleveland to Newark, she resurrected an animated lineup of past boyfriends. During the layover, my mother—my frugal mother, wearing the same faded jeans and clogs she'd had since I was born, with the original suede skinned off the toe—treated me to an epic airport feast: steak frites from the flashiest, most overpriced grill in Cleveland international, topped off with a brownie sundae that was probably illegal in some states. She stopped short of carrying my luggage; I asked at baggage claim, whiny with exhaustion, and she gave me a look equivalent to a sharp kick. At home, she babied me for a few weeks—doing the laundry, making my favorite minestrone soup—before telling me it was time that I decided what to do next, and I better not think about living alone.

"What other choice do I have?" I asked. "I don't know anyone."

I was sitting on the couch in my dad's old sweatpants, eating Funyuns out of the bag, and I couldn't decide whether I was pleased or disgusted with myself.

"Find a roommate on Craigslist," she said. "People do it every day. Or call Hannah, from high school."

"How?" I asked. "We didn't have cell phones back then—I wouldn't even know how to reach her."

My mother sighed and walked out of the room. When I heard the quick patter of her footsteps on the stairs, I figured she was giving up on me. But less than a minute later, she reappeared in the living room doorway and tossed a heavy, spiral-bound book at me. It landed at my feet with a self-satisfied smack.

I picked it up: the old Mills directory, an impressive inch and a half thick, which included a dense section on the school's rules and history before getting to the good stuff. Having everyone's home address and phone number felt deliciously valuable then, as benign as it seems in today's obsessively public, networked world: I remember crowding over a San Francisco map with Hannah to look up her crush's address and repeating Gabe's home phone number in my head until I had it down by heart. But the directory was almost a decade old now. The phone number listed for Hannah rang so long that I was about to hang up, convinced that her parents had sold the farm, when there was a plastic clatter and her mother's melodious hello. I could still picture her soft pale braid, her browned and callused palms, the way she bent over the rosemary bushes in the garden as if checking on sleeping infants.

Hannah wasn't there; she was in Berkeley, her mother said, with more than a touch of pride, after finishing culinary school in New York. She'd spent a year working on an organic farm in Canada, and now she was an assistant chef at a vegetarian restaurant. Ingrid asked how I was ("Er, fine") and gave me Hannah's cell phone number. I was worried we wouldn't know what to say to each other, but Hannah was so enthusiastic, Stevie Wonder playing in the background, that my nerves dissolved ("Hang on a sec, let me turn that down—I've got my pump-up music on, you know I can't wake up otherwise— Sylvie! Jesus Christ, girl, it's been ages!").

She was living in a squat, sixties apartment building in the Gourmet Ghetto ("Hideous—we're talking wood-paneled walls and orange shag carpeting, but what can you do?") with her ex-boyfriend, a chef at the same restaurant ("Don't ask— it's about as terrible as it sounds, but it's only for another nine weeks, not that I'm counting, and on the upside, he's obsessively tidy and does all of my dishes"). Their lease was up at the end of July, and she needed a new roommate.

"I'd love to have you, obviously," she said. It was nine in the morning in California, and I could hear her bustling around the kitchen: the clink of a knife, plates rattling, the swift wheeze of a window being pushed up. "But what would you do here?"

"I've been thinking about going back to school, actually," I said. It was true—I still had that damn application for readmission, and it was becoming clear that this was my best option. I knew that if I lived with my parents for much longer I'd become self-pityingly depressed, and I needed a college degree. "I could come out in August, get a job waiting tables while I work on my application. Maybe I could start up in the spring semester."

And that was what happened. I spent the early summer tying up loose ends in Newark, not that I had many: I packed my bags, trashed my mementos of Snake Hollow and my photos of Gabe. I ate more consecutive dinners with my parents than I ever had as a kid. In June, Rodney came home from college, where he was studying creative writing; in the evening, we kicked a Hacky Sack around as the sun's golden yolk smeared the backyard. After weeks of apartment hunting, Hannah found a turrety little Victorian just blocks from her restaurant. She sent me photos via e-mail: two bedrooms, a turquoise-tiled bathroom, space for a garden.

I could put Gabe out of my mind during the day, but at night, memories of him throbbed beneath my skin. I dreamed of his off-kilter smile, the particular tenor of his voice, and woke sweaty and gasping. I didn't pick up his phone calls, though each one was a fresh puncture, followed by a dull ache that lasted for days. If he asked me to come back, if he told me again that he loved me, I didn't trust myself to move to California. It would be so easy to slip back into our life together before I even knew I was doing it—to edge quietly through the door like a teenager returning after a long night out, to climb the stairs and take my old, soft place beside him in bed. He would wake up to find me there, fold his body around mine in habit before the surprise of it registered. But I would have to return to Keller, too—to the bare halls of the lab, the perpetual exhaustion, and the stagnant, indoor air. I felt as if I'd spent years within the glass segments and cyclical view of a revolving door. Outside, I was so dizzy that I could probably have fainted on command, but at least there was wind.

Gabe wasn't the only one who called me. My cell phone rang constantly, the area codes ranging from Madison to Massachusetts, and the voice mails were all from Keller. In the beginning, they were curt—*Sylvia, it's Adrian; I need you to call me*—but as the days passed, his voice became strained, an undercurrent of panic impossible to cover up. He called from the private number at the lab, his Boston-based cell phone, and eventually, from pay phones. Ignoring him made me feel sickened and blasphemous, but I never picked up.

Instead, I wrote a letter. The silver lining of Anne March's

trial was that it gave me a prepackaged excuse. I can still recall, with mild embarrassment, the convolution of the first
paragraph: *Though the past three years of my life have been
dedicated to my work with you, and I have believed in that work
as ardently as my conscience has allowed, certain events of late
have forced me to see our research, and its terrible complications,
in a new light. It is with great sadness that I recuse myself from
an effort in which I have been so profoundly invested, but I can
no longer ignore the evidence that suggests our work has been of
primarily negative consequence to the lives of our participants
and their loved ones.*

I wrote that I wouldn't share the details of our work with
the media or the police, and I've kept that promise, though
I've never been able to figure out whether it was for their sake
or my own. In return, I asked Gabe not to tell Keller what I'd
learned. I've no idea whether he honored his part of the pact;
in any event, when the case against Anne came to a sudden
close later that summer—Anne changed her plea to guilty
and was sentenced, without a trial, to twenty-six years in a
federal prison for women—Keller's calls dwindled to a stop.

Maybe even he knew by then that an era was coming to
a close. While in Berkeley, I followed him and Gabe from
afar. They continued on for another two years, traveling like
vagabonds from one college town to the next. They spent the
fall after I left in Ann Arbor, the spring in Bloomington. From
there, the universities became more and more obscure. After
the 2005-2006 academic year, which they spent in a small
New York college so far upstate that it bordered Canada, their
work was no longer tied to any school at all.

I've often wondered how they felt in those final months,
when the East Coast was just beginning to wake after a winter
in hibernation. Were they filled with despair, so incongruous
when the outside world was in bloom? Or did they surrender
quietly? They must have known that their time had come and

gone. As the twenty-first century continued, nobody wanted to learn how to live in their dreams—they just wanted to stay asleep. Out was the touchy-feely naval-gazing of the eighties and nineties; when gas prices were soaring, ice caps were melting, and resources were becoming thin, insurance was the best thing money could buy. *You'll Sleep Like a Baby*, one mattress ad promised—and what was more attractive, more elusive, than that sort of ignorance, harder-won in adulthood but no less blessed?

I should have felt a sense of redemption when Interactive Lucid Dreaming finally dissolved, but all I felt was mourning. Until that moment, the research itself had stood as witness to my life, both personal and professional. When Keller dropped out of the academic landscape, his work as brief and brilliant as a species gone extinct, it was as if none of it had ever happened at all.

# 20

Five months after I left Madison, in October of 2005, my mother called on the half-broken Nokia I'd brought to Berkeley. A letter had come to my parents' house, addressed to me. At least, it appeared to be a letter: it was a thick, large envelope, taped shut over the tack. Three stamps were pressed in the upper left corner. The return address was Gabe's. She had mailed it to me.

"Don't read it," said Hannah. "It'll only torture you. Who cares what he has to say?"

Hannah was, and still is, the only person who knows the story in all its humiliating detail. I had already told her about how I'd reconnected with Gabe and had left school to join him, but she knew nothing of my work with Keller until our first night in California. We were sitting on the living room couch, eating takeout from the vegan place down the block whose utter lack of cheese and meat made it clear I was no longer in Wisconsin. The room was hedged with boxes, and I barely recognized Hannah: the slight, wiry girl I'd known at Mills had became tall and womanly, butter skinned, her curly hair piled in a bun and held with chopsticks. She had gained weight, but it suited her: with her sturdy, round thighs and flushed cheeks, she looked as if she had grown into the body she was always meant to have. I couldn't help it. I began to cry.

"What is it?" she asked, setting her seitan on the ground.

Before I could stop myself, I was telling her everything. She listened to me with quiet focus, her blue eyes wide and barely blinking. The gentle attention of an old friend, of someone who wanted nothing from me, was enough to make me cry harder. I blew my nose so loudly that Hannah leaned away, laughing until she snorted.

"She's still got it," she said.

When Gabe's letter came, she stood between me and the counter where it sat like a parent separating two warring children. For the first few days, the curiosity gnawed at me so badly that we stuffed the envelope in a shoe box in her closet. Soon, though, I realized I had more power if I didn't know what was inside it. What if Gabe revealed something new? What if he asked me to come back or let go of me completely? I wanted none and all of these things to be true. And for the first time in my life, I learned the value of ignorance. We drove to the beach boardwalk in Santa Cruz and drank cheap, warm beer, sitting on the dock with our feet in the surf, screaming as the Giant Dipper dropped. We huddled in dive bars with her coworkers deep into the morning; hours later, I hiked across campus to gather signatures for my readmission forms and course preferences, as sleep deprived and coffee-high as any other undergrad.

I was twenty-five and a college senior, but I didn't feel like either one of them. I'd been so serious about college the first time around—even my relationship with David had felt like a kind of work-study. Now, if only to take my mind off Gabe, I was determined to have fun. On weekends, Hannah and I took BART into San Francisco and went dancing downtown. I had never been so close to that many bodies at once, writhing and shouting en masse; with the music pounding and dizzyingly sweet drinks coursing through my blood, I could almost forget myself. It was a tradition of ours: even years later, when I finished my undergraduate degree and began the PhD, we made a monthly pilgrimage to our favorite spot. On one of these nights, Hannah spotted a curly-haired man with a suit jacket thrown over his shoulder, standing at the bar and eyeing us with amusement. "Go on," she said, "he's smiling at you"—so I marched over to the bar, brave with vodka, and flirted with him so flagrantly that he asked for my number before pulling me onto the dance floor.

With Gabe's letter tucked safely away, I had tricked myself into believing that I could control whether and when news of him came into my life. In fact, after four years in Berkeley, I had practically forgotten the letter itself. But one afternoon in May, when I had just gotten home after teaching a section of Abnormal Psych—all grad students were required to TA introductory courses in return for tuition remission—Hannah bounded through the door. She was breathing hard, one hand still on the knob.

"You'll never guess who I saw on the train," she said.

"The guy from the club?" My curly-haired dance partner hadn't called, not that I blamed him—I could barely remember what we'd talked about, though I did remember stepping on his shoes so many times that he asked whether it was my signature dance move.

Hannah shook her head. "Michael Fritz."

The name hit me like a rush of cold air. Michael Fritz—one of Gabe's best friends at Mills. Hair the color of flame and a snigger of a laugh.

"Yeah?" I asked, feigning casualness. I was stirring pasta water, and my hand on the wooden spoon was already clammy. "What's he doing here?"

"He's working for a start-up. Something to do with data technology." Hannah closed the door and kicked off her clogs, walked to the couch. "Hey—sit down with me for a sec, will you?"

The pasta had two minutes left, but I turned off the water and drained it, dumped it into a bowl with a powdery packet of orange cheese. I sat down beside her and picked at the shells. Hannah's breath was shallow, her cheeks flushed.

"Gabe has a kid," she said.

The pasta was underdone; it crunched between my teeth, stiff and rubbery as plastic. I spat it out, my heart rattling.

"What?"

"I know, Sylvie," said Hannah, putting a hand on my knee. "I wasn't sure if I should tell you, but I thought—in the long run, you know . . . I thought it'd help you move on."

"Who is she?"

"It's a boy."

"The mother," I said.

"Oh." Hannah nodded, inhaling. "Apparently, he met her in upstate New York, when he and Keller were working at that college—the one near Canada?"

"Was she a researcher? Or a student?"

"No, no. I think she worked in the town. Sarah something? Works as a receptionist in a dental office—or maybe it's a chiropractor, I can't remember. Anyway, he met her there and stayed. Mike visited them on a business trip last year— drove up from Albany. She's nice, he said. Laughs a lot. Gabe seems happy."

I nodded and walked to the window. I couldn't bear the weight of her gaze. When she left for the restaurant that evening, I waited only minutes before going into her closet. I found the shoe box beneath a stack of winter sweaters, Gabe's envelope on the bottom. I couldn't wait to bring it to my room; I sat down against the closet wall, Hannah's white work shirts grazing my knees, and ripped the envelope open. I wouldn't admit it, but I hoped to find a plea—Gabe begging me to come back to him, moving on only when he received the silence of my answer.

I tore open the top of the envelope. Inside were two paintbrushes. The wooden handles were caked in color, but the bristles had been newly cleaned. They were my favorite brushes, ones I'd had since Mills. Gabe had wrapped them in lined paper, and when I unfolded the page, I saw he had scrawled something inside it.

*I hope you're still painting, Sylve, and that you're not*
*covering them up anymore. I never wanted you to.*
                                        *Love,*
                                        *Gabe*

*P.S. I'm so sorry.*

I put it on the floor of Hannah's closet with the brushes on top, my throat constricting. I was about to throw the envelope away when I noticed that something else was crumpled at the bottom. It was a glossier piece of paper, folded and unfolded so many times that it was now as soft as fabric. When I smoothed it open, I saw that it had been ripped from Mills's fall 1999 alumni quarterly. Gabe had circled a photo that took up half the page. *Such Great Heights*, read the caption beneath: *The class of '99 watches an eclipse.*

And there we were: David Horikawa making an ill-fated tower of apples, Michael Fritz balancing his tray on his head, Hannah pointing at the moon with her head thrown back. I was kneeling beside her, following her hand. Only Gabe sat apart from the larger group. He was leaning back on his arms, several feet behind us, and he wasn't looking at the sky. He was looking at me.

In the pit of my stomach, I felt a low swirl of mourning. If I could arc back through time and begin again, winding the spool of thread back to that hill and the gaping blackness of the sky—if I could change what I'd said when Gabe asked me to come with him, what would I do? I pictured the gate to Keller's garden, the bloom of the doubled flower, the whole ache of possibility. And I knew that I still would have followed him.

• • •

To my surprise, the guy from the club called that weekend. His name was Jesse. He lived on Polk Street, and he wanted to take me to dinner. I borrowed and belted one of Hannah's floral dresses—at seventy-eight degrees, San Francisco was in the middle of a heat wave—and took the train to the city. Like a giant steel caterpillar, it wound through the lit world of the Castro: past the brightly colored banners and the men in leather, the neon signs of stores with names like Does Your Mother Know, and uphill, into the muted and staggering streets by Randall Park. I got off at Alamo Square—lights threading through trees, the smell of sweat and barbecue ember—and walked to the seafood bistro he'd chosen. He was already there, an open menu on his plate, his chin resting in one hand.

Jesse: a cherub's curly, close-cropped hair, a small space between his two front teeth. When he smiled, the skin around his eyes crinkled like cellophane. He grew up in the Hudson Valley, the only child of parents who owned an outdoor theater company, and ran as far away as he could: all the way to law school in California, where he'd never have to sweep another stage or play Mustardseed—"Five lines, yellow tights"—when there weren't any child actors available. I worried that he was too normal for me, but when I told him I'd spent most of my twenties doing experimental dream research, he looked up from his mussels and grinned.

"Few weeks ago?" he said. "I had this dream that I lived on a sex farm run by Carol Burnett."

"A sex farm?"

"And here I thought you were going to give me shit about Carol Burnett."

"We'll get there," I said, my laughter a release; I hadn't realized how nervous I was. "But really—what *is* a sex farm?"

"Not a clue. In the dream, of course, it was clear as day—sorry, couldn't resist—but when I woke up? Damned if I could tell you."

He rode home with me on BART, even though I told him I wouldn't let him stay over. ("I gave you the wrong impression, that night at the club," I said as we hurtled through the pitch-black underground, our hands in our own laps. "I usually don't step on a guy's feet until at *least* the third date.") But when we climbed into bed, our bodies tenting the sheets, it was he who buttoned the top of Hannah's dress back up and suggested we just sleep.

*Gabe has a child*, I said to myself. *Gabe has a son.* Beside me, Jesse's breath was deep and slow, his body exquisitely unfamiliar. I pictured Gabe's bulldog jaw, his broad palms, in miniature—pictured a baby with someone else's nose and a troll tuft of hair on Gabe's shoulders, reaching for the ceiling as they walked. The two of them building a house of Lincoln Logs or splashing in the tub, surrounded by rubber creatures and soap scum. I knew he would tend to the kid with the same dedication he did our research. He would stay up late reading parenting books; he would teach the boy to spot poison ivy, to catch bugs in jars, to turn over stones. He would point to the busy, roiling worlds beneath them: the ants seaming the mud, the dogged wildflowers, here a newt. He would take the tender, green body in both hands and hold it up to the light, for however long it would stay there.

# 21

MARTHA'S VINEYARD, MASSACHUSETTS, 2010

To the east of Martha's Vineyard lies the small incorporated island of Chappaquiddick, accessible only by way of a three-car ferry. Technically a part of Edgartown, Chappaquiddick feels separate, wilder and less traveled than its mainland counterpart. The roads are mostly unpaved, and the houses are farther apart. Dune grass and poison ivy braid along its coast. In the relative absence of human life, the beaches have flourished: they crawl with hermit crabs and ticks, the water full of foot-long, iridescent bluefish. Perhaps people were scared off by the Chappaquiddick incident of July 18, 1969, when Senator Ted Kennedy drove off Dike Bridge into the rocky water below—where his only passenger, a teacher named Mary Jo Kopechne, drowned.

Digital modes of tracking and detection have made it more difficult for someone like Keller to live off the map. I found him on Instant Checkmate, a website that gives paid subscribers access to the phone number and address of anyone in the United States. With Keller's equal appetites for intrigue and solitude, I was not surprised to find him on this island. His house is in the northwest corner of a large, grassy knoll. A woman bicycles down the road as I sit in the car, the engine idle. When she passes, the street is empty.

I put the car into park and turn off the ignition. It is four thirty in the afternoon, the sun hazy and diffuse. I've checked out of the motel in Edgartown. After this, I'll turn around again and begin the long journey back west. Just as I'm about to unlock the door, a wave of heat rolls through my body, and my vision goes starry. It only lasts a second, but it's enough to knock the air out of me. I count to ten, inhaling slowly, and then I take out my cell phone. Hannah picks up on the first ring.

"I can't do it," I say. "I'm terrified. I just had a fucking hot flash."

"Jesus, Sylve, what is it with the hot flashes? You better not be going menopausal on me." But there is warmth in her voice, and I can practically see the dimples in her cheeks, distinct as fingers pressed in dough. "You *can* do it. I'm positive. You wouldn't have made it all the way to his freaking house if there was a shred of doubt in your mind. Remember why you're there."

"Why am I here?"

"To get closure," she says. "To show him that you're different now, that you're strong. That you're not hiding or ashamed."

I nod, though I know she can't see me, and look at the house. It's smaller than many of the others in this area, beach mansions made New England–modest by their lack of distinction, but it has the same white trim and cedar shingles. They haven't yet turned to silver, which means the house can't be very old. I wonder how recently he moved here. Did he build the house himself? To calm myself, I picture Hannah sitting on the paisley couch we found at a church rummage sale with a bowl of cherry tomatoes in her lap, looking out at the used bookstore on Shattuck. Hannah with a leg tucked underneath her and a red bandana holding her hair back. A brush of flour on her nose, her old cut-off jean shorts.

"Sylvie?"

"I'm here."

"Good. Was worried you might have fallen asleep on me."

"Screw you," I say, laughing, and something in my chest is gratefully dislodged. I think of quarters shaken out of a vending machine, their palmable brilliance. Something to keep with me. "Okay. I'm going in."

"That's my girl," says Hannah. "Oh, and one more thing. If it's appropriate? Give Keller a kick in the balls from me."

"I can pretty much assure you that won't be appropriate."

I pop the lock on the door and step out, smelling the salt in the air, the sweetness of the warm grass.

"Stranger things have happened," Hannah says.

When we hang up, I don't let myself hesitate. With the sun hot against my arms, I walk along the wooden fence that separates the hill from the road. Though I could easily climb over it, I decide to go through a low gate, latched but unlocked. The grass on the knoll is uncut, swaying knee-high with the breeze, and there is no path to the house. Does Keller want to deter people from coming here? Or does he rarely leave the house himself? There is a small gray door with a lion's head for a knocker. But before I can reach for it, noises of movement come from inside the house: slow and creaking at first, then faster and deeper in pitch, as if the building is waking after a long hibernation. The doorknob begins to shake, coughing rust, and then the edge of the door is pulled back into the house.

And there he is. I calculated on the ferry that he must be fifty-seven. He has changed, I see now, in ways that only someone close to him would notice: a thinning of the face, a slight droop in the skin around his eyes.

"Ah," he says. He takes off his glasses and squints; his

irises, a clear and watery blue, seem to widen as the lids contract. "Sylvia."

He smiles. At once I feel a rush of affection for him. He wears a pair of scrub pants and a collared shirt, a canvas apron wrapped around his waist. This is, in part, what I have come for—proof that he has aged, that he is no longer almighty.

Then he puts his glasses back on, and the old feelings return: the resentment, the terror—the sense that he has visited me, and not the other way around. All feelings I've come here to do away with.

"You've found me," he says, "how sly of you"—and now he is opening the door all the way, ushering me into a front hall filled with the fading natural light of afternoon and the dank smell of soil.

"I should have given you warning."

"No, no, that's all right. You've every right to surprise me."

But he doesn't look surprised. He is, I can tell, in one of his lighthearted moods. I expected him to be caught off guard, to ask me why I've come. Instead, he is playing host, as though I'm simply an old friend who has stopped by on the way elsewhere.

"Sylvia," he says again, leading me into the living room. "What a pleasure. Can I get you a drink? Water? Or something else?"

"Water is fine."

This side of the house is mostly in shadow. He walks through a low entryway into the kitchen, and from there he flicks on a light that brings the living room into view. There is a small brown couch, a reclining chair, and an old table piled with books. Everywhere else, though, are plants: trees potted in the corners, succulents hanging from the ceiling, flowers climbing the walls. Their leaves are pungent and fleshy, grotesquely ripe. All over is the close, moist smell of growth. I can't help it; I cover my nose with my sleeve.

Keller returns to the room and hands me a glass of water.

"So you've found my perennials. Gorgeous, aren't they? They get just enough sun. I've never had a green thumb. But the terrific thing about succulents"—he takes a seat in the reclining chair, gesturing toward the ceiling—"is that they prefer neglect. Truly: they thrive on it."

His affect is still one of ease. But he's talking too much, too quickly. I see now that what I thought were the contours of the chair is actually the imprint of his body. He fits perfectly inside it, like rubber in a mold.

"I can't stay for long," I say. "But there are a few things I want to say first."

Am I imagining it, or does a sudden blankness come over his face—an instinctive absence, the chalkboard wiped clean?

"First," I say, "I don't want to talk about Gabe."

"Very well. He told me he tried to reach you—years ago, it must be now."

"He wrote a note."

"And you didn't reply."

It isn't an accusation, but it's not a question, either—just a scientist's habit of blank-filling and estimation.

"No. I didn't."

He waits for me to continue. I shift on the couch, warm. Despite the weather, I've worn pants.

"I drove past Snake Hollow yesterday," I say.

"I'm sorry to hear that." He smiles. "It's hideously changed, of course. I'd rather you be able to remember it as it was."

"I'm sorry you sold it. It was Meredith's, wasn't it? Your wife's?"

"It belonged to her family, then to her. And when she died, it belonged to me."

"They didn't mind when you gave it up?"

He raises an eyebrow.

292 · CHLOE BENJAMIN

"It was their suggestion, I'm afraid. Too many bad memories associated with that house—and worse, perhaps, too many good ones. They were in favor of selling it right after she died. I held on a little longer. But everything, good and bad, must come to an end."

Keller cocks his head. His lenses flash with light.

"Does that make it less alluring to you?" he asks. "No family drama, no bitter struggle?"

Again, the clinical voice—the weighed curiosity of a professor, imbued with just the right amount of mildness. Still, I'm startled into silence. He stands and walks to the kitchen. When he returns, he holds a green watering can with a bulging belly and a thin, long spout.

"She was very much like you, in fact." He waters the soil around a ficus, dirt splattering his hands. "Very inquisitive, especially when it came to her own mind. A touch of obsessiveness—later, of course, more than a touch of it. And the capacity for self-destruction."

"Everyone has that capacity."

"You're right. But in some of us it goes unfulfilled." He stands the watering can upright and wipes its nozzle on his apron. "Still, I wasn't referring to your disorder. More, I would say, your inability to let go."

"And you don't think that's what Meredith did?"

"My wife didn't kill herself to let go. She did it to hold on—to life as she knew it, to herself as she was."

The surprise is wearing off, and now I'm eager. He has given me license; I've wanted a fight.

"Is that why you left San Francisco? Holed up in a small town in Northern California and began to teach high school students? Or was it that they were easier to control?"

"It's true that I left the university when my wife died." His voice is clipped, and I can tell I've prodded him. "I thought I could live a quieter life at a place like Mills. But it began to feel cowardly, such an obvious lie. So I returned to my research. I tried to do it in her honor. Moving forward, all while respecting the past—it's a delicate balance, Sylvie, and I don't claim to have mastered it."

"In her honor," I say. "Or was it that you got inspired again? At Mills, you had a whole new group of subjects. Stu Cappleman. Me. You'd be nothing without your patients, but the saddest part is that you haven't helped any of us. You want to know what Meredith and I have in common, Adrian? You. You wrenched us open and used your tools to rummage around in our minds until everything inside got squiggly and confused. It's just like what happened to Anne March. You left us worse off than we started."

"Oh, Sylvie." Keller frowns in disappointment, as though I've failed an easy test. "That's very simplistic. I thought I'd at least taught you that life is never so black and white. Besides, look at you now. You're, what—thirty years old? You went back to school. You seem to be thriving."

"Which has nothing to do with you. Those were my accomplishments." I pause. "And how did you know?"

"I've followed your success. You spoke at the ceremony, didn't you?"

The year I finished my undergraduate degree, I was asked, along with two other nontraditional students, to give a speech at the commencement ceremony. The university wanted us to paint them as a progressive institution, embracing of difference and alternative paths. The fact that Keller can still follow me, however benignly, triggers the paranoia that sits under my skin like an implant.

"Don't worry," he says. "No bugs. I saw an article in the *Chronicle*. I meant to write to Mills, in fact. I thought your story might be of interest to the alumni quarterly."

"I'm glad you didn't. My story isn't yours to hand out."

Keller opens his mouth as if to speak, then closes it again.

He looks at his lap, his lips pursed in what is either a gesture of contemplation or a small smile. I wonder, suddenly, if he's slipping, his mind fraying with age. In that case, it could be difficult to get much from this visit at all.

"Sylvie," he says quietly. Then he stands, wipes his hands on his apron, and walks toward the kitchen. "Can I get you anything else? Something to eat? A piece of fruit?"

"I won't be staying long."

He waits in the doorway to the kitchen.

"Fine. A piece of fruit."

He returns with an apple and places it on the table in front of me. Then he settles back into the recliner again.

"I've been afraid of this," he says. "Afraid you'd come to me. Not for my sake—you can ask me whatever you like, and I'll answer you. But I doubt there's anything I could say to give you the closure you want."

"You can let me be the judge of that," I say. But already I feel the wind stilling inside me, sails beginning to fold in defeat.

A faint ticking noise comes from the kitchen. Through the open archway, I see an octagonal wooden clock. The hands point to the place where five o'clock should be, but the numbers are heaped in a jumble at the bottom of the clock's face. At the top, in block letters, are the words WHO CARES?

"I want to understand how it happened," I say. "I want to know how I did what I did."

"I doubt I can tell you anything that you don't already know." He takes off his glasses and rubs his nose—that old, familiar gesture. "You were unusual; you had both the fine motor skills of a sleepwalker and the vivid dreams of an RBD patient."

"Parasomnia overlap disorder," I said.

Keller nodded. "A fascinating case. As a sleepwalker, you were remarkably skilled: your mobility and speech as advanced as I've ever seen. An observer—uninformed, of course—might have thought you were awake."

"I tried to figure out whether I was dreaming. I thought I must have been, because I kept seeing Meredith. How was that possible?"

Keller raised his eyebrows.

"Sleepwalkers can interact with the real world, but visual hallucinations aren't uncommon. You were dexterous and agile, clearly able to communicate, but you were still asleep. It stands to reason that your mind would incorporate some things that were real and some that were not. That's part of the reason why the disorder can be so dangerous." He sighed. "But you were on the brink of lucidity. If you had only stayed with us until the end of the semester—even another month—I think you would have achieved it."

"Yeah? And what would have happened then?"

Keller's eyes were far away. He stroked the skin beneath his chin.

"My guess is that an opportunity would have been created—space for your conscious and subconscious minds to reconcile. Once you became consciously aware of your subconscious activity, your sleep disorder could have resolved—and, aired in the aboveground arena of the consciousness, your repressed urges might have followed suit. Lucidity could have made you aware of the moment when you left your bed for the neighbor's house, for example; ideally, you would have been able to stop yourself. But if I knew with any certainty, I doubt we'd be sitting here now."

"No. You'd be the head of the neuroscience department at a cushy university, wouldn't you? Sitting in a choice office with a spectacular campus view? And where would I be?"

Keller doesn't blink. "In the office down the hall."

"That's absurd. You really think you would have gone to the university, put out a press release, told them your most successful experiment revolved around your assistant? The scientific community would have laughed in your face. And there's something else I don't understand."

Keller is quiet. He watches with interest as I inhale and begin again.

"There were too many clues. That's what I keep thinking about—how I didn't figure it out sooner. You knew I was assigned to the file reorganization project, but you didn't hide Meredith's file. You asked me about my nightmares, and you had Gabe drop hints, ask me whether I was lucid or if I saw my hand."

The hall falls into shadow as a cloud passes over the sun. Keller settles farther back in his chair.

"So I have this theory," I say. "I think you wanted me to know about it. I think your time was running out, and you were getting impatient. So you nudged me. Dropped a hint here and there. Tried to get me to realize something I wouldn't on my own."

"We were experimenting," says Keller, "with methodology."

"Methodology. You should be jailed."

His face still doesn't change. But he crosses one leg over the other and clasps his hands, pulling his elbows toward the chair, as if retracting into himself.

"You're lucky," I say. "You're lucky I still have a shred of loyalty to you. I can't say why."

"Sylvie. What is it you wanted out of this visit? Did you want to see me stripped, displaced, an old man living alone?"

"I want to know what you've *learned*," I hiss. "Your wife kills herself, you manipulate your own researcher, you're practically an accessory to murder, and then you abscond to Martha's Vineyard. So what did you learn, Adrian? Where has all of this high-minded research gotten you? Was it worth it?"

I stand, my jaw locked with something like despair. I've

fantasized so many times about saying these things to him—telling him off, cutting him down, watching his face fall and his veneer crack. In real life, though, it doesn't feel good. It feels humiliating—for each of us individually, for both of us together. I think of the time in my sophomore year of college when, home for the holidays, I opened the bathroom door to find my father getting out of the shower. He squawked, pulling the shower curtain around him, but it was too late. The curtain was clear. We never spoke of it again.

Keller stands, too, pushing with effort out of the recliner.

"I have to believe that it was," he says.

The sky is warming in color: the sun rusty and smudged, the horizon line a ribboned, bloodshot red. When I was driving from Berkeley to Martha's Vineyard—beneath the orange stalks of the Golden Gate Bridge, through Nevada's feverish lights and across the northern plains of Missouri—I imagined how I would leave Keller's house: a slammed door, a final word, a look I'd make sure he'd remember.

Reality, though, is never so satisfying. He walks me to the door and opens it. Then he pauses, one hand on the knob.

"I'm terribly sorry," he says.

Perhaps it is an act of generosity: the gift of closure, however belated. Perhaps, pulled by the yoke of conscience, he wants deliverance himself. But I detect, too, the peevishness of a child pushed forward by a parent and forced to apologize.

I look at him without responding. Then I step outside into the wild, green dune grass and climb back to the car. I'm ready to go home.

# 22

SEATTLE, WASHINGTON, 2009

A year ago, I visited Rodney in Seattle, where he works for a start-up that develops games for smartphones. All of the games are supposed to offer mental and physiological benefits. Rodney had spent the past year developing ShepherdZZZ, a game that is literally supposed to put you to sleep: the objective is to shepherd a lost, hyper sheep back to its herd via a battery of dizzying obstacles so overstimulating that most users are exhausted in less than fifteen minutes.

Rodney picked me up at the airport in a Zipcar. He'd inherited our father's height and our mother's quick hazel eyes; his hair was shoulder length, tied back in a short ponytail. He looked more mature than I'd ever seen him and also, somehow, impossibly young.

"It's basically a dream job," he said, pulling onto the highway. "Initially, there were like, four employees, and now there are thirty of us, running around like gerbils. But the really great thing is that it's so innovative. It's like a baby Google. Baby Apple. I mean, we get *creativity* time. And paternity leave!"

"What's creativity time?"

"You know," he said, waving one hand. "Creativity time?

A bunch of companies are doing it. It's basically half an hour each day when we can play Ping-Pong or read for pleasure or wander around, lost in creative thought. It's supposed to be really generative. We get paid for it."

The week before, Rodney had e-mailed me the link for ShepherdZZZ, along with an employees-only free download code.

"It'll save you the five dollars," he said. "You need it."

"The app or the five dollars?" I asked.

"Both, probably," he said brightly. "Grad school and all."

Rodney was hired right out of college. Now he lived with his boyfriend, Peter, in a loft in Belltown. Downstairs, Peter ran a trendy ice cream company that sold counterintuitive, savory flavors: sweet arugula, prosciutto and fig, olive oil ribboned with red veins of balsamic. He had recently received a write-up in the *Seattle Times*, and now, on warm days, the line coiled around two blocks.

"Try the sweet arugula with the olive oil and balsamic," Peter said when we arrived, swinging open the door of an industrial freezer. "It's the most popular thing on the menu! I call it the Naughty Salad."

While Rodney was at work, I hid out in a massive deli in downtown Seattle, where the patrons were as hopelessly unhip as I felt. As large as a school cafeteria and stubbornly devoid of any cultural identity, the deli was home to a bewildering buffet: there were bagels, sushi, a Chinese noodle bar, a sandwich station, eight steaming trays of Indian food. It was cheap and crowded, dully safe, the kind of place where people only came to disappear.

I sat at a long bar in front of the window with a plate of chicken tandoori and a Chinese dessert, translucent and shaped like a drawstring pouch. Outside, it was somber and drizzly; the two umbrella buckets in the deli's entrance were stuffed to capacity, and a pile of additional umbrellas lay to one side. I had just finished eating when a tall figure came through the doors and stopped.

He wore a slick black raincoat and expensive-looking, Italian-looking shoes—the golden-brown color of scotch with leather tassels at the toes. The bottoms of his slim slacks were drenched, and his strawberry hair was thinning; at the crown of his head was a pink bald spot, dappled with raindrops. He hunched as if the ceiling in the deli were slightly too low.

There was a moment in which we both weighed the costs and benefits of pretending we hadn't seen each other. Then he sighed and offered a small, grim smile.

"Sylvie Patterson," he said. "I thought it was you."

I was stunned numb. Like the second in which a toe is stubbed or a finger jammed, I felt the impact but not yet the sting. I glanced at the tables nearby, but the people around us were unconcerned, engaged in conversation or tabloid magazines or the complicated disentangling of wads of chow mein.

"I never knew your last name," I said. "That's strange, isn't it?"

"Perkins."

"Perkins. Thom Perkins."

"That's it," said Thom. "I never thought I'd see you again."

His voice had the same playful inflection I remembered, but it was effortful now, his smile wooden, like an actor forced to play a part he had long ago outgrown.

We regarded each other. I wondered if I looked as old to him, as changed, as he did to me. His eyes were sparsely lashed, a chilly, arctic blue. The skin of his cheeks looked translucent and exposed.

"I suppose there are a few different ways this could go," he said.

I had no idea what he thought of me—whether he was resentful or bewildered, whether he'd passed me off as crazy. Through the years, I'd remembered snatches of my time with

Thom, and I had stitched the story together square by square. Scratching a mosquito bite, I saw my head against his crossed ankles, our bodies making an L shape on the floor and crumpling with laughter. Going through a turnstile at the BART station, I remembered crawling under the broken fence plank, Thom helping to pull me through. We stole through the yard and tugged the basement door closed, the moon swallowed like a lump in the throat.

A subway train squealed its approach, and I heard Louis Armstrong on low as we clung and spun together, Thom singing a hushed harmony. *The way you hold your knife; the way we dance till three* . . . A drizzly Thursday morning in October, pouring hot water into a packet of oatmeal: *You promised you'd show me,* he said, *you promised*—and we were wrestling, knees scraping the concrete floor, until I let him peel my fingers open and out fell a small yellowed photo in a plastic frame. Solemn gaze, ketchup fingers, the bangs my mother cut below a bicycle helmet: the only childhood photo I have.

And this: A tinkle of Christmas bells. Our hands on a glass door, breaths drifting through the air like parachutes. Inside, we took our gloves off and raked our cold red fingers through the candy aisle. It was the twenty-four-hour gas station on Williamson, blocks from our houses. We were attached at the neck, a thick black scarf of Thom's wound around both of us at once. I blew the fringe out of my mouth. He chose a Twix. *Why do* you *always get to pick?* I asked. *Last time it was the—*

Snatches. Half memories: pathetic, wispy things. Often, they'd leave off like this, in the middle of a sentence. But it didn't really matter how I finished the sentence. What mattered was that now I could remember I'd said it.

It occurred to me now that I'd never told him good-bye.

"Do you want to sit down?" I asked.

Thom paused. Then he set his briefcase down and shook off his coat, hanging it on the back of the chair beside me.

"I only have a few minutes," he said, sitting down. "I have a meeting."

"Where do you teach?"

He looked at me quizzically. "Teach?"

"I just—I assumed you were a professor."

"Ah." He laughed shortly. "No, I don't teach. Had to give up the old Romanticism when Jan was born. Grad students don't make very much money. Neither do professors, for that matter—not unless you get lucky. I didn't."

"I'm sorry."

"Don't be. I was never going to finish that dissertation, anyway."

We sat side by side, looking out at the street. Men in suits and sharp-heeled women passed interchangeably in front of us. There must have been two feet of space between our chairs.

"Jan," I said. "Is that your son?"

"I hope so." There was a glint of his old puckishness, a lightbulb swinging in the dark. "He's my oldest. Then there are the twins."

He rooted around in his pocket and came up with a battered leather wallet, flicking it open. Inside a clear sleeve was a family photo, taken against a marbled studio background. Thom sat in a stiff-backed chair with a child on his lap. The boy looked to be four or five, with fiery red hair and a solemn gaze that matched his father's. Janna sat beside them, wearing a puff-sleeved floral dress and a canary-yellow, off-kilter hat. Her hair was cropped short, and it was a pale, diluted blond—what must have been her natural color. At her feet were twins, a boy and a girl, both in suspenders and shorts. Their hair was white-blond and cowlicky, and they had familiar smiles: catlike, toothy, the incisors crooked and sharp.

"Henrik and Inger," said Thom, pointing. "Hooligans, those two."

I didn't ask about Janna, but neither did he ask about Gabe. He put the photo away.

"How did you end up here?" I asked—I couldn't help myself. "I never thought I'd see you in a place like this."

"A place like what?" he asked, one eyebrow arched.

"I don't know—like *this*." I waved a hand, looking around at the people reading newspapers at single-person tables or eating the miniature pickles that came free with each sandwich. "It's so—corporate."

"Snob. Have you tried the chicken tandoori?"

"I have, in fact," I said, gesturing to my empty paper plate, where orange oil had melted into psychedelic pools.

But the routine had become tired. It took an extraordinary amount of effort to make our conversation appear so effortless, to conceal the strain it took to ignore the subjects that stood so persistently between us.

"No," said Thom. "The story's not very exciting, I'm afraid. When Janna got pregnant, we both decided it would be best if I left the university. My cousin found me a copywriting job here. I've been in pharma ever since—that's pharmaceuticals to you outsiders. Basically, I write the little black script at the end of commercials and magazine ads, the stuff that reminds you not to take your antidepressant while operating heavy machinery or drinking like Dylan Thomas. It's a rare trade— requires years of apprenticeship. You may have seen my work in last month's issue of *Cosmopolitan*."

"I'm sorry you had to leave the PhD," I said again. I felt embarrassed and guilty, as though it were my fault.

"Let's face it. I didn't know what I was doing." He turned to me, his eyes level with mine. "Did you?"

"Know what I was doing?"

He nodded. The door opened, and a chill passed between us, ruffling the hair on Thom's forehead.

"With me," he said.

It was too late to withdraw. In ten minutes, Thom would leave the deli, and I would probably never see him again. If I wanted to ask him anything, I knew I had to do it now.

"In a sense," I said. "Did you know I was asleep?"

Thom flinched. He looked down and began to smooth a crease in his pants with both hands.

"You were woozy, sometimes. You got confused. Goofy. But so did I—it was three o'clock in the morning. I didn't expect you to act the way you did during the day. I just chalked it up to the hour. The way we were together."

"How were we?"

"I don't know. Uninhibited. Sometimes we fell asleep together. Other times we just laughed. We were always laughing."

His ears were pink, his eyes shifting.

"You knew," I said. "You did."

Once the words were out, I could tell I was right. A flush climbed his throat. He still wouldn't look at me.

"I don't want to do this now," he said, his voice low.

"Oh, Thom, be honest. Please—just tell me the truth."

"Why?" His voice was hoarse, and there was something in his face I didn't recognize—dread or shame or thinly veiled panic. "Do you really want to know? What'll it do for you? For either of us? The truth's a bitch, Sylvie. Always has been. Better to let her lie."

"Better for who? It's already done. I know you don't owe me anything, and maybe you're angry at me. We fucked up, Thom, but we fucked up together. If there's anything left—if there's one last thing you'll do for me—"

My face was hot. It was humiliating, this groveling. And even as I asked him, I knew he was probably right. What was the point of knowledge, won so late and given over so reluctantly? What could I do with it? I was about to tell him to leave it when Thom shook his head, in wonder or in resignation.

"Okay," he said. "Okay."

He ran a hand through his hair, smoothing it down where it had blown aside.

"There was this night," he said. "What was it—November? A few days before Thanksgiving, past midnight, and I was working in the living room. It was excruciating. The dissertation wasn't coming, and I felt like a fucking fraud. I couldn't breathe. I went outside to feel fresh air in my lungs. That's when I saw you.

"You were walking around your backyard. No shoes on, these funny little shorts, an old T-shirt despite the cold. I asked if you were okay. You came toward me like a hologram—you were swaying, and your eyes flickered. But every so often, they sharpened, and you looked at me like you really saw me. I didn't know what to make of it. I thought you were on drugs, which was funny at first—I thought, *Goddamn, Sylvie, you?* You seemed so square. But you were making me nervous. I told you to go inside, get back to bed, but you didn't want to. You were so damn stubborn that I finally just hopped the fence. You were shivering; I walked you to the door with my arms around your shoulders. I kept worrying that Gabe would see us, or Janna—that somebody would ask me what the hell we were doing. But nobody saw us. Nobody asked."

It was one thirty now, and the lunch rush was thinning. Several of the deli employees were taking their break, crowded into a nearby booth with plates from the buffet. They laughed rowdily; one of them threw a grape into another's mouth.

"I saw you again a few nights later," he said. "Your arms were hanging over the fence, and you were looking into my yard like you were waiting for me. I came outside and asked you what you were doing. 'Let's go,' you said. 'Let's go away.' I think I started laughing, but I stopped when I realized how serious you were. I'd figured out by then that something wasn't right. You can't blame me, can you? I knew you were

306 · CHLOE BENJAMIN

researching dreams, sleepwalkers, strange conditions. You had told me all about it—it was like you *wanted* me to know. Still, I helped you through a broken plank in the fence. It was early in December, and you kissed me. I'm not blaming you—I didn't pull away—but you want the facts, don't you? It was the first snow of the year. Frigid outside. Little crystals on your eyelashes and your nose."

Thom shook his head, brusque.

"Anyway, it was too exposed out there. You didn't seem to care, but I was paranoid that we'd be seen. So I took you down to the basement. From then on, that's where we saw each other. I knew I should have made you go home, but I couldn't. You were magnetic. You spun these long, fascinating stories—these *yarns*. You told the dirtiest jokes I'd ever heard. You kept on surprising me. I knew I was taking advantage of something, but I didn't know what. In a way, I felt like you were taking advantage of me."

"That's a convenient read." The guilt I'd felt before was gone, replaced by an ugly fusion of anger and shame. "You had realized by then that I was sleepwalking. I obviously wasn't myself. How could I have taken advantage of you?"

"Don't you understand?" asked Thom. "I was entranced by you. I would have done anything you wanted. And who was I to say you weren't yourself? How was I supposed to know what that looked like?"

I couldn't answer. I smarted with shame. Still, I marveled at myself. Here it was: the truth of what I had done, laid out before me. If I chose to believe him.

Thom checked his watch—a fat silver watch with large links, slightly loose. He shook his wrist until the face was visible.

"I should go," he said.

"All right."

"Are you going to be okay?"

"I will be. I am. I've developed a pretty high tolerance for surprise."

Thom smiled, if slightly. He stood and pulled his raincoat on.

"Despite all that—everything I said." He paused. "I really did like you. I thought we understood each other."

"Probably we did, in some way. Though I'm not sure what that says about us."

"Probably nothing good."

"Probably not."

The tension between us collapsed. Perhaps it was only momentary; in all likelihood, the sway of regret would soon return. For now, though, we were directionless. We floated. We left our embarrassment behind, like clothes cast off on the sand. Caught in the moorless place between young adulthood and middle age, we were just learning how to forgive ourselves.

Thom nodded at me, briefly but not without genuine acknowledgment. Then he picked up his briefcase and left the deli, wind rushing in to meet me as the doors shut behind him.

• • •

Even now, there are nights when I skip along the surface of sleep like a flat stone on water, when I feel pulled in two directions. Like moths and mosquitoes, like migrating birds and microscopic fish, a part of me will always be attracted to the sun. But I'm drawn, too, to the deep drop of dreams, the plunge into an ocean where, thousands of feet below, creatures make their own light. Perhaps this is why Keller's theory of simultaneous potentialities still makes sense to me, for I am not of one mind. In moments of decision, it seems as though a thousand versions of myself branch and spread like a deck of cards. One of them I select. Then they are once again stacked, facedown, and put in their box to await the next shuffle.

On particularly bad nights, when I can't help but look backward, one memory calms me. During my final days in Madison, I slept on the couch, half-packed boxes all around me. One night, I felt Gabe jostling me by the arms. His hold on me was both firm and gentle, the way a parent might wake a small child.

"Sylvie," he whispered. "Sylve . . ."

I sat up, shrinking away from him, as my eyes adjusted to the darkness. Seventy-two hours later, I would step onto the porch with my suitcases and look back at his face for the very last time.

"You told me you wanted to see the stars," he said.

Slowly, his face materialized in front of me. It was the face of a younger Gabe, the boy who had something to show me—the boy who knew we called him Napoleon behind his back but who marched ahead anyway.

"So that was real?" I had a groggy memory of shaking Gabe in bed—or was it Thom?—and asking where the stars had gone.

Gabe nodded. And though I can't quite say why, I decided to go with him. It was one in the morning. We drove through the night—past Middleton, past Janesville, to a small public park with a sloping hill.

I'm not sure what we did when we got there. Gabe unrolled a blanket, maybe, or took off his coat, spreading it open on the grass. There was nothing to point out to each other. We knew the constellations—the Big Dipper, Gemini's twin legs, Lyra and her harp—and we could see them clearly. Perhaps he laid his head on my lap, the way he used to at Mills when we stole out to Observatory Hill in the evening. Perhaps we didn't touch at all. His eyes were trained on me in their intent, entreating way, or they flickered like a bulb going bad; or he had already closed them, had fallen asleep beneath the cape of dark sky and its light shop of stars.

Probably I've chosen not to remember it. After a while, Gabe suggested we return to the car to sleep off the last few hours before daybreak. Soon, he was dozing in the passenger seat, but I couldn't fall asleep, so I stumbled back out to the field and laid my head in the grass.

What I do remember is that at some point in the very early morning, I woke up, and my mind was entirely blank. For the first time in months, I couldn't remember my dreams or their aftertaste; the feeling was so alien that if it weren't for the change in the light, I might not have been sure I had fallen asleep. I felt just-born, or born again—the night's transgressions washed clean, my ignorance the purest blessing.

In the pinkish glow of morning, I could see spring's first daisies dotting the hill, their fragile petals peeled back and glistening. When I was young, I wove them into crowns, using my fingers to split each stem at its wet, fibrous center. And though I remember myself as a practical child, I imagined I was different when I wore the flower crowns: holier, or supernaturally powerful, as if I could spell myself new just by wanting it.

But this time, I didn't touch them; I left their roots in the ground. I laid my head on the grass and returned to the same deep, vacant sleep. I knew there was nobody watching me.

# Acknowledgments

There are so many people to whom I have the honor of giving thanks.

First, to my marvelous agent, Margaret Riley King at WME, whose skill and unflagging support carried me through multiple drafts of this book (and moments of mild panic). All first-time authors need someone to take a chance on them, and I am so lucky you did.

To Daniella Wexler, a dream of an editor: your belief, advocacy, and keen editorial insight brought this book into being, and I will always be grateful.

To Judith Curr: you gave this book a home, and it means more to me than I could ever express.

To the rest of the incredible team at Atria, thank you for all the phenomenal work you've done on my behalf. At WME, my thanks too to Britton Schey, for first supporting my work; Ashley Fox, film agent extraordinaire; and Tracy Fisher and Cathryn Summerhayes in foreign rights, among others. At both Atria and WME, I feel immensely lucky to be in such good hands.

To the mentors I've had throughout my writing life: Kiese Laymon and Paul Russell at Vassar, and Lorrie Moore, Jesse Lee Kercheval, Amy Quan Barry, and Ron Kuka at UW-

Madison. A special thanks to the extraordinary Judy Mitchell, my MFA adviser and mentor, who rallied at my side through each step of this process. There are writers, and then there are teachers. It is my privilege to have learned from all of you, who are both.

To the pioneers whose research informed my book: Sigmund Freud, Carl Jung, Stephen LaBerge and the Lucidity Institute, Rosalind Cartwright, Robert Stickgold, Deirdre Barrett, and others. This book would not have been possible without your contributions to the field.

To my bighearted, brilliant friends, from the MFA and beyond: Bri Cavallaro, Alexandra Demet, Alexandra Goldstein, Andrew Kay, Nick Jandl, Angela Voras-Hills, my UW cohort, and many more.

To my family: how can I ever thank you enough? Mom and Dad, Ellen and Molly, Jordan and Ty, Grandma and Papa, Bob and Kate, and all the rest—you know perhaps more than anyone else how much this means to me. Your unconditional support and love, your belief in me and in the value of the arts, are the great gifts of my life. I share this accomplishment with you.

And to Nathan: for your passion, your love, your wisdom, and your partnership—which is not to mention your excellent copyediting skills and your willingness to listen patiently as I rattle off my dreams each morning. You are my person, and it thrills me every day.

# THE ANATOMY OF DREAMS

## CHLOE BENJAMIN

### An Atria Reading Group Guide

Young couple Gabe and Sylvie are lured into a controversial sleep study by their charismatic boarding-school headmaster, injecting mistrust into the trio and revealing the immense, uncontrollable power of our dreams.

## Topics and Questions for Discussion

1. Think about Sylvie's relationship with Gabe from meeting at Mills to parting in Wisconsin. How does their relationship evolve over the course of the novel?

2. How did you first react to Dr. Keller and his influence over his students? Why are Gabe and Sylvie attracted to joining Keller in his controversial, secretive line of work?

3. How does painting help Sylvie process her feelings?

4. Why do you think Sylvie decides to go with Gabe when he suddenly reappears in her life? Do you think she ever trusted him after he disappeared from Mills?

5. How does Gabe change in the years between high school and Wisconsin?

6. Why do you think the author used nonlinear storytelling to give insight into Sylvie's life? How did this influence your understanding of the storyline?

7. Consider the themes of privacy and intrusion throughout the novel. How does the issue of privacy play into Gabe and Sylvie's relationship? How does it affect their work?

8. Think about Sylvie and Gabe's first interactions with Thom and Janna. Why does Sylvie end up telling Thom so much about their work?

9. Sylvie and Gabe can't really have close friends due to the secrecy their work requires. How does this loneliness and isolation affect Sylvie? How does it affect Gabe?

10. Thom argues that the subconscious is perhaps best left alone, that it's dangerous to make people aware of their darkest dreams and subconscious desires. Do you agree with Thom? Why or why not?

11. How do the interactions with Jamie and Anne change the relationship between Sylvie, Gabe, and Keller?

12. How did you react to the revelation at the novel's climax? Do you think Sylvie suspected something all along?

13. Why doesn't Sylvie confront Keller and tell him the real reason she left Wisconsin?

14. Does Sylvie get the closure she needed from Keller? From Gabe? How is she affected by the chance meeting with Thom in Seattle?

15. Consider the last scene in the book, when Sylvie gazes at the stars and considers Keller's theory of the conscious and subconscious minds. Do you think Sylvie still believes in Keller's work? Why or why not?

## Enhance Your Book Club

1. Experiment with keeping a dream journal. Put your journal next to your bed and record your dreams as soon as you wake up each morning. Look for interesting patterns or themes, and share some of them with your book club. For help with decoding your dreams, visit www.DreamMoods.com or www.TheCuriousDreamer.com.

2. Take a painting class with your book club at a local community center, school, or art store. Try your hand at painting representational interpretations of your dreams, just as Sylvie does in *The Anatomy of Dreams*.

3. Learn more about the author at chloebenjaminbooks.com. Catch up with Chloe's other writing, connect on social media, and check out Chloe's book recommendations on her blog!